# INTRODUCTION

THE ALICE EQUATION
*Sometimes love is complicated*

*Three months of fake-dating your friend to help him secure his dream legal job.*
   *How hard can that be?*
   *Pretty damn hard if you've been secretly in love with him for the past five years…*

Alice Montgomery's life is like Groundhog Day. Five years after graduating, she's still working in her Mum's bookshop, hiding her stash of romance novels under the bed and pining for the gorgeous guy who helped her over a panic attack before her final uni exam.

   Aaron Blake, loves to party – *hard.* His idea of commitment to anything other than his legal career is strictly three months. Until landing a job with the most prestigious law firm in town means he has to convince the partners he's committed to family values.

Aaron needs a fake date fast—and who could be safer than shy, bookish Alice?

Soon Alice finds herself dating her secret crush, sporting a daring new look of vintage frocks and itsy-bitsy lace underwear.

Now the heat is notching up. Aaron's feelings for his fake date are proving anything but safe, and Alice is discovering her inner sex-goddess.

But when secrets are revealed and lies uncovered, both Alice and Aaron will have to work out the hardest equation of all — what this crazy thing called love is all about.

## ALSO BY DAVINA STONE

The Polly Principle

A Kiss for Carter

The Felicity Theory

Print ISBN: 978-0-6450065-0-6

Ebook ISBN: 978-0-6450065-1-3

Cover design by Bailey McGinn, Bailey Designs Books

Edited by Abigail Nathan, Bothersome Words

Proofread by Vanessa Lanaway, Red Dot Scribble

# THE ALICE EQUATION

## SOMETIMES LOVE IS COMPLICATED

DAVINA STONE

FEATHERS AND STONE PUBLISHING

**Equation:**
*A difficult problem that can only be understood if all the different influences are considered.*
*(Cambridge English Dictionary)*

~

This book is written in Australian English.
Therefore the spelling of some words may be slightly different from US English.

And being Aussie,
the slang tends to be a bit different too!
Just saying, mate.

# CHAPTER 1

"So, Aaron, tell us all about *you*."

Caught in the combined stares of the partners of Trojan, Bendt and Fink, Aaron resisted the urge to fiddle with his cufflinks.

He'd been sure they were about to be offer him the senior associate position.

Obviously not.

"Consider this an off the record chat," Archibald, *"call me Archie,"* Bendt of the iron-man handshake continued.

"Just to check our values and yours sit well together," Charles Fink added, stretching a sinewy arm towards the bread rolls.

Aaron swallowed hard. "Right. Of course. Sounds very reasonable."

Geoff Trojan, the senior of the partners, leaned across the restaurant table. "You know we will own you, don't you, Aaron? If you work for us, you will have no secrets left." He burst out laughing, joined seconds later by his colleagues.

*Christ! What were they playing at?*

Aaron knew he'd nailed the interview last week; an hour

and a half of curly litigation questions he'd answered thoroughly to much head nodding. He'd even injected some well-timed humour. So when the call came inviting him to lunch to "discuss the details", he'd allowed his fantasies free rein: his name on the door of an office with river views; the heady thrill of a partnership offer. Okay, so a partnership wasn't imminent, but landing the senior associate position made it within grasping distance.

No way was he going to blow it now.

He took a sip of his water; placed it down next to his meagrely filled wine glass. Smiled until his teeth ached. "What would you like to know?"

"Well, of course, we're all familiar with your background," Trojan said. "Your father's a clever guy. Fantastic podcasts. I listen to them on my way to work. But right now we want *you* to impress us, Aaron; tell us what makes you tick. Likes. Dislikes. Hobbies. Current relationship status."

Aaron's veins turned icy.

*Relationships?*

As in, *flings*. As in, catch a whiff of commitment and Aaron was out the door so quick even his shadow was caught unawares. *Shit on wheels.* He was going to have to think fast.

Charles Fink gave a faux apologetic smile. "To be honest with you, Aaron, we're down to the wire; it's between you and one other candidate. So, now's your chance to pip the opposition at the post."

Aaron cleared his throat. This better be good. "I run marathons, for charity mostly. I enjoy working out. I guess you'd call me something of a fitness fanatic, I find exercise keeps my mind disciplined. Other than that; spending time with friends, family, er... travelling. Dislikes, not many, though I've never really been keen on oysters."

The air at the table vibrated with expectation. They were wanting more.

The *relationship* stuff.

And that's when a brainwave struck him, as brainwaves

2

sometimes do when you're backed into a corner. Christ! Would she go along with it? It would stretch the bonds of friendship to put it mildly, but desperate circumstances required desperate measures. Aaron threw caution to the wind. "And I have a girlfriend, Alice."

"Fantastic," Trojan beamed. "How long have you been together?"

"Four months." Not the right answer, clearly, judging by their stone-eyed stares. *Four months doesn't qualify as long-term in their books, fuck-wit.* He gave a flimsy laugh. "Wow, time flies; it only *feels* like four months. Must be at least a year." He frowned. "Come to think of it, probably closer to two."

"Any plans to tie the knot?"

Aaron nearly reeled back in his chair. When would this torture end? "I'm keen to, but she's... she's..."

*About to kill me? Probably.*

Trojan's brows waggled. "She is?"

"Oh, you know." Aaron waved a vague hand. "Slower than me on the marriage thing. Death do us part and all that... I mean, don't get me wrong, she's very committed, but, yeah, she's being mature about it all."

"And what does Alice do, Aaron?" Trojan clearly wasn't letting up.

"She works in—" Should he say she was career-minded? Keen to have babies? His gaze fixed on Archie Bendt's wedding band as he played with the stem of his wine glass. Definitely they'd have to want kids. But probably not straight away.

"She works in her mum's second-hand bookshop." Perhaps take that up a notch. "They own it together, and the books aren't *second-hand* as such, they focus on rare books, first editions, that sort of thing. Alice graduated with first-class honours in English. She could do anything she set her mind to, but she's choosing to build up the shop; she's pretty ambitious."

Geoff Trojan frowned. "Hopefully not *too* ambitious. We are totally affirmative of women in the workforce, but since we're all men together, I'll be frank. They can't expect to have it all. Delia was climbing the ladder in a family law firm, but once our first was on the way, we had the 'talk'. Four children later and she's a stay-home mum. I'd be lynched if I said this in public, but our kids are well-adjusted. No drugs. No sex. They tell us everything. Once you tie the knot, you've got to make the decision on who's bringing home the bacon. As a team."

"Enough lecturing, Geoff," Archie remarked. He'd started drumming his fingers on the checked tablecloth, his wedding ring gleaming in the ambient light.

Luckily their entrees arrived and conversation halted briefly. Aaron tried to breathe normally as he skimmed his fork over blobs of black caviar drizzled around an artichoke heart and a few coiffed leaves of mesclun. His appetite was shot. He was usually good at talking his way out of awkward situations. But right now, it felt more like he'd dug an enormous hole and was shovelling shit all over himself.

The partners had started chatting about a corporate corruption case, including him in the discussions with encouraging glances, to which Aaron hoped he nodded in all the right places. Meanwhile his head was spinning like a washing machine on a super-fast setting.

He needed to brief Alice. She'd understand. She was used to bailing him out of tight situations. Besides, it was unlikely she'd ever have to meet them. She'd just have to agree to him calling her *"sweetie"* or *"hon"* if he took a call from her in the vicinity of the partners. As soon as he was past his probation period, she would ditch him. He'd get the haunted look of a man who'd lost his one true love, valiantly performing to spectacularly high standards despite a broken heart. Then he'd quietly saunter off to his previous nefarious ways. After all, he'd have the perfect excuse. A guy who'd been dumped didn't want to re-commit in a hurry, did he?

Aaron dived into the second course—a slab of super-rare steak—with a lot more gusto. For the rest of the meal he made sure he asked intelligent questions, showed off his superb knowledge of legal precedents. Flashed his winning smile.

As the afternoon wore on with no more awkward questions, he sensed his usual buoyant confidence returning.

Finally, the partners stood, chunking up in size from small to medium to large, like the three bears of the legal establishment. Aaron was tall, but even he had to tip his head to look up at Archie. The man must work out daily. For hours. How did he find the time? Oh, of course, a loving and devoted wife. And a state-of-the-art home gym with panoramic views over the ocean most likely. Aaron felt a pang of envy. Fit-Bods twenty-four-hour gym looked swish but smelled constantly of sweaty socks and pheromones. Suddenly his workout regime didn't hold quite the same appeal.

But hey, wasn't that why you clawed your way up the corporate ladder?

Because it smelled like roses at the top?

At the door, Archie pumped his hand until Aaron's metacarpals twinged. "Impressed. Very impressed with you, young man."

"Time for a serious chat amongst ourselves," Trojan said with a smirk to his colleagues.

"Expect a call this afternoon," said Fink.

Archie Bendt gave Aaron a wink. "We're all looking forward to meeting *your* Alice."

Aaron's mood, which had been riding high, promptly crashed.

Alice bagged up the copy of *The Green and Gold Women's Institute Cookbook* and handed it to Esther Brown.

"There you are, Esther. And I've emailed Mum to ask her to look for a first edition of *Mrs Beeton's Household Management* for you while she's in the UK."

Esther came in every Friday evening because she was

widowed and lonely and the Book Genie, with its Tiffany lamps and cushion-strewn sofas, was always welcoming.

Esther beamed. "Fancy you remembering that throwaway comment. Thank you, my dear."

Warmth spread around Alice's chest. Wasn't this exactly what she loved about her work? It wasn't just the books, important though they were. Giving out an extra dose of happiness in a smile or a recommendation as she handed over a leather-bound copy of *Middlemarch* or a 1970's Penguin edition of *Pride and Prejudice* was what made her truly happy. They might be small things, but wasn't it the little gestures that made the world a nicer place?

Then she glanced up and her happy heart twisted into a pretzel. Because there, standing behind the balding man with Asimov science fiction titles piled up to his chin, was Aaron.

Nor was he looking his normal suave and—a secret that she'd only ever shared with her best friend, Polly—*gorgeous*, self. Dirty blond hair that usually flopped casually over his forehead sat at odd angles around his head, and his blue eyes held none of their usual laid-back charm. In all honesty, he looked completely frazzled.

She cast him an enquiring smile, at which point he bared his teeth and jabbed a finger at the man in front as if to hurry things up. Alice quickly counted up the pile of books, tallying the price on the computer. The man struggled to fit them in a little string bag that wasn't quite big enough for five fat tomes of Isaac Asimov. All the while she could sense Aaron ready to explode behind him.

Suddenly it dawned that he must have had *the call*. Alice nearly dropped the man's change. Did that deranged face mean he hadn't got the job?

"Hi," she said as the man exited.

Aaron's energy practically vaulted over the desk.

"Can we talk?" His gaze flew around the book-lined walls. "Like—not here."

Alice nudged her glasses up her nose. "I can't leave the

shop. Mum's away on a buying trip. It's only me here until closing time."

"In the storeroom then."

"Seriously?" *That bad, huh?*

"I just need a couple of minutes," he hissed.

Alice cast a glance around. There was a lull. If she left the storeroom door open, she could still see if a customer came up to the desk. "Okay." Her heart was hammering as they squeezed into the tiny book lined room behind the counter. The smell of musty paper and old leather was so familiar she barely noticed it anymore, but now all her senses seemed oddly elevated. She crammed her back against the counter that held the kettle and her elbow sent a mug flying.

Aaron didn't seem to notice. He was dragging agitated fingers through his hair.

"I got the job," he blurted.

"Oh, Aaron, that's wonderful." Any other time she would have hugged him, but in this cramped space a hug suddenly felt too intimate. She reached out and tapped his bicep instead.

"I heard this afternoon." His gaze landed on her heavily and for some reason her cheeks heated. "There's just a small problem; kind of related."

He paused, his gaze shifting to her forehead. "I need your help with something."

Alice rolled her eyes. "What now?"

"I need you to be my girlfriend."

Alice blinked. Time stood still. A pulse hammered madly in her neck. Her mouth went dry and little stars formed in her vision. So, it was true, your body *did* do strange and wonderful things when the words you'd dreamed of hearing forever were suddenly real.

"I... oh—" she stammered, her cheeks burning now.

Aaron's face broke into an embarrassed smirk. "That came out all wrong. I meant I need you to *pretend* to be my girlfriend."

It was like a movie clip had come to a grinding halt with

Alice freeze-framed, her jaw hanging open and a stupid adoring look on her face.

Another hideously long moment passed before she managed to scoff, "Well that's a huge relief. I'd have had to turn you down."

Aaron grinned, clearly relieved. "I know, kind of weird, huh?"

*Weird. Of course. Silly me.*

"The problem is, I sort of stuck my foot in it with the partners. They were asking about my personal life, whether I had a relationship, and—"

"Oh."

"Yeah. They were really turning the screws, said it was neck and neck between me and one other candidate." Aaron stepped back against a pile of journals and nearly lost his footing. He glared down at the mess at his feet. "Jesus, where does Rowena find all this stuff?"

"Back copies of *National Geographic*. Very sought-after. Go on." Alice tried to sound nonchalant even though her heart had shrivelled to the size of a pinto bean. Here they were again; Aaron in a fix, Alice to the rescue. Sensible, practical Alice. Same old, same old. Meanwhile, her brief fantasy lay smashed at her feet, along with that pile of musty old magazines.

"Okay, well I told them I had a steady girlfriend. Namely—um—you."

Oh, boy, this one took the cake.

"Why on earth would you say that?"

"I know, I know. It was seriously dumb of me. I panicked. The words were out of my mouth before I thought it through. I just needed to present a solid, dependable image and—"

"I was the most solid, dependable girl you know. I see." Could he tell her molars were at risk of grinding to pulp? "And how long exactly do you envisage this arrangement lasting?"

"Three months, just to get through the probation period. Then you can dump me."

"You want me to pretend we're dating for *three months?*"

Aaron winced. "Yes."

Alice's mind was doing cartwheels. Did pretend girlfriend mean pretend handholding? Pretend kissing? Pretend... oh no, she must *not* go there. Now she was hot all over.

In the space of five minutes it felt like she'd been ravaged by a band of marauding pirates. Right now, indignation was bubbling to the surface. But wasn't that what Aaron always did? Turned her into a maelstrom of emotion? Most of which she'd quietly locked up inside herself for years. She just needed to do the same thing now.

Somehow, she stopped her voice from shaking as she said, "That's the most ridiculous idea ever."

Aaron's face fell.

She crossed her arms over her chest. "I mean, they're hardly going to sack you if you don't have a girlfriend. It's illegal for a start."

Aaron shoved his hands into his pant pockets and stared at the ground. "I wouldn't put it past them. But at the very least if I don't fit with their values, they could seriously sideline me. They're far more establishment than I thought. Carrying on about family and kids and how behind every great man is a great woman."

"Well that's true enough," Alice muttered. "The answer is no, Aaron."

His crestfallen look turned to sheer panic. "Shit, Al, they want to meet you. They suggested drinks next week."

"And you said yes?"

"What else could I do without looking suspicious?"

Alice bent down and busied herself tidying the *National Geographics* into a pile. Her eyes came level with Aaron's thigh, the outline of his hand in his pocket curled into a tight fist, and a little knife went through her heart.

Why was she such a sucker for this guy? Five years and counting. Polly would despair of her.

By now Aaron had ducked down to help her, his eyes so close she could see the strands of midnight in the sky-blue.

With his pupils dilated and his gorgeous full lips within kissing distance it would be so easy to let her mind play make-believe. He smelled of *him,* spicy aftershave and soap and something else she couldn't quite place but that always made her feel good.

As he handed her a magazine a little shot of magic sped up her arm. A magic only she'd ever felt, of course. She pulled away sharply.

"Please, Al. At least think about it?"

"It's fraud."

"See it as a game. We'd have a laugh. I tell you what—" he stood up. "Let's go out for dinner tomorrow night and talk it through?"

Alice slapped the last *National Geographic* onto her haphazard pile. "I'm working all day tomorrow. I'll be too tired to think straight by the evening." She stood up and dusted down her jeans.

"Sunday, then."

"I'm going to an exhibition at the art gallery."

"What's showing?"

"As if you care."

"No really, I'm interested."

"The Pre-Raphaelites."

"Great. I'll come."

Alice gave a snort. "You hate art."

Aaron had the grace to look sheepish. "But I owe you. For helping me practice for the interview at least. Even if you don't agree to the other."

"I won't."

"Okay, okay. I'm sorry I asked. But I still want to come to the exhibition."

Flustered, she knew she had to get out of here before she completely lost her cool. She glanced past him into the shop. "I have to go, there's a customer waiting."

His gaze remained steady on her face. "What time on Sunday?"

Alice shrugged. She'd just said no to an Aaron request, an almost unheard-of phenomenon. He'd apologised. Even seemed to accept she wouldn't do it. What harm could there be in going out with him on Sunday? Okay, so she'd been trying to back off lately, telling herself to accept the fact that if it hadn't happened between them by now it never would, but... hey, he was still her friend. "Okay then. Make it three o'clock."

"Great, I'll take you out for a bite after."

"We'll see," she managed, dodging past him into the shop and sighing with relief when she was out in the open.

Aaron sauntered past as she was answering the customer's questions about Daphne du Maurier hardbacks. His expression under his blond fringe was back to it's familiar mischief.

"See you at three on Sunday. Outside the art gallery," he called out as he left.

Alice kept smiling sweetly at the customer and pretended she hadn't heard.

# CHAPTER 2

P olly's forkful of julienned carrots and celery hovered mid-air between the plate and her mouth.

"Let me get this straight. He told the partners of this new law firm he has a long-term girlfriend called Alice. And now he wants you to play the part until he gets made permanent?"

Alice nodded.

They were sharing veggie and rice noodle salad at the kitchen table because it was Polly's day two of the 5:2 diet before a weekend splurge. Alice knew she'd have to attack a bar of chocolate in her bedroom later to make up for it, but she liked to keep Polly company.

It felt good to support your friends.

Unless they'd just asked you to be their fake date. That she would never, ever do. Which was why she was now telling Polly the afternoon's events. Saying it out loud, she figured, would cement her refusal.

"So how long's his probation period?" Polly asked.

"Three months, apparently." The strand of noodles she'd managed to twirl around her fork coiled back onto Alice's plate with a small *slurp*. "I said no, of course."

Polly's eyebrows flew up as her fork slid into her mouth.

"Why?" she asked, chewing. "Isn't this what you've always wanted?"

"*Poll*!" Alice spluttered. Only the other week Polly had advised Alice to put some distance between her and Aaron. Suddenly it felt like she was being encouraged to skip into the forest like Little Red Riding Hood with a basket full of goodies.

"It's a *fake* relationship," Alice said pointedly. "The last time I checked the word fake, it meant *sham.*"

"Well, yeah, but—"

"But what?"

"Maybe it's time to re-think the whole Aaron thing."

Polly's volte-face was unbelievable.

"There's nothing to re-think."

"Except your diabolically long-standing crush," Polly pointed out, skewering a celery stick with gusto.

"I'm almost over him," Alice muttered. "Your advice to not answer his calls really helped."

"Sure did." Polly munched loudly. "He's never been at the house so often."

"That's only because Mum's away."

Alice's mum, Rowena didn't like Aaron much. Not that Alice had ever whispered a word about her feelings to her mum. Imagine the fuss! The fact that Aaron only read legal textbooks and Instagram posts made Rowena's hackles rise. "How can you have anything in common with someone who doesn't read novels?" she'd once asked Alice in an outraged tone.

"And I guess because I was helping him practice for his interview." Alice nearly went boss-eyed trying to wind the noodle back onto her fork.

"Good one." By now Polly was grinning her head off. When Polly grinned, her corkscrew curls bounced ever so slightly like they were having their own personal snicker. "I think we need to workshop this over a drink." She pushed back her chair.

"It's your fasting day."

"Extenuating circumstances. I'll stop eating. That'll make up for the extra calories."

Alice threw her fork into her half-eaten dinner. "Why am I suddenly feeling anxious?"

"Because, Munchkin, anxiety is your default mode."

Alice sighed and stared at her plate. Polly, as usual, was right. Though where the anxious gene came from was a mystery. Certainly not from Rowena, who socialised with more ease than she breathed air. Maybe from her dad, but trying to find anything out about him was like sending a space probe into a black hole. Alice had given up years ago.

"You'll be glad to know I maintained my cool admirably." True enough, considering she'd teetered on the brink of major humiliation.

"Well done." Polly uncorked a bottle of white wine at the kitchen bench, poured them both a glass and sprawled back in her chair. "So, when are you going to let him talk you into it?"

"I'm—he's not. I *may* have mentioned in passing I was going to the art gallery on Sunday and he said he'd like to come, but—"

"I rest my case: he's desperate. And you're still hopelessly smitten. That's why there needs to be a revision of the plan."

"What sort of revision?" Alice asked suspiciously. Polly was known for her wildly spontaneous approach to dating. And admittedly Alice enjoyed watching it all—from a safe distance. But this was feeling suddenly way too close for comfort.

Polly grabbed a pad of paper that happened to be on a pile in the middle of the table along with some shopping dockets, a dying pot plant and a couple of Alice's hair scrunchies.

"Okay. This is how it works." She scribbled something on a page, tore it off and handed it to Alice.

*Alice*
——— + *amazeballs sex = true love*
*Aaron*

Alice frowned. "Is this a joke?"

"Nope. If you take on this girlfriend gig, the game changes."

"Hardly. It's no different from all the other times I've bailed him out," Alice remarked glumly, but her eyes were drawn to the words *amazeballs sex* like iron filings to a magnet.

"Yes, it is. It makes for a completely different dynamic." As a social worker, Polly spent vast swathes of her day doing family counselling at the hospital she worked at, which meant she threw out words like *dynamic, symbiotic* and *co-dependence* as if they were pronouns.

"Nothing will change the fact that the person I want doesn't want me back."

"In all fairness, you've never rigorously tested the hypothesis."

"Five years feels like a pretty thorough experiment to me."

"Yeah, right. With you being the eternally patient advisor for all his girlfriend problems, letting him crash on your sofa, making him hot-chocolates, cooking him hang-over brekkies— get the picture?"

"I'm just not his type. You know as well as I do Aaron goes for blondes with legs up to their earlobes and big—" Alice gave a wave at the region of her chest. "Not small brunettes who wear glasses and have no—"

'Tits," said Polly matter-of-factly. "You've got great tits, but you choose to hide them under T-shirts that read *I prefer my book boyfriend.*"

"I only ever wear that one to bed," Alice rebutted indignantly.

Polly sighed heavily. "Face it, Munchkin. You've friend-zoned yourself so spectacularly you don't know how to get out of it. Here's the perfect opportunity to show Aaron a whole lot more than your mind, and you're working yourself up to a panic attack."

Sure enough, Alice's palms were clammy and her heart pounded fit to burst through her ribs.

She hadn't felt like this since university, when she'd had to regularly shove her head between her legs to stop from hyperventilating before lectures.

"I—no—oh, no—I wouldn't know where to begin. And then, what if something does happen and… oh god, how would we look at each other the next day?" She gulped in a breath. "Nope. I'm really happy with the status quo."

"Intense sexual frustration, you mean?"

*Yowch.* Polly always went for the jugular. Or, in this instance, somewhere else a fair bit lower.

"Let me explain before you freak out." Polly scooted her chair over to Alice's, and circled their names with her pen. "Alice over Aaron, that's a given. Unless you prefer Aaron over Alice, but really, missionary position is so *yesterday*."

Alice winced. She'd got used to Polly's detailed descriptions of her own sex life, but when it came to focussing on her own more or less non-existent one, she wanted to squirm.

Polly's pen hovered over *amazeballs sex*. "You two have had this weird, sexually charged friendship since uni."

"Really?"

"Sure. I've watched you laughing at each other's awful jokes, WhatsApping those stupid cat pictures to each other, running tabs on who's winning at Monopoly and just 'hangin' out' for years. And Aaron still hasn't worked out he's mad about you." Polly sniffed disdainfully. "Typical male brain."

"Why, if you thought that, did you tell me to stop contacting him?"

"To see what he did."

Alice fell silent, thinking. What he'd done was text her daily asking if she was okay.

That was the problem. If she'd only ever seen Aaron as a shallow, ridiculously good-looking womaniser, she'd have shaken free years ago. But there were times—frequent enough to keep her hooked—when Aaron showed her a different side altogether. A kinder, softer side. A side the other women never got to see. Or at least, Alice hoped not. Somehow, she'd convinced herself that meant they had something special. And then she'd been dumb enough to think that was enough.

Polly continued, "Besides, if you and Aaron aren't a happening thing, isn't it better to know? If it doesn't work out, you'll be free to go off and do all the things you've been talking about: travel the world, apply for that job in publishing you've always wanted."

"There aren't any jobs. Not now that everyone's self-publishing."

"You're being Eeyore again."

"And you're being Tigger."

"Better to bounce through life than drag your ears through the mud," Polly countered with a grin. "Now, let's tackle the amazeballs sex."

Alice pulled a face. "Couldn't we start with true love and work backwards?"

"Okay, if the sex bit is weirding you out, we'll tackle love first." Polly drew a heart around the words *true love*. "Think of all the friends-to-lovers movies. *When Harry Met Sally, Friends with Benefits, One Day*—"

"Not *One Day*!" Alice protested. "I *hated* that movie. Twenty years of angst, only to be knocked off your bicycle and die when you finally get together." She shuddered. "It was *horrible*."

Polly rolled her eyes. "The point is, friends *do* fall in love all the time. Remember Bella and George?"

"From the newsagency?"

"Yep. I was kind of behind that."

Alice's eyes rounded. "You were?"

"Uh-huh. Every time I went in to buy a lottery ticket, Bella would talk about George not getting a decent meal, and on her day off George would carry on about Bella's smile. I got so sick of it I arranged to meet them both at the pub, then didn't show. That was it, they yabbered away until closing time, went home together, and... well, you know the rest."

"You never said."

17

"I wanted everyone to think it was fate. Sometimes fate needs a little helping hand. That said, you and Aaron probably need an earth-mover."

Alice felt her shoulders slump and Polly reached out and gave her arm a reassuring squeeze. "Just joking. Now to the sex bit."

Alice braced herself. It wasn't as if she hadn't spent hours dreaming about kissing Aaron, but she rarely let her mind go "all the way". She simply couldn't cope with the consequences in her body when she did.

Polly had her professional face on. "In my substantial experience, the most mind-blowing sex is always best-friend sex. You're so attuned to each other the physical stuff automatically follows. There's none of those awkward moves and wrong angles. It's like your bodies just *fit.*"

"Is that how it is with you and Jake?"

Jake was Polly's long-term go-to when the Tinder scene was fallow. Their friends with benefits arrangement seemed to keep them both very satisfied.

"I guess."

"Why don't you fall in love with him, then?"

Polly whipped her hand off Alice's arm and grabbed her wine. "Because I don't want to. I get my kicks from helping other people fall in love."

Alice opened her mouth then shut it. Polly had left home at sixteen after her parents' messy divorce. She'd always made light of it, but she was adamant that all that love stuff was never going to be her gig. Weird then, that Polly got so much pleasure out of seeing other people fall in love.

"And what if it doesn't work? Our friendship's blown for good, isn't it?"

"Not necessarily. Sometimes it clears the air. But view this from another angle, Munchkin; how much longer can you go on like this? I'm worried you'll self-combust."

"That's a possibility." Alice took a sip of wine. Placing her glass down, she chewed thoughtfully at her lower lip. "Where would I start, Poll? I mean, I can't even fathom the basics of flirting. What am I supposed to *do* to actually seduce someone?"

*Let alone someone I've been madly in love with for years?*

"Well, first you have to throw Aaron off-balance, shake him up a bit. You're in the perfect position to do that now. You've well and truly got the upper hand."

"That sounds awful. Like a scheming hussy."

Polly grinned. "Where do you get those sayings?"

"Regency romances," Alice muttered. She had a pile of vintage Georgette Heyer novels hidden under her bed that she re-read whenever she felt sad.

"I prefer the term *strategy*," Polly said airily. "All you're doing is making sure the conditions are right for *lurvvv*. I've already got an idea." She caught Alice's worried frown and raised her hand to stop her protests. "Don't shoot it down in flames before you've heard it." She jumped up. "First we need to give you a makeover." Before Alice could even register what was happening, Polly had grabbed her by the hand and was dragging her across the hallway to her bedroom.

Motioning to the bed, she ordered, "Sit down."

Alice did so and watched as Polly started to grab dresses out of her crammed wardrobe.

"Remember that buying spree I went on when I reached size ten for a whole week?" Polly said, piling garments gleefully over her arm. "There's all this stuff I can't squeeze into that will fit you perfectly." Flicking a strand of ebony curls off her face, she grinned over her shoulder at Alice. "It's dress-up time, Munchkin!"

At the bar of the Shamrock Irish pub, Aaron stared into his pint of Guinness. Next to him, Carter Wells, his friend since they were fourteen, flipped a beer mat between a bony finger and thumb.

"Can you stop doing that?" Aaron grumbled.

"It's that or jiggle my knee. Lucy hates me jiggling my knee."

"I hate you flipping beer mats."

Carts, as he was known, gave Aaron a baleful look. "Right now, Lucy's opinion matters more than yours."

"Why? She's more or less ditched you. And I'm—for some reason I still can't work out—your best mate." Aaron cast a look up at Carts; "up" being the operative word. Even seated on a bar stool, the top of Carts' head skimmed the shelf of glasses above the bar. He'd hit six foot five at fourteen and added another inch a year later, which had earned him the title Stick Insect, swiftly shortened to The Stick. It had been Aaron who'd insisted on calling him Carts instead, and who'd made sure the name stuck with their peers. He guessed that proved he wasn't a completely selfish bastard. Because for some reason the memory of Alice's shocked expression this afternoon kept tweaking his gut and tarnishing the day's win.

*User*, a voice said inside his head. In an attempt to ignore it he asked, "Any developments with the Lucy thing?"

Carts' face brightened and *hallelujah*, the mat-flipping stopped. "She's agreed to meet me."

"What for?"

"I think she's realised she's made a mistake."

Aaron swiped condensation off his glass with the pad of his thumb. Lucy had developed a crush on her personal trainer, intense enough that she'd packed her stuff out of Carts' house and left two weeks ago. Aaron had seen the writing on the wall months ago. She'd been telling Carts that he needed to beef up – a sure sign of a woman on the move. Brawn had clearly won over brains and she wasn't coming back anytime soon.

"I had a Eureka moment last night," Carts continued, clearly not noticing Aaron's silence. "I'm going to surprise her with an engagement ring."

Glass at his lips, Aaron nearly spluttered Guinness everywhere. "What the hell for?"

"I figured her leaving probably had something to do with me not taking things to the next level. If she knows how I really feel—I mean, this guy, he's just playing with her, right? He's not offering her anything."

"Apart from a great time in the sack."

"Absolutely nothing's happened between them. She told me. Nothing. It's just an emotional connection."

Aaron bit his lip. Swallowing his cynical scoff was probably the kindest thing, because frankly, however much advice Aaron gave him, Carts was a sucker for women who took pleasure in draining his bank account only to scarper when a better offer came along. At least with Lucy, Carts had got laid over the past year, which was more than could be said for his luck with the two before her. Though from Carts' account it was usually in the dark and never on a weeknight because Lucy was always too tired. Hence the naturopath and a personal trainer that Carts had obligingly forked out for.

"You don't believe me," Carts burst out.

"I didn't say a word."

"Exactly."

"Okay," Aaron prevaricated. "For what it's worth, I don't think it's a great idea to offer an engagement ring after the horse has bolted."

"That's not a nice analogy."

"Metaphorically speaking."

"Oh. Right." Carts picked up his glass. "What's wrong with it?"

"Because... because..." *Because she's clearly not into you enough, mate, that's why.* "Maybe see what she has to say first. Get a feel for if the split was about her wanting more from you. Then take it from there."

Carts gave this a moment's thought. "That's a pathetic idea. I shouldn't even be listening to you. You wouldn't know love if it hit you in your freakin' balls."

Aaron grinned. "If that's where it hits, I'd say I'm pretty much an expert."

"Yeah, well, what d'ya know? Certificate of excellence for the one-night shag awarded to Aaron Blake for his endeavours in the field." Carts waved his glass in Aaron's face, then downed the contents and slammed it onto the counter. "Same again, mate," he called over his shoulder to Paddy, the Shamrock's barman.

Paddy sauntered over. "Any news on the job?" he asked with a raised eyebrow at Aaron.

Another weird gut contraction. What was wrong with him? He should be shouting it from the rooftops.

He forced a smile. "Yeah, actually. I had lunch with the partners today and got the call this afternoon."

"Dude. Why didn't you say? I've been droning on about my own crap, and you've just landed the job of a lifetime. Congratulations." Carts uncoiled from his stool and gave Aaron a slap on the back.

"What's with the bromance?" A bright red head bobbed into Aaron's field of vision. Dan Roach, the last member of the school-friend trio, dragged up a bar stool.

Paddy cracked his knuckles. "Aaron's had some good news. You're buying the next round, mate."

Dan's eyes rounded. "You got it? Seriously? Shit, you *did*. You're going to be a big swinging dick around town."

Caught in a headlock that only a rugby left-sider could deliver, Aaron managed to croak, "Thanks, mate. Now take your filthy hands off me and buy me a drink."

For the next hour, maybe two—seriously, who was counting on a Friday night when you'd landed a kick-arse job?—the three of them downed pints, discussed what Aaron's new office would look like, analysed why Dan's last rugby match had them relegated to bottom of the league and ribbed Carts for thinking the idea of marrying Lucy had any merit whatsoever.

But after a further sojourn at the bespoke rum bar near the quay, when his friends suggested going to the casino, Aaron hesitated. He was already a bit wasted and a trip to the casino meant getting home in the wee small hours and spending his weekend feeling less than sharp. And he needed to stay sharp for Sunday with Alice.

A wave of nausea rose up his throat. Yep, he'd definitely had one too many.

"Guys, I'm going to call it a day."

"Wuss!" said Dan.

"Yeah, you wimp," Carts seconded. The conversation was clearly deteriorating to an earlier phase of the life cycle. Based on past experience, Aaron knew things would only get messier from here.

Aaron downed the last mouthful of his rum.

"Nah, I'm off. I've got a busy weekend lined up."

"Still coming to watch us beat the Kicking Roos on Sunday?" Dan's eyes were two pools of blue swimming in bloodshot whites.

Aaron hesitated again. How was he going to keep his mates out of this fiasco? The Shamrock was the closest pub to Trojan's. What if his work colleagues turned up there on a Friday night and the conversation gravitated to Alice, his *girl-friend*? Dan and Carts wouldn't buy it for a second, unless— unless he gave them a hint that he was actually interested in Alice *that way* already. A hard one to pull off, but... "Sorry, can't. I'm seeing Alice," he heard himself say.

Carts' elbow slid along the bar; stubbly chin hitched onto his fist. "I think I could fall for Alice," he mused hazily. "If it wasn't for Lucy, I'd probably ask her out."

Aaron felt his spine stiffen. "You're not her type. Besides, she'd only come up to your waist."

"An advantage if I was like you, but luckily for the entire female population, I'm not." Carts' eyes focused with sudden suspicion. "You're looking shifty; you better not be planning to come on to Alice."

"Of course not." Aaron gave an unconvincing laugh. "Though, I guess Al and I have been spending a bit more time together lately." He searched around for his suit jacket and

23

swung it over his shoulder. Dan grinned and elbowed Carts in the ribs. Carts looked even more peeved.

"See you next week." Aaron waved airily and made for the door.

Outside he took a breath. Pulled out his phone. No messages.

He'd tried to phone his dad earlier to tell him the news. A standard, *busy now, will call you later,* text had been shot back. No missed calls registered. Aaron dialled, and the phone cut to: "You have reached David Blake of Blake Financial Services, please leave a message and I will get back to you as soon as possible."

Aaron flicked "call end", then scrolled to his stepmum's number. Andrea picked up after a couple of rings. "Aaron, how are you?"

"Great. Is Dad around?"

"He's at dinner with a client. Have you tried his phone?"

"Yep. No answer. Standard Dad."

"Can I give him a message when he gets home?"

Aaron hesitated. What was he hoping for? The great big hoorah, the *I'm so proud of you, son,* virtual slap on the back? Of course, it wouldn't happen. It hadn't after he'd graduated law school, or when he got the job with his last firm. So why now?

"Just tell him I got the position."

"The one with the big litigation firm?"

"Yeah, that one."

"Oh, Aaron. That's marvellous. Your dad will be chuffed."

They both knew she was lying. Andrea was good at papering over the cracks. At best David Blake would grunt something about it being high time Aaron thought seriously about his future. "Yep," he said. "Thanks, Andrea."

"I'll get him to ring you when he gets home." Andrea's voice had that too-bright sheen to it.

"Don't bother. I'm off to bed. Tomorrow will be fine."

"Of course. And congratulations again."

"Thanks, Andrea. Bye."

As he brought up the Uber app on his phone, Aaron found he was once again dwelling on Alice. The weatherboard cottage her mum owned was a mere ten-minute walk from here; the sofa bed in the spare room more appealing than usual. Alice would open the door wearing that ghastly checked dressing gown and pink slippers with rabbit ears. She'd take one look at his face, give him an exasperated eye-roll over the top of her glasses and throw a quilt at his head. Maybe if he grovelled, she'd make him a hot chocolate.

He pulled himself up short.

*What the fuck are you thinking?*

That was a seriously bad idea. Alice wasn't at all happy with him right now; he couldn't recall ever seeing such a stunned look on her face before. To be honest, it had slightly dented his ego. Not that he'd ever want Alice to look at him like *that*—god no, it would be like dating your sister; well, maybe not your sister, more like your first cousin—was that even legal?

Wasn't that why he'd thought of Alice in the first place? Because she was completely safe territory? He'd just have to promise to make it up to her; art house movies, as many as she wanted for the next year; eating out at those weird vegetarian restaurants she loved. It'd be fine, absolutely fine; their friendship was bigger than this.

So why was there this uneasy feeling in his gut?

Probably he was just pissed because Dad couldn't be bothered to return his call.

That had to be it.

Shrugging it all off, Aaron punched in his location for the Uber.

# CHAPTER 3

Outside the art gallery people greeted each other with hugs and laughter. A group had gathered to watch a clown on stilts, and Beatles songs floated over from a busker on the other side of the square. Alice fought off the tightness in her chest. She just needed to stand still and let the crowds flow around her; breathe in for two and out for a count of three.

She'd texted Aaron to let him know she was standing to the left of the entrance behind a pillar, but omitted any mention of what she was wearing. It was hidden under her old grey coat anyway. A vintage 1950s dress patterned with peacock tails in shades of blue and turquoise and green, cinched in at the waist and with a low neckline (well, low for her). She'd had a fight with Polly over whether to add a scarf, which Polly had said made her look terminally frumpy. Finally, they'd settled on Alice's strand of freshwater pearls, even though Alice thought they drew too much attention to the glimpse of cleavage that peeped over the neckline.

Reflexively she fiddled with her coat buttons. It was a warm day for the middle of winter, the sun smiling out of a clear blue sky, and already she was hot under the thick fabric. She'd been reassuring herself that she could keep her coat on inside the gallery if she lost her nerve, but not if she was going to melt into a sweaty puddle.

She was checking her phone to see if she'd missed a message when a familiar voice sent shivers scooting down her spine. "Sorry. I missed my train by thirty seconds."

Suddenly she was engulfed in an Aaron hug. A moment of powerful biceps and hard pecs. Like always, she didn't even have time to return it properly before it was over.

He pulled back and smiled down at her.

Alice let herself be dazzled. His blond hair had returned to its effortless style, short at the sides, longer at the front so that it fell casually over his forehead, accompanied by a flash of perfect white teeth and oh, those cheekbones!

Did he have any idea just how utterly *regency rake* he was? How wonderful he would look in a cravat, or galloping across a barren moorland on horseback?

No, of course he didn't.

This was Aaron. The guy who thought Charlotte Brontë wrote *Pride and Prejudice*.

Alice stifled a wistful sigh. "I was a bit worried you wouldn't find me."

"Is it too busy?"

She flapped a hand. "No, no, it's fine, really."

"If you want to go to a café first, we could come back when the crowds thin out."

"Thanks, but I'll cope."

How could she hate her anxiety when it was how she'd met Aaron in the first place? Head bent over her knees, mid-panic-attack, she'd been huddled on a wall behind the lecture theatre. It was her final exam, and she had been about to blow it spectacularly. She remembered looking up and blinking into the eyes of a guy who'd ducked down in front of her and was asking if she was okay. Something—maybe the deep blue of his eyes, or the lopsided hitch of his lips as he smiled at her—must have stopped her heart for a moment, because when it started again the crazy pounding was not nearly as intense. She'd gasped out something about having an anxiety problem. He'd nodded like he understood, handed her a bottle of water, and stayed until her lungs had finally filled with air.

When she put down her pen three hours later, having written the best essay she could ever remember in her whole three years of English literature, Alice knew this was it.

She'd fallen head over heels in love.

"The line over there looks shorter." Aaron gestured towards one of the three queues. "I'm paying, by the way."

Alice fumbled to get her purse out of her bag. She never let Aaron pay; they always split things. "No, you aren't. Besides, I'm a Friend of the Gallery. I'll get both with my discount and you can pay me back."

"Okay then, I'll buy dinner."

She was about to protest vigorously when Polly's voice blasted through her head. *"Don't insist on being politically correct all the time. It's not sexy."*

"I—er, we'll discuss that later," she mumbled.

"No strings attached, if that's what you're worried about," Aaron said quickly.

Alice tried to return a sensual smile. The effort almost made her eyes water. At least she'd held out against Polly's insistence that she wear contact lenses; that would have been too much of a makeover. The dress was enough of a diversion from her usual jeans and T-shirt.

Luckily, Aaron didn't seem to notice her failed seductive look as they exchanged cash and tickets. "Okay, give me your coat and I'll hand it in."

"No—I'm fine."

"It's really hot in here."

She shrugged.

His eyes scanned her face and homed in on her mouth. "Are you wearing lipstick?"

Alice felt her cheeks firing up. "Just a touch of gloss."

Aaron's gaze stayed fixed on her lips. The heat from her

cheeks migrated to a spot much lower down. It made her want to hop from foot to foot.

"It suits you," he said. "Now, give me your coat."

Alice resisted the urge to wrap her arms around her midriff. Damn it, Polly was right; it was now or never. She peeled off her coat, handed it to him and then fidgeted with her purse.

Aaron stepped back, giving her a very obvious once-over.

Her gut contracted. "What's wrong?"

"Nothing. I don't think I've ever seen you in a dress before, that's all." For a beat his gaze rested on her chest, then he snapped his head up. A dull flush suffused his cheeks.

A rush of adrenaline whooshed through her. Nothing at all like a panic attack.

She said, as nonchalantly as she could, "I decided it was time for a change."

"It's certainly very different." A pulse ticked in Aaron's jaw. She couldn't resist an internal high five as he turned abruptly and strode over to the cloakroom, shrugged off his jacket and handed both garments to the girl at the counter. Alice watched the girl's lips lift in a coy smile. No doubt Aaron was flirting outrageously. And just like that, her moment of elation sputtered and snuffed out. Who was she trying to kid here? One glance at her cleavage meant nothing. It was merely a reflex. Aaron loved women's bodies and Alice guessed hers—being presentable enough—would elicit a reaction when she showed it off. It was no more significant than your pupils dilating when the light changed.

Resisting the urge to rush over and wrestle her coat back, she forced herself to go and buy a program instead. When Aaron joined her, she made sure she was engrossed in reading about Dante Gabriel Rossetti and William Holman Hunt.

"I hope you're going to interpret. You know what a philistine I am." He grinned. Alice gave an exaggerated eye-roll as they shuffled their way through the crowds into the first room of the exhibition.

Once inside, the problem was there were so many people

squishing up to see the paintings that firstly, Alice couldn't see much from her five foot two height (even though a pair of heels she hadn't worn since a cousin's wedding two years ago elevated her another couple of inches), and secondly, she was nudging elbows with Aaron so frequently her body was refusing to behave in any way close to normal.

Aaron leaned closer, his breath warm against her neck. "Do you want me to lift you up so you can see?"

"That's sizeist."

"No, it's realist. Next best thing, then." His hands landed on her shoulders and he manoeuvred her gently forward. Then didn't let go. Alice teetered on her heels, which somehow nudged her body against him. She felt the warmth of his chest on her back and his fingers tightened briefly around her shoulders, then loosened.

Quickly, she stepped forward and, scanning the signage, said, "This is *Beata Beatrix*."

She knew that, of course. *Beata Beatrix* was her favourite of all Rossetti's works.

"Hmm. So, what's the story?" Aaron said.

There was no need to flick through her program; she knew everything about the painting, but she did so anyway because her whole body felt like a lit-up Christmas tree. Her nipples tingled as they nudged at the tight fabric of her dress. Was this what wearing a vintage dress did to your libido? No wonder Polly had such a good sex life.

"It's a portrayal of a thirteenth century poem about lost love," she explained primly. "Rossetti painted it as a tribute to his partner, Lizzie Siddal, after she died of a laudanum overdose."

"That's a bit morbid."

"I think it was his gift of atonement. Lizzie had a miscarriage and sank into depression. Rossetti left her alone for long periods while he painted and had affairs with other women. Lizzie wanted to be an artist too, but she never got the chance; women didn't in those days."

"He sounds like a prize dick."

Next to them, a bearded man glared. Alice gave him an apologetic smile. "Probably," she conceded. "Though at least he paid a tribute to Lizzie with *Beata Beatrix*. Look at her, she's absolutely divine."

"She reminds me of Polly."

"What makes you say that?"

Aaron waved a hand at the painting. "The pouty lips thing. It's completely over the top."

Alice pulled her mouth into a tight line. She'd been trying to emulate Polly's sensational pout. Obviously not the right move. Lip gloss or no lip gloss it wasn't going to cut it with Aaron. He went for the cool Scandinavian model look. And she was never going to be able to copy that, not with Rowena's Yorkshire genes and her dad's… well, god only knew.

She let out an exasperated huff. "I give up, you don't take anything seriously."

Aaron gifted her a lopsided smile. "I'm sorry, I really meant to try this time. Okay, let's move on. What's this one about? Looks like a woman lying in a pond fully clothed. But correct me if I'm wrong."

"Ophelia. You must know what play she's out of?"

"Macbeth?"

"*Hamlet*, you dunce." She gave him a little swat on the arm with her program. "She went mad and drowned after Hamlet jilted her."

"And did the artist's model die a terrible death too?"

"Well she's dead now, obviously. This was painted in the 1850s. There's a scandal behind this one. Effie Gray left her husband, John Ruskin, for John Everett Millais, who painted her here as Ophelia. Effie's marriage to Ruskin was never consummated."

"You're kidding? They never had sex? Why not?" Aaron looked at her sideways from under the thick sweep of his lashes. They were probably longer than hers, which was monumentally unfair.

"Apparently, so the rumour goes, Ruskin didn't like... that was, he didn't expect... a woman would have *pubic hair,*" *Alice* finished in a louder whisper than she'd meant.

"What was he wanting—a Hollywood?"

Alice giggled. "Keep your voice down. And what's a *Hollywood* anyway?"

"The full works. *Zrrrppppp.*" Aaron made a zipping motion below his waist. "All gone. Or, so I've heard."

Alice bit her lip and stared at the garland of flowers around Ophelia's neck. She guessed Aaron had probably seen everything there was in that department. She thought of how untidy *down there* she would be in comparison if... if... she tried to control the blush that was riding across her face, but it was too late, their corner of the gallery suddenly felt like a sauna.

Fanning her face with her program, she tried to slow her breathing. "According to some art historians—though all their correspondence disappeared so we don't really know for sure —John Ruskin couldn't consummate the marriage because Effie didn't live up to his ideal of what the female body should look like naked."

"That's pretty weird."

"Ruskin was an intellectual, he was probably more into his books than, well, you know... more *earthly* pursuits."

"Like someone else I know."

Before she could stop herself, she rebutted, "Are you implying I don't like sex?"

For a moment their eyes locked. Alice tried to control the crazy little zaps that seemed to be prodding her in very intimate places. Once again, a dull flush sat high on Aaron's perfect cheekbones. "No, not at all."

"Well, good."

He grinned. "Just not with hairy men."

"Oh, you—" Her words jangled around the gallery and again the bearded man cast them an exasperated look. If she'd come on her own, Alice knew she would have been like him, deeply immersed in studying the art, the beauty of the brushstrokes and the nuances of light and shade. But now all she could think of was how her skirt swished delightfully around her legs when she walked and the warm glow that wouldn't let up in her belly every time Aaron looked at her.

For once in her life she was having too much fun to care what Mr Bearded Man thought.

After that, the afternoon seemed to pass in an enjoyable haze of vibrant colours and light banter. By the time they were back in the foyer and fetching their coats, it was hard not to feel a frisson of excitement about the evening ahead. It wasn't as if they'd never been for a meal together; they had, more times than Alice could count. Especially when Aaron was between dates and she was, well... her drastically dateless self. She'd only ever had two boyfriends, and neither had proven earth-shattering experiences. But this felt different. Anticipation bubbled in her stomach. Despite his no-strings-attached promise, she was sure the fake date was on Aaron's agenda; why else would he have subjected himself to two hours of non-stop art appreciation? And what if he didn't raise it... would she have the courage to?

By now they were out in the rapidly cooling late afternoon.

"That was more fun than I expected," Aaron said, raking his fingers through his hair as he surveyed the buzzing art precinct. "It's still early but I skipped lunch, so if you're happy to eat, you can choose."

Alice's eyebrows flew up. "Me choose?"

"Yeah, why not?"

"Last time you said you'd never let me decide where we ate ever again."

"Oh come on, be fair, raw zucchini noodles in a pad Thai? What's a guy to do? I had to grab a kebab on the way home." Aaron gave his stomach a light thump. His shirt barely indented against the ridge of his abs and Alice suddenly had the overwhelming urge to reach out and touch them.

She curled her fingers tightly round the handle of her bag

instead. "Okay, Japanese then. There's that place we went to for Carts' birthday. It's near here somewhere."

"You're on."

She'd started to walk briskly down the steps towards the restaurant strip when Aaron's hand on her elbow startled her. She halted and their bodies bumped. They'd touched more in one afternoon than they had in the last couple of months. It felt odd. And wildly exhilarating.

Aaron swivelled her round and, for a second, they faced each other. She gazed up at his mouth, his full lips slightly parted, his eyes glittering down at her in a way she had never seen before. A pulse started drumming in her neck. Was Aaron going to kiss her?

Alice tilted her chin.

Then he turned her another ninety degrees, and said, "Your sense of direction is shot. It's this way."

As a plate of sizzling Teriyaki beef arrived at the table, Aaron's mind was working a lot faster than his facial muscles. He was good at not giving away what was going on in his head. He'd learned to do it after his mum died. A very useful strategy, he'd finally realised in his mid-teens—his face a blank canvas on which he'd perfected the laid-back smile, the heavy-lidded gaze; one elbow hitched over the back of a chair, accompanied by the full torso slouch. Add the casual flick of hair away from his eyes and he'd found out he was seriously onto something with the opposite sex.

Carts had called it his *come-fuck-me look.*

The issue was, Aaron had never dreamed of using his *come-fuck-me* look with Alice. Only now it seemed he was more than a little tempted to. And even more alarming, he was even enjoying the idea. Alice blinked at him over the top of her glasses. He'd always known vaguely that her eyes were brown, but they looked suddenly bigger... wider... darker.

"Don't wait," she said. Her lips seemed fuller too. They had drawn his attention all afternoon in the gallery. "I'll wait for the tofu."

He poured her a glass of wine. "Still doing your vego thing?"

She gave a little shrug. It made the small spheres of her breasts tip towards him. Aaron swallowed the saliva gathering in his mouth, filled up his own glass and put the bottle down. He must be hungrier than he'd thought.

"Yes, more or less. I think I'm what's called a *flexitarian*. We've got some flexitarian cookbooks in the shop. They're very popular."

"What does that term even mean?" Aaron said. Food fads annoyed the hell out of him.

"Mostly vegetarian, but sometimes not. And it sells books, I guess."

Aaron dug into the bowl of rice then handed it to Alice. Her dish arrived; squares of fried tofu floating in a golden aromatic gravy, garnished with spring onions. Not so bad considering there was no meat in sight.

"Polly's on the five:two," Alice commented.

Aaron snorted. "I prefer the caveman diet. What's it called?"

"Paleo."

"Yeah, that one. The idea of spearing my food and ripping it apart with my teeth has a certain appeal."

"I can't see you doing that." Alice smirked. "It would leave blood on your designer shirts." She busied herself spooning tofu onto her plate. He took the opportunity to watch her. Her hair was tied into its characteristic ponytail, but little tendrils of chestnut had escaped and fell softly around her neck. How come he'd never noticed that little indent at the base of her throat? The soft v of her collarbones? His eyes slipped to the curve of her breasts once more and he found his mind toying with an image of her nipples. Small and rosy, he'd guess.

Something stirred in his groin.

*Shit!*

This was *Alice*, for Christ's sake.

Aaron shifted in his seat, skewered a slice of tender beef with a chopstick. "Obviously I would wear nothing but a loin-cloth while hunting."

Alice made a strangled sound. He glanced up. "Are you all right?"

She grabbed a napkin and dabbed at her mouth. "I just choked on my tofu."

"At the idea of me in a loincloth?" He cast her his best heavy-lidded look.

Alice placed her napkin down and her mouth trembled into a smile. "Maybe. It's not something I've really thought of before." She cast a glance at him over the top of her glasses again, and he suddenly had the urge to reach over and remove them.

He drew in a breath.

Maybe this would be as good a time as any to bring up the dating issue once more. Given how their afternoon was panning out, he might get a more favourable response.

He was about to open his mouth when Alice leaned forward and planted both elbows on the table. Two bright spots of colour flared on her cheeks.

"I'll do it," she said.

Aaron eyed her cautiously, not sure whether by *it*, she meant what he thought she did.

"The girlfriend thing," she rushed on. "I've decided I'll do it."

"*Really?*" A little bubble of unease made its way up his throat. He'd expected this to call for some serious persuasion tactics. Somehow it all seemed too easy, and Alice appeared, well, kind of—*agitated*. She picked up her glass and took a large gulp, then another. He watched her throat move as she swallowed. Contents drained, she plonked the glass back down next to her plate.

"Yep." She gave a little hiccup, followed by a hand slapped

over her mouth and a giggle. "Sorry, I don't normally do that. Tastes disgusting. I do have a request though, in return."

He shrugged. "Sure. Fire away." Honestly, how hard could an Alice request be?

Slender fingers fluttered to the string of pearls at her neck. Her gaze dropped away and she seemed fascinated by the paper tablecloth. "I need you to teach me how to flirt."

"W-what?"

"You know, *flirt*," she said, her cheeks now beetroot. "I need to learn how to do it."

"Why?"

"So I can get a boyfriend."

Aaron blinked. Alice flirting with men wasn't something he'd ever really contemplated. As for a boyfriend? Apart from a couple of short-lived relationships, Alice had always been a boyfriend-free zone. Free and available whenever he needed her. He pulled himself together. "That's ridiculous, you've had boyfriends before. You managed to find them yourself without any help."

She flashed him a twisted little smile and started pleating the tablecloth. "Two boyfriends, Aaron. I'm twenty-six years old and I've only had two boyfriends. And neither of them stuck around for long. That's not a great track record, is it?

He cast his mind back. "There was what's-his-face... the guy who studied quantum physics."

"Quentin."

"Yes, and... Joseph, wasn't it?"

"Jeremy."

"That's right, Jeremy, who used to come to the pub on Fridays with you. Wasn't he heavily into gaming?"

"But not heavily into me. That's the problem, I don't seem to inspire full-blown lust."

"Full-blown lust?" He was beginning to feel like a parrot.

She nodded. Grabbed the wine bottle.

There was a long, drawn-out silence while he watched her fill it to the brim. "What help do you think I would be..." His voice trailed off as her fingers slid up and down the stem of her glass.

"Well, you're experienced at dating. And you also happen to be my closest male friend by miles. So I figured, that's a good combination. You know what appeals to guys. Besides," she continued, picking up her wine glass, "it's water-tight, because it won't get *awkward* between us. After a few tips from you I'm sure I'll feel okay to put my profile on Tinder." She flashed him a bright smile. "Come to think of it, you could help me write it."

"Tinder!" he almost yelped. "Alice, I really don't think—"

She raised an eyebrow. "Why not?"

"It's full of guys out for a quick shag."

"Like you?"

"Yes, I mean—no!"

"Well, I'm not averse to a few practice shags."

Aaron almost winced, the word sounded all wrong coming out of Alice's mouth. He had no problem with anyone else saying it, which made him a complete hypocrite, didn't it?

"I have to get to first base before I can get to second base, right?" Alice chimed.

He shot her a dark glance. "Do you even know what that means?"

She beamed. "It's a good analogy isn't it? Sort of like climbing Everest. If I want to scale the dating mountain, I have to navigate the base camps."

"There is another connotation."

"Really?"

Was Alice playing with him? Or was she seriously this naïve? Alice didn't play games, so it had to be the latter. Which made it even more imperative he didn't let her throw herself to the wolves.

"As in, first base." Aaron plastered his palms on his pecs; forced his eyes not to stray to her chest. "Second base is... lower..."

She cocked her head. "How much lower?"

"Like your..." He swallowed hard. "Like your..." Normally, if he was with the lads, he'd say *pussy*, no problem, but Alice and he had never had these kinds of conversations—at least, not in direct relation to each other's bodies.

Aaron felt a flush of embarrassment riding up his neck. "It used to be called second base at school when you got inside a girl's undies."

Alice's eyes skittered away but her lips tilted. "No wonder I've never heard the term before. I bypassed the school groping stage."

Thankfully the need to reply was interrupted by the waiter arriving with a plateful of sushi. Aaron stared at the plates piling up on their tiny table. This flirting thing was a dumb idea. But then asking Alice to be his date in the first place, was —as she'd pointed out the other night—a pretty dumb idea too.

Maybe they should just forget the whole thing.

Then he thought about next Friday's drinks with the partners and his stomach clenched. How would he explain the absence of a girlfriend when he'd said Alice was so excited to meet them?

He forced a smile. "How do you want to go about this?"

Alice wriggled forward in her seat. "Okay, well—I thought that for every date I have as your girlfriend, you could return the favour by giving me flirting tips."

"Like what, exactly?"

"Oh, I don't know... I was thinking I could practise with you, like method acting classes, and you could tell me whether what I'm doing *works* or... um... doesn't. You know, be my coach."

"I see." He didn't. What he did see was trouble looming that he couldn't quite put his finger on.

"Or better still, since we're supposed to be dating, we could practise 'on the job', so to speak."

He shot her a dumbfounded look. Alice lifted her chin and returned his gaze, and still two bright pink spots rode her cheekbones. Aaron stifled the desire to call the waiter for the

39

bill. Whether he liked it or not, he was stuck between a rock and a hard place. As for the tightening sensation in his belly, if he'd been prepared to explore it—which he definitely wasn't, since he didn't believe in navel gazing in any shape or form— he might have been forced to admit that the thought of giving Alice flirting lessons wasn't *entirely* unappealing.

He binned the thought and picked up his glass. "Well, I guess we should toast to that."

Alice flicked her ponytail over her shoulder. "To us. Fake dating and flirting lessons," she said sweetly, and he watched as, once again, she sank the whole glass.

"To us," he answered.

He hadn't got a clue what Alice and he were anymore.

# CHAPTER 4

"Here." Polly thrust a miniscule lacy bra at Alice. "Wait—this one's gorgeous too. Try both."

They'd only been in the lingerie department at Myer for five minutes and already Alice was almost buried under scraps of lace and silk held together with wire and annoying little hooks that would take her forever to do up.

Polly had the look of a kid in a candy store as she zigzagged between the rows of bras and panties, her fingers flicking gleefully through the garments.

Considering Alice normally went to Target and grabbed cotton T-shirt bras, the same ones she'd been buying since she'd finally made it to a B cup at seventeen, this was all completely new and, frankly, daunting territory.

"Okay, start with these, and if they don't work, we'll progress."

"How long is this going to take?" Alice glanced nervously at her watch over the pile in her arms and a couple of bras slithered to the floor. "I've put the back-in-ten-minutes sign up. Mum would hate it."

Polly gave her an exasperated look as she picked up the

bras. "Your mum is on the other side of the world and you're worried she'll notice if you close the shop on a Monday when there's never any customers? Think of me, I've got to help our occupational therapist run a macramé group on the ward this afternoon."

Alice brightened. She would love to try her hand at macramé. All those lovely hanging plant holders that cost so much in posh interior design shops. "Lucky you. Can you teach me later?"

Polly glowered. "Not on your life, you know I hate craft. Unless you call applying nail polish a craft. Call me when you've decided on the top three, I'll be looking at the Spanx. I need to get something to hold back the tummy tide."

Alice rolled her eyes. Polly's curves were beautiful. Not that she'd always felt this way. When Polly came to work at the Book Genie when they were teenagers, Alice had been terrified of this beautiful, gum-chewing creature squeezed into jeans and midriff-baring tops, with her red lips and purple nails. She was like all the popular girls at school who ignored Alice. Which was why when Polly actually talked to her, let alone seemed to want to spend time with her, it had seemed weird. At first she'd resisted the friendship, pretending she wasn't jealous when she caught guys covertly glancing at Polly from behind their copies of *The Seven Habits of Highly Effective People*. They all bypassed Alice, even though she knew so much more about books than Polly, just to ask Polly where the business section was (despite the fact it was staring at them in big bold letters because Alice had spent hours re-doing the signs). But of course, none of them actually *wanted* books on assets and mergers, they just wanted to gawk at Polly's assets.

In her cubicle, Alice undid her shirt buttons one by one and stared at her own modest assets neatly encased in white cotton. How was she going to make these stand out? They were so unspectacular. She undid her bra and slipped it off. Hesitantly, she ran the palms of both hands over her nipples. They peaked into two hard little pebbles. She shivered as an image of

Aaron's hand cupping one of her breasts, his thumb pad rolling over one tip, sprang into her head.

Blushing wildly, she grabbed the first bra. It was a gorgeous shade of deep blue with a tiny pearl-studded rose between the cups. She struggled with the clasp but finally, surveying herself in the mirror, marvelled at how her breasts seemed suddenly so rounded and, well… *lush*. Something stirred inside her. That treacly warm sensation that had been a rather constant companion since Sunday at the art gallery with Aaron.

They'd got over the embarrassing flirting discussion at dinner and had moved on to drama series as they walked back to her house. They always had robust discussions over whether the English made the best shows. Aaron was heavily into Nordic noire. Alice liked period dramas, was onto her second re-run of *Downton Abbey,* and would likely watch an episode or two to take her mind off Aaron later. They both agreed that the English had the advantage when it came to black comedy— something about their ability to combine humour with just the right dose of pathos. By the time they'd reached the steps up to her veranda, Alice was relieved they seemed to have got back into the swing of their usual banter. She'd flicked the light switch before realising the porch lamp had broken, and there ensued an awkward minute or two while she scrabbled in her bag for her keys and their breathing seemed to be amplified. Eventually Aaron suggested her coat pocket and sure enough, the big plastic key fob in the shape of a Rubik's Cube was in there. She'd smiled ruefully up at him and in the semi-dark, the glint in his eyes had made her heart do a crazy flip.

After that, she'd scurried inside, purposefully not asking him in for a hot chocolate, saying she was "dead beat" with a big yawn and had an early start, to which Aaron replied he'd be pumping iron at the gym at 6 a.m. so wouldn't have stayed anyhow.

She'd had to rapidly shut down the image of Aaron in T-shirt and shorts, all sweaty and panting, to avoid any more hot flushes.

"Have you decided?" Polly's voice jogged her back to the present.

"I've only had time to try the blue one."

"There's five others."

"I like the blue one." Alice gave her reflection another admiring glance. "I could buy two like this."

Polly groaned. "Try the red and black one."

"Oh god, I'd look like a harlot."

"Harlot is very in at the moment, I've heard."

Alice stuck her head out from behind the curtain. "Are you laughing at me?"

"Your weird Victorian vernacular? Possibly." Polly stood back with her hands on her hips. "If you want an opinion, I do need to see more than your face."

Alice drew the curtain back a smidge. Polly gave a tug. Alice stopped her shoulders from drooping, a habit from too much reading combined with an abject lack of self-confidence. Nevertheless, she couldn't stop her hands from clasping in front of her belly to preserve some sense of modesty.

"Very pretty." Polly nodded approvingly. "I think that's a definite seduction starter."

"Won't it show through if I wear light colours?"

"Yep, hopefully. We'll find something silky in a lighter blue and with this underneath it's bound to 'pop' enough to tanta-lise Aaron's tastebuds."

"I can't wear something see-through to drinks with Aaron's bosses!"

Polly shrugged. "Can't or won't? But okay, we can keep this one for when you go clubbing."

"I am not going clubbing. Strobe lights and loud music are palpitation hell."

"Okay, then we'll have a party."

"What do you mean 'we'?"

"At our place."

"No way." Alice shuddered at the thought of all the

smashed Victorian crystal glasses that were Rowena's pride and joy.

"Boring," Polly snorted. "Try the champagne-coloured one with the padding, that'll definitely take you up another cup size."

Fifteen minutes later, Alice was paying for three new bras that she was quite sure were a scandalous extravagance, when Polly whispered, "Don't look now, but there's Carts immersed in Victoria's Secret."

Which meant Alice had to look, naturally.

Carts and lacy undies were as incongruous a combination as her and lacy undies.

Carts was bent forward, squinting at some tiny French briefs splashed with scarlet roses. Alice watched as he gingerly pulled them off the rack and held them up like he was trying to work out some difficult mathematical problem. The shop assistant handed Alice back her credit card and, before she knew it, Polly had left her side and was navigating the aisles towards Carts like a she-wolf after her prey.

Carts nearly jumped out of his skin as Polly touched him on the arm.

His face turned almost the same colour as the silk panties he was holding.

Alice's heart went out to him. She really needed to save him from Polly. Grabbing her bag of bras, she hurried over to them.

"Hi Carts, do you need some help choosing?" Polly's green eyes were twinkling with mischief.

"Oh, no, um, thanks, I think I've decided."

"Who are they for?"

Carts didn't answer and Polly grinned. "They're too small for you, Carts."

Carts' eyes landed on Alice and his blush went up another notch. "Just... someone."

"You don't have to tell her." Alice tried to sound reassuring. Poor Carts. Sometimes Polly didn't read the signs. Or if she did, she delighted in ignoring them. "If you want to keep it private, that's your choice."

Carts shuffled and flicked at his long fringe with the back of his hand. "Ah-erm—oh, so what if you know? They're a present for Lucy."

Polly's brows rose. "You two are still an item, then?"

Carts' laugh was altogether too jolly. "Why wouldn't we be?"

Polly smiled sweetly and didn't say a word. Her trick, Alice knew all too well, of using silence to make someone jump in with the very thing they didn't mean to say. Sure enough, after a beat Carts finished: "We've just been having a little time apart before we take things to the next stage."

Polly's smile said *gotcha*. "Is this part of an engagement present?"

Carts cast another glance at Alice. His brown eyes reminded her of a pleading puppy. "Not exactly," he mumbled.

Polly relented on the teasing. "Well, it's a lovely gesture, regardless of what's going on between you. But with Lucy's colouring, you need to be careful what red you choose. Go for neutrals, or if you think she might like something more vibrant, emerald green would suit her skin tone." With that, she raced off to the seriously expensive section, leaving Carts and Alice to trail behind.

Carts concertinaed his torso towards Alice and whispered, "Myer should give her a commission."

Alice grinned. "She's managed to get me to buy up half the stock in my lunch break."

Carts' gaze filled with sudden curiosity. "If you don't mind me being personal, what did you buy? It's just, I'm trying to be better at understanding women's tastes."

Alice swung the plastic bag around in her hand. "Oh, you know, just everyday practical stuff. Sports bras." Somehow, on the downward swing, the bag caught and got tangled in a suspender and G-string set on the "Passionate nights" rail, grinding her to an abrupt standstill.

Carts stopped too and immediately went into action trying to free her purchases.

Why was it that embarrassing things always happened when you told porkie-pies, Alice wondered as, on Carts' final tug, the bag did a backflip and a plethora of bras landed in a brightly coloured heap between them.

Carts bent down and scooped them up, then handed them back to her, the tiny red satin and black lace number taking pride of place like the cherry on top of an ice-cream sundae.

Alice's scalp prickled.

Carts, to give him credit, kept a straight face—though one of his eyebrows twitched.

"Thanks." She crammed the offending articles into her bag as Polly joined them, holding up a cameo set in a soft shade of cream with offsets of coffee-coloured lace.

"Now this," Polly said, waving it in front of Carts' face as Alice stuffed the offending bag behind her back, "is pure class."

Where was she? Aaron's palms were sweaty. It was twenty minutes before the scheduled drinks with the partners—and their *wives*—and they still had to walk from the station to the beachside house—bound to be a freakin' mansion—where Archie Bendt lived. Alice had texted to say she was on the train but that was fifteen minutes ago. He glanced impatiently at his phone and wished he'd insisted on meeting her at work. But Alice was having to wait for Polly to fill in for her at the shop and Polly had to get there from the hospital and blah, blah, blah.

Christ, how come he was *this* nervous? It was just, well, he needed to make a great impression, needed it to look like he and Alice were a loved-up item. What if she let something slip that made it clear they weren't... or turned up looking a bit too casually Alice-ish in jeans and sneakers? It would let his image down.

A strange heat made its way down his spine and landed alarmingly close to his groin as he thought about their outing on Sunday. She'd looked okay then, hadn't she? No, go on, admit it, she'd looked great. Hot. *No!* Not hot. Classy. Pretty. Cute.

Whatever. Just don't use words with overtly sexual connotations.

Aaron did a turn of the station platform and saw the train lights in the distance. A minute later, Alice was alighting with a gaggle of other commuters.

Aaron's breath whooshed from his lungs. She wasn't wearing her glasses. She looked so different without the heavy frames that he couldn't take his eyes off her. Alice was synonymous with spectacles. That's how it was. Except not tonight, clearly. Her face without them formed a perfect heart shape; delicate brows fanning above the biggest, softest, brown-sugar eyes. Her nose, which reminded him of a squashed button with the scaffolding of her glasses bridged across it, was unobscured, and perfectly tip tilted. Somehow the whole symmetry of her face had changed. To top it off, her hair swung in a silky curtain to her shoulders, gleaming in the combination of the winter dusk and station lighting.

Holy cow. Alice was—almost—beautiful.

She wrinkled her nose as she gazed around the platform, then spied him and her lips turned up. She waved a hand close to her side, a typically Alice gesture that grounded him, at least for a second, before the dispelling crowd allowed him to take in the rest of her appearance. A short black jacket over a dress in a flattering shade somewhere between blue and green, and though he was no expert on women's fashion, the way it moulded to her body as she walked held him in thrall. His eyes dipped lower. Slender calves were accentuated by the glimmer of sheer stockings and black shoes with little bows adorned her feet.

Why did he suddenly feel like he was screwed?

As she drew up in front of him, Aaron ground his molars

together and slapped on a smile. Alice cocked her head and smiled back. Should he kiss her? He should kiss her. There was the flirting deal to consider. Better they did it in public, otherwise there could be consequences... unwanted, potentially disastrous... consequences.

"Hi," he said and pecked her cheek. She smelled great. Her skin felt like silk against his lips and his body stirred an alarming response. He moved abruptly away as she murmured "hi" back.

"We'd better get going, it'll take us a good ten minutes to walk it from here." He turned and strode off, trying to ignore the tightening against his fly. Alice fell easily into step.

"How's your week been?" he asked after a moment.

He was ridiculously aware of how close she was, the *tap-tappity-tap* of her heels, the rustle of fabric as she walked. The fact that, if he were to put his arm around her, her head would nestle perfectly into his armpit.

Alice shifted her bag strap over her shoulder and he felt her casting him a sideways glance.

"Pretty busy. What about yours? Did you hand in your notice?"

"Of course."

"How did they take it?"

"I'd say not overjoyed. We're in the middle of a big case that I've been doing the groundwork for, so it's inconvenient for them."

"They value you, Aaron."

"They value how many billing hours I can squeeze into a day," he snorted.

"What did your dad say when you told him?"

Mutual parental grumbles had always been Alice and Aaron's home ground. Rowena drove Alice mad too, admittedly for very different reasons from Aaron's dad.

Aaron shrugged. "He made the right noises, when he could finally be bothered to phone me back. Andrea would've had a word."

49

"Have you told Oliver?"

"He phoned me on Monday. Full of fake congratulations."

"Aaron. That's mean. Oliver has always believed in you."

"Oliver has always been a condescending arse."

He dared to glance at her now, and she frowned and pushed out her lower lip. Alice thought his older brother was wonderful. But then, didn't everyone? Including Oliver's massive following on social media, who lapped up his blog posts, his YouTube videos and TED talks, and who were eagerly awaiting his new book on ethical investing for millennials.

Aaron gave himself a mental shake. God, what the hell was the matter with him? He should be happy, ecstatic. Was it anxiety about the evening ahead making him so grumpy? Or was it Alice? Sans spectacles. And practically gift-wrapped in her pretty new dress.

He shoved his hands in his pockets and walked faster.

They made rather awkward small talk until they found themselves outside Archie Bendt's palatial home on the esplanade, directly facing the ocean.

"Thought as much," Aaron said, with grudging admiration.

"Don't worry," Alice responded brightly. "You'll own one just like it in a few years."

Silently he had to agree with her. That was the game plan. He'd show Dad and Oliver what success really meant.

This was it. Time to start acting.

When he glanced down at Alice he saw she'd gone pale and was holding her purse over her chest like it was shielding her from harmful gamma rays.

Sucking in a breath, he said, "Okay, let's do this."

She nodded, lips tight.

Another breath and he grabbed her hand. It was cool and a little clammy, but not unpleasantly so; he tucked it firmly in the crook of his arm and squeezed to reassure her.

Together they marched up to the gate. Aaron pressed the bell and they waited.

A second later a woman's voice drifted over the intercom. "Yes?"

"Hi. Aaron Blake here, and Alice."

"Our guests of honour. Welcome." The voice warmed up a notch and the buzzer signalled the unlocking of the gate.

Aaron braced his shoulders, opened the gate, and strode up the path, almost pulling Alice with him. Before he had time to think anything more, the front door flung wide and an immaculate blonde woman with super-toned arms and legs stood beaming at them.

"Come in, come in, I'm Miranda Bendt." A hand with a very large diamond ring squeezed his shoulder as she kissed the air close to each of his ears and then gave her full attention to Alice.

"And Alice, welcome to the firm." She threw back her head and laughed, "Wow, that sounds like the mafia, doesn't it, darling?" And with that she kissed the air on either side of Alice's head too.

Alice returned a shy smile. "Wonderful to meet you, Mrs Bendt."

"Oh, for goodness sake, not Mrs. That makes me sound ancient. Miranda, please. Now come, I can't wait to introduce you to the other wives."

Aaron's blood ran cold. Heck, it *was* like the mafia, he thought as Alice cast him a look that seemed to contain the same element of alarm that he was feeling.

They followed in Miranda's wake, towards the sound of voices and laughter. A vast hallway opened up into an even vaster room equipped with an uber-modern kitchen where a chef was arranging food onto serving platters. In the living area couches were placed strategically around artefacts and exotic plants in huge pots. While Aaron was taking it all in, Alice was whisked away in a flurry of feminine oohs and aahs.

Geoff Trojan descended, then Archie, who handed Aaron a glass of champagne and muttered, "Beer later, out the back, once the girls aren't watching."

Aaron flashed his teeth, the way he'd watched Archie do at lunch. It had struck him as charming and disarming, the sudden wide, almost cheeky, grin emerging out of a deadly serious visage. He intended to perfect it. Improve on it, even.

A waitress shoved a platter of tiny little canapes at him. He raised an eyebrow and she ventured, "Sea vegetable mousse, topped with fried green ants on a tuile of Albany seaweed."

Aaron took it and wondered if it would be possible to dispose of it anywhere but in his mouth. He guessed the pot plants were out of bounds.

"Not sure who to introduce you to first. The whole team are here and eager to meet you." Archie's piercing steel-grey eyes scanned the room. "Now, where's Alice?"

Why was it that so far everyone seemed more interested in Alice than in him? Yes, this confirmed it, he *had* joined the mafia. One big, happy family.

He pointed with his champagne glass to where Alice was now seated neatly on a sofa and two other women were leaning forward, eagerly talking at her.

"Ah-ha. The petite brunette. Lovely." Bendt nodded.

The quieter of the three, Fink gave a rare smile. "Perfect foil for you."

How the heck would they know? They hadn't even met her yet.

Aaron nodded, turning the canape around and around in his fingers. "She is." He jumped as something tugged at his trouser leg. He looked down to see a brown and white pooch, with a very snub nose. It was making weird grunting noises.

Aaron couldn't help wondering if it might fancy a canape.

# CHAPTER 5

M iranda Bendt was stunning.
Alice found it impossible not to gawk.

Her thick copper tresses were piled into an up-do that defied gravity, dark lashes framed her china blue eyes, and her skin shone like a burnished peach. Everything about her *glowed.*

Of course, the other two wives, Delia Trojan and Natasha Fink, were also attractive and immaculately groomed—they made Alice think of thoroughbred horses. But Miranda was, without question, the jewel in the crown of the Trojan, Bendt and Fink wives club.

After doing the introductions, Miranda had thrown herself nonchalantly back against the cushions of a plush sofa. "Just look at that husband of mine." Her lips curled indulgently. "Putting Aaron through his paces already."

Alice gave a weak smile and let her gaze stray to where Aaron was standing ramrod stiff in his dark blue suit next to a broad-shouldered Nordic god and a dark-haired man who looked whip-smart. Natasha Fink gave an elegant little snort. "Mark my words, any minute now they'll disappear."

"And where will we find them?" Miranda slid one bronzed leg over the other, showing a glimpse of toned thigh beneath her figure-hugging black dress.

Delia Trojan, the slightly older of the three, shook her head. "Raiding the beer fridge, without a doubt."

Miranda gave a little shrug. "They never really grow up, do they? Happiest in the shed cracking beers and sharing bad jokes."

There was no way, Alice thought, there would be anything remotely resembling a shed in the grounds of this palace.

"Honestly," Natasha laughed, "I don't think Charles would know how to iron a shirt. Or boil an egg. Where would they be without us?"

"Lost." Miranda smiled like a cat that had just licked the saucer clean out of cream. She played with a sparkling diamond on an (obviously white gold) chain around her neck. "So, Alice, Archie tells me you and Aaron have been together a while now?"

Alice sipped her champagne and rifled through the memory of her debrief with Aaron. "Nearly two years." God, how she hated lying. "But we've known each other since uni."

"How did you meet?" Natasha asked.

*While I was hyperventilating behind the lecture theatre* probably wouldn't sound the best. "Oh, you know how it is. We sort of spotted each other around, and then we got chatting and... One thing led to another."

"I can't say I blame you." Miranda's gaze followed Aaron as he sauntered around with Archie, shaking hands with his new colleagues. "He's a cutie."

Alice stomped on the green-eyed monster.

She knew that admiring look. She'd got used to it from countless women. But really, what was the point letting it worry her? Aaron was no more her boyfriend now than he'd ever been.

Earlier, with Polly's enthusiastic thumbs-up following her out of the Book Genie, she'd felt confident, attractive—even a little bit sexy in another of Polly's hand-me-downs; an Audrey Hepburn-style classic. And when Aaron's eyes had nearly propelled out of his head at the sight of her, followed by a kiss on the cheek she was sure lingered for just a second more than was necessary, well. Her heart had done gymnastics for a moment.

But now... among these women for whom beauty and obscene wealth were obviously considered a birthright, she felt like a fraud.

"So, Alice, you own a bookshop, with your mum. How deliciously quaint." Miranda leaned forward and refilled Alice's glass as she spoke. Alice stared at the red and gold label and Miranda's immaculately manicured hands as she placed the bottle carefully back on the alabaster coffee table.

She could hardly own up that the Book Genie—other than some virtual shares that she really had no idea what to do with —one hundred per cent belonged to Rowena. Always had, always would. It was her mum's pride and joy.

"I inhale books. It's my outlet now I don't work," Delia commented, almost wistfully. "What's your shop called?"

"The Book Genie," Alice said. Miranda and Natasha stared at her blankly. "It's in Northbridge. We sell second-hand books."

Miranda tinkled out a laugh. "Oh, I never buy second-hand *anything*. And if I read, it's on a device. Other than the books in Archie's study all our books are really just for decoration. And old books have that smell, don't they?" She wrinkled her nose.

Delia gave Alice a warm smile. "I love old books. I really should come and have a snoop. Could you get hold of a copy of *North and South* for me? Now, who's the author..."

"Elizabeth Gaskell," Alice supplied, feeling like she had something to offer at last.

"Yes, of course. Remember that BBC series—with that sexy broody guy, oh, what was his name?" Delia snapped her fingers. "You know, who played the lead. Probably way before your time."

"Richard Armitage." Of course Alice knew, she'd lost count of how many times she'd watched it. "I've got the series on DVD. Wasn't he amazing?"

"Swoon-worthy." Delia sighed. "Maybe they'll do a remake. I mean, I don't know how many versions of *Pride and Prejudice* I've watched. Though my favourite Mr Darcy will always be Colin Firth. That scene where he walks out of the lake dripping wet. Ohhhh, myyy god."

Miranda interjected. "Personally, give me Travis Fimmel from *Vikings* any day."

"That's because he looks just like Archie." Natasha Fink laughed.

"Isn't it wonderful," Miranda purred, "that I only lust after men who resemble my husband?"

As if they shared thoughts by symbiosis, all three turned their eyes now on Alice. "Any wedding bells on the horizon for you and Aaron?" Natasha Fink asked.

Alice nearly choked on a mouthful of champagne. "Um, not quite yet."

Natasha's eyebrows rose. Miranda stared, unblinking. Delia looked like maybe she got it as she said, "You want to focus on your career for a bit longer, right?"

Alice grabbed it like a lifeline. "Yes. Mum and I have got some really exciting things planned; we're hoping to expand the shop, maybe start a franchise." That was kind of true, Rowena had been talking about another shop for a few years. "And with Aaron wanting to establish himself first, you know..." She trailed off.

"Don't wait too long." Natasha pursed her lips. "A woman's fertility drops dramatically after thirty. How old are you, Alice?"

"I'm twenty-six," Alice said as she took a delicate-looking morsel from the waitress and shoved the whole thing in her mouth. Time to change the subject. She chewed, swallowed.

"Mmm, these are delicious. What were those little crunchy bits on top?"

"Fried green ants," Miranda supplied sweetly.

∾

After what seemed like forever listening to the wives exchange advice on the best private schools and Botox specialists, Alice managed to excuse herself and escaped to the toilet.

She sat on the loo and counted breaths, then reeled off a wad of toilet paper, tried to rewind it and failed miserably. In the end she gave up, begged the recycling fairy for forgiveness, and stuffed it down the toilet before flushing.

In the mirror, as she washed her hands, her reflection stared back at her. She really hated looking at her face without her glasses. It was akin to running around with her top off.

Sad eyes, she thought. Maybe that's why she hid behind frames most of the time. Or perhaps they were just sore from the contact lenses? She forced her lips to smile but her eyes stayed sad. She'd read in a book on emotions that fake smiles used far fewer muscles than real smiles and people could usually tell the difference. She reckoned there were a lot of fake smiles around here tonight.

She reapplied her lipstick, opened her compact and dusted powder on her nose. This make-up thing was a whole new ball game. But then, fake dating, lying through your teeth and mixing with people who were as rich as trolls was all new too.

And, frankly, horribly stressful.

Maybe she should tell Aaron she was out of the deal. Forget Polly's stupid idea that she stood a chance with him and that silly equation about amazeballs sex. Scuttle back to her smelly old bookshop and hide behind crushes on her nineteenth century book boyfriends.

*Gah!* She flung the lipstick and compact back in her bag and stuck her tongue out at her reflection before flouncing out. Straight into a hard chest. And a familiar tantalising spicy smell.

"*Ooophh*—Aaron." Strong fingers closed around the tops of her arms to steady her.

"There you are, I was just coming to see if you were all right."

"Fine, never better actually." She tried to pull away, but his grip was remarkably firm and, if she was honest, reassuring. She gazed up into the clear blue of his eyes, detected the tiny wrinkle between his eyebrows that happened when he was half amused and half questioning, and her resolve to tell him to take a hike evaporated like rain drying in the sun.

"Are you having fun?" he asked.

"Kind of. Are you?"

"Yeah. They're a great bunch. I've met all the team. I'll be under Archie the first year, it seems."

"Not literally, I hope."

His eyebrows shot up then he laughed. "Idjit."

He looked relaxed, happy. His face was a little flushed, bringing out every nuance of his spectacularly handsome features. She smiled. Forcing it to be genuine. Using the right muscles.

"Ah, here you both are."

Suddenly Aaron's arm was hunkered around her shoulders and she found herself sandwiched up against his side and swung around.

Archie Bendt smirked down at them.

Close up he *did* look like Travis Fimmel out of *Vikings*.

But meanwhile, she had to contend with the way her body was responding to the warm pressure of Aaron's, the feel of his arm around her and oh, gosh, what was that…? A soft tanta-lising stroke around the collar of her dress. Her skin goosebumped.

Aaron's fingers shifted under her hair and kept moving, agonisingly sweet, slow strokes of his fingertips against the sensitive skin at her nape.

Her legs nearly gave way and she found she had to slump against him to stop feeling like her bones were made of rubber.

Archie extended his hand in greeting. She managed weakly to put hers into it and found on top of everything else she now had to contend with her arm being practically shaken from its socket.

"Sorry I didn't say hello earlier, busy talking shop. Dry as dust so I hope the girls amused you. I understand that you're Aaron's biggest fan."

Aaron demurred. "I never said…"

"You don't need to. I can tell, just looking at you both together." Archie let go of Alice's hand and waggled his brows. "He'll need your support these next few years. We work our lawyers *harddddd*."

The twitch in Aaron reverberated through her and she wondered—not hoped—just *wondered*, if he'd be requesting an extension on the three month dating deal.

After a few more pleasantries, none of which Alice remembered a word of due to her energy being expended in ignoring the pulse that had started up in her lady bits, Archie strode off and she extricated herself from Aaron's embrace.

He kept up with her as she hurried off. "You sure you're okay? I've done the rounds of everyone important and so… you know, if you want to go?"

They'd reached the fringe of perfectly groomed guests and Alice stopped abruptly. A wave of heat whooshed from her stomach right up to her scalp, followed closely by two heart beats in quick succession. Oh god, not now… She pressed a hand to her chest and gave him a look that probably showed her horror. A full-blown one hadn't happened in ages, but then, when had she honestly subjected herself to the circumstances that would set off one of her panic attacks?

Ostrich therapy had proven very effective for years.

The trouble was, playing the part of doting girlfriend in front of all these perfect people and then having the disconcerting—and delicious—interlude outside the bathroom had probably overloaded her nervous system, sending it into complete overdrive.

"Oh—I," she gasped, leaning against the wall. "You stay, and I'll let myself out."

"That wouldn't look good." He frowned. "Are you having a—?"

She bit her lower lip and nodded while trying not to crumple in half to get her breath.

Aaron's mouth tightened. "Okay, stay close. I'll get you out of here."

His arm circled her waist as he propped her up and she tried to ignore the black dots in front of her eyes. As they walked towards the partners, then the wives, she heard his voice strong and firm, as if from miles away. It was award-winning Aaron.

"My brother is flying in from London tonight. Not the best timing but we promised to meet the plane. Yes, yes, Oliver Blake, the one and only. Yes, he's amazing. Following in Dad's footsteps." A deep, throaty laugh. "Anyway. Thank you so much, this has been truly wonderful... I am so excited to be..."

Alice somehow managed to pull herself together enough to handle the hugs and goodbyes.

Finally outside, Aaron walked her across the street to a seat facing the dark expanse of the ocean.

"Head down. Now, breathe. Hold for two, breathe out one, two, three."

Alice clung on to his instructions as he crouched in front of her, his expression serious and focused. The sound of the waves pounding rhythmically on the beach below, a lone insomniac seagull circling in the darkness over their heads and the cold night air on her face finally calmed the internal storm.

Aaron was breathing with her. Just as he'd done that first day at uni. No wonder she'd fallen head over heels in love. Wasn't it true that you were always at your most vulnerable when you were at your lowest ebb? She'd seen a documentary once where baby ducks saw a human before they actually set eyes on their mother, and forever after believed the human was their parent. Followed the human around. Ignored their real duck mummy.

Maybe the same happened when you fell in love? You were primed and ready, in a state of emotional rawness, and *wham*, there you were: hook, line and sinkered… forever more. Alice slumped over her knees and was finally able to take a breath.

It felt like she'd run a marathon. Aaron sat down next to her, knowing that silence was best for a few more minutes.

Finally he asked, "Better?"

Nodding, she managed, "Yes, thank you. About tonight, I'm sorry—"

"Best to leave while you're ahead when you're the new kid on the block." He gave her a lopsided smile. "Dancing on the table at 2 a.m. before you've even started working for them probably wouldn't be a good look."

"Not when the tables are made of Albanian marble." Alice managed a weak giggle. "There was a lot more alcohol flowing than food, that's for sure."

"Oh god, did you try a canape?"

"Seaweed and ants?"

"Yeah, seriously weird shit."

"I quite liked it until Miranda Bendt told me what it was, then my stomach nearly flipped it right back out." Alice managed a weak giggle.

"I fed mine to the pooch."

"Aaron, no."

"Yep, when I came to find you I still had it in my hand; the dog followed me, breathing like a miniature Darth Vader, so I handballed the canape to it."

"It'll probably vomit it up on one of their priceless Persian rugs."

Now they were both laughing. Her body felt limp like a newborn kitten. In this state it was possible to appreciate the way one of Aaron's legs swung so close to hers, the sting of salty air in her nostrils, the flash of a ship's lights out on the horizon. "Oliver isn't really coming to Perth tonight, is he?"

"Tomorrow."

"Has he been in London?"

"No. He's arriving from Sydney. But meeting him from overseas added more gravitas."

"Why's he here?"

"A book festival gig. Also I think him and Dad are hatching a double-act publication. Blake Financials Inc. conquer the world."

Alice cast him a sideways glance. "Does that still bother you?"

She sensed him shrug next to her. "Not now I'm—as Dan christened me—the new *big swinging dick* in town." He gave a little bark of a laugh. "I'll probably be saving their arses when they're caught recommending dodgy hedge fund investments."

"They wouldn't!"

"Probably not. But it's a nice revenge fantasy."

Alice didn't say anything. They'd had enough discussions about how differently David Blake treated his two sons. Oliver, the golden boy who could do no wrong and Aaron, who only had to say hi the wrong way and his dad's nose was out of joint. From what she knew, it had got worse after Aaron's mum died, but Aaron had always been vague about that period of his life. Said he didn't remember much, even though he was twelve years old when his mum had the car accident. Polly, in one of their frequent "Aaron dissections", had said that maybe Aaron being blond and blue-eyed like his mum was too much of a reminder for his dad. Who knew?

Polly had a theory on everything and some of them were way off the mark.

"I think I stuffed up the girlfriend thing."

"No, you didn't. They loved you, particularly the wives."

"Apart from Delia Trojan, who said she enjoys reading, they all thought I was a freak. They called owning a bookshop 'quaint'."

"That fits. You are kind of quaint."

Alice elbowed him. Elbowing had always been admissible contact.

Silence.

"I owe you a flirt," Aaron said.

"Hmm, payment for services rendered." Now she was blushing in the dark.

Another silence.

"So how do you want to do this thing?"

She flipped her bag over and over in her lap. "You did quite a good job with—um—my neck."

Aaron gave a snort. "Yeah, and you responded with a panic attack."

"I guess that would have the potential to scare a guy off." The tension crackled between them; she almost expected to see sparks fly off into the night sky.

"Besides," she said, almost gruffly, "that neck-stroking thing would, strictly speaking, be described as *you* flirting with *me*, whereas I thought the deal was *I* get to practise on *you.*"

"Okay, go on then."

"What, now? *Here?*"

"Why not? It's as good a time and place as any."

"It's way too public."

"All right, we'll go down on the beach."

Aaron got to his feet. "Up you get," he ordered.

She did and wobbled, her leg muscles the consistency of half-set jelly, partly residue from the panic attack and partly... Amazing how excitement and fear could make your body feel almost the same.

She let him loop her arm in his and they walked down the steps onto the sand. Finally, in a pool of light cast from the beach volleyball floodlights, Aaron turned to face her, shoved his hands in his pockets and looked down at his feet. He really was behaving very oddly.

"I had a great time tonight, thank you."

She looked at him, perplexed. "You did?"

Aaron grinned. "We're *flirting*, Al. Pretend I'm a guy you've

63

just been out on a date with. I'm keen. You've got to give me a bit more than that."

"Like what?"

"'So did I' would be a start. Reciprocate a bit."

"Okay. So did I."

"Put more emotion into it."

Alice flapped her bag at him. "Can't we just get the lines right and practise the emotions later?"

"God, you're hopeless."

"What sort of advice is that?" Alice protested. "I mean, if Thorpie had that level of encouragement from his coach, he wouldn't even have made it to his school swimming carnival, let alone the Olympics."

"Okay, okay. Try again. I'll be nice."

Alice shuffled her feet. There was sand in her shoes but she wasn't going to spoil the moment by taking them off. She cleared her throat and held her bag against her stomach.

Aaron pushed her hand gently down to her side. "Don't guard your body. That definitely says *not interested*."

Oh lordie, if only he knew the half of it.

Alice stood to attention. Aaron rubbed one of her arms briefly, which was probably meant to reassure but made her feel weak as a kitten again. "Relax your stance a bit, you look like you're on parade."

"Could you stop touching me? I haven't given you the cue yet," she replied, far more sharply than she meant.

His lips quirked. "Sorry." He dropped his hand from her arm.

Alice pulled herself together, cleared her throat. "Okay, here goes. I'm in character now."

"Go for it."

*Think sexy, think sexy.* She pursed her lips and glanced up at him from under her lashes the way she'd been practising in the mirror for the past week. "I really had fun tonight—with you."

Aaron leaned towards her. It made a shiver cascade all the

way down her spine. "Yeah, so did I," he murmured. "Maybe we should do it again sometime?"

"That could be pleasant."

"No, no. Come out of role for a sec."

Alice blinked, momentarily disoriented. "Don't say *could*," Aaron said. "Could is too vague. Would is more positive. And get rid of the word pleasant. It's meh."

"I'm trying not to sound too keen."

"Why?"

"I—I, it's not cool."

"Who says?"

"I read somewhere it puts guys off."

"Yeah, maybe if you texted him a dozen times after the first date or followed him home from work, but you've got a lot of wiggle room here. Here's this guy panting for you and you're behaving like the vicar's wife out of *Midsomer Murders*."

"Sorry, sorry. I'll try again."

For a second, she closed her eyes. Then, with all her might, she channelled Polly. The habit Polly had of kicking out one hip, the angle of her head, the way her eyelashes swept over her eyes just before she went in for the kill.

"I'd love that." *Gosh!* That was almost a Marilyn Monroe *"Happy Birthday Mr President"* purr!

Their eyes locked. She heard Aaron's intake of breath, sensed a sudden wired tension in his body.

"Great. I'll call you." Was she imagining it or had his voice dropped an octave? Her heart was pounding so loudly, surely he could hear it?

His eyes searched her face, lasering into her soul, laying all her secrets bare. The five years she'd pretended she found him nothing more than good fun, laughed too hard at his jokes, teased him about his conquests. Died a little inside each time.

Every last skerrick of her crazy blind love for him, exposed.

No, she couldn't risk it.

Alice twisted away, her feet scrabbling for purchase on the

sand. From somewhere inside her bag, her phone started to play the opening riff of "Crazy Little Thing Called Love".

"Oh, I—that'll be for me." She dived for it, feeling for all the world like an ungainly seal pup. Finally, she located her phone and saw the word *Mum* light up the screen. She pressed the green icon.

"Ah, there you are, darling. Did I wake you up?"

Alice mouthed *Rowena* at Aaron. He rolled his eyes.

"I'm at the beach."

"Good lord, it must be dark. What are you doing at the beach?"

"Nothing much. Just taking a walk."

"A walk! It's nearly 9 p.m. where you are. Are you feeling okay?"

"Yes, Mum, fine really. I'm with a friend. We've just been at a party."

Luckily Rowena didn't ask which friend or even comment on the party bit. There was something to be said for having a mother who never really noticed the important milestones in your life, she supposed. Rowena gushed on. "I'm in Devon, darling, I've just been to Daphne du Maurier's house. On the river—it's divine. Then I got a tip-off that the Oxfam shop in Tiverton had acquired a collection of books from some Lord whatsisface after he died, and I've got some amazing first editions. You would love England. You really must get over this flying phobia thing you have, it's so limiting."

"I know, Mum. Where are you going next?"

"Cambridge, bit of a trip down memory lane."

"Lovely," Alice said. Rowena had done an exchange year at Cambridge as a postgrad student. There were yellowing photos of her all over the house: Rowena on a bicycle with her college scarf flying behind her. Rowena in a ballgown that made her look like a wedding cake, posing on the Bridge of Sighs. Alice was sure Rowena secretly saw herself as the next Germaine Greer who'd somehow missed out on her big break.

"Is there anyone you know still there?"

There was a moment's pause. "Oh, maybe one or two. These days we're scattered all over the globe."

Alice feigned excitement. "Perhaps you'll bump into Emma Thompson. Or what's the guy out of *House*? Hugh somebody-or-other? Weren't they both at Cambridge?"

She knew she was keeping Mum talking so she didn't have to go back to the awkward flirting thing. Aaron had moved away and was skimming pebbles across the waves. His back muscles rippled in his suit jacket as he lifted his arm.

There was a pause before Rowena said brightly, "They were a bit before my time. Besides, I met so many people, it's hard to remember them all."

"Mmmm," Alice traced a pattern in the sand with her toe, realised it looked like a heart and quickly scrubbed it out. "Did you get my email about the Mrs Beeton book?"

"The one for Esther? Yes, and I'll make sure I find her a copy. Now sweetie-pie, is everything all right at home? Polly and you haven't broken any of my antique glass collection, I hope?"

"We're not toddlers, Mum."

"And the shop's going well? Lots of customers?"

"Yes, pretty steady. I'll send you the end of month financials next week."

"Perfect. Well, darling. Better go, I have a train to catch. Though knowing how things work here there will be a delay due to something, or somebody, falling on the line."

"Mum!"

"Well, it happens. I'll let you get back to your friend. Hope he's nice. Kiss-kiss."

"Oh, it's not like—" Alice protested.

But Rowena had already hung up.

# CHAPTER 6

Aaron stood on the doorstep, a bottle of shiraz in one hand and a bunch of orange gerberas in the other.

He sucked in a breath. He always needed to fortify himself before seeing Dad; add Oliver into the mix and it felt like he had to impersonate the Sydney Harbour Bridge—more steel than human.

A second later the door swung open and Andrea was enveloping him in a warm hug. She smelled of vanilla icing and rosemary roasted lamb. An odd combination unless you understood that Andrea spent most of her days in the kitchen, cooking. As she was a successful food blogger, the aroma was understandable. And they'd always benefited from trialling the results after the photos were taken. Andrea's food was something he had to look forward to tonight, at least.

Aaron handed her the gerberas and wine.

"Thank you. So thoughtful. We've missed you, Aaron, it's been a while."

He ignored the stab of guilt. Andrea was just making the right noises. It wasn't like Dad even noticed. And Andrea was fond of him, sure... but it wasn't as if they were flesh and blood... she didn't have to feel *obliged*. "Sorry, with finishing up at Fishers, you know... it's been crazy."

"I can imagine. Come on in. Your dad is with Oliver in the study and Gran will be here shortly."

"Gran's coming?"

"Yes, you know how she adores Oliver. A driver from the residential home is bringing her. Your dad will take her back after dinner."

"I could have given her a lift."

Andrea gave him a funny look. "She's a bit more confused lately. She had an *incident* the other day."

"What kind of incident?" Aaron stepped inside and stripped off his jacket. The hallway was as minimalist as ever; expensive artwork was showcased at measured intervals on vast white walls. A huge vase of fresh cut flowers in subtle variations of white stood on the elegant marble hall table. Guess he'd got the colour choice wrong. Andrea took the flowers with a murmured thanks and whisked his jacket over her spare arm, ready to secrete it away in some allotted space probably marked 'visitors'.

"She was on the way back from playing bridge," she continued, closing the door. "From what I can gather, she tried to kiss the cab driver; you know—a proper lip lock. I guess he must have looked like Gramps when he was young. It did give the guy a bit of a shock."

Aaron felt his lips twitch. Dear old Gran. She'd been sharp as a tack until Gramps died two years ago. A fall and a broken hip had landed her in a home, and since then her life had obviously descended into a strange time warp.

"I'm about to temper the chocolate for dessert. It's always tricky. Go and join them in the study—they're expecting you."

As Andrea bustled away, Aaron turned down the corridor to his dad's study. His stomach tightened. There it was, that familiar feeling, like he'd done something wrong.

Outside the door, he waited, listening to David Blake's big laugh followed by Oliver's, laid-back and mellow, but with the same cadence and rhythm. Aaron turned the door handle and there they were. Team Blake.

David Blake was a big man, still handsome but a little heavy around the jaw from his penchant for fine reds. Oliver, in comparison, looked like he'd stepped out of the pages of *Esquire* magazine. Perfectly put together. Dark to Aaron's fair, brown-eyed like their father, but where David Blake sported a square jaw, Oliver had their mother's chiselled bone structure. His body was lean and muscled, clad in understated designer labels; the whole look topped off by a jaw of meticulously crafted stubble to give just the right appearance of edginess.

A dazzling smile slashed his face.

*Smug bastard.*

"Hey there, bro." Oliver jumped up from his chair with what could only be described as panther-like grace. "Good to see you."

*Bro?* Was this the new "cool" Oliver designed to impress his fan base of eager millennials? Well, Aaron wasn't buying. He knew Oliver hovered on the brink of OCD. Oliver's bedroom used to resemble an operating theatre. TGFZ: totally germ-free zone.

Aaron submitted to an oddly painful back slap just below the shoulder blades before Oliver beat a retreat, launching himself gracefully back into the winged chair on the other side of the fire.

"Hi," Aaron replied through tight lips.

David Blake got up and clapped a hand briefly over Aaron's shoulder. "How's the new position going?"

"Haven't started yet."

"Oh, really? I thought they were keen to get you in there as soon as possible."

"I finish at Fishers next Friday. They're paying out the annual leave they owe me, so I'll start the following Monday at Trojan's."

"So proud of you, mate," Oliver said as David Blake sauntered over to the drinks cabinet.

70

"Mate" now? Better and better.

"What'll it be, Aaron?" Their father raised a brow.

Aaron noticed they were both drinking whisky on the rocks. "Got any beer?"

He was sure his dad stifled a wince. "You'll have to go to the kitchen if you want beer. I don't keep any in here."

Aaron shrugged. "Gin and tonic then."

While his dad organised his drink, Aaron had no choice but to pull up one of the formal chairs kept next to the huge mahogany desk for visitors. He sprawled onto it, slouching down the padded back, one vertebra at a time.

Oliver crossed his long legs and swirled the amber liquid in his glass.

To deflect any more fake bonhomie, Aaron said, "Remind me, what's the event you're here for?"

Oliver cast him The Look. The one that said he was the infinitely more considerate brother. The brother who *remembered* stuff.

"The International Authors Fair at Perth University."

"Right."

"Have you read the copy of my new book I sent?"

"Not yet."

Oliver gave a miniscule shake of his head, then took a swig of whisky.

David handed Aaron his drink. "Planning to squander our substantial pay increase on drinking and clubbing, are we?"

Aaron ground his back teeth together. He'd be spending it on cosmetic dental treatment at this rate.

"Have you got an investment plan in place yet?"

"I'm onto it."

"And I assume your superannuation contributions are all sorted?"

"I've filled in the paperwork, yes."

"I meant, are you topping it up? Salary sacrificing."

"Okay, Dad, let up," Oliver interjected smoothly. "I haven't seen you guys since Christmas. Let's start off on the right footing, shall we?"

Aaron jabbed his finger into his drink to stir it. He knew it gave Dad the screaming shits. "How's Lee-annie?"

"*Leonie.*"

"That's the one."

Oliver grinned, ignoring the jibe. "Five years together coming up next month. In fact, I've got some news... No—on reflection I'll save that until everyone's here."

David gave an encouraging throat rumble.

Oliver raised a hand. "No, Dad. Gran and Andrea will want to share in this. Anyhow, quick segue: what's happening in the romance stakes with you, Aaron?"

The doorbell trilling "Greensleeves" prevented the need to answer, but not before a pulse had started up at Aaron's temples accompanied by another one... well, never mind where. Both of which were clearly intent on disturbing every last ounce of his peace of mind.

The truth of it was he'd been reflecting too often these past four days on the weird interaction with Alice at the beach. He thanked his stars that Rowena had called, because if she hadn't... well. There had been a serious risk that he could have been tempted to... kiss Alice.

He'd never been so disturbed by the idea of kissing someone in his life. Kissing was something he excelled at. He'd been doing it with great alacrity since he was fourteen, which had soon led to first base, then... second base. Aaron almost groaned, remembering his discussion with Alice on exactly that subject. It used to be so easy talking to Alice about his girlfriend issues, particularly when they went pear-shaped. She'd always been really creative at helping him come up with exit strategies. And when he was single again... Well, they'd just go back to the status quo. Nights spent on Alice's couch. Alice returning his car keys the next day and squirrelling him a bacon sandwich. Aaron tiptoeing out—making sure he didn't step on the floorboard in the passage that squeaked, before he got sprung by Rowena or Polly.

Alice was comfortable, homey, safe.

So how come, these past two weeks, being with Alice—hell, even *thinking* about Alice—felt anything but safe?

"Did I touch a raw nerve?" Oliver's voice cut through his thoughts.

Aaron's spine snapped straight. "No, why?"

Oliver smirked. "Thought for a moment there Mr Commitment Shy had the smitten look about him."

Aaron gulped down the rest of his gin and tonic and slammed the empty glass onto Dad's teak desk.

"Gran's here," he said, and stalked out of the room.

Polly getting ready to paint her nails was like Napoleon preparing for Waterloo. An exercise in strategy. Various metal devices that looked remarkably like implements of torture were laid out on the bathroom vanity, followed by the biggest tray of nail lacquers Alice had seen outside of the nail parlour in their local shopping mall. She'd never been in there, but every time she walked past, the interior with its rows of brightly lit workstations reminded her more of a nineteenth century sweat shop than a place you'd go to get pampered.

Alice stifled a shudder; she had trouble getting her head around all this beautifying stuff. Even the hairdresser's was an ordeal she put off until absolutely essential.

Polly, naturally, had no such problems. She'd done a course in acrylic nails, paid for with her earnings from the Book Genie when she was seventeen. Then she'd tossed up between being a beautician and a social worker, but in the end Polly's vocation clearly stretched to bigger things than putting flower transfers and glitter on people's extremities. Polly was born to help people out of the knots they'd managed to tie themselves into.

"What's the plan, then?" Polly asked as she rifled through

bottles of colour. "Quick, before we get started—Granite Sapphire or Purple Haze?"

Alice wrinkled her nose. Since it was going on toes only, due to it being a Wednesday and Polly only ever painting her fingernails at weekends, she guessed either would be fine. It was winter anyway, it wasn't like they'd be on show, but Polly said it made her happy looking at her pretty toes in the bath.

"Purple Haze. I don't know what Granite Sapphires look like."

Polly smirked. "Think dark grey and deep blue mixed together."

"Sort of sludgy clay then."

Polly eye-rolled and grabbed the bottle of Purple Haze and shook it. "So, like I said, what's the plan?"

"I don't have one," Alice replied glumly. "I'm just waiting to hear from him."

"That's the typical passive stance women take early in relationships. Checking their phone every five minutes and hoping and praying he'll call."

"I am not hoping and praying. Well, not praying. Maybe hoping. A bit."

"Did you know," said Polly, unscrewing Purple Haze with a firm twist and tapping a glob of the colour into the pot, "that hoping and praying is a recipe for depression."

Alice frowned. "How so?"

"It removes all your sense of empowerment, like giving over your destiny to a higher being instead of believing in your own capabilities. That makes you feel helpless, and feeling helpless can make you depressed."

Alice pondered this. As a kid she'd watched *Aladdin* too many times to count, and every night for months had closed her eyes tight and wished Aladdin would swoop through her window and whisk her away on his magic carpet. Oh, and yes, she could never go past a wishing well, even now, without throwing in a coin and making a wish.

But she'd never got depressed. Just anxious.

Her frown deepened. "Can being a dreamer lead to depression?"

Polly shrugged. "Depends what you do with your dreams, I guess. If you go after them, definitely not. Now let's recap. You think Aaron is avoiding you since the almost kiss on the beach?"

"I might have read that completely wrong. It might not have even been close to a kiss."

"From your description of his body language: lingering eye contact, voice deepening, stepping closer... it sounds promising. You weren't aware of anything nudging into you, were you?"

Alice took a second to comprehend this then, eyes widening, "No, absolutely not! No! God, Poll, what a suggestion!"

"Guess you need to factor in how well-endowed Aaron is," Polly mused, admiring her handiwork. "And how close he was standing at the time."

Alice blushed fiercely. Polly, totally oblivious, continued, "All in all, I think that was most definitely a close call on a kiss."

"If it wasn't for Mum phoning—"

"That was probably for the best," Polly replied briskly. "Neither of you are emotionally equipped yet to deal with a kiss, it's too soon; the whole thing would likely have ended up a shit sandwich."

"It has already!" Alice wailed. "I mean, he's only sent me one text since then, saying when he's settled in the job he'll let me know what the next step is. And we could barely talk to each other afterwards. I just pretended I was exhausted from the panic attack and needed to go home. I've never seen him look so relieved to see an Uber. He shoved me in it and headed off in the other direction."

Polly's chin rested on her knee as she slicked the brush over each nail. "You need to step back and take a wider view of this. When did you last see Aaron awkward around a woman? Like never. He's always in control. Now he's not. In fact, it sounds like he's floundering. That's a good sign. But he needs more time to acclimatise."

"Acclimatise to what? He's known me for ages. There's nothing to get used to."

Polly shook her head. "Munchkin," she said with the patience of a mother who's just found their toddler grinding playdough into the carpet, "*you* don't have to get used to anything because you've been in love with him for years. This is all new and weird for Aaron. Suddenly he's got all these disturbing feelings zapping around inside about someone he's always thought of platonically. Besides, he's crap at relationships. You are, in point of fact, his only true girl *friend*. Right now, he probably feels like he's swallowed glass shards."

"Wow! That sounds enticing."

"Feelings are messy. Shit-bags! Look what I've done." Polly stared horrified at the slash of purple smeared across the edge of her pinkie toe. "All this love talk is making me lose focus."

"Sorry," Alice muttered, handing Polly the nail polish remover and a cotton bud.

Polly glanced up as she took it, her smile reassuring. "Don't worry, you're in the hands of the *lurvvv* expert. We do need to get things back on track, though. You can't afford to lose your mojo after all this prep."

"Retreating feels so much safer."

"Falling in love is never safe." Polly sang the opening riff of "Love is a Battlefield" way off key, but then, Polly did everything with so much confidence she somehow got away with it. She was always the first up on stage at Shamrock karaoke nights and the last to leave to enthusiastic applause despite torturing everyone's eardrums.

Alice couldn't think of anything worse than performing on stage. Except, possibly, the performance she was trying to pull off with Aaron. She straightened her shoulders. Sitting on the edge of the bath wasn't the most comfortable place for a counselling session.

By now Polly had finished the first coat and she extended

her legs and flexed her feet. With the red foam toe separators in place, her feet had taken on Minnie Mouse proportions.

"You need to bombard him with the new you," Polly mused. "Subtly."

"Isn't subtle bombardment an oxymoron?"

"Meaning?"

"A contradiction in terms."

Polly smirked. "Probably. That's the point though, isn't it? Aaron has to want this new you like crazy without knowing why. You've got to erase the way he used to feel about you; scramble his synapses, force his brain to lay down new pathways."

Alice frowned. Sometimes Polly's fascination with brain physiology made her own brain feel like a waterlogged sponge.

"Stop blinding me with science. Just tell me how to go about it."

Polly started on her second coat. The colour took on more depth and complexity.

"Okay, well first we need to engineer another meet-up. Very soon. Maybe this Friday at the Shamrock."

Alice cringed. "That would look too obvious. It's his last day at his old job. He'll be out for goodbye drinks with his team."

"Hmmm, you're right. Maybe not the best time." Polly screwed the top back tightly on Purple Haze and popped it in the box of polishes. "Didn't you say Oliver was here for some book launch thing?"

Alice screwed up her face. "Yes, I think that's what Aaron said." To be honest it was hard to remember; the night had turned into a rollercoaster of highs and lows.

Polly grabbed her phone off the vanity and started to scroll through search engines.

"Yep. Saturday morning at 11 a.m. Listen to this: *Ethical Investment. How to save for your future and save the planet.*" Polly chucked her phone back on the vanity. "We'll just *happen* to be there."

"What if Aaron doesn't show?"

"Aaron will show. Despite all his bravado he wouldn't let the Blake side down. He'll want to be associated with the movers and shakers now he's about to become one."

"Should I text and let him know?"

"Nope. Absolutely not. You need the element of surprise."

By now Polly was working on the final touches, a transparent coat of colour protector. Her toes shone a rich shade of purple and Alice suddenly got the appeal. It was like those little flaps on the end of your feet finally had purpose and meaning. No longer dispensable bits of flesh, best hidden inside thick socks and slippers; they knew what they were meant to do—they were meant to *shine*.

"Polly," Alice said after a moment's deliberation. "Would you paint my nails?"

"Sure, Munchkin. Choose a colour."

# CHAPTER 7

Aaron bumped the woman's knee as he squeezed past, muttered an apology and tried to control the jolt of pain that shot through his temples.

He was seriously late. The room was full. And he had the mother of all hangovers. He slumped onto the only spare chair in the packed-out venue, which happened to be in the middle of a row in the middle of the room, and tried to drown out Oliver's voice.

It grated on his ears like nails down a blackboard, reminding him of school assemblies when he'd had to block out his brother's smug Head Boy addresses and keep his head down to avoid the teacher's frowns that clearly said, "Why can't you just be more like Oliver?"

Aaron jolted in his seat. He hadn't thought of that period in his life for years. Not since uni, in fact. Probably the lack of sleep this last week, tying up all the loose ends on the workers' compensation case he'd been handling with Fishers. They'd bled every last drop out of him and he'd crawled out of the office close to midnight and grabbed a takeaway before dropping into an exhausted sleep.

He'd decided to make up for it last night, though. And hell, was he paying the price now.

"… Investment in renewables is at an all-time high and their future has never looked brighter or, for that matter, more urgent. Millennials get this, investing more than…"

Aaron transcribed "blah-de-blah-blah blah" over Oliver's voice. He dropped his chin to his chest, crossed his arms to stem the nausea barrelling around his stomach, and cast a glance at the row in front.

And froze.

Polly freakin' Fletcher. He'd know those curls anywhere—a fountain of tiny black corkscrews cascading off her head and down her back. And next to her… Fuck.

Alice. His stomach lurched. Not the Alice he was used to, either, hair neatly tugged into one of those hair scrunchies she always wore; oh no, this was the new shiny version of Alice, glossy deep chestnut hair falling straight and heavy around her shoulders. Without even thinking, he leaned sideways to try and see if she had her glasses on. The woman next to him shot him a you-are-invading-my-personal-space look.

He couldn't blame her. He'd dragged on his crumpled black jeans from last night and a T-shirt that had been in a basket of unironed but hopefully clean clothes.

He probably still smelled of bourbon and coke.

He could hardly fumble in his pocket for a mint, either—she'd definitely think he was trying to grope her. Who made chairs this small and put them so close together? Someone with an extremely poor understanding of personal boundaries, obviously.

And why couldn't he stop gawking at Alice? He tried but he couldn't seem to control his eye muscles.

A guy seated three down from him let out a loud chortle. Had Oliver actually cracked a joke? Alice's head swivelled to look at the guy, a smile hovering on her lips.

Nope, no glasses. Big Bambi eyes. Kiss me eyes. Eyes she wasn't *allowed* to have.

And then he did the dumbest thing. He lifted his hand and gave her a wave.

It must have caught in her peripheral vision because her head twisted that bit further and their eyes met.

Her smile widened—he guessed it was a smile. To be honest, her mouth opening and shutting like that was more reminiscent of a goldfish. Then her head snapped to the front.

Aaron hunkered his elbows onto his knees and sank his head into his hands.

Before he knew it, a loud round of applause thundered in his ears. He hadn't registered a word of Oliver's presentation because his addled brain had been trying to work out a damage-control strategy. His inclination was to run, but that would look weird, particularly now Alice had spotted him. He stood up abruptly; the woman next to him was still seated, talking to her friend. He sat down again and rifled a hand through his hair. The wait was killing him.

Glancing up, he spotted Dad and Andrea at the front with a group of people lined up for book signings. He had a vision of vaulting over the rows like hurdles, but he'd probably throw up if he tried that stunt.

By now, Polly had turned around and was grinning at him. He flicked his gaze away, pretending he hadn't seen—only to spot Carts standing against the far wall, accompanied by his equally height-enhanced parents and younger sister, lined neatly up near the door like sentinels. The Wells family never sat at events because no-one could see past their heads.

*Shit on a stick. He was surrounded.* He took a breath. Think this through. He was a god-damned lawyer. He needed to tamp down this illogical fear inside him. Nothing had happened between him and Alice. They'd had a *fun* evening. She'd adequately measured up in the girlfriend stakes, despite the slight mess-up with the panic attack. He'd returned the favour with some harmless flirting practice... then they'd gone their separate ways.

Fine. Everything was fine.

It just didn't feel fucking fine. It felt like they'd ripped each other's clothes off and made out wildly in the sand dunes.

Was that why he couldn't face her? Because his imagination had gone off on a weird tangent? And now it seemed the whole thing was being blown out of proportion by the hangover that was threatening to gouge his eyeballs out from the inside. He lifted his head. Polly called out something that sounded like, "You look like shit." But he might have misheard.

The woman beside him finally rose and the row emptied out. Alice's back was still turned. Was she doing it on purpose? Maybe she was keen to avoid him too? He frowned and another red-hot needle spiked into his brain. There was nothing for it. He'd just have to tough it out. After all, there was potentially another three months of this ahead of him. He stood up again. His head spun slightly and he steadied himself with a hand on the chair in front.

"Hi Polly," he managed to croak. "Didn't quite catch that?"

"I said"—Polly's grin spread across her face—"you. Look. Like. Shit."

∼

"Tea or coffee?" the fresh-faced young man behind the table asked.

"Um, tea, please." When she took the cup from him, Alice noticed her hand shook slightly. But her fingernails glittered in a shade called Moon Shimmer, so she forced herself to focus on how pretty her hands looked instead.

She'd put on the ring her mum had given her for her eighteenth birthday, silver with a large moonstone that she always thought was too ostentatious—much more Rowena than her—but she had to admit it did look good with her ensemble: a silky white blouse tucked into a circular skirt with a wide waistband in a lovely shade of cherry red. She should feel pretty and sophisticated, but there remained this niggle she couldn't quite let go of that she was a kid play-acting in a world full of grown-ups.

Maybe if she didn't lose her nerve, like Polly said, the new Alice would superimpose itself over the old one. Emerge like a phoenix rising from the ashes to claim Aaron's heart. Except judging by the way they were both circling each other like a couple of sharks with toothache, she wasn't at all sure this was going to work out.

"Biscuit?"

"Oh, thank you." Alice smiled at the young waiter.

"They're Andrea Blake home-made," he added.

"Oh, my!" Polly exclaimed at her side. "Andrea's jam drops are to die for." She promptly grabbed two.

Alice took a chocolate and almond biscotti and placed it neatly on the side of her saucer. She turned around to say something, but Polly was already off catching up with some colleagues she'd spied from work.

"Alice, is that you?"

She swung round to the sound of Carts' voice, warm and friendly—perhaps a little warmer and friendlier than usual.

"Hello Carts."

Carts' eyes were on stalks. "It *is* you. I barely recognised you. Have you met my parents before?"

"I think so, at our university graduation, wasn't it?" Alice looked up at their smiling faces. Carts' dad was almost bald; hard to imagine Carts would ever go that way with his unkempt dark locks. "And this is my little sis, Avery." Avery was definitely over six foot. But she looked petite compared to the rest of the Wells family. Everyone did the hand-shaking thing.

Carts couldn't seem to stop staring at her. "Wow, you look" —he gave a nervous laugh—"gorgeous." Followed by a blush. "Am I allowed to say that?"

Alice felt her cheeks heat in tandem. "Yes, of course, why not?"

"You have to be careful not to offend. We had a seminar on

respecting female colleagues last week. You know—what I might think is a compliment may not be okay with you..."

"I am not offended, Carts. On the contrary. But thanks for checking. Did you enjoy Oliver's talk?"

A figure flitted past Carts' shoulder. Without even looking she knew it was Aaron. Since the awkward wave earlier he'd clearly been avoiding her, which was making her feel like she'd made the most humungous mistake in coming here.

Somehow she managed to keep up a polite exchange with Mr and Mrs Wells about investment, which would have been relevant if she'd ever earnt a decent salary. On paper it looked okay but more often than not Rowena funnelled a chunk of Alice's wages back into the shop.

When the figure zigzagged past again, her jaw clenched. And suddenly, there was Aaron at Carts' shoulder, flicking a strand of blond hair out of eyes that looked decidedly red around the edges.

"Didn't expect to see you here." Aaron thumped Carts' arm with a playful fist. "You were in a worse state than me when I left."

"I've got more critical mass to spread the alcohol over," Carts retorted good-naturedly. He certainly did look better put together this morning than Aaron, in a smart jacket and neatly ironed striped navy and white shirt.

Aaron grunted, stuck his head around Carts and gave a salute to his parents. "Hello there, Carts' parents."

Alice could sense Avery preening. "Don't forget to say hello to me, Aaron," Avery squeaked. Despite her height, Alice guessed she was barely fourteen if she was a day. Obviously the Aaron effect struck young.

Aaron gave an easy grin. "Hi there, Avery."

Alice stared into her teacup. She should acknowledge him. It would look weird if she didn't.

"Hi Aaron," she squeezed out of tight lips.

Aaron's brows shot up in feigned surprise. "Oh, Alice, hi! Didn't notice you standing there." *Thunk.* What a put-down.

Yet somehow his eyes gave a different message as they met hers and held on tight.

Not knowing what else to do or say, Alice gulped down some lukewarm tea. The rest of the conversation was a meaningless drone; she was too busy not looking at Aaron's face. Her attention pinned onto the crumples in his jeans, the way he'd obviously tucked his T-shirt very haphazardly into his waistband. His dishevelled state was disturbing. Like he'd just tumbled out of bed. An image of Aaron's naked chest, his mouth so close she could almost taste him... and...

*No, no, no!* Bed and Aaron must *not* occupy the same thought bubble.

Alice's cup clattered into the saucer, spilling tea onto her biscotti.

She was just wondering whether needing to replace one of Andrea's biscuits was a viable excuse to extricate herself when a deep voice said, "If it isn't our new recruit and the lovely Alice." Alice's shoulders went rigid. Archie Bendt, one arm draped around the beautiful Miranda, had joined their group and was flashing big white teeth at them.

It was like someone had waved fairy dust all over Aaron.

He snapped to attention, shoulders back, spine straight. A quick hand through his hair and it all fell into place. His smile sparkled. How could he go from vaguely grotty to frankly gorgeous in less time than it took to blink?

Aaron magic, she decided. Fatally flawed but irresistible, nonetheless.

"Archie, Miranda, great to see you here. What did you think of my brother's advice?" Aaron said, as smooth as butter melting on hot toast.

"If you're half as talented a legal attorney as your brother is a financier, we've invested in gold," Archie said.

"I will do my best to imbue the organisation with the Midas touch."

From anyone else, that statement would come over as swollen-headed, but delivered with just the right dose of self-deprecating smile, Aaron, as always, stonkered it. Everyone laughed. Alice stifled a twinge of resentment. She'd told Aaron the story of Midas. He wouldn't have a clue about Greek mythology if it wasn't for her.

Well if Aaron could pull this off, so could she, damn it. "Thank you so much for the other night," she spiked in brightly. "It was lovely to meet everyone. And the canapes were *divine*."

Miranda preened and Archie gave her an indulgent smile. "Such a pleasure, Alice. We really are one big family, so we welcome you aboard. That's what's always delivered Trojan's edge in the market. Family values at our core."

Next to her, she was sure Aaron blanched.

Carts looked from her to Aaron with a perplexed frown.

After Aaron had made impeccable introductions between the Bendts and the Wells family, and a few more pleasantries were exchanged, Alice excused herself. The soggy biscotti had swollen to take up most of the saucer of tea slops and it wasn't a good look.

She slid the cup onto a table and wondered whether she should go and say hello to Oliver. She listened to his podcasts but hadn't seen him in a couple of years, and despite Aaron bagging him, she'd always really liked him.

Polly zoomed up and whispered loudly in her ear. "How's it going?"

"Awful."

"Don't be negative. Who's the goddess and the Travis Fimmel clone?"

"The Bendts. They were the ones who hosted drinks the other night."

"Oh-ahhh." Polly's eyes were like chips of emerald. "Well, get back in there, girlfriend, and strut your stuff. He's going to have to go along with it now he's in front of his boss."

"What should I do?"

"Link your arm in his, rub your cheek on his bicep."

"God, no, not with Carts standing there. He's already suspicious."

"It won't hurt to drop Carts into the mix; it'll shake things up even more." Polly stared over her head and mused, "Maybe I'll go say hi to Oliver. He gets more divine every time I see him."

Alice followed Polly's eyes to where Oliver was posing for a photo with an acned teenage boy, being taken by the proud dad. "Don't you dare. He's got a girlfriend."

"How do you know?"

"Because he's been with the same woman for years. He's the opposite of Aaron. Loyal," Alice hissed back.

Polly pulled a face. "O-kaaay, won't waste my money buying his book, then."

"You are so shallow." Alice rolled her eyes.

"Just *go*. Stake your claim and leave me to my own mischief." Polly gave Alice a little nudge in the small of her back.

The Wells family were leaving. Carts' eyes searched her out across the milling crowd with a questioning smile that made his lean face almost handsome. Alice sighed. If only she could fall in love with someone like Carts—a solid, dependable, respectful guy. As she neared them, she saw Aaron throw back his head and laugh at something Archie said. It showcased the play of muscles in his neck.

Solid, dependable and respectful flew out the window.

As she drew to a halt just shy of Aaron's elbow, his scent tickled her nostrils, the warmth of his body soaking into her like sunshine. She sensed him glance down at her but she kept her gaze pinned sweetly on the Bendts.

"Well, I guess Alice and I should get going—we've promised to meet some friends for lunch."

They had? Alice felt her head bobbing on her shoulders like those nodding dogs people used to put on the dash of their cars. The next moment she froze as Aaron's hand circled her waist.

His fingertips felt like they were burning a hole in the silk of her blouse, right through to her skin. "Hon, we mustn't be late for Jason and Sash. They've reserved a table at Seashells." He made an apologetic face at Archie and Miranda. "Birthday gig."

*Who the heck were Jason and Sash?*

"No problem," Archie said. "See you at the office on Monday, Aaron. I've allotted a time for us to meet and go over cases. 7 a.m. sharp. I'll make sure my P.A. puts on croissants and coffee."

"Perfect. Can't wait get started." And with a charming farewell to Miranda, Aaron was propelling Alice towards the door.

"Shouldn't you say goodbye to Oliver?" she queried when they were out in the foyer.

"Nope."

"How about your Dad and Andrea?"

"Nope."

"That's a bit churlish."

"They won't even notice. They're too busy basking in Oliver's reflected glory. Come on."

Aaron's hip jostled hers as they walked. In fact, wherever there was a contact point it felt like a zap of lightning had hit. His hand on her waist, the light pressure of his arm around her back, the nudge of his armpit against her shoulder. It made her want to melt into him and rip her body away all at once.

Outside, she catapulted out from under his arm.

Aaron looked at her, perplexed. "That bad?"

"What?"

"Do I smell?"

*Yes, delicious.* "No. Why do you say that?"

"I drank too much last night. I cleaned my teeth but..." He fumbled in his pocket and got out a packet of tic-tacs. "Want one?"

Alice shook her head.

He shovelled a handful of mints into his mouth.

"Al?"

"Yes?"

"I'm not feeling the best right now."

"How much did you drink?"

"I really have no idea." His voice was muffled from the tic-tacs. "A lot. It's been the week from hell. Kevin Fisher insisted I finish off all the court notes for that negligence case I told you about. I worked fourteen-hour days, ate crap all week and drank too much coffee, and then, you know, we had to do the farewell drinks thing, and after that I went out with Carts and Dan to celebrate at the Shamrock, then to Rumbubba on Elizabeth Quay, and then I think—" He scratched his head, frowning. "I think we ended up at the casino."

"Oh, Aaron—" *This* at least was familiar territory.

"I need a hangover fix." He glanced over at her, his expression that mix of wicked and contrite that always made her feel like someone had dumped runny honey into her veins.

"Do you want to join me for a seriously greasy brunch?" he asked.

Honestly, how could a girl refuse?

When they were finally seated in a small café nearby, after Aaron had taken a few mouthfuls of BLT dripping with tomato relish and Alice was onto her second cup of tea for the morning (if you didn't count the two she'd had when she woke up, which were really a life-support system), she said, "That was a bit awkward, meeting the Bendts."

Aaron gave a whimsical grin between chews. His face seemed to be regaining more of its normal colour with each mouthful. "Should have expected it, I guess; it was like the who's who of Perth. I really didn't think I'd see you there, to be honest."

"Thanks a lot."

"I didn't mean it like that. It's just you've never shown an interest in investment strategies."

"I was there to support Oliver."

*Liar, liar pants on fire.*

"Oliver doesn't need your support."

89

Piqued, Alice countered, "I thought if you landed this job, you might iron out that chip on your shoulder."

"Oliver only gets to me when he's in Perth. I can tolerate his existence as long as he stays on the other side of Australia. And when he doesn't send me a signed copy of his latest book with a photo of him on some palm-fringed beach, then expect me to actually read it."

"Maybe you should now you'll be earning squillions," Alice retorted. For some reason she wanted to needle him.

Sure enough, Aaron gave her a dark look. "Don't you start. I had the Spanish inquisition over my finances from both of them the other night before dinner."

They sat in silence for a moment, while Alice fought an overwhelming urge to keep niggling and Aaron studied his sandwich as if two bits of toasted bread, greasy bacon and a limp lettuce leaf were the most fascinating thing he'd ever seen in his life.

He took another bite, then shoved it back on his plate.

"Sorry," he said. "I'm being shitty, aren't I?"

She nodded and straightened her spine. She needed to take control of the situation, not play victim. She let her lips curve into a smile as she glanced up at him. "Yes, actually, you are."

"Guess I'm a bit wired—you know, about the new job. And hungover to buggery. I probably should have taken a break between contracts, but I didn't want to put a foot wrong."

Alice relented. "I get that."

He was still staring at her weirdly as he picked up his food again. "Look, this girlfriend gig, it really won't be much of a deal at all. I just need you to phone me from time to time, maybe join me if there's some sort of social gathering after work. You can start to cool off within a few weeks; that will give them more reason to think things aren't so great between us by the time you dump me."

The idea of dumping Aaron nearly ripped a hole in her heart.

"So what's my reason?" she asked.

"Reason?"

"For dumping you. I mean, don't you think we should work out what goes wrong between us? You know, so we can keep our stories matching." This was ridiculous. Discussing the end of a relationship they'd never even had. She wouldn't be so miffed if they'd actually experienced some good bits first. Or maybe she'd be even more miffed…

"Good point." Aaron put down his sandwich again and picked up his steaming cup of black coffee. He took a mouthful. "Why don't *you* come up with a reason? After all, you'll be doing the dumping."

"It takes two to make a relationship fail, you know," she responded.

"Not always. Sometimes one person cares more than the other."

Alice felt a blush creeping up her throat. "Okay then, you've been unfaithful. That's the obvious choice."

"God, no! That would make me out to be a complete bastard."

She couldn't help thinking there were probably quite a few women around Perth who would agree with that definition. "Right. Okay then, I'm sick of your narcissism and selfish attitude."

Aaron's eyes rounded. "That's almost worse. How about you're going off to travel the world and find yourself?"

"How about I fall in love with someone else?"

Aaron wrinkled his nose. "You wouldn't." His expression was so hurt-puppy, Alice couldn't help a giggle. "Would you?" he finished.

"Quite possibly." Again that look lingered between them for a second longer than necessary and made strange hot feelings dart into parts of her that really weren't used to this many strange hot feelings in close succession. She shifted in her seat and looked out of the window. "There's only so many nights on the couch and demands for bacon sandwiches a girl will put up with from her boyfriend, you know."

"I never knew that bothered you."

"I—it doesn't. I'm acting my part."

Aaron laughed and then winced. "Ouch, that was not a great idea."

Alice resisted the urge to reach in her bag for some paracetamol. Sex sirens did *not* mother men. They seduced them. And she'd better start remembering that.

As Aaron finished his sandwich, she pulled her purse out of her bag. His gaze latched onto her hand. "I've never seen that ring before. Who gave it to you?"

If she'd been more scheming she might have pretended it was from an admirer, but out it came. "Mum."

"You never wear it. Nor, come to think of it"—he reached out and before she knew it her hand was clasped gently in his warm one and turned over—"have I ever seen your nails painted before."

"It's called Moon Shimmer," she gasped, her heart skidding against her ribs.

Quickly, he dropped her hand and his jaw tightened momentarily before he asked casually, "How long is Rowena away for?"

She tried to ignore the tingles and focus on his question. Her mum's visit to England was a bit open-ended and somewhat shrouded in mystery. Alice was used to Rowena's spontaneous overseas trips, but usually her mum filled her in on every last detail. There had been fewer phone calls this time, and not as many photos on Facebook. "At least six weeks. She was a bit odd about it. I hope she's not going to purchase a bookshop in some quaint little English backwater and tell me I should come and help her run it."

"Your mum's eccentric, not crazy."

"I don't know. She's never got over her halcyon days studying in England. I think she almost blames me for the fact she couldn't stay longer."

"How could she? You weren't even alive."

"No, but she was pregnant with me, that's the reason she came back."

Aaron's eyebrows shot up. "I don't think I ever knew that."

Alice flicked open her purse and dragged out a ten dollar note. "Guess I never thought to mention it." The old feeling of guilt kicked at her gut. As if she were responsible for Rowena's happiness, even as an embryo. "Anyway, I really should be going, I have to relieve Amanda at the shop. She needs to be gone by midday to take her son to hockey practice."

"I'll get this," Aaron said.

"We'll split the bill."

"It's *my* hangover brunch." Playfully he grabbed her purse and made to shove it back in her bag. A scuffle ensued. "While you're my girlfriend, I pay."

Alice pouted. It actually felt quite good.

"Besides," Aaron added, zipping up her bag and placing the strap over her shoulder, "my new salary is eye-wateringly large and I have to spend it on something."

"To which David and Oliver Blake would respond…?"

"—that I am a hedonistic and immature fuckwit…"

By the time they'd tumbled onto the street, still making jokes about the many ridiculous things Aaron could spend his newfound wealth on that would drive his dad and Oliver to despair, Alice's sides ached from laughing. But wasn't that part of the problem? The fact that despite everything, Aaron always made her laugh?

As they stood on the pavement, it seemed to Alice that they'd spent an inordinate amount of time facing each other in public places lately and pretending that the eye-contact thing between them wasn't indicative of anything unusual.

*Eyes are the windows to the soul.* And clearly, to another place south of her waist. Why hadn't she ever realised before that there was an eyes-to-vagina superhighway? She'd never felt anything like this when Jeremy had looked at her. Or Quentin, who hadn't really looked at her at all; he'd had this disconcerting way of staring at a freckle above her eyebrow that did nothing at all for their sex life.

But now, *that* place between her thighs was begging for attention.

She shuffled her feet.

Aaron popped a mint in his mouth and rocked on his heels.

It was all so… strange and… kind of *cute*, but for the imminent risk of her melting in a puddle on the pavement.

"So, I call you at work, is that the plan?" she asked, trying to sound vague and disinterested.

"Yeah, I'll message you the best time to phone. Maybe at the end of the day when I'm walking past the partners' offices. Wouldn't look great if I took too many calls while I'm in full-on billing mode."

"Okay, I'll be on stand-by." A pause, more internal firecrackers. "Well, thanks for brunch."

"Thanks for coming, I feel a lot better now." He gave an exaggerated pat to his stomach and she cast a quick glance down. Was that an inordinately large bulge in the front of his jeans?

Alice jerked her head up, heat winging into her cheeks.

Aaron's mouth twisted into a grin, the one that carved the dimple into his left cheek.

*Do it, do it, do it…* a devilish little voice chanted in her head.

As if in slow motion, Alice saw her hand come up, felt her fingers curl around his forearm, registered the tiny twitch in his muscles.

She went up on tippy-toes and arched her neck.

The kiss was meant for his cheek but somehow—maybe in surprise—Aaron jerked his head and her lips landed softly on the corner of his mouth. Coffee mingled with mint and the sharp graze of stubble. His response was almost imperceptible, a tremor in his lips, a shifting of his energy towards her, even though if you were watching you wouldn't have noticed a thing.

A surge of feminine power shot through her as she drew

back and dropped her hand. Drawing in a breath, she dared to take a peep at his face. He looked completely stunned; his pupils drowning out the bright blue of his eyes.

Quickly, Alice stepped away and said, "Today's flirting practice." Hoisting her bag strap up her arm, she tossed her head, enjoying the swing of her hair around her neck. "Hope I did okay. Bye, Aaron."

As she walked away, she felt his gaze drumming into her back.

It was impossible not to smile. A real, genuine smile using all the right muscles.

# CHAPTER 8

Thump, *thump, thump.* Aaron's feet pounded the treadmill. He notched up the speed and incline and the treadmill whirred and clunked. His legs matched the rhythm of the machine, sweat beading his brow. Outside the expansive windows of Fit-Bods gym, the city streets shone wet and the rain continued to dump great sheets out of big blousy clouds. It had been too wet and windy these past few days to take his normal loop around the river and back to his apartment, but he had to run to stop his thoughts from whizzing around inside his skull.

*Thump, thump, thump.* Faster and faster. Until finally he registered nothing except the gyrating bodies on the wall-mounted screens and the rhythm of the pounding music. But then... somehow, fragments of the week slithered into his mind. And within no time what started off as a trickle had turned into a flood.

He'd got his head around the computer system at Trojan's relatively easily. But the amount of cases he was expected to take on was mind-blowing. Phone call after phone call to clients. Meeting after meeting after meeting. The names and issues merged. The billing—ha, well that had been the only light relief, trying to work out who to charge eating his sandwich to during his lunch break. Not that you could call it a break. He'd eaten at his desk. He'd never shied away from working his ass off—in fact, he'd realised at uni he needed the pump of adrenaline to keep focused. As well as his regular exercise routine… and sex.

Shit, where did that just come from? Angrily he notched the speed up another level, and then another. When had he last had sex? Not since he applied for the job at Trojan's. He'd been too busy spending time with Alice going over interview strategies.

Fuck… there he went again.

Every night when his head hit the pillow chasing sleep, all he seemed to see when his eyelids closed were Alice's huge brown eyes, as he imagined the softest pressure of her lips against his. He'd even caught himself touching that spot on the corner of his mouth and that's when he'd deduced he was going out of his fucking mind.

Sweat dripped off his hair and along the bridge of his nose. A glance at the timer told him he'd been running for forty minutes. He'd make the hour, then pump weights until he was wrung out like a rag.

As he left the gym a while later, he felt like he'd been purged. He could think about Alice with her glasses on and her hair tied back and not really react at all. Tomorrow he would message her, get her to call him and do the "hi hon" thing in front of Trojan or Fink's office. He was sweet with it. Totally cool.

He was almost smiling to himself as he swung his bag over his arm and walked through reception.

"Hey, Aaron. Didn't know you were a member."

His brows furrowed as he tried to place the guy. That's right, Hamish Lender, one of Fink's legal team. Nice guy. Eager beaver. He'd met him briefly at the drinks party. Hamish had been with Trojan a year already and had been more than happy

97

to fill Aaron in about some dos and don'ts. Seeing him in his workout gear instead of a suit had thrown him for a moment.

"Hey, there." Aaron drew to a halt. "How you going?"

"Good. Just doing my obligatory workout. Jacinta says I'm not worth living with if I don't get Trojan shit out of my system before I come home."

"Oh." Aaron had hoped maybe Hamish, muscle-bound and good-looking, could be a partner in crime once this probation hell was over. He could imagine they'd have similar taste in women. "Jacinta?"

"My fiancée." Hamish grinned.

"I didn't see you with anyone at the drinks do."

"She was on a girls' trip to Bali. Good to have her home, though. Quite frankly I don't think I'd have survived this last year as a Trojan lacky without her."

That ruled out Hamish, judging by the rather soppy expression that had just spread over his previously rugged features.

Were there any real men left in the world? Aaron tried to smile away the irritation. Hamish's face suddenly lit up as if with a brainwave. "Hey, why don't you come to dinner? You and Alice. Jacinta's always complaining we don't have people around nearly enough. No time like the present. What are you doing Saturday night?"

"Urm. Saturday. I, er—" Aaron's mind drew a blank. Maybe he had overdone his workout because he couldn't think of anything he'd be doing Saturday night. "Oh, look, wouldn't want to put your fiancée to the trouble, especially if she's only just got back from overseas..." he trailed off lamely.

"No dude, seriously. I'll text her now." Hamish pulled out his phone and was madly thumbing at the keypad. "Cinta loves cooking. We've got another couple we have to invite— about to pop out a baby. It'll be the last outing before they're tied down with a little human ball and chain."

*Ball and chain. Very apt.*

Finally, the accommodating Cinta having come back with

an enthusiastic yes, Aaron said his farewells to Hamish and headed as fast as he could towards the door.

A couple of messages pinged on his phone. The first was from Oliver: "Hi bro, when are we going to catch up, just you and me?"

He flicked to the next one.

It was from Dan. Aaron frowned as he read it. "At Shamrock with Carts. Lucy's shoved the knife in. Come join us."

He let out an exasperated huff. He'd been meaning to go home, tidy up his apartment, fold his washing and make himself a huge bowl of pasta.

But Carts would be gutted at yet another kick in the balls from Lucy. With a shake of his head, Aaron rode the lift down to the underground carpark. He threw his kit bag in the boot, got in, then started the engine.

Guess it would be another late night.

When he arrived at the Shamrock, Dan's red buzz cut caught his eye straight away, secreted in their usual spot at the bar. Sure enough Carts was next to him, shoulders stooped in the abject manner of a man who'd been right royally fucked over by a woman.

Aaron's ribs constricted. *This.* This was exactly why he didn't let himself get involved. Look at the guy. He was a train wreck. You had to make the choice to never let a woman mess with your heart. Not that he'd ever seen it as a conscious choice. His indifference to all that mushy stuff was just there, like his arms and legs were just there, a part of what made him who he was. Almost in protest at Carts' posture, Aaron bracketed his shoulders wide and strode over to the bar.

"They are never worth it, mate." He slapped a hand on Carts' shoulder. Carts looked up at him with flat eyes. "Who told you?"

"Dan texted me as I was leaving the gym."

"You didn't need to come." Carts sighed heavily and downed the dregs of his glass.

"Yeah, I did. What happened?" Aaron swung his butt onto a stool and motioned to Paddy.

Obviously it was Guinness night. A few pints of draft black diamond would hopefully drown Carts' sorrows.

Carts bent down and placed a plastic bag onto the bar. He turned it upside-down and shook it and out spilled a tiny little pair of lace briefs and a miniscule matching bra. "I went over to give her these. Tell her I'd made a huge mistake not being there for her enough, that I wanted to make it up to her." He delved into his pocket. "Oh, and this…" A small blue velvet box skidded across the bar.

*This* could only mean one thing…

Carts waved a hand dismissively in the direction of the box. "Go on, open it."

Gingerly, Aaron picked it up and flipped the top. In the light from the bar the large diamond ring seemed to gloat back at them.

"Oh, fuck," Dan exclaimed. "Is that thing for real?"

Carts nodded, his lips tinged green.

"Well, at least you didn't give it to her," Dan said, trying to find the silver lining in a cloud of plutonium.

"It gets worse." Carts gave a visible shudder. "I rolled up at her place. She opened the door and she was wearing her—her dressing gown."

"What time was that?" Aaron asked.

"Just after work. I dunno, sevenish, I guess. Anyway, I didn't think too much of it, Lucy always has a shower and changes after work. I handed her the bag and she lifted out the undies and kind of made this weird little noise, which I thought was, like, a happy sound. I took that as my cue, went down on one knee and brought out the ring. It was nerve-racking, I just wanted to get it over and done with. And then I heard the toilet flush."

Dan's brows beetled down. "So?"

"She doesn't have a flatmate," Carts replied. "So, in the midst of my proposal there it is, the fucking toilet flushing, and she's, like, trying to slam the front door, and she's going all red and blotchy in the face. Except she jams the foot of my bent leg in the door, which hurt like hell, so I'm howling and she's squealing and the next thing I see are these great big hairy calves strolling out of the bathroom at the end of the hallway."

Carts' voice had risen almost to a shout and by now quite a few heads had turned their way.

"Whose were they?" Dan looked like he was waiting for the next episode of his favourite Netflix show.

"Her freakin' personal trainer. Joey, or Joshy, or Joss-stick or whatever his fucking name is."

At that moment Paddy landed three more pints on the bar with an expressive eyebrow raise. Aaron grimaced a reply. Carts would likely regret his rant later when he realised most of the Shamrock regulars had witnessed his humiliation. Maybe it would be good to remove him but it was still bucketing down and the beer garden would be a swimming pool by now, so Aaron guessed they'd just have to ride it out. Carts stopped and gulped in a breath. "Why didn't she tell me?" He looked at Aaron as if he was the Oracle.

Aaron shook his head. Why couldn't women be more honest? Why had Lucy carried on about just needing some space, when what she should have said is, "Dude, it's over." It would have been hard to hear, yes, but kinder in the long run.

But who was he to judge? He'd never done that, had he? Never been truthful. He'd ducked and weaved and not returned their calls in the hope they would get the message. He'd been confronted by teary-eyed women and done the "it's not you, it's me" thing. He guessed at least he'd never been trounced with another girl. He hadn't stooped that low.

But when all was said and done, he wasn't a whole lot better than Lucy.

"Why aren't you saying anything?" Carts asked morosely. "Usually I can count on you to make me feel better." He gave Aaron a suspicious look. "Except you've been seriously weird lately." He peered over his Guinness and Aaron found it hard to meet his eyes. "Are you up to something? Is that why you're keeping schtum?"

"W-what?"

"You heard me. Something's going on between you and Alice, isn't it? You put your arm around her at Oliver's talk. I had it in mind to call you and say what the hell... but the Lucy stuff took over."

There was no way he was letting Carts deflect to the Alice issue. "Maybe right now we should focus on what's going on for you, eh, mate?"

"If you do any of your crap moves on Alice... I... I will..."

"Leave it out," Aaron parried, more sharply than intended. "We're here to discuss your love life. Not mine."

"That's practically an admittance of guilt." Carts' eyes bulged. "You're dating Alice."

Aaron hesitated. He had to keep this looking real, didn't he? For the next month or so.

"Maybe, sort of."

Carts glowered darkly. "You know I like Alice; I told you the other week. If it hadn't been for trying to sort things out with Lucy..."

Aaron slammed his glass onto the bar. "Jesus, Carts, you've just been trying to give your ex an engagement ring and you're telling me you've got the hots for Alice. What's that about? Using Alice as your rebound fuck?"

"I don't use women. That's you, mate." Carts' eyes sparked angrily. "You'll treat her like dirt and discard her."

"Guys, guys." Dan stepped forward and sliced a big hand between them. Aaron hadn't even noticed Carts had slid off his stool and that, somehow, they were facing off, chests puffed out. "You're just wanting to let off steam. I get it. But cool it, okay, both of you." Dan had his rugby voice on. The voice that, on the rare occasions he used it, turned him from big and goofy to big and authoritative.

Aaron backed off. How come he'd let himself get riled so quickly? Carts was clearly not thinking straight. He was gutted, of course he was. Aaron needed to remember whose side he was on.

"We're just having a bit of fun between dates," he said evenly. "In a mature kind of way." A frisson of something tingled down his spine. He slammed it into lockdown.

Carts had slumped back in his chair, a stricken look on his face. "Sorry, dude. That was out of order. Guess I should keep out of it; I realise you came here when you didn't need to. Thanks, I appreciate it. Here, I'll buy the next round."

Things calmed down after that. Aaron bought a burger from the bar menu, which saved him from more hangry outbursts, and they had a couple more Guinnesses. Within no time, they were slapping each other on the back outside the Shamrock, declaring that the brotherhood was far more important than any woman could ever be.

"Ah, shite. Better take this back to the shop tomorrow," Carts said, tossing the ring box in the air before pocketing it. "What am I going to say?"

"That you got a better offer." Aaron grinned.

They all burst out laughing, and with another thump on the back, Aaron watched his best mates stride off, one as wide as the other was tall. Yeah, the brotherhood; they stood by you through thick and thin. When he got home, he threw himself on the sofa, exhausted, eyed the piled-up basket of clothes and the washing up he hadn't done from last night and grabbed the TV controller.

His phone beeped with a message. Please, god, not Oliver again. He picked it up off the coffee table and a strange little tingle travelled over his scalp when he saw the message.

Alice: *How's the week going?*

Aaron: *Hard. How's yours?*

Alice: *Ok. Shop's busy. End of month financials.*

He smiled. Alice hated anything mathematical. She'd once told him she was allergic to numbers. For some crazy reason he felt the need to share the evening's events.

Aaron: *Carts and Lucy are over for good. Messy as shit.*

Alice: *Poor Carts. Is he ok?*

A feeling pierced him just below the ribs. Unfamiliar. He didn't like the idea of Alice caring how Carts was feeling. Which was kind of bizarre and mean-spirited of him.

Aaron*: Not great. Dan and I cheered him up.*

Alice: *u r good friends to him.*

Aaron: *Told him women aren't worth it.*

Alice: *Speak for yourself.*

Aaron: *Maybe with one exception.*

Alice: *????*

Now he was blushing. Actually blushing and there was no-one to see him. He bit down on his lower lip.

Aaron: *Stop fishing. What r u doing?*

Alice: *Reading*

He thought she wasn't going to elaborate, then he saw three blinking dots.

Alice: *Georgette Heyer.*

—More dots. He waited.

Alice: *Regency romance.*

He grinned. Typical Al. Off in nineteenth-century lala land. He sent a yawning face emoji. His fingers itched as they hovered over the keys.

Aaron: *We've got a dinner invite Saturday night r u free? Colleague from work.*

A long, long pause. Now he felt itchy all over. He got up and started to pace the room.

Alice: *Ok. What time?*

Aaron: *Not sure. Let you know.*

He wanted to keep texting. Worse, he badly wanted to call and hear her voice. He forced his fingers to type the words "Night, sleep tight". Before he knew it he'd added a kiss-blowing emoji. He grimaced. They had an unspoken code when it came to emojis. Nothing even vaguely romantic. No hearts. No kisses. All others were game. Frogs, monkeys, cats, though eggplants were only ever in relation to someone behaving like a dick. Never, ever sexual.

Exasperated at himself, he was about to turn off his phone when back pinged a kiss-blowing emoji, followed by *zzzz*.

His fingers crept to the corner of his mouth, remembering how soft her lips had felt. He whipped his hand away, flicked the phone to airplane mode, threw it on the coffee table and grabbed the TV controller.

A good dose of visual Valium. That's what he needed right now.

# CHAPTER 9

Oh, *poo*! She'd missed a piece.

Alice grabbed the torn scrap of paper and slapped it on top of her pile—the result of the times she'd done a scribbled calculation instead of entering a cash sale on the computer system, which now meant finalising the end of month financials was going to be a complete nightmare. She chewed on the end of her pencil. Would she ever learn? Most likely not. As soon as there was a queue of more than three people, her brain seemed incapable of using technology. Add to that her mind being occupied these past couple of weeks with Aaron thoughts and she was scattier than usual.

She stabbed the numbers into the calculator again. This time she *would* get them to tally.

Then all she had to do was add these onto the spreadsheet and email them to Rowena.

"What do you have to do to get service round here?"

Her head jerked up, horrified she hadn't noticed a customer.

Oliver Blake stood in front of the desk smiling at her with a twinkle in those almost black eyes.

Polly was right. He *did* get more gorgeous with each passing year. And yet... Alice's heart wasn't doing crazy somersaults when she looked at him. Not one.

Her palm landed on her chest; fingers splayed. "Oh, Oliver, I thought you were a real customer."

He stuck his lower lip out in a mock pout. "Better than that. I'm the bringer of books."

He must have read her perplexed look as he added, "Albeit, slightly damaged ones." He gave a little flourish towards a large box next to the counter. *"The Earth Investor: How to Get Rich and Enrich the Planet While You Do It."* He gave a self-deprecating smirk. "There were boxes of them sent by my publisher to mainstream booksellers around Perth, but somehow this lot got damaged on the way over. Bent spines and the like. Nothing major. But I thought the Book Genie might like them."

"Thank you, Oliver." Already Alice had circumnavigated the desk and was eagerly slitting open the box with her penknife. "How much do you want for them?" she asked, pulling out a copy. She hadn't really focused on the books at Oliver's talk last week, too engrossed in other things, she supposed. But now, staring back at her, was Oliver's amazing bod in cut-off shorts, shirt open, arms stretched wide on a pristine beach in paradise. She hoped he'd done carbon offsets for the flight to wherever it was, then chided herself fiercely. She was sounding as mean as Aaron.

Oliver's next comment made her feel even more bitchy. "Nothing. They're a gift." He cast a glance around the empty shop. "Where's your lovely mum?"

Oliver used to come into the Book Genie years ago when he still worked nearby, soon after Alice had first met Aaron. Rowena and Oliver had hit it off—another black mark against Aaron that his brother, in Rowena's words, was "so utterly charming, and he's read *Brideshead Revisited* twice, sweetie."

"She's in England for a couple of months," Alice said, carefully keeping the relief out of her voice. Mum and Oliver's mutual admiration club could get a bit hard to stomach at times. "She'll be sorry to have missed you."

Oliver had already started to unpack the books. "Where would you like me to put myself?"

Alice swiftly cleared a space on her paper-cluttered desk. "Here for now. I'll have to work out a price." She cocked her head at him. "Would you like a tea or coffee?"

"Sure, why not? I've got nothing until a book launch this evening in the city. Black coffee no sugar, thanks."

As Alice disappeared into the storeroom, busying herself filling the kettle, Oliver sauntered over and leaned on the door frame. She had none of the skittering heartbeats that she'd experienced when Aaron was in here. Oliver just felt warm and safe, like a big brother. Or at least, how she imagined it would feel if she had one.

"How are you and Aaron going?" Oliver asked.

Alice nearly dropped the kettle into the sink. On second thoughts maybe Oliver wasn't safe at all.

"Sorry, what?" She laughed nervously, buying time by putting the kettle back on its base and flicking the switch before answering. "Same as ever. Why do you ask?" That was dumb. Never ask an open-ended question if you want the subject closed. Out the corner of her eye, she saw Oliver's elegant shoulders shrug.

"Oh, just a vibe I got on Saturday. I happened to look up and you two were looking pretty cosy and I *thought* I saw Aaron's arm around you."

Alice laughed. Oh heavens, she sounded like a braying donkey. "It was a joke."

"Joke?" Oliver's face was sceptical.

"More like a dare."

"Really?"

"Yes, um, someone made a joke—dare I mean—that if Aaron put his arm round me, I would slap it off immediately. They laid money on who would give in first. Me or him."

"Hmm. Right."

Clearly, Oliver didn't believe a word of it.

"I've only got instant coffee." She flailed. "I'm saving up for one of those capsule machines. But I guess you probably disapprove of all that plastic waste."

She poured water over coffee granules and went to hand him the mug.

He was still staring at her out of unblinking eyes. "You know you're the only girl Aaron's ever got close to, don't you?"

She glanced down at the mug in her hand. *Don't wobble, don't wobble.* Oliver took the mug and she gave what she hoped was a dismissive little snort as she turned away. "Well, that doesn't mean much considering Aaron's track record, does it?"

She busied herself untangling an Earl Grey tea bag from the rest of the pack. What was it with tea bags and those annoying little labels getting all snagged up in the strings?

"You're referring to his Teflon-like sticking power in relationships?"

"I guess."

"It's because of what happened to Mum," Oliver said quietly. "At least, that's what I put it down to."

Alice couldn't help a surprised glance over her shoulder. "You mean when your mum died?"

Oliver nodded. "He's talked to you about it, right?"

"Not really. Just that it was a head-on collision with another car. And that he doesn't really think about it anymore."

"Guess that doesn't surprise me, I don't think he wants to remember." Oliver released an audible sigh. "The day it happened, Aaron was supposed to get a lift home from footy practice with another parent, but there was an information glitch and the woman left without him. So he phoned Mum. She was on the way there when... it... happened. Pretty hard on Aaron, knowing that."

A long pause followed. Alice dunked the tea bag until her tea went murky brown. "Were they close? Your mum and Aaron?"

Oliver nodded. "Oh yeah, Aaron was definitely her

favourite. I was Dad's, that was pretty much a given. Those two just can't seem to get along, no matter how hard they try." Oliver stared broodingly into his coffee cup. "You know Aaron never cried? After she died. Not once. Not that I ever saw, anyway. And then his behaviour became a nightmare for a while. He drove Dad nearly insane with worry. That only made things worse between them, of course."

Alice sipped her tea. It felt like an electrical storm was travelling up and down her spine and spiking into her brain. Why was Oliver suddenly confiding all this to her? Why had Aaron never told her any of it?

"When Andrea came on the scene it helped," Oliver continued. "Well, by that I mean she helped Dad deal with Aaron better. And then, I don't know, maybe because Aaron can't stand competition, but when I graduated high school with good grades, he pulled himself together enough to do okay and get into university." He lifted his head and smiled sadly at her. "And there he met you."

*Rescued me*, she thought silently but didn't say.

"You're the only girl he's ever brought home to meet the family." He gave a short laugh. "The only person who could get all of us round a Monopoly board. We're not great at relaxing together, being playful... but we did manage to when you came around."

Alice felt a warm glow bracket her heart like a hug. "Thank you, Oliver, that's really nice to know."

They sipped in silence for a moment before Oliver said, "To be honest, we've all kept hoping..."

Alice's fingers pincered round her cup. "Hoping what?"

"Oh, you know, that you two would get together eventually."

She took a slurp of her tea and nearly choked.

Oliver didn't seem to notice. "So when I saw you at the launch together looking—more than a little friendly, I guess, I nearly shouted hallelujah. I even pointed it out to Dad and Andrea."

*Bother, bother, bother.*

"I've been trying to get Aaron to meet me for a drink—not that he'd tell me anything, of course—in fact, I'm sensing he's avoiding me. So, when these books arrived, I thought, why not come here and get the truth from Alice?"

Alice put her cup down with a clunk, and did her best to peg together the pieces of herself that had been flying off in all directions while Oliver talked. "I'm sorry to disappoint you, Oliver, but the truth is there's nothing going on between me and Aaron. Never will be."

Oliver looked truly disappointed. Sudden hot prickles beset the back of her eyelids. Thank goodness she was wearing her glasses.

"That's a real shame." He gave a grimace. "Especially since my life is so on track, I was hoping Aaron's might finally be." A sudden smile lit up his face. "I've just got engaged."

Alice let out a squeal, partly to hide her breaking heart but also because the part that wasn't fatally damaged was over-joyed to hear it.

"To Leonie?"

"The one and only amazing Leonie." Oliver grinned; his tanned skin flushed with delight.

He took another sip of his coffee and Alice was sure he was disguising another grimace at the taste. He put the cup down next to hers on the bench top. "Odd, isn't it? There's me, a one woman for life kinda guy, and there's Aaron, who can't settle with a woman for more than five minutes. A psychoanalyst would have a field day."

Alice decided to only focus on the good news. "I'm so happy for you. Congratulations, Oliver." Spontaneously, she gave him a big hug. His body was a lean, mean powerhouse of muscle and still—luckily—all she felt was the warm and friendly vibes she always got around Oliver.

He'd make a wonderful husband.

Unlike someone else she knew.

A lump formed in her throat and threatened to join forces

with her prickly eyes. She swallowed around it. "How much longer are you in Perth?"

"About a month. Dad and I are collaborating on a project and it's easier and pleasanter doing it together. I was hoping Leonie would get over at the weekend but she's a wedding planner and there's the society wedding of the year coming up."

"No, Oliver, the society wedding of the year will be yours."

"That will be next year's." He grinned.

"Well, I hope you get that drink with Aaron," Alice said airily as she picked up the cups. "There's no need to grill him about us; you know the full story now."

"Who won the bet?"

"Sorry?"

"The bet. Did he take his arm away first or did you push him off?"

"Hahahahah." The *donkey bray was back.* "Me, of course."

Oliver shook his head. "You know the trouble with you two?" he said. "You can't see what's staring you both in the face. Great to see you anyway." He gave her a wink. "Hope I sell well." And with that he sauntered off.

Alice dumped the cups in the sink and hurried back to her desk. Her heart was heavy in her chest as she looked at the disarray.

She'd have to go back to the beginning and recalculate.

Who was she trying to fool? It wasn't all these harmless scraps of paper making her heart feel like a lump of lead, was it?

No, it was something a thousand times worse.

With pursed lips, Alice grabbed the calculator, a wad of papers and started all over again.

The prongs of the fork skittered across Aaron's plate and a spray of peas arced across the table. When would he learn to take Andrea's advice and scoop them onto the back of his fork instead of spearing them? It was just... so counterintuitive to do that. Like winding spaghetti around your fork, when everyone knew what really worked was to shovel it at speed into your mouth and ignore the sauce spills until after.

He gave an apologetic smile to Jacinta. "Sorry, me and peas —never a good combo."

Jacinta tossed a blonde tress over her shoulder and tinkled out a laugh.

Alice, in his periphery, was shepherding her peas neatly into a corner of her plate. "They're delicious," she said enthusiastically. "I've never tasted such nice peas."

"Fresh," Jacinta replied with obvious pride. "It took me hours to pop them out of their pods, but with the salmon and horseradish the flavour is *so* divine." She gave a pointed look at Aaron. "It's an Andrea Blake recipe. I was so excited to hear from Hamish she's your mum."

"Stepmum." Aaron turned his fork over and managed to balance three peas on it.

"Oh, your parents are divorced then?"

The peas plopped back onto the plate. "My mum died."

Jacinta looked stricken. "I'm so sorry."

Silence fell across the guests and Aaron felt the need to elaborate to ease the sudden tension, which was particularly emanating from Alice. Why would she worry? She knew the story. Well, as much as he'd ever told anyone, which was practically nothing. "A car accident, when I was twelve."

"Oh, how awful, I'm sorry."

"To be honest, that time in my life is pretty hazy." He tried again and this time the peas got to his mouth safely. He chewed, swallowed. "Andrea has been my stepmum since my mid-teens; the benefits are obvious." He waved his fork at his plate and beamed out his best smile. "Though I have to say I don't think I've tried this one in her repertoire. Delicious."

The conversation moved on quickly to when Stella's baby was due, and the imminent baby shower.

"Alice, why don't you come? You must come." Stella's grey eyes were full of genuine warmth.

Alice let out the sound Aaron had often heard her make when she didn't know how to respond. A little musical hum with a kind of question mark on the end.

Aaron jabbed at his salmon. If he had known how cosy this whole thing was going to be... how smug and adult and *committed* everyone was... he'd have had his excuse not to come much better prepared.

Except... damn it, he'd actually been looking forward to seeing Alice after his crazy first week at Trojan's.

He stole a glance at her. She'd put her cutlery down and a forefinger hovered close to the bridge of her nose, then dropped away. His lips twitched despite himself. She thought she was still wearing her glasses and had gone to shove them up her nose. A wave of nostalgic longing hit him. He missed those glasses.

Earlier, when he'd picked her up, he couldn't bring himself to look in her eyes as she answered the door. She was wearing another outfit he'd never seen. A cornflower blue dress with a little knot over the centre of her breasts, the material falling in soft folds from there, stopping a few centimetres short of her knees. Cute knees. And cherry-pink lipstick that defined the full outline of her upper lip. He'd carefully kept his eyes off her after that. He couldn't risk any more action in his groin.

In the confined space of his car they'd made polite and stilted conversation about his work.

When they got here, he'd grabbed Alice's hand as the door opened and was sure he felt her flinch. She'd removed it swiftly to give her coat to Jacinta and had kept a careful distance since then.

Well, damn it. Good. That's what he wanted. Right?

It suddenly occurred to him that maybe Alice would want some flirting practice after this as payment. He shifted to try and re-arrange himself in his seat.

"So how about you two?" Stella pressed her pregnancy-engorged breasts against the table, leaning eagerly towards him and Alice. She placed her chin in her hands and popped her eyes wide. "Will we hear the patter of tiny feet any time soon?"

"No!"

"No!"

Everyone was staring at them. Almost without thinking, Aaron reached for Alice's hand and brought it to his mouth, planted a kiss on the back of it, then intertwined her fingers with his. He felt the moment of resistance then a tentative pressure as she returned the squeeze, and once again the sensation of her hand in his made his cock stir.

But he couldn't drop her hand. Not without looking like a complete... well... *dick*. He cleared his throat, but his voice came out weird and husky. "What Alice is trying to say... what we mean is... *this* period of our relationship is so special, we don't want to rush into..."

The words ground to a halt so he replaced them with a stupid grin. And still his body refused to behave anywhere close to normal. Swiftly he let go of Alice's hand.

He sensed Alice's smile was superglued on and everyone made *ooh* and *aah* and "that's cute" noises. Blain, the father-to-be, looked at Aaron with a tinge of envy.

Willing the throb in his groin to take a hike, Aaron focused on his food.

Alice kicked him under the table.

And that, thankfully, seemed to do the trick.

When they were walking back to Aaron's car after what seemed like hours more of torturous dinner party conversation, Alice said, "I can drive if you've drunk too much."

He probably had. After the baby discussion incident he'd needed to fortify himself and he'd guzzled down more red wine than he'd meant to. Luckily they'd done the table swap thing for dessert and Alice had been hustled to the women's end of the table to discuss all things baby-related, while he, Hamish and Blain had talked work. Blain was a cabinet maker and it felt kind of good to talk to someone who worked with his hands and couldn't give a rat's about who around town was ripping off who for the most money.

Aaron tossed her the car keys. "Okay. I could be over the limit."

"I think you probably are."

He settled himself in the passenger seat. Alice had driven his car, even picked him up enough times after a wild night on the town, for this to feel familiar.

"So, shall I drive you to your place? I don't mind Ubering from there."

He paused. "Is Polly home?"

"No, I think she's out with Jake tonight."

He slunk low in the seat. "Let's go back to yours. I fancy one of your hot chocolates."

What the hell had he just said?

"Really?"

He did his best to sound nonchalant. "Yep, I'll sober up and be able to drive home after."

He sensed her shrug as she manoeuvred them out of the parking spot. "Okay," she said casually. "Though I can make up the sofa bed if you prefer."

Aaron's scalp prickled. Supposing his dick ruled his brain and he sleep-walked into her room? He nearly laughed at the sheer craziness of it, or maybe he did actually laugh out loud because she looked at him again, quizzically. "What's funny?"

"Nothing, why?"

"You kind of let out a *glumph*."

"A *glumph*?"

"Yeah, the snorty sound you make when you're amused."

"Well, if you must know, I was thinking about the noise you made when they asked you to the baby shower." He imitated her high-pitched tone. "*Hmmmm-umm?*"

"Only because I've never been to one before. I don't know

how you conduct yourself. Even the name is kind of weird. I have images of dousing a poor little baby's head with a garden sprinkler."

Aaron laughed. "Even I know it's to shower the baby with gifts."

"How domesticated of you."

Aaron slunk even lower in his seat and muttered, "Never."

That stopped the conversation dead.

They drove for a while in silence, Alice supposedly concentrating on the road. Aaron flicked a glance at her legs to see the hem of her skirt riding way above her knees. His car was a manual—all the best sporty numbers were—and the tensing and relaxing of her thigh as she pumped the gears made him want to turn the air-con on full blast.

He switched his eyes to the front and stared at the oncoming lights of cars. Where the frig had the ease they used to share gone?

Finally Alice questioned, "Have you seen Oliver recently?"

He flicked her profile a glance, but her little nose and the sweep of her upper lip gave nothing away. Even her tone was bland. "Not since his talk last Saturday. Why?"

"Oh, just... Nothing really, except he said he was trying to reach you."

Now he sat up. "When did you see Oliver?"

Alice drew up at a red light and glanced at him. He tried to wipe the surprise off his face.

"He brought in a box of his books to the shop; they got damaged in transit so he donated them to us."

"Nice of him."

"It was," Alice protested.

"I meant it." For once he actually did, but he guessed his attitude to Oliver was like the little boy who cried wolf. When he was being genuinely nice, he was suspected of being a bastard.

"He said he was trying to catch up with you for a drink."

Aaron thought about the stream of messages from Oliver

he'd ignored all week, until finally sending a curt, "Maybe next Monday or Tuesday I could do, after work". Which Oliver had come back to with such enthusiasm, it churned the old guilt-knife in Aaron's gut. He even found himself wishing for a moment that he could drop the blanket of antipathy, call a truce even, but he'd held on to it for so long, he wouldn't actually know what to put in its place.

"I'll catch up with him early next week," he said brusquely.

"That's good." Alice's tone was clipped. They turned into her street, rows of neat little weatherboards all with containers of vegetables growing on the verge outside. Only Rowena had a lawn. And roses behind her white picket fence—a nod, she'd once told him proudly, to her English heritage.

"Hot chocolate time," said Alice, way too chirpily as she killed the engine.

"Hot chocolate time," Aaron repeated, wondering why his nerves felt like they'd been torched.

He'd been to Alice's place a million times before for hot chocolate.

This time wasn't any different, right?

Ten minutes later and the *different* feeling wasn't letting up. By now Aaron had slung his jacket over a chair and was standing at the kitchen window pretending to stare at—well, nothing much—it was too dark to see anything but blobby shapes in the garden.

He said, "Are you looking after Rowena's roses properly?"

He could hear Alice rustling around behind him. When they'd got here she'd disappeared into her bedroom and come out shortly after wearing her pink fluffy bunny slippers, which made her look like a Disney character with her bright blue dress. It also made her smaller now the heels were shed and… hellish appealing.

Which was why he had to maintain his vigil at the window.

"They don't need much care in winter. It rains nearly every day."

He heard her open the fridge; he didn't need to look to

know she was getting out a carton of full cream milk. Next the pantry cupboard door banged. A spoon clunked, then *click*, the drinking chocolate tin lid was prised off. In a minute she'd whip up the milk until it was thick and frothy and then she'd whisk in the chocolate, and finally sprinkle some on top.

*Jesus Christ, he sounded like those domesticated couples from dinner.*

A sharp stab hit him in the chest. He coughed and pumped a fist in the centre of his ribs and the feeling receded enough for him to get his breath.

"Are you okay?" Alice asked.

Suddenly he needed something much stronger than hot chocolate. "I need a drink."

"Be patient," Alice laughed. "It takes a little while to make it how you like it."

"No, I mean a real drink." He turned and propped his hips on the kitchen bench and folded his arms over his chest. "What have you got?"

"I—um, don't want to raid Mum's wine collection. Maybe we've got some spirits... somewhere..." She turned, and up on tippy-toes, foraged through a cupboard. Aaron tried not to be mesmerised by the pert spheres of her buttocks under the flimsy fabric of her dress. He was still staring when she turned triumphantly with a bottle in her hand.

Flicking his gaze to the label, he grinned with relief. "Ah. Good one. Tequila."

# CHAPTER 10

Alice eyed Rowena's antique crystal liqueur glasses, the ones that were kept well out of reach for a reason, then, steeling herself, grabbed two of them off the top shelf of the pine dresser. She had to stop worrying about consequences. Live in the moment, like Polly did. As she turned around, Aaron was wielding the bottle of tequila, a smile on his face that made her toes curl against the fluffy insides of her slippers. Consequences. To hell with them. *Carpe diem.* Pleased with herself that she'd recalled the Latin version, she stepped back to the table and plonked the glasses down in the centre. Reflexively she ran her damp palms down her thighs. Aaron's gaze followed the movement and the sense of dampness intensified… not only in her palms it would seem.

The silence hummed between them. Finally, Aaron said, "Okay, so you're up for a lick, sip, suck."

"A what?"

One corner of his delectable mouth hitched. "It's the best way to take a neat shot of tequila. Unless you've got ginger beer, in which case I could make us slammers."

"Polly threw out all the mixers last week. She reckoned the sugar was gravitating to her thighs."

Aaron laughed, picked up a shot glass and held it up to the light. "These look a bit classy."

"They're all we've got. It's fine, as long as we're careful."

"No going wild and smashing them against the wall, then?"

Her mouth went slack as she fumbled for some appropriately pithy, *flirty* response.

Aaron got in first with a brisk, "Okay, we need lemons. And salt."

"Oh, yes, of course." Alice roused herself and scampered back to the cupboards, her body vibrating with the sense he was still watching her. It couldn't have felt more potent if he'd tiptoed his fingers down her back.

She grabbed the salt-shaker and checked the fruit bowl. "Oh, wait—no, I think Polly put the lemons in the fridge." She ducked her head inside, thankful for the brief waft of cold air on her fired-up cheeks. She found a couple of shrivelled lemons and pulled a face. "Not the best, I'm afraid."

"Knife?" Aaron moved towards the cutlery drawer and their bodies bumped in passing. She jumped, but Aaron simply sauntered back to the table and busied himself quartering the lemons on a board. He poured an equal amount of golden liquor into each shot glass, exquisitely self-assured. Alice groped her way towards a chair and hung on to the back until her knuckles whitened.

"Give me your hand," Aaron ordered.

Already? Oh, no, she needed a drink first. Two. Maybe three…

Nevertheless, she reached out and his fingers, warm and firm, gloved hers. Little tingles of sensation buzzed around her pelvis, before finding home in the apex between her thighs.

He turned her hand so that the back of it was uppermost and she watched from under her lashes as he sprinkled a measure of salt on to it.

"What's this for?"

"Put your hand to your mouth and lick the salt." His eyes traced her lips as she obeyed. He grabbed her other hand and placed the shot glass into it. "Knock it back in one."

The tang of salt on her lips turned into fire burning down her throat. She gagged and groped for the slice of lemon that had appeared between her fingers.

"Now suck."

Her mouth puckered as she put the lemon slice to her lips. A sharp tang followed the burn. A cauldron of sensations bubbled on her tongue and down her throat. Salt, heat, sour. She raised wide eyes to Aaron's.

"What's the verdict?" he asked, removing the lemon and shot glass from her hands.

"Oh, wow!" she exclaimed with a dawning smile. "I think I liked it. After I got over the initial shock."

"Good." Aaron went through the same motions. He didn't pull any of the faces or make any of the noises she had. Just swallowed it down like it was the most natural thing in the world.

As he smacked his lips their eyes met with shared mischief. Alice let out a gurgle of delight.

She tossed her head and her hair spun around her shoulders. "Can we do it again, please?"

Like this, she was too gorgeous to take his eyes off. Cheeks glowing, a dusting of salt crystals on her lower lip and her body swaying slightly as she steadied herself with a hand on the chair back. All he wanted was to reach out and touch.

Somehow he resisted the urge. Already he'd made a bit too much of handing her the refilled shot glass, giving and taking lemon slices, holding her hand longer than strictly necessary as he shook on the salt. When he'd neatened the edges of the little pile of crystals, he'd stroked the silkiness of the back of her hand with his thumb and felt her shiver. Was she cold? Maybe he should put his arm round her?

Her head kicked back as she skulled the tequila, followed by the cutest boss-eyed look as her lips pursed over the lemon. She'd just downed three tequila shots in not many more minutes and he knew from experience Alice's alcohol tolerance had always been abysmal.

Reaching out, Aaron prised the lemon wedge off her; she giggled and her head, as if suddenly too heavy for her body, dropped forward. She looked like a puppet that was in danger of losing its strings.

"*Whoa,*" he said, his arms coming out to steady her. Her chin bumped his chest and her eyelashes fluttered as she gifted him a crooked grin. They were close now, really close, and he marvelled at the softness of her breasts, the patter of her heart-beat. She was slighter, yet more curvy than he'd ever realised. But then, he'd never realised a lot of things about Alice... A steady throb started south of his waist and he shifted to minimise contact with his groin; he didn't want to alarm her.

Gently he pushed the heavy curtain of her hair away from her neck and whispered in her ear, "You all right?"

"Mmm, never better." Her voice was muffled against his chest. Now her hips bumped his groin and his cock jumped from interested to ready for action.

Holy cow. He was up shit creek.

And what's more, he didn't seem to care.

When his arms circled her she snuggled even closer. Gently, he let his lips nip down her neck. Alice inhaled sharply, followed by a little mewl of encouragement. He let his mouth slide lower and her neck extended into his kisses. As her hands sneaked around his waist a growl rumbled up Aaron's throat which he tried to turn into a cough. Who was he kidding? His lips had reached her collarbone by now. She was pressing into him, *down there,* and down there everything was hot and swollen and aching.

He should stop. He should... should... *not stop.*

Suddenly, Alice's head lifted and she looked up, eyes huge and questioning. But something else, some dark little devil was dancing in there too and it made him want to devour her mouth.

"Is this part of the flirting practice?" she asked, her voice thick as melted chocolate.

For a moment he stared down at her, losing himself in her particular brand of beauty; elfin, delicate, ethereal in a way that he'd *thought* didn't appeal to him, but which now he found... mesmerising... enchanting. The kind of beauty princes scaled ivy-clad castles and slayed dragons and swam across alligator-infested moats to get to.

Tequila-fuelled or not, he totally got it.

"I think we could call it that," he returned huskily, lowering his head. Their noses nudged, once, twice... then the fire took hold inside him and he smothered her mouth with his.

Soft, soft, soft. Moist. Soft. Wet. Ohhhh—*Jesus Christ*.

The kiss went on and on. Holding his libido back like a dog on a chain, Aaron ran his tongue tip slowly around Alice's quivering lips. Little moans escaped her; her lips clung to his. She did the same to him. And suddenly he couldn't stop from diving in headlong.

Tongues slid and danced and duelled and every cell inside him lit up. Not just his groin, which he'd always thought sex was all about, but everywhere—his scalp, the small of his back, right down to the soles of his feet.

Even his toes tingled. As if he'd been waiting for Alice to press some magical button inside him and *wham*...

And then all thoughts were gone as lust hijacked his brain.

Better, so much better than she'd ever dreamed... ever hoped... The taste of him, tequila and lemons and salt, the feel of him, his lips a perfect fit with hers, and oh, when his tongue met hers... their kiss had got so urgent their teeth clashed wildly before Aaron softened it, deepened it, unravelling her inch by inch...

And all the time strong arms anchored her as she threatened to spiral off into outer space; his pecs squishing her breasts, the beating of his heart... and... oh *gosh,* a rod of steel pressing against her belly.

Alice's fingers itched to sneak down, to outline the size of that ridge. Get the feel of his dimensions... she giggled at the total Polly-ness of the urge.

Aaron dragged his mouth off hers, his gaze heavy. "What's funny?"

"Nothing." She pulled his head back down before the weirdness of what they were doing struck Aaron and he stopped. It wasn't weird to her. It was like she'd just won the superball in Saturday lotto.

She giggled again. This time he laughed with her before nibbling her lower lip.

And then she stilled. One of his hands was exploring tentatively up the front of her ribs. Her nipples pebbled in anticipation as his little finger nudged the underside of her breast. She angled her body to let her breast push out and sighed as she felt the heat of Aaron's hand palming around the swell of it. His fingers slid under the front of her dress, below the lace of her bra, brushing one engorged nipple. He squeezed gently and the eye-to-vagina superhighway, Alice now realised, had nothing on the nipple-to-vagina superhighway. No, not just her vagina, more precisely the bud of her clit, vibrating in unison with Aaron's fingers gently tweaking and moulding her nipple.

A whoosh of warmth flooded her panties.

Aaron's head swooped and the next moment his mouth enveloped her nipple.

And sucked.

Alice was quite sure she had died and gone to heaven.

~

The clatter of a chair hitting the kitchen floor jerked his head up. He blinked. Somehow they were semi-sprawled over the tabletop, and if he'd had a skerrick of common sense left inside his head—which he didn't—he might have stopped right there; but surveying the damage also meant seeing the ball-boggling sight of Alice, one pink nipple exposed over her lacy blue bra, lips bruised from their kissing frenzy, pupils dilated... hair tousled... by him... All of this—*his* doing.

He watched her small teeth indent her lower lip; her eyes riveted to his crotch. The air huffed out of his nostrils before their bodies crashed together again. With a grunt Aaron hoisted her butt onto the table. Immediately she pinned him to her, and his gaze dropped to the dress riding up her thighs... Christ, she was wearing suspenders! He glanced around to where her legs clasped his buttocks and something about the sight of suspenders at one end and those ridiculous bunny slippers at the other was so erotic his balls drew tight and his cock bucked.

"Oh... god... you... are..." he muttered as Alice pulled his head down to her mouth again with a whimper. "Beautiful," he got out in between deep kisses. He pushed into the v between her legs; another whimper that could have been his name. Her panties were slippery and warm against his crotch. Surprisingly nimble fingers worked his zipper... an invitation for him to return the favour. He let his palm shift up her thigh until his touch skimmed the soft skin above her stockings, flicked aside the gusset of her panties.

"Oh, oh. Oh, ahhhh!" Hot sweet breath tickled his ear as she ground herself into his fingers. Christ, she was soaking wet.

Heat and moisture, the musky scent of their shared arousal and he had to taste her, right now. He pulled away and kneeled between her legs... his mouth hungry as hell.

*Slam. Tap tap tap. Thud, thuddity thud.* Two pairs of footsteps on the hall floorboards and Alice had catapulted off the table before he'd even quite registered she'd gone.

Shit on wheels. Polly and...?

Jumping up, Aaron was over at the window in two strides,

willing his erection into oblivion while his hands dug deep in his pockets to give his strangled cock more breathing space.

Polly's voice split the air. "Well, hello there—have we just interrupted something?"

"Oh, no, not at all," Alice squeaked from some distance away. How had she got that far that fast? "Aaron was just leaving, actually."

*More like coming…* Hell, this really wasn't the right time for his brain to manufacture wisecracks. He'd been caught teetering on the verge of cunnilingus with Alice on her kitchen table. Not smart.

Dumb. As. Fuck. In fact.

He forced a smile onto his lips and glanced over his shoulder. "Poll. Oh, Jake. Hi there." He feigned surprise. Why, he didn't have a clue, everyone was used to man-bun Jake and Polly. A non-item who often ended up an item.

Guess this was an item night.

By now the lid on his libido was snapped safely shut, but in its place came the oddest empty feeling. Like he'd lost something precious. It roiled low in his gut. He made the mistake of turning around and casting a furtive glance at Alice.

Even though her hair looked like a family of magpies had just vacated and her chafed mouth looked like someone had painted clown lips on her, he still wanted to make love to her so much it hurt.

*Make love to her?*

Rationally, that was nonsense.

Except it didn't *feel* like nonsense.

Pushing off the bench, he went to grab his jacket off the chair. "Yeah, I'm off." His mouth still tasted of Alice's. "I came back for one of Al's hot chocolates because I was too wasted to drive. But, ha-ha"—his laugh was as dry as bark—"the plan went a bit wrong, seems we polished off your tequila, Poll, sorry." He cocked a casual eyebrow at Alice. "Keys, please?"

She looked at him horrified. "You can't drive, not after…" Her words trailed off and she went beet-red in the face.

He tutted his lips impatiently and saw her features pinch with hurt. "I'll grab a cab. Give me the keys and I'll come and pick my car up in the morning; that way I won't disturb you."

"Don't leave on our behalf." Polly was clearly concealing a smirk, as was bun-man.

Aaron raked a hand casually through his hair, located his phone and busied himself with tracking an Uber ride. Luckily, there was one three minutes away. Alice was foraging around in her handbag; she took out his car keys and walked towards him without looking at him.

"Sure you don't want to join us for a beer?" Jake said as he raided the fridge with the confidence of a guy who came here often.

*Jerk.* Aaron shook his head.

Alice plonked the keys with a *thwack* into his outstretched palm and flounced towards the door. "I'll see you out."

He didn't need her to see him out, but it would seem odd if he refused. Alice always walked to the door with him, usually laughing at some shared joke. But now it was like they were on an expedition to the South Pole as they silently trudged down the hall. Alice fumbled with the door handle and for a brief second it flashed into his head to swing her round and kiss her again. Start where they left off. He forced it out of his head.

Alice held the door open, peering into the street with feigned interest. "Here it is," she said as a car slowed down and stopped outside. "Guess I'll see you around, sometime," she muttered, staring at her slippers.

He swept past her and somehow their elbows bumped. His nerve endings surged like she'd slapped him.

"Guess so. I'll call you."

"Sure. See you, Aaron."

"See you."

He heard the door shut. Not a slam, exactly, but a definite closure.

He got into the back seat, gave the guy his address.

His eyelids were stinging. Probably the result of too many

tequila shots. Or maybe he'd rubbed lemon juice into them. A headache brewed behind his temples as he laid his head against the back of the seat.

Tomorrow he'd work out what to do about him and Alice. Right now, he just wanted to pretend it had never happened.

# CHAPTER 11

S o. So. Awful.

With each word, Alice banged her head on the bathroom cabinet. Which only made it hurt more. Was it possible
for your head to split open and your brains to spill out from a
hangover? Or was this what happened when you were hit by a
tsunami of shame and self-loathing?

When she'd awoken this morning there had been one brief
second of the most amazingly syrupy feeling blanketing her
body and then... she wasn't sure which came first— the sense
that her skull was an egg being cracked repeatedly with a
spoon, or the raft of memories that assaulted her brain.

A kaleidoscope of hot lips and feverish fingers, of smell,
taste, touch. The feel of him thick and hard, straining against
her hand as she fumbled with the fly of his pants, and the
knowledge that all she'd wanted was to lie back and let Aaron
do all kind of unimaginably wicked things to her.

Then do unimaginably wicked things back.

She gagged and, avoiding her reflection, flung open the
bathroom cabinet and fumbled around for some painkillers.
She shook two into her hand from the bottle then shoved them

into her mouth, cupped water into her hand and gulped them down before sinking onto the edge of the bath.

She needed to talk to Polly.

But Polly was probably still holed up in bed with Jake and wouldn't surface until late morning. Especially with Rowena away. And meanwhile Alice would probably have to put on some loud music so she didn't have to hear their morning coitus routine. Which would do nothing for her splitting temples.

Polly wasn't self-conscious about making a lot of noise when she orgasmed. She said being vocal intensified it.

Not that Alice would know.

Amend that. She recalled being pretty vocal last night with the things Aaron was doing to her nipples. Not that there had been an orgasm. Such events were rare and self-induced. Very quietly in the dark. But oh god, she'd been teetering on the brink... even... before...

A sudden image of Aaron's tousled blond hair nestling between her legs, and despite her utter state of misery, her sex sprang alarmingly to life. She was beginning to feel like a fairground ride down there, one of the slam-dunking big dipper kinds that left you wobbly kneed and terrified but still wanting to go back a second time... and a third.

She groaned and covered her face. How would she ever be able to look him in the eye again?

A tap on the door startled her.

"Alice. I need a pee."

Polly? Up already? Alice scrambled up and her stomach rose in tandem, but she gulped hard and unbolted the bathroom door, then peered around it.

Polly's face, flushed and framed by even bouncier curls than usual, met hers.

"Not feeling so great?" Polly grimaced sympathetically as she slipped into the bathroom.

"I want to die." Alice slumped back on the side of the bath as Polly wriggled her kimono-style dressing gown up her thighs, sat on the loo and happily tinkled away, still watching her with bright, sympathy-laden eyes.

"Please don't look at me like that," Alice moaned, hands over her face once more.

"Oh come on, Munchkin, you've seen me in this state often enough."

"What, peeing?"

"No, silly. The post-sex state."

"*You* might be. I'm not."

"Very close though, am I right?"

*Arghhh.* Alice shook her head then grabbed her forehead. It felt like her brain was dislodging.

Polly clucked her tongue. "I'll take that as a yes."

Done and dusted, Polly shimmied over to the basin and washed her hands. "Go and get ready," she said briskly. "I'm taking you out for breakfast."

"God no! I'll vomit. Besides, aren't you and Jake—"

"Jake had an early shift at the café, so he's gone—sadly. And you should know, after your countless hangover brekky preparations for a certain someone who shall remain nameless, that the best cure is fat and carbs."

Alice almost retched.

"Strong coffee, at least," Polly compromised. "You or me in the shower first?"

"You first," Alice said feebly. "I'm going to get an ice pack."

By the time she had tucked into her plate of a half serve of the full vego brekky and a soy long mac at the Hole in the Wall café two blocks down from their house, Alice was beginning to feel human again.

Polly sat opposite, drinking black coffee. She'd over-indulged in more ways than one last night, apparently. "I always get the munchies after good sex." She sighed. "I sent Jake out to buy hot chips from the burger van on East Street."

"What on earth time was that?"

After Aaron had left, Alice hadn't been able to face either of their enquiring glances and had gone into her room and thrown herself face-down on the bed, where the choice was howl like a banshee or pass out. She'd chosen the latter.

Polly shrugged. "About 11ish, I guess."

"How do you do it, Poll?"

"Do what?"

"Get them eating out of your hand like fledgling birds."

Polly laughed. "I'd hardly call Jake a fledgling. More like a big cuddly bear."

"Psychologically, I mean; they're like baby birds pecking up any crumb you graciously throw to them."

"Not really." Polly shrugged. "Though I guess it could have something to do with the fact I'm not interested in anything long term. Guys pick up the scent of a woman who's too needy pretty damn quick. There's no way I'm going to go all soft over a guy. So yeah, maybe they get that about me and, I dunno, perhaps, perversely it makes them keener."

Alice sipped miserably at her macchiato. "Clearly, I've wrecked it with Aaron on all counts, then."

Polly's eyes twinkled. "The rules change when you're both in as deep as each other. Then everything gets a whole heap more complicated."

Alice frowned. It still hurt her head, but not quite as fiercely as before. "You've lost me as usual."

"Well, it's like this, right. Once the emotional connection is already in place and you add sex, it's like, *whoof,* light the blue touch paper and stand well back. It's seriously deep shit. He can't go back from here. Mind you, he won't have a clue how to go forward either." Polly gave a sudden wide grin. "Remember *Doctor Dolittle*?"

"Yes of course, I read it a hundred times."

"Me too. And the movie, I loved it. Remember the Push-Me-Pull-You? That's what it's like for Aaron right now. He's pushed and pulled by his feelings, which means he's stuck until he finally accepts he's in love with you. And here's the thing: you're going to have to give him a bit of help."

133

Alice stared miserably into her coffee. The enormity of the task was like scaling Everest in a pair of stilettos.

"I just want to go back to how we were before. I knew where I stood then."

Polly threw her hands up in the air. "Yeah. Invisible."

"It was safe. Easy."

"You're right; safe *is* easy. Safe is boring. Safe is your life slipping through your fingers. Go on, Munchkin, hightail it back to safe before you really get to *feel* like you're alive."

Alice squinted across the table. "Sometimes you are so mean."

Polly leaned forward and placed a hand on her arm and stared earnestly into her eyes. "Because you're my best friend and I love you. Which means I want you to grab every opportunity that could make you happy, not live a small, mean little life buried under old books and rescue cats."

Alice shot upright in her seat. That wasn't a nice image at all.

"I love you too," she said, and shovelled in a hasty mouthful of hash brown. "Even if you are a prize cow sometimes." The food tasted good—really good—and as she ate more, the gnawing feeling in her stomach receded.

"Do you think it's because I don't have a father?" Alice mused after a while.

Polly, who'd been eyeing up the waiter's pert buttocks, asked, "What is?"

"The fact I'm scared of everything. That I can't, you know, do the normal things other people our age do without even thinking twice? Mum told me the other day I needed to get over my flying phobia. She's right. I've never travelled—never gone anywhere except down the coast on a bus trip. I got first-class honours and here I am, still working in a bookshop five years after I graduated. Living in Mum's house. Living in Mum's shadow. Aren't girls supposed to gain courage from their fathers being in their lives? Has not having one stunted my emotional development?"

Polly shrugged. "I think no father is better than a useless one."

Alice pinned her lips. Polly had no time for her own dad and his drinking problem. The way he had finally pushed her mum away. And his only daughter, too. Polly used to hate him, but she'd learned to drop that down several notches to indifference.

"Maybe," Alice agreed. "But it would be nice to know some basic facts."

"Surely Rowena's told you *something*?"

"Yes, that he had brown eyes, she *thinks*. And wasn't very tall, because she remembers she didn't have to look up at him. He was a one-night stand at a party and she's pretty sure his name was Andrew and that he was from Basingstoke."

"Surely she could have traced him?"

"Apparently it was at some big house party in the countryside and he'd just come for the night with a group of friends and left first thing the next morning. She reckons by the time she found out she was pregnant it was too late to find him."

"Or she chose not to."

"Exactly."

Alice put her knife and fork down neatly in the centre of her plate. She'd had enough to eat. The trembly feeling and nausea had gone.

"I just wonder if having no father has made me hang on to the *dream* of Aaron all these years. Maybe I love him because I've never had a good male role model."

"Then invent one."

"That's silly."

"No, go on. Invent how you want your dad to be. Since he's not around you can imagine him any way you want to. What's he do for a living?"

Alice smiled. Polly's ability to find the seed of positivity in every situation was sheer genius.

"He's a writer. No, better still, a movie director."

Polly raised a brow. "Impressive. What's he look like?"

"Handsome, in a lean, haunted, underfed kind of way. You know, the Ralph Fiennes look. He lives in a castle in Scotland. He has a slight limp from falling off a galloping horse at a young age. Oh, and a quite disfiguring scar across his left cheek from an accident with clashing swords."

"Swords!"

"When he was directing a remake of *The Three Musketeers*. He got in between the actors during a particularly nasty parry."

Soon they were both laughing, and Alice realised her dark mood along with her hangover had almost completely lifted. She just had to erase last night from her mind. Inventing a father seemed to be doing the trick quite nicely.

As they strolled back home, arm in arm, Polly said, "Okay. Don't call Aaron, or text him for several days. Let him stew."

Alice felt her neck tensing up again at the return to the subject of Aaron. "He won't call me. Not after the way we left each other. It was like the Cold War."

"That was simply a mutual failure on both your parts to process the enormity of the situation. Let things brew for a while. If you want I'll hide your phone so you can't keep checking it."

"That will not be necessary." Alice stuck her nose in the air. "I am bigger than that. I am the daughter of a Scottish laird who directs Oscar-winning movies despite living with horrendous pain from his injuries on a daily basis."

"Cool," said Polly. "Piece of cake, then."

~

"He'll be with you shortly. Just finishing up an important phone call." Archie Bendt's P.A. glanced up from her computer as she said these words with a perfectly synchronised smile.

Aaron feasted his eyes on her. She was beautiful. Totally his type, the leggy Swedish look, lean bone structure and long legs, pale blue eyes perfectly framed by long lashes. Her nose didn't wrinkle when she smiled and her mouth was catwalk model material—not somehow reminiscent of a rosebud that tasted like icing-sugar-coated marshmallows.

He flashed a wide smile, showing off his teeth. He'd met Lauren quite a few times at the photocopier and she'd made the odd remark that could have been construed as vaguely flirtatious. Not that he'd go anywhere with it, of course. He never dated women he worked with; well, okay, there had been one time that led to an awkward month or so early on in his career. In the end it had been a face-off to see who would leave the company first. Luckily, she did.

No. All he wanted was to feel the familiar stirring of interest in the right parts of his anatomy for the right kind of woman.

But there was nothing. Zip. Zero. Zilch.

Even more disturbing was how the libidinous pathways in his brain appeared to have got badly scrambled. Whenever he looked at an attractive woman, an image of that *other* mouth, those *other* eyes, one delectably swollen pink nipple would flash in front of his eyes like some erotically charged one-armed bandit.

And he couldn't even claim the jackpot.

So he sat and eyeballed Lauren Donovan in a way that was crass and professionally unsound. And might even get him reported if he didn't keep it in check, but for the fact his intentions were harmless.

He just wanted the old him back.

Archie suddenly burst out of his office and strode over to Lauren's desk. He came to a halt behind her, and confident hands landed on the back of her chair as he leaned over her shoulder.

Aaron caught the way she twirled a lock of silvery blonde hair as she looked up at him, and something... some kind of energy between the two of them made his scalp tighten.

He disregarded it. He was in a heightened state of arousal at the moment... not towards Lauren, obviously, he was simply more hyper-aware of bodies right now... a rather unfortunate consequence of being in a state of coitus interruptus since last Saturday night.

"Get the invoices out on this one will you, Laurie," Archie said. "And then we're pretty much done and dusted on the De'Bel case after that."

"Cool. No problem."

Archie's fingers drummed out a beat on the back of Lauren's chair and she swivelled slightly more his way. They gifted each other a grin. A collegiate, *professional* grin.

"C'mon in, Aaron." Archie jerked his head towards his office. "We have some serious stuff to nut out on the Willoughby-Green trial. Have you got your iPad to jot notes on?"

'Right here." Aaron patted the device and, jumping up, followed Archie's expensively suited back into the office. Just before he closed the door, he glanced at Lauren.

Her eyes were focused past him. On Archie Bendt's incredible shoulders.

～

Behind the door of the men's toilet at Trojan's with the bright red Alpha sign emblazoned on it, Aaron tugged on his running shorts. Exasperation warred with exhaustion. The meeting with Archie had gone on for more than two hours and he'd found it hard to concentrate on all the details required for the court report. It had been like this all week. His concentration slipping, and an underlying restless energy coursing through his veins.

Fear surfaced. What if... What if he was slipping back... Christ, that had been another lifetime. He'd been barely in his teens. He'd been fine now for years.

That was why he was running, right? Pounding himself to a pulp all the way into the city. And all the way back at night. Every day so far this week. Because exercise did the trick, calmed him down, helped him focus.

He hung up his suit neatly in his locker, then scrunched his shirt in with his toiletries and laptop in the backpack; he'd still have to do some work tonight at home to get up to speed. Trainers on, laces tied and he was out the door, slinging his pack on his back and jogging on the spot, waiting for the lift. Lauren sashayed through the automatic glass doors of Trojan's with her bag and a coat slung over her arm and waited.

"That's a disciplined routine," she remarked as they got in the lift.

He stood still with difficultly and grinned at her, feeling rather stupid—though why, he couldn't fathom. He tried for a mild version of his *come-fuck-me* look but there was no *come-fuck-me* energy flowing between them, that was blatantly obvious.

He gave her a casual wave as he made his way across the vast marble floor of the foyer and heard her heels *clack-clacking* in the other direction.

And then he was out on the city pavement, his earbuds in place and all he had to do was focus on the rhythm of his playlist and his running feet.

Finally, panting and dripping, he was feeling around for his keys in his pocket and staring absently along the street when he saw a red Golf GTI zip into a parking place just down from his block. Dad had one of those in his stable of cars under the house... Frig, surely not? Dad never visited him in his "little rabbit hutch", as he so kindly referred to Aaron's apartment.

He waited and within a minute a familiar male form had vacated the car, clicked the remote and was strolling, hands in pockets, towards his apartment.

Oliver. What was he doing here? Annoyance churned in Aaron's stomach.

He didn't want to see his brother right now. Oliver never managed to put him in a better mood. Right now what he needed was a shower, a cold beer and a couple of episodes of his latest Nordic noir series, before working on his laptop until the early hours.

But hand in hand with the annoyance came a stab of guilt. He had meant to phone Oliver and tee up a time to meet, but all week he'd put it off and put it off; ignored the messages from his brother after quickly checking they weren't from Alice. Then ignored the dent of disappointment that they weren't from Alice.

He jiggled his keys as Oliver reached him. "What are you doing here?"

"I got a bit sick of being deflected." Oliver smiled good-naturedly.

"Sorry. I've been mega busy. But now you're here... if you don't mind me having a quick shower, stay and share a beer." He tried to sound as hospitable as possible, given he was covered in sweat.

"Sure. Or we could go for a bite to eat. Is there still that great Indian restaurant around here?"

"Vavoom Vindaloo?"

"Yes, that one."

Vavoom Vindaloo was one of the best Indian restaurants north of the river and it was cavernous enough inside that it never failed to seat the people who regularly queued up outside. So, some time later, duly showered and changed, here Aaron was, seated opposite his immaculate older brother, sipping Kingfisher beer. He was fast running out of questions about and, quite frankly, interest in the book on investing for retirees Oliver and Dad were hatching up.

"And then we'll do one for teens," Oliver went on. "I'm hoping to get it into schools. Maybe even onto the national curriculum."

Aaron nodded, wringing out a last grain of enthusiasm. "Sounds like your usual entrepreneurial self."

"It's not all about me." Oliver sounded slightly offended. "I'm thinking of mine and Leonie's future. Our kids. The broader future of the planet for generations to come."

*Oh my god, Oliver the omnipotent.*

Aaron cast him what he knew was a mean-eyed look.

"Don't try and make out you don't earn a nice tidy sum as well."

"I never pretended not to. You can gain wealth through ethical means, in case you hadn't noticed."

"Are you implying litigation isn't ethical?"

Oliver shook his head disbelievingly. "Jeesh. There was no criticism, implied or otherwise. Why do you always take what I say the wrong way?"

Aaron poked at a piece of butter chicken with his fork. "It's your tone."

"What about my tone?"

"Kind of smug and supercilious. Like you know better than anyone else."

Oliver thrust back in his chair. "Boy, oh boy. This goes back to another time, bro. Put it back in its box."

"Which box, Oliver? You have enough of them." *And all of them neatly colour-coded.* By the thinning of Oliver's lips, he got the inference. Suck on that, *big bro.*

"The one marked 'in the past', mate," Oliver said grimly.

Aaron stared at his plate, his body tightening. One point to Oliver. An awkward silence ensued.

In a kinder tone, Oliver finally said, "Look, I know you had it rough after Mum died. And that I kind of backed off from you and let you get on with it. But we were both going through some pretty difficult stuff at the time." He sighed. "Being four years older than you, I should have tried harder, but..."

"I know. I was shit to live with. Dad never lets me forget it."

"Dad wasn't great either; he really didn't have a clue and he was grieving for Mum too. He was way too hard on you. All the stuff you went through—it wasn't your fault. Dad realised that, after you'd..." Oliver paused and took a sip of his beer. The energy was spiky like it always was when Oliver tried to unpack that time. Just because he'd had therapy, he liked to shove the fact down Aaron's throat.

"Do you still take medication?" Oliver asked, then quickly added, "That's not a criticism, by the way. Whatever works."

"Nope." Aaron shifted in his seat. Not going there. Not with Oliver. Not with anyone. "No. I got off it at uni. I exercise instead."

"That's great." Oliver resumed eating. "This food is even better than I remember. As good as most of the Indian restaurants in Sydney."

Aaron resisted the urge to mutter that some things in the west were a damn sight better than over east. But another barbed comment might bring Oliver back to trawling through the past. The past that Aaron apparently hadn't sorted. And Oliver had. Urgh.

He was just going to do the right thing and ask how Leonie was when Oliver said, "I saw Alice the other day."

Aaron's spine stiffened. He knew that, of course he did, after Alice had mentioned it the other night. He had just been hoping Oliver wouldn't bring her up. But trust Oliver, always finding a new scab to pick at. He kept focusing on his plate.

"I took some damaged copies of my book to the Book Genie. We had a nice chat."

Aaron heaped saffron rice onto his fork. "How was she? Haven't seen her for a while."

*Apart from spread out like a feast on Rowena's kitchen table.*

"She's looking great. Though she was a bit evasive. How's things with you two?"

"Same. Why do you ask?"

"No reason. Except you walked out of my talk with your arm around her."

Aha! Now he saw the great big hook Oliver was dangling. Well, he wasn't fucking biting.

Aaron shrugged. "She was feeling a bit panicky, you know, with the crowds, so I gave her a bit of support."

"Funny, that's not her account of things."

*Shit.* "Oh really?"

"Yes. She said it was because of some bet or other."

A bet? Surely she hadn't told Oliver about the fake girlfriend/flirting thing? Besides, that was an agreement, not a bet.

And then he found himself irrationally hurt that she would want to put Oliver off the scent. Didn't she want his family to suspect something was going on between them? Come to think of it, she'd certainly given him his marching orders when Jake and Polly turned up. Like she was ashamed to be associated with him *that way.*

Aaron shoved a forkful of curry and rice into his mouth and chewed. What did it matter? The last thing he needed was Alice getting a crush on him. Ergo, any little fib Alice had told Oliver was irrelevant.

Forcing a laugh, he flung the fork down. "Ah well, you know me and Al; always trying to get one up on each other."

Oliver merely waggled his eyebrows. "Andrea's inviting her for afternoon tea on Sunday, by the way," he added casually—*too* casually. "She's trialling a couple of new cakes for Gran's ninetieth and she reckons Alice has the most discerning tastebuds." Oliver waited, as if for Aaron to own up to something. "You'll come, of course?"

He could find an excuse. So damned easy. He had a million and one other things he should be doing this weekend. Come to think of it he'd probably have to go in to work and get up to speed on the case before Monday.

He opened his mouth, and out came the words, "Sure, I'll be there."

# CHAPTER 12

I t was Wednesday and she'd been good.

Her phone was—for the most part—secreted in a spot right up high where they kept the stationery, which meant she couldn't keep flicking a look at it. Alice allowed herself to check it at coffee time. Nothing. Lunch time. Still nothing. And then refused to look until she was locking up the shop each day.

Nothing.

It helped considerably thinking about her imaginary dad. All those things he'd been through. It pegged up her spine and put vim and vigour into her interactions with customers.

She was the result of good strong stock. Yorkshire miners— on Mum's side—who'd made good and, well, who'd have known it—Scottish aristocracy. So poo to Aaron and his English and Dutch origins and the smidgin of Italian on his mum's side, three generations back. By the middle of the week, however, the imaginary dad story was getting a little thread-bare and her edges were fraying. So, a little frisson of illicit excitement had shot through her when she'd heard her phone ring that afternoon.

It was Andrea. Alice had always loved Andrea. She was the kind of woman who should probably have been a saint. Saint Andrea. Kind, even-tempered, unconditionally giving. If she had ups and downs they never showed or got mixed into her cakes and beautiful sourdough bread and amazing stews with their weird and wonderful secret ingredients like five spice or cacao.

Alice had often gone around to the Blake family home when she first knew Aaron and he was still living at his dad's, but since he'd bought his own apartment it was rarer—the odd family dinner or when Aaron and she swung by after a Sunday brunch together. She and Andrea hadn't actually seen each other—if you didn't count the sighting over the heads of the crowds and the soggy biscotti incident—for months.

She answered with slightly shaking fingers.

"Alice?" Andrea's soft voice always had a breathless quality to it.

"Hi, Andrea, how are you?"

"Good, good. How are you? I spotted you at Oliver's talk with Aaron but by the time I'd extricated myself to come and see you, you'd both left."

Had Andrea seen Aaron's arm around her, Alice wondered? Yes, she had. Because Oliver in his wisdom had pointed it out. But Andrea was too tactful to dig around.

"I'm calling to invite you to tea on Sunday," Andrea said. "I want your opinion on a couple of cake recipes I'm trying out for Gran's birthday party. The family will be there, David and Oliver and hopefully Aaron, but not Gran, because obviously I want it to be a surprise."

"How lovely." Alice tried to sound calm. "How old is Gran now?"

"Turning ninety. Can you believe it?"

Gran was Aaron's mum's mum. It was lovely that Andrea had become almost as close to her as a real daughter. Another tribute to Andrea's sainthood and Gran being pretty much the sweetest person to walk the earth after Andrea.

145

"I'd love to," Alice said enthusiastically. Who cared if Aaron was there or not? She was doing this for Andrea. And Gran. A celebration of three generations of women.

The next day Alice was going through a consignment of books, trying to work out how many to give a credit note for, when her phone trilled in her handbag. She'd forgotten her rule and had left it under the counter. She hesitated, then grabbed it. A little breath punched out of her lungs when she saw Aaron's name on the screen.

"Hi *sweetie*, how are you?" Aaron's voice had the I'm-with-the-partners ring to it.

It was tempting to hang up on him. She held the phone away from her ear as he blabbed on about some drinks thing it was a pity she couldn't make it to, which made her want to stab him in the ear with a virtual needle.

"I can't talk now, I've got a customer," she snapped. The shop was full of browsers, but that did not constitute buying, of course. Sometimes she'd have to go and stand near one of them and pretend she was sorting books to stop them reading a whole novel. The record was two hours and thirty-three minutes for *Harry Potter and the Philosopher's Stone*.

She should be tougher. Rowena always shooed them out or made them buy. Well, she was practising her shooing skills on Aaron now, wasn't she?

"Wait." His voice changed; he'd obviously moved away from the group, though she could hear droning conversation and the odd burst of laughter. "Are you going to Dad and Andrea's on Sunday afternoon for tea?"

"I may be," she hedged.

"Andrea wants you to taste her new cake recipes."

"I know, she phoned me. That's why I'm going. Obviously." She tried to drip icicles down the line.

It seemed to work as he said awkwardly, "Okay. Well I guess I'll see you there if I can spare the time. I'm up to my freakin' eyeballs with work here. Huge case getting ready to go to court next week. Don't think I've slept all week."

She nearly broke her phone case squeezing it to stop herself making sympathetic noises.

"Okay, well, I'd better go. Catch you—maybe—Sunday then," she said briskly.

A moment's pause. "Yep. Sure. See you if I see you."

She threw the phone on the desk and fought the stupid urge to burst into tears. No mention of Saturday night; no, "that was great, let's do it again some time."

As if… It had been a tequila-fuelled mistake. Really, had she gone soft in the head?

With fast and angry fingers, she rifled through the pile of moth-eaten books. They were total rubbish. Soiled. Badly written pot boilers. Not worth cutting down trees for.

She wrote on the box in red texta, *No credit note. Return to sender.*

Yes. She could be a hard-nosed bitch when she chose to be.

~

Aaron tucked his Moschino shirt into his jeans. Pulled it out, ripped it off and put on his ancient Cold Chisel T-shirt, with the hole in the front. It was entirely appropriate for a guy who didn't give a fuck and it wasn't as if it was Gran's actual party. Just a casual get-together to taste cakes. He tucked it in to his jeans. Pulled it out. Out looked better.

He'd put product in his hair, which made it spike rather than flop. Taken a lightning-fast shower. Not thought about Alice. Thought about Alice. Resisted doing anything about the massive erection staring up at him. Got out and dried himself until the towel burned his skin. Trimmed his stubble. Doused his underarms in deodorant and splashed on one of his more subtle colognes.

So here he was, having barely spent any time on prep. Because it was only Alice. And after today he wouldn't feel like his head had been stuffed full of cotton wool balls and wood chips. Meeting her over afternoon tea would be a civilised way for them to get back on a more even keel.

He grabbed his car keys and phone and exited his apartment, his usual confidence re-emerging... along with something else that reminded him of the popping candy he used to put on his tongue as a kid. Though how it had got into his bloodstream was beyond him.

At Dad's, there was no street parking so he used his remote to open the underground garage and parked his car between David Blake's 1954 Daimler and the Golf GTI Oliver had turned up in the other day. He flicked a glance at Dad's other two classics, a 1962 convertible E-Type Jaguar and a 1973 classic Porsche.

Seriously, Dad had money to burn. The cars, the speedboat moored at the river he hardly every had time to use, the imposing house in the most elite part of town. Except... wasn't that exactly what he, Aaron, wanted? To be like the David Blakes and Archie Bendts of this world?

He shook off a vague queasiness as the image of Archie leaning over Lauren's chair came into his head. Since that day, he'd noticed a few more incidents. His imagination was way too active at present. Look what had happened in the shower. One fleeting thought about suspenders and bunny ears and all the blood had migrated to his dick.

Taking the lift from the garage he found himself in the elegant hallway. The flowers were shades of pink and apricot today. Delectable scents of cinnamon and vanilla and something else he couldn't work out wafted from the kitchen. Voices. Andrea's soft and melodic, and another laugh that made his toes tingle.

He paused, nearly switched on his heels to go the other way towards the study and then realised he was stuck. He didn't want to see Dad and Oliver any more than he wanted to see Alice.

Except he *did* want to see Alice. He was desperate to see Alice... to put things straight between them, he told himself firmly. He missed their easy banter, the way he didn't have to put on a performance in front of her... except now... yeah, he'd really put on a performance the other night, hadn't he? With agitated fingers he smoothed his hair and willed his pulse to slow. Pressing his mouth tight, he ambled into the kitchen.

Dappled light shafted through the big windows and hit the state-of-the-art appliances and gleaming white cupboards. Outside, a watery sun peered from heavy winter clouds and Andrea had the lights on—modern glass pendants that hung low over the kitchen island bench. They lit up a cast of beautifully iced cakes.

Behind the bench stood Alice and Andrea fussing over cutting up a large, fluffy sponge covered in thick pink buttercream icing. Alice had a smudge of icing on her finger and she licked it off and rolled her eyes heavenwards. His gaze got stuck on the lips enveloping her finger and a sudden flash of those same lips going through similar motions somewhere else had him shove his hands abruptly into his pockets.

*Not. Here.*

He must have made some kind of strangled sound because both women's heads shot up. Two pairs of eyes zoomed in, Andrea's warm and hazel, Alice's huge and dark and utterly unreadable.

Launching into the room, he hugged Andrea, hyper-aware of Alice standing ramrod stiff next to her, hands now clasped neatly in front of her. He stepped back and gave Alice a nod. Andrea frowned at him. Okay, so maybe he should be a bit friendlier. Leaning forward he pecked Alice quickly on the cheek and tried to ignore the floral waft of her perfume, the same one she'd been wearing the night they... they... lurching back, he bumped into a stool and nearly lost his footing. How could a guy who spent as much time as he did in the gym suddenly feel like a puppy trying to navigate an ice rink? Bracing through his heels, palms on the benchtop, he stared at the array of cakes. "Wow, Andrea, you've done yourself proud."

Andrea pointed her spatula. "Classic Victoria sponge, hummingbird cake, and this one is an angel cake. We've just decided we're going to put violets on the one we choose, because violets are Gran's favourite flower."

"We were trying to work out whether we should make the violets out of confectioners' icing or marzipan," Alice said matter-of-factly.

He cast her a quick glance. "Are you helping Andrea?"

"I am the chief assistant pastry chef, yes." Alice's tone was haughty. He hoped it was joke-haughty. He wanted them back where they were supposed to be. Teasing, playful. Easy. Not all these clunking sharp edges.

"Can I taste?" He ducked a hand out, but Alice slapped it with a wooden spoon and it actually hurt. He drew back. "Ouch."

She let out a snicker. Their eyes met for a second and it was like he'd been punched in the solar plexus. "Still wearing your contacts," he muttered.

"Don't you love Alice's new look?" Andrea chimed in. "Such beautiful eyes she's been hiding from the world all these years."

Alice gave a coy smirk. Aaron wanted to take the wooden spoon and rap Andrea over the knuckles with it.

Just then David Blake entered the room, filling up the space with his big energy. "Oliver and I are taking a break from writing. So, when you're ready... we're ready... Hi Aaron..." His eyes alighted on Alice and his face lit up. "Hu-llo, Alice." He bounded round the island bench, circumnavigated Aaron and enveloped Alice in a big hug. "One thing I miss about my younger son moving out is not seeing you around the place." He held her away from him and frowned. "You look different, your hair, maybe?"

"It's not in a ponytail." Alice beamed. "And I'm not wearing glasses."

"Doesn't she look great?" Andrea said. And off they went again, like a pair of noisy galahs.

Aaron chewed the inside of his lip until it tasted metallic. "Hi, Dad," he said finally.

David glanced at him with that look he got around Aaron, like he was waiting for the disappointment to hit. "Hi, son, how's work going?" he asked.

"Busy as hell."

"Well, don't complain, it's what you wanted."

Aaron's skin smarted. "I wasn't complaining. Just stating a fact."

For a second he felt Alice's eyes on him, then Andrea picked up a plate and shoved it into David's ample stomach. "Stop grousing and take these into the lounge. Alice, sweetie, could you bring some plates? You carry this one in, Aaron, there's a dear." She handed the grand three-tiered pink thing to him.

"Are you fattening us up for Christmas?" he asked, trying to sound as light as Andrea's sponge cake.

"Always." Andrea laughed.

~

Alice's stomach felt like a balloon. Nerves had made her cram way too much cake into her mouth. It was delicious, as was everything Andrea created, but her mouth was so dry she could barely swallow and she'd kept refilling her tea from the pot to wash it all down.

Aaron, meanwhile, sat opposite her looking like some seedy lead singer in a grunge band; probably she should know some names, but she didn't like grunge. She liked all the old stuff, like Simon and Garfunkel and Van Morrison, particularly "Brown-Eyed Girl"—it always made her think of how it might have been between her and Aaron.

She balanced her plate on her knees and cast another glance at him. He was talking with Oliver, quite good-naturedly for once, and she could take in the way his T-shirt, grunge or no grunge, seemed to hug his pecs and outline his flat abs; the sexy way his bicep bunched as he put his plate back on the coffee table. Her mouth went even drier as she thought about what she'd been doing with that body only a few short days ago…

"More cake, Alice?" Andrea asked.

"Oh, no, Andrea, I couldn't." She patted her tummy. "I've eaten so much already."

"The verdict?"

"By a whisper, I think the angel cake."

Andrea nodded. "I think so too. So you reckon if we put the violets on top of that one, we've got our winner?"

"Yes, most definitely."

They discussed a time when Alice could come and help make them. She wasn't averse to the idea of learning the art of confectionery. It was a thin thread that still connected her to Aaron. Because, admit it, that's all there would be from now on. She dug her fingernails into her palm to stop the miserable inner dialogue.

After a few more minutes of conversation about how to make violets, Alice said, "I really should be going, it's a couple of buses home from here, so—" She stood up.

Aaron jumped up. "I can give you a lift."

"That's not necessary."

Suddenly Alice was aware of three pairs of eyes homing in on her. "All right then," she said and went to search for her coat and bag with Andrea.

In the lift, Alice wedged herself into a corner while Aaron hummed and looked at the roof. Her anxiety threatened to turn into panic. That morning Polly had come up with a genius idea that was now burning a hole in her handbag. Alice had given up on the idea, deciding no way would she do it after Aaron seemed so disinterested. Until the offer of a lift home. And suddenly here was her chance. So what if it didn't work? Her hands went clammy. But hells bells, there were icicles forming in the space between her and Aaron right now. What did she have to lose?

As they got out of the lift, Alice tilted her bag until the small pad of notes and her purse fell on the ground. She picked up the purse. Aaron bent and picked up the notes. He looked at them with a frown on his face "What's all this?"

"Oh, nothing." She made to grab them from him, then forced a giggle. "Just some ideas Polly and I were putting together for my Tinder profile."

He scanned the notes, harder this time. She wanted to rip them off him, but somehow she tethered her hands to her sides.

"'Quiet, but curious petite brunette'... I don't think you should use 'curious'." Aaron recited.

"Why not?"

He shrugged, but he was still frowning. "Guess it depends what kind of guy you're wanting to attract."

*You, only you.* "Someone nice, friendly. A bit intellectual."

He read on. "'... who loves literature, would also love to meet someone to unleash her—'" Aaron's brows had tightened into a ridge across his nose. "Christ, Alice, *unleash*?"

"Why not? Isn't it about getting lots of swipes right—or is it swipes left? I've forgotten."

"Sure. But not... I mean, this is going to attract a certain type of guy, not the sort you're looking for."

"I see. You're the expert on what I'm looking for now, are you?"

He fell silent. The air was so thick Alice could barely inhale it.

"Look, why don't you come back to my place and we'll re-write this. Polly's ideas won't work for you."

"That's a lousy pick-up line."

His cheeks flushed. "I am *not* trying to pick you up."

About to fire back, Alice remembered Polly's advice to stay quiet and mysterious. Let him do the leg work. "Equanimity," Polly had said. According to Polly it was an esoteric term for keeping your shit together.

"Okay," she said after a moment. "Not for long though."

"I haven't got long." It was almost a snarl. "I've got to go into the office later."

"On a Sunday?"

"You don't know my workload right now." He glowered at her.

Well, whoopee-doo. Things were going to plan. *Not.*

In the car Alice tried to ignore the way Aaron changed gears, which happened to show off to perfection the shift of muscles in his arm, the way his chunky metal watch hung low on his wrist, the tiny spray of dark blond hairs. Which led her to wonder what colour his hair was lower... *oooff...* well, that just sent equanimity up in smoke.

She snapped her head the other way and stared out at the large posh houses changing into large posh apartments as they circled Riverside Drive and finally arrived at the denser, inner-city, trendy apartmentsville Aaron lived in.

Once inside, Aaron flung his keys on the hall console and mumbled an apology for the mess. Alice let her gaze roam around. It *was* a mess. She'd been here so many times and never seen it in this much disarray. For a guy, Aaron was relatively neat. But unironed shirts spilled out of washing baskets, boxer shorts dried over the backs of chairs and dishes were piled haphazardly in the sink. She nearly tripped over a mangled towel in the middle of the floor. She peeped in his bedroom. The bedclothes were tumbling off the side of the bed. She guessed it could put off a lot of women. It certainly didn't look like he'd been entertaining lately. Which made her inappropriately happy.

"Tea, coffee, beer, wine?" he asked, head in the fridge, already pulling out a beer.

"I'll have a spritzer, please."

He busied himself making it, brought the wine glass over to her and flung himself down on the sofa. Alice perched herself in the easy chair opposite him; their respective seats whenever they played Monopoly. Monopoly had always been a bonding experience. But now it felt like she was a stranger here. Maybe she should suggest they forget all this stupid stuff, play a game instead, and everything would go back to how it was before. Her eyes skittered around; no Monopoly box in sight.

Aaron ruffled the hair on the back of his neck with one hand. "So," he said. "You're serious about this… Tinder thing?"

Face it, the game between them had changed. Whatever happened now, it would never add up to how it was before.

"Yes, of course."

He gave her a dark look. "Okay, give it here." He motioned impatiently for the notebook. She handed it over and he started to scribble, a little smile beginning to quirk at the corners of his mouth. After a minute he handed the paper to her and she read aloud: "'Petite, introverted 26-year-old with a secret passion for bodice-ripping romance and Victorian artists with kinky hang-ups, seeks like-minded-male for hot intellectual pursuits.' What does 'hot intellectual pursuits' mean?"

"You said you wanted an intellectual and I'm assuming you —er—don't want just conversation, so I kind of combined them. The right person will read between the lines."

"I don't like it."

"It's better than your and Polly's attempt. If you want some kind of weird sexual deviant, go for it properly."

She gave a nervous laugh, took a sip of her spritzer and wrinkled her nose at the bubbles. Aaron was watching her steadily and it made her blood feel very like the spritzer. She leaned forward and tried to grab the pencil. He held it away from her. She got up and stood over him, kinked one hip the way Polly did.

"Give it to me," she demanded.

He sprawled out in front of her, legs wide in a gesture that made her go hot all over. She bent forward and their fingers grazed as she plucked the pencil from his grip. She pulled her hand away— no, that was still too uptight. Sitting back down, Alice forced herself to cross her legs in a way she remembered Miranda Bendt doing. Her skirt rode up her thigh and she saw Aaron's gaze dart there, his Adam's apple bobbing as he looked away.

That *worked.*

She crossed out 'introverted' and added in 'thoughtful'—it was the only thing her addled brain could come up with.

Back and forth the pad of paper went, each time getting a little more scribbled on… the suggestions from Aaron getting ever more outrageous.

"How about S & M? Bondage? Ménage?" He kinked an eyebrow at her.

"I'll just stick to normal practices, thank you."

"Plain vanilla? C'mon, Al. How about butt plugs?"

Her eyes grew wide. "They sound ghastly. What even are they?"

Aaron was grinning his head off. "Exactly what they sound like, to intensify your…"

She felt herself blushing madly. "Oh… really?"

"You can choose your own tail. Fox, bunny rabbit. Kind of cute, not sure it would appeal to me, but each to their own."

"I think we can stop this right now." Giggling despite herself, Alice flailed a hand and grabbed the page. Aaron held on. The piece of paper ripped off the pad and he jumped up, thrust open the window and went to throw it out.

Laughing, she raced after him. "You can't hurl butt plugs and bondage requests onto an unsuspecting public."

She grappled a handful of his T-shirt in her fist; Aaron lost his footing and his arm grabbed hers as he steadied himself. For a second they wobbled. Then they stilled, suddenly facing each other. His eyes, deep blue and unblinking, stared down into hers. She wasn't one iota tiddly… there was no excuse to feel like the ground was opening up under her feet.

Without even thinking, her head tilted up, her lips parted. She felt Aaron's fingers at her nape, the pressure of his hand cupping the back of her head. His face swam out of focus.

Alice closed her eyes and gave herself to his kiss.

# CHAPTER 13

H oly *shit!*
        In the space of a week, they were kissing again. Kissing like they'd never get enough of each other.

Lips clung, tongues thrust, everything hot and wet and *ravenous.* He ripped at the buttons of her shirt as her hands burrowed up under his T-shirt. His skin goosebumped. His scalp tingled. Hearing her little gasps and moans only heaped fuel on the fire—how could he be so close to blowing when she hadn't even touched him below the waist?

Alice had his T-shirt bunched in her hand and he aided by ripping it over his head. She stared at his bare chest, her mouth momentarily slack. He had to squeeze his eyes tight shut to hold his shit together as she began palming across his pecs, his abs. Lower.

He pushed her shirt off her shoulders, her bra straps went next. With a groan he buried his head between her breasts then went from one nipple to the other, nipping, sucking; pulling back to gaze briefly at the perfection of them, before diving in for more.

They were still in full view of the window. Some distant

part of his brain registered there were apartments across the street that might be enjoying the view, but he couldn't give a toss.

He kept kissing and nuzzling and not having enough hands and lips to explore every glorious inch of Alice. When her fingers cupped him over his jeans he bucked like a rodeo horse.

"Shit, Alice, I don't think I can hold—"

"Shall we go somewhere—?" She was glancing towards his bedroom; a room he would never have thought to take her to, what, a mere month ago? But things had changed so radically, he had no idea what the rules were anymore.

"You're sure?"

She nodded, her teeth edging her lower lip. He kissed her right there.

With the mess of his apartment, it made more sense to scoop her into his arms and carry her than have them trip over a pile of socks or a pair of his running shoes. She was so light, so soft and yielding with her head nestled against his chest, that a weird protective caveman vibe gripped his heart.

He laid her on the bed and kneeled over her with a great stonking erection tenting the front of his jeans. He guessed there could be no mistaking his intentions. But he still needed to check.

"You're absolutely sure?"

She nodded. "Just, um—condoms?"

Of course. He was an idiot. He hadn't thought to ask if she was on the pill and he always wore protection regardless. Though it had been a while... even by his standards.

He frowned, trying to remember where he'd put them.

"YOU MUST HAVE A CONDOM, AARON!"

He burst out laughing at her flushed, indignant expression.

"Yes, Al." He pressed a kiss on the tip of her nose. "I have condoms. Somewhere. Despite my reputation I haven't required one for a while now."

She hitched up on her elbows and watched him and he couldn't help casting hungry glances at the upturned peaks of her nipples as he zigzagged around the bedroom throwing open drawers.

No luck.

Bathroom. Yes, that would be it.

Items flew out of the bathroom cabinet. Floss. Cotton buds, a packet of razor blades. Finally he found a pristine, unopened pack. He grabbed them and hurled himself back onto the bed beside her.

She snuggled into him. "Sorry. That was a bit out of character for me." She giggled sheepishly, which made him grin.

Why was this so easy? So… *fun?* Sure, it was kind of weird as well, knowing Alice as a person before he discovered all these other surprising delights, but…

All thoughts stopped as her fingers found his zipper.

Who was this sex goddess? Honestly, Alice had no idea. It seemed that since last week and the kitchen table incident, a sex fairy had sprinkled some kind of magic libido-enhancing dust over her and suddenly… she didn't feel shy. She didn't feel anxious. She felt horny. A word she'd always found distasteful before, but it fit now they were wound all around each other, skin sliding against skin.

In fact, it felt like the most natural word in the world.

Aaron was kissing her over and over, his very large—very beautiful—penis thrusting against her thigh, his hand… oh, oh, *yes*. Alice arched her back and moaned as his fingers ran an erotic path between the folds of her sex, then came back and focused where all the sensations had bunched together and were screaming for attention.

"Is this okay?" His breath fanned hot in her ear.

"Uh-huh." She nodded, chewing her lip.

"Firmer? Softer?"

He actually cared! He was holding back and pleasuring her… first.

It blew her mind. But she couldn't let it be all about her. She reached her hand down, curled her fingers around the hot tip of him, felt the slide and slip of moisture. A man had never been wet for her before, not as far as she'd noticed. Gently he removed her hand, kissed each finger, then slid them into the warm cavern of his mouth.

Her sex spasmed and he laughed as the hand nestled between her legs registered it. "No, no you don't. Not yet."

His grin was pure lasciviousness. Her very own regency rake. No, better still, her very own Greek love god. Cupid. No, Eros... then her mind turned to gloop as he murmured, "You might like this more."

And with that his mouth trailed a path down her body... stopping to briefly suck each nipple, circling her belly button with his tongue, lower. Lower... lower... until he found the magic spot. Applied the perfect pressure. Clever fingers joined his mouth, sliding in and out of her, circling, then swooping back inside. Enticing her orgasm out of hiding with every skill he possessed.

Ripples of sensation flooded through her pelvis. Her hands puckered the sheets, her hips rocked, and she couldn't seem to stop from pushing up into his administrations, writhing, calling his name, begging for more. Aaron's tongue sped up at her little gasps of "oh yes," and "right there," and "pleeeease, more," his fingers in perfect harmony, until all there was, was this. *This...*

White light flashed behind her eyes; a cry wrenched from her lips as her orgasm hit, breaking her into tiny pieces, a zillion stars bursting all at once. Going on forever.

Slowly, slowly Alice drifted back to earth; her senses as light as spun sugar, her limbs leaden, utterly sated.

Finally, she cracked open an eyelid. Lips glistening, hair sticking out at angles around his head, Aaron grinned back from the apex of her thighs.

It took her a moment, but as he shifted up her body and she

felt the steel of his erection on her thigh, she knew it wasn't over. Oh, no, no, there was so much more…

With hands still trembling from her orgasm, Alice pressed him down on his back and they kissed some more, deep, explorative, tender kisses.

"See how nice you taste?" he murmured, and her body hummed with the need to pleasure him back.

She sat up. "I'm going to return the favour."

He reached out and cupped a breast, thumbing her nipple, which peaked obligingly. "My stepmum's faith in your tastebuds is clearly warranted."

"Yes, hitherto untested on penises."

His hand went to her arm, staying her. "What, never?"

She shook her head.

"And you? Didn't either of them ever…?"

"Nope."

"Jesus." He threw his head back and gave a disbelieving scoff. "Were they insane?"

"Just not very interested in the finer details, I guess." She slid her lips down his amazing torso, admiring every inch until she reached the head of his erection. She held it to her mouth, tasted his salty tang, revelling in the way his hips arched, the way his fingers rafted into her hair, the deep gritty sounds he made in his throat. She licked and sucked and rolled, then took him deeper.

"No. Oh, god, no, Al, no more." He brought her back up to him. "I want to be inside you this time."

Her heart twirled. Did that mean there would be other times? But even if there weren't, how could she ever regret this?

He was ripping open the condom pack feverishly, a veil of sweat on his brow. She wanted to help but needed it to be quick, so she lay back, watching as Aaron rolled the condom down his impressive length. His hair was dark blond down there, nestling around the base of his cock, framing his balls.

*Cock. Balls.* She let the words play in her head. She'd never said those words out loud. "I love your cock," she murmured, and it sounded wonderful. Empowering.

His eyes narrowed. "And I love when you talk dirty to me, baby."

"You haven't heard anything yet." She giggled against his damp neck as his weight shifted over her.

She opened to accommodate him. Felt the push, the stretch, the deep, deep satisfaction of taking him inside her.

"Oh, Shit. Al-ice. You feel A-maz-ing."

She flung her legs around him, squeezing her thighs around his buttocks to bring him closer… closer…

Her head thumped the headboard and Aaron lowered her effortlessly down the bed; threaded their hands together above their heads to steady them as his rhythm quickened. His skin flushed; his eyes lost focus. She felt his heart slamming into hers. It was like he filled every one of her cells.

A moment later and Aaron's features contorted. He shouted "Alice!" and she held him while his body spasmed and finally sagged against her.

For long moments afterwards she stroked his hair, as his breathing slowed.

Clearly he needed a little help to return to earth, too.

When he rolled off her a shard of fear pierced her belly. What if he just got up, and left her bereft?

But he didn't. He did a little neat disposal trick with the condom, turned on his side to face her and his gaze held hers steadily.

He leaned over and kissed her eyelids, her lips and said, "I think that might have constituted a bit more than flirting."

With every item of clothing he put back on, the magic seemed to be slipping away. With every moment spent away from his bed, both of them getting ready to face the world again, it was like an arctic cold was taking over his heart. It had felt so good. But now it all felt wrong.

Aaron rummaged around for a clean T-shirt. He'd offered to take Alice home on his way to the office. He had to brief the barrister first thing tomorrow and he couldn't afford to get it wrong. Nor could he wear Cold Chisel with a rip in it, smelling of sex. Just in case a partner came into the office. Besides, he didn't want to sit in the office and be reminded of Alice tearing it off him, her perfume lingering, driving him nuts while he tried to focus on writing up a report. She was bending over, putting on one of her shoes, flicking a strand of hair behind her ear, and he looked from her to the bed with a pang of longing.

In bed they'd talked and laughed and kissed and...

In his bed they'd shared the best sex ever...

His body tightened, his thoughts a scrambled mess. Alice and he... were *friends*. You didn't have sex with *friends*.

"Okay, I'm ready." She was smiling at him now, her eyes too bright. His gaze alighted on the torn piece of paper by the window with their notes on it and his throat closed up. Her Tinder date. Some guy in her future. Not him.

"Great, let's go," he got out of tight lips.

She picked up the shreds of paper and put them in her bag before following him out. He didn't allow himself to dwell on the implications of that. They didn't speak on the way down to his car. They didn't speak as he drove out of his car space or on the road to her place.

How were they going to navigate this now? It had got complicated, he'd let it—no, for Christ's sake—he'd *encouraged* it, orchestrated it, even. At the traffic lights he drummed the steering wheel with his fingers, turned on the radio. It was some soppy love song and he turned it off pronto.

After a minute more of agonising silence, Alice asked, "What have you got to do at the office?"

He launched into a spiel of boring shit about the case he was working on and how the barrister was a complete pompous arsehole and on and on, blab, blab, blab.

She made polite noises. How come they couldn't maintain a remotely normal conversation anymore? They were behaving for all the world like complete strangers who'd struck up a conversation at the bus stop.

They'd turned into Alice's suburb with its main street full of Thai and Vietnamese and Korean restaurants; ones they'd eaten at so many times. Would they ever do that again? A dark chasm opened up in his chest and his spine turned rigid.

Suddenly Alice said, "Aaron, I'm fine. You don't have to worry."

"What was that?" He forgot not to look at her, and the way her head tilted, the angle of her chin, the soft curve of her cheek made his balls ache all over again. Was that a hickey? On her neck? Jesus Christ, he'd bitten her, bruised her, and he hadn't even realised.

"Just in case you were worried," she said. He had to force himself to focus on her words. "It doesn't need to change anything between us."

What was she talking about? It had fucking changed everything.

"Oh—um—good."

"I mean, you know, we're friends, right?" Her lips tilted up at the corners as she met his eyes, a little shy, a little challenging. "Whatever happens from here on, we'll always be friends."

"Yes, of course." The car juddered as his foot slipped slightly as they took off from the lights.

"Well, then, why not be friends with benefits?" Her voice reminded him of a compère on a game show. "Like Polly and Jake. If you want to, that is. I mean, only until I've met a nice guy on Tinder, and you meet someone you—"

*Ngggggg.* Now he was biting the inside of his lip so hard he'd probably drawn blood. He battled to pull himself together. He did casual brilliantly, for Christ's sake. He was the king of casual. So how come Alice was all of a sudden beating him at his own game?

Aaron forced his shoulders to relax, his foot to stop

cramping over the pedal. This was good news. Perfect, in fact. They had another couple of months of the fake dating thing. Why not add in sex? His cock bounced in agreement.

"That... could... work." The words came out in slow motion. His brain was having trouble playing catch-up. Already they were in Alice's street and he had to focus on navigating the tightly parked cars before coming to a standstill just past Rowena's house.

"I mean, if we're *supposed* to be dating, we might as well go the whole hog." She was gathering up her bag and before he knew it, she'd leaned over and pecked him on the cheek. "It will be more convincing that way, don't you think?"

He turned and looked at her. Her face hovered, like she might kiss him again, and if he wanted, he could lean forward and take that rosebud mouth in his, pull gently at her lower lip with his teeth, lick it better. He shut out all the things he wanted to do to Alice. Would another two months be enough?

It would have to be.

He forced a smile, and for a second he thought he saw a shadow pass over her face. But then the perky smile was back in place. "Give it some thought," she said and waved her bag at him as she got out. "Thanks for the Tinder tips. I'll probably use some—minus the butt plug."

Their eyes held for a beat more and he felt like he was drowning. Then he pulled himself together. Gave her his best cheeky grin, the slightly lopsided one he knew got women every time. "Thanks for today," he purred. "I enjoyed it."

Understatement of the century. But she'd never know. He'd never own up to how much it had blown his mind.

She snagged at her lower lip with two little white teeth. "Me too."

For a second he watched her as she sashayed up the path. Only for a second. He couldn't cope with the way it made him feel to see her walking away.

∾

The queue for banh mi rolls was longer than usual. Alice flicked an impatient look at her watch. She'd locked the shop, put the *back in ten minutes* sign on the door and followed her urge for a treat at the Vietnamese bakery three doors down from the Book Genie. Call it comfort food. Honestly, who cared. Today was not a vego day. She wanted—*needed*—banh mi with beef spilling out the sides and extra fresh chilli. She had to sweat out some sexual tension.

Sure, she was still proud of herself. She'd managed to survive the most amazeballs sex of her life (Polly's description was right on the money) with the man of her dreams and not make a complete idiot of herself afterwards. When she'd walked into the house and collapsed on the sofa where Polly was watching what was probably episode 2043 of *Outlander* with a box of assorted Lindt chocolate balls in front of her, Polly had raised an eyebrow and observed, "Now here's a woman who has just been right royally shagged."

Which meant Alice had to spill the beans on how the plan had worked perfectly. Not every technicolour detail, of course, but enough for Polly to get the gist. Afterwards Polly had crowed, "Brilliant. You little sex goddess, you."

Except now it was only Monday lunch time—*only* Monday; it felt like a century had passed—and her sex goddess status was slipping with each hour that went by with no contact from Aaron.

"Yes, please?"

Startled, she realised she had somehow got to the front of the queue. She ordered, her mouth watering as she watched customers disappearing out the door with their paper-bag-wrapped rolls. The problem with the friends with benefits arrangement, she decided as she stepped back to wait for her order, was that it changed the rules. Suddenly you weren't just friends who contacted each other with a funny YouTube clip or some outrageous bit of world politics, you were... something else. Something that hovered between a friend and a girlfriend without the clear status of either.

166

The concept that had seemed a stroke of genius was now making her want to devour seriously spicy food and donuts in large quantities. Who was she trying to fool? She wasn't Polly. She'd never have Polly's sexual panache. Her phone vibrated in her pocket. Her heart did a roller coaster, dumping her hard when she saw who it was.

Why did Rowena always have the worst timing in the world?

"Hi Mum."

"Darling. How are you?"

"Good, how's England?"

"Raining. Do you know it's rained every day so far in July?"

"Everything must be very green."

"Very. Now look, sweetie, it sounds busy there so I'll be quick." Alice didn't bother to enlighten Rowena she was in a café, not the Book Genie. "I wanted to alert you to a package I've sent you."

"Books?"

"Not exactly." Rowena's voice boomed with more than its usual decibels. It actually hurt Alice's ear. "Some documents you might find interesting."

Goodness, what if it was purchase information on a shop in some sleepy little village with a hyphenated name, a plethora of cats and a teashop called the Copper Kettle?

"What kind of documents?" she managed after a moment.

"Best if I let them speak for themselves, darling. Then we'll Skype. I've sent them to the house, not the shop. They should arrive in about a week, I'm guessing."

"Okay, Mum, I'll look out for it."

"Oh, and can you tell Esther I've found her a copy of *Mrs Beeton's Household Management*? I'm sending back the most interesting array of books you have ever seen."

"The shelves are pretty full already."

Rowena laughed. "We'll fit them in. What's all that kerfuffle? I've never heard so much noise. Have you put a sale on you haven't told me about?"

"No, of course not." Alice walked outside and changed ears.

"Oh, that's better," Rowena said.

"Are you still in Cambridge?"

"Yes. For a few more days, then I'm going to your cousin Beatrice's in Burton-upon-Trent. She's the one who keeps ferrets and had a bit-part in *Pride and Prejudice*, remember? Anyway, darling, I'm planning to be home in about three weeks."

*Three weeks?* What would that mean for her and Aaron? Under Rowena's eagle eye, romance was hardly going to blossom, let alone rampant sex. Maybe it was time she moved out, found her own little pad.

"But you're having fun, aren't you, Mum?" she asked. "It's been a worthwhile trip?"

For a second she felt Rowena's hesitation, which was odd because Rowena had the crashing enthusiasm of a Pamplona bull about everything in life. "It's been, interesting—challenging." Rowena's voice drew out the last word, her tone almost pensive.

Was Mum having a mid-life crisis?

Alice looked back through the window of the shop and saw An ho, who owned the café, waving a paper bag with what she was sure was her roll in it. An ho spotted her through the window and beckoned.

"I'd better go, Mum. Customer."

"Bye, darling. Let me know you got the package, won't you?"

"Yes, Mum. Bye."

"Toot, toot, sweetheart."

Honestly—where did Rowena get these weird phrases?

Alice tucked her phone into her coat pocket and entered the café, saliva building in her mouth as she took her banh mi from An ho with a smile.

She walked back to the Book Genie nibbling her banh mi around the edges. Clearly she needed a dose of iron and B12 because she would happily have ingested it through a drip. Could that be due to the extra activity she'd done lately? Blushing, she pushed the thought away.

Back in the shop she let in a couple of regular browsers, placed her banh mi roll on a plate in the storeroom, where it was easy to nip in and out for a quick bite, and flicked the kettle on for a cup of tea.

"Hey, Alice?"

She ducked her head back round the door. "Carts, what a lovely surprise."

Carts looked somewhat unkempt, she thought, and thinner than usual, which wasn't good because he'd never been what you would call well-covered. His jacket hung like it was on a coat hanger rather than shoulders, and his trousers were too short. She remembered the break-up with Lucy. She'd been meaning to text and ask how he was going but the Aaron interlude had completely dislodged it from her mind.

"Are you okay?" Alice pulled up a stool. He really looked like he needed to sit down. "I heard about Lucy."

Carts gave a resigned nod. "Who told you?"

She couldn't lie. "Aaron."

"Not all the sordid details?"

"No, just that it hadn't ended that well."

Carts lowered himself onto the stool and hooked his feet on the rungs. A gap between his socks and his pants hem gaped, showing off bony ankles. Alice had the sudden urge to hug him or take him shopping. Possibly both.

Carts huffed air out of his lungs. "Guess I should have seen it coming. But, hey—" He brightened, his grin, always his best attribute, lighting up his face. "My wounds will heal. And at least I got the money back on the ring."

Alice's jaw dropped. "I didn't realise you got engaged." No wonder he looked so down-hearted.

Carts fidgeted. "Not exactly. Probably best not to go into the finer details. Anyway..." He slapped a palm on his knee. "I'm not here to whinge." He was suddenly looking at her intently.

A little sheen of heat built on the back of her neck. "I was wondering..."

Alice stepped back, knocked a stack of books she'd been pricing earlier off the counter, and busied herself picking them up off the floor. "I was wondering if"—he bent over, coiled out an arm, picked one up and handed it to her—"you'd like to come to a quiz night."

At that moment a customer strode up to the counter and Alice had to focus on totting up their eclectic mix of Stephen Kings and Sufi poetry.

Once they'd gone, Carts was still looking at her out of large, moony eyes.

There was clearly no escaping a response to his question. "What kind of quiz night?" She must have sounded a little sharp because he looked taken aback.

"It's for my sister Avery's school orchestra trip. They're going to Japan. Maybe you didn't know but she plays the flute; she's really good—the school's encouraging her to apply for a scholarship to the Paris Conservatoire." The hurt glint still underpinned his features and now Alice felt horribly mean. Carts wasn't going to do anything silly, like ask her on a date. She was getting tickets on herself.

She gave him a dazzling smile. "Oh, that would be fantastic; of course I'd love to support her. When is it?"

"Thursday of next week. I could pick you up—"

"This looks cosy." The deep timbre of the voice that had interrupted made a shiver skitter up Alice's spine. She spun round to see Aaron standing behind her. Telltale heat swamped her cheeks. How come she hadn't noticed him come in?

And even more odd, Carts and Aaron weren't surveying each other with any of their usual camaraderie. In fact, they were both glowering from under beetling brows.

"What brings you here, Carts?" Aaron's tone held a definite note of accusation.

"Could say the same to you, Blake-o. You don't work near here, last time I checked."

"Neither do you."

*What in heavens name?*

Alice tugged at her ponytail and made clucking noises. She felt like a librarian dealing with two recalcitrant schoolboys. Aaron didn't look at her—he didn't need to, the air between them was vibrating. He dug his hands in his pockets and rocked back on his heels. "I was at the law courts, so I thought I'd take the opportunity to come and buy myself a book."

Carts scoffed. "What for?"

Aaron's lip curled. "To cut my back teeth on. Seriously, what do you think?"

"You never read books," Carts muttered.

"I've started to enjoy quite a few new pursuits lately."

The colour heightened in Alice's cheeks. If that was meant for her it sure hit the mark.

Still Aaron's gaze pinned Carts with the ferocity of a puma. "What's your excuse?"

Alice's eyes rounded and her breath shortened. Aaron was almost staking a claim. Which was outrageous, even if the adrenaline spiking round her system told another story.

Carts was pushing out his chest and his lower jaw at the same time. "I've asked Alice to Avery's fundraiser."

Aaron cocked an eyebrow. "What's she fundraising for?"

"Her school trip to Japan. Raising money for the orchestra."

"What are they doing?"

"A quiz night," Carts mumbled.

A sudden wolfish grin swept across Aaron's features. "I love quiz nights. I'll come. When is it?" Carts' mouth dropped open. "I'd love to support Avery," Aaron added, smooth as silk.

"Bet you would," Carts muttered darkly.

"That's below the belt, mate." Aaron's eyes smouldered.

For all the world they were behaving like two prize fighting cocks about to rip out each other's feathers. And it really wasn't on. Alice didn't need all this testosterone flying around the shop this early in the week. She started to slam pens in her pen holder to try and defuse the tension. As if realising he was out of order, Aaron gave an easy laugh and punched Carts lightly on the shoulder. "Seriously, mate, I am the king of useless information. I'd love to join you."

Wheels were turning in Carts' brain, you could tell. Alice felt his pain. To say no to Aaron when Carts had just invited her would look suspiciously like only one thing... maybe Carts saw that too, as he conceded grudgingly, "Okay, mate. Come if you like. But you'd better be worth the invite. Our table better win, or you're history."

Aaron smirked. "History was my finest subject at school. We'll smash the other teams."

For a while they stood talking, the energy between them still as spiky as broken glass. Finally, Carts got up from his stool with clear reluctance. "I have to go. I've got a meeting. Why don't you walk back with me?"

"I'm in the law courts all afternoon," Aaron said, as if he'd been cemented to the spot.

Carts' mouth took on a sullen hue, his shoulders sagged. Then, as if giving himself some internal talking to, he stood up to his full height. A tug of sympathy pulled behind Alice's ribs. Sometimes, Carts reminded her so much of herself. Except for the height differential, of course.

"Bye, Alice." To her surprise, Carts swooped and planted a stubbly kiss on her cheek. "I'll text you the details. Bye shit face," he muttered to Aaron as he loped off.

Painfully aware that the shop had emptied out towards the end of lunch time, Alice fiddled with some paperclips on her desk. Her stomach growled loudly.

"Do you mind if I eat my lunch?" she said. Aaron standing so close was making every one of her cells zing, as if her whole body was starving. And not for a banh mi either.

"Sure, go ahead," he replied with a shrug.

As she scooted into the storeroom, the hairs on the back of her neck told her he'd followed her. When she glanced around he was leaning on the door frame, one ankle casually crossed over the other.

*Stay cool. Don't blow it.* She released a slow breath through her nostrils. She was Aphrodite rising from the waves, pure minted sex goddess material. She just had to remember that.

"So, how've you been?" she asked as she sank her teeth into the soft sweet bread and tore off a mouthful. She had to wipe a dribble of sauce off the side of her mouth with a fingertip and saw his jaw tighten as he watched her.

"Since yesterday?" His voice was gravelly. "Kind of been thinking of what you said, actually."

Oh no! He was going to turn her down. Now the heat of shame was prickling her stomach, the back of her neck, up into her cheeks. A lump of bread stuck halfway down her throat and she barely managed a gasped, "Ah-hmmm?"

"Yeah, so…" The grin widened as he watched her near total meltdown. "I was wondering whether tomorrow you'd like to…?"

*Oh, golly gosh… was he suggesting…* that *soon?* All she could do was give a little nod, clasping her roll in two tight fists.

Aaron shifted off the door and strolled towards her. "Maybe we could go for a quick bite to eat after I finish work, then back to my place…"

She needed to play it cool; nigh-on impossible when she was burning up inside. As she stalled, searching for words, a slice of beef drooped out the side of her roll, then flopped to the ground.

Aaron smirked. "Nice tofu?"

"Oh—I—I needed some meat." As she realised what she'd said, the heat from inside spread out in a red-hot blush.

Aaron gave a snort of laughter and Alice couldn't help bursting into a giggle of her own, dropping her banh mi onto the plate. He was standing whisper-close now. Her legs turned boneless, her body screaming out for his touch. His fingers curled softly around her waist and her eyelids fluttered as he dipped his head and murmured in her ear, "I could suggest something else you could eat—"

"Aaron!" Her eyes flew open, the laughter bubbling, stopping when beyond Aaron's shoulder she saw Esther Brown, her neck craning to peer into the storeroom.

"Alice," Esther called out querulously. "Are you in there?"

Flustered, Alice broke away. "I have to go."

"Why don't you meet me at my work?" Aaron's voice was thick, laden with promises. Her body brushed against his, felt the pressure of him against her as she exited. "Let's say 6 p.m.?"

"Okay." She was barely able to see straight as she flew out to the counter. "Esther, I've been meaning to call. Mum's found that copy of *Mrs Beeton's Household Management* for you."

# CHAPTER 14

I t should have been fascinating. His first big case of serious negligence against a national organisation. A whistle-blower, coercion, and a culture of systematic bullying uncovered. The barrister, though a pompous git, undoubtedly knew his stuff and sliced and cut with precision to get exactly the information he needed, drawing his pound of flesh from each witness.

But Aaron wasn't concentrating. He was dreaming about Alice's hot kisses, her welcoming body, the little mewls and squeals she made when he touched her just right; the way they both laughed when their bodies made those lewd smacking noises during more strenuous movements, and how none of it, *none of it*, had detracted from how totally mind-blowing making love to Alice had been… And then he would have to focus on John Ventwhistle's clipped consonants and legal speak, just to stop his hard-on bursting through his zipper.

As his scalp tightened and a vague sense of panic threatened at what he was doing with Alice—*Alice!* —he calmed himself with the memory of her as cool as a freakin' tumbler full of ice cubes, telling him it only needed to be a friends-with-benefits arrangement. By the time he'd escaped, done the debrief, nodded in all the right places and said all the right things to Ventwhistle and his team, Aaron's heels were practically skidding on the marbled foyer of the law courts. Racing to get the hell out of there and hightail it back to work, dump the files—and meet Alice.

She was already sitting in Trojan's reception as he strode through the doors. His heart started up a rap behind his ribs. She stood up and Aaron, seeing Charles Fink walking out with a client, went and gave her a lingering kiss on the lips. The soft return pressure of her mouth made him want to keep on going. Reluctantly he pulled away and was rewarded with a rare smile from Fink and a wave.

One notch on his belt for commitment to family values.

Next, Lauren sashayed past with Archie.

"Goodnight, Aaron," Lauren purred, her eyes flicking with interest to Alice.

Alice seemed to stiffen as she returned Lauren's gaze with a tight smile. He guessed he should introduce them, but Archie was at Lauren's side, his torso bent towards her as she tilted her face up to his. Aaron decided to give it a miss. Turning back to Alice, he caught a slight furrow between her eyebrows before it switched to a bright smile that made his insides catch alight.

"I'll just dump some of this stuff and be straight with you."

She nodded and sat back down, crossing her legs. He wanted to walk his fingers up her calves, over her knees, her thighs, see if she was wearing stockings... Aaron belted through the open-plan area to his office like a man possessed.

A quick visit to the cloakrooms followed, where he slicked back his hair and ran a hand through his stubble. He'd shaved this morning; not wanting to leave too much of a stubble rash on Alice's skin. He was about to leave when he caught the expression in his eyes. Downright soft. He'd seen the look on Carts' face before and thought he looked like a pussy-whipped idiot. He pulled himself up short, tugged off his tie and pocketed it. Firmed his lips. *Friends with benefits,* he reminded himself as he strode towards reception.

In no time flat they were out in the city and at the bar he'd already fantasised taking her to. A cosy little joint with velvet curtains closed against the winter night and strange artefacts like teapots and bizarre hats scattered around the place as décor.

"The Mad Hatter," Alice said approvingly as her eyes scanned the interior. "Great name, I love it."

"I thought with your literary background, it would probably appeal." Being early in the week, the place wasn't too crowded, so they sat at the bar, their knees almost bumping on the stools. Aaron handed Alice the cocktail menu, trying not to focus on the little gap between her thighs, where her skirt had ruffled up. She looked over the top of her glasses and read "Dodo Daquiri, White Rabbit Rum Punch. Ooh, I love the names. What are you going to have?"

"Beer probably."

"What a waste! I should have a mocktail... But—" She gave him a wicked little smile. "Maybe I'll try the Queen of Hearts, with kaffir lime, ginger and pink grapefruit liqueur."

Aaron couldn't resist a grin. "Personally I prefer the more tried-and-true."

"Such as?"

He avoided her eyes. "I don't know... maybe a Slow Comfortable Screw Against the Wall."

When he glanced at her he saw her lips twitch.

"You asking?" she purred in a totally un-Alice-like voice. Well, not the Alice of old. Now, with her hair tumbling around her shoulders but her glasses on, he felt like he was caught between two worlds... naughty librarian images swirled behind his eyes.

He cleared his throat. "I could be. You offering?"

"I might be."

Aaron looked down at their knees, almost touching, and

sandwiched her legs between his thighs. She pushed gently back, and right on cue blood rushed to his groin.

He waved with a sense of desperation at the waiter. He needed the formalities over. He needed her naked. Soon. Or they might actually be at risk of screwing up against the wall. And the way he was feeling right now... forget slow. Or comfortable. It would be fast and furious.

One drink each and they both agreed to go. They found themselves walking out into the lane with its brightly coloured bobbing lanterns and then Alice was pulling him into a side alley with a little grin on her face. Her hands were on his jacket lapels, tugging him into her, and shit, he needed no encouragement.

"Maybe we should make good on that suggestion," she murmured, her eyes dancing behind her glasses.

He arched back to look at her. "Here?" he said, wanting to kiss her mouth so much it hurt.

"Just a little appetiser," Alice murmured and held her lips up to his.

They kissed for what seemed like forever. He'd never been so turned on just kissing. Okay, not just kissing, because all down his body Alice was pressed against him, her thighs shifting and moulding with his. The softness of her breasts, the feel of her fingers at the nape of his neck.

Eventually he pulled away, if only to draw breath before diving in again for more kisses, and did something he'd never done with any other woman: he cupped her face gently between his hands and gazed deep into her lust-drunk eyes.

"My place?"

Alice did her cute nose-wrinkle thing. "Have you tidied up?"

"I have. The weekend was an aberration. A glitch in my usually impeccable housekeeping record."

She trailed a finger down the buttons of his shirt, wiggling one through the gap and swirling his chest hairs. Pressed her hips into his rock-hard cock.

"Okay then," she said, and bit his neck.

~

He couldn't wait for the Uber to deliver them home, couldn't *not* kiss her in the back seat, couldn't stop his thigh from riding between hers.

All of it, he told himself, because they were simply friends enjoying the here and now, and when the time came they would shake on it and go back to where they were before.

Monopoly. And sitting through three hours of interminable artsy movies and eating at cheap and cheerful restaurants and lamenting politics and pretending that this hadn't ever really happened.

Which made it all okay to keep on doing it.

At his place they tumbled in a hot mess through the front door. Alice ripped off his coat, his shirt went next. She twirled around to let him unzip her skirt, which got stuck so he shimmied his hands up her legs instead and almost shouted with triumph as he peeled back the gusset of her panties and found her drenched for him.

They made it, not very steadily, along the wall to his room, not even bothering to turn on the light.

Light from the street illuminated the bed as he feverishly pulled off her blouse, her bra. She gasped and her nipples hardened under the brush of his palm, her skin goosebumping under his fingers.

How could you want to do so much to a woman's body all at once? He stood up, ripped off his pants, and she launched herself laughing onto the bed. He kneeled over her and crawled up her body; took off her glasses and placed them carefully on the bedside table. Alice waved her hands around in front of her, screwing up her face. It struck him he'd never seen anything so cute and sexy in his life.

"Where are you? I can't see you." She laughed. And then he was kneeling over her.

"I'm here," he said, kissing one taut nipple. "And here... and here." He went lower and flicked his tongue into the dip of her belly button. "Oh, and right—" Nuzzling away the elastic of her knickers, he buried his face in her soft curls. "Here..." came out muffled and he felt her back arch like a cat, her sigh of total satisfaction as her fingers twisted into his hair.

"You have my permission to stay *right* there."

～

She awoke to the wonderful sensation of not being alone. The sound of slow, steady breathing, a heavy arm around her waist. The slightly sticky but delicious feel of two naked bodies who'd slept the night spooned together.

Two halves making a whole.

Alice lay there, wondering what day it was, what time it was, even. Wondering if it mattered.

Her hand came up and stroked the fingers curled around her waist and she opened her eyes to see the dim light of morning creeping through the curtains.

She glanced down at the hand, the fingers, long and fine-boned, that she'd looked at so wistfully so many times, thinking they would never be hers to feel, to be pleasured by. And now look... *so* much pleasure.

He'd woken her once in the night to do it again.

And then she'd woken him.

They were totally quits. *How many orgasms... let me count the ways...*

Aaron stirred, his phone alarm went off to a rap riff with somewhat vulgar lyrics—something about doing it and doing it and doing it.

With a grunt, he waved his hand around and found his phone. He angled away from her and bashed it, then lay back down and snuggled right back into her. Kissed the nape of her neck, which sent spasms of delight into places that were definitely a bit sore but totally willing to overlook that fact.

She *was* a sex goddess.

"What time is it?" she asked reluctantly.

He stirred. "Dunno." Then shot up. "Crap, I have to be in court again. Ball-blaster Ventwhistle will go me if I'm late." He kissed the back of her shoulder. "I'll make us some coffee, you use the bathroom, then we'll swap."

It felt easy, totally natural. But then, why wouldn't it? Aaron had stayed over at her place enough times, tiptoeing to the bathroom from the spare room in nothing but a towel. She'd had to avert her gaze from that gorgeous chest and the line of hair running from his belly button towards his crotch, but now she could look. He was hers to gloat over—at least for the moment.

As Aaron sprang off the bed, her eyes were drawn to his impressive morning glory. What a shame they didn't have time for her to help him out with that...

When he left the room, Alice got up and padded to the bathroom. A quick shower, a teeth clean with the toothbrush she'd hidden in her bag the day before, feeling like she was doing something really wicked and totally illicit, and soon she was seated at the breakfast bar in Aaron's small kitchen.

He handed her a coffee, the box of muesli, a bowl, spoon and milk carton. Not exactly five stars, but the performance earlier had been so Alice forgave him. As he moved past her, he took her hand and let it hover over his crotch.

"See what you do to me?"

She let her fingers curl around that impressive bulge, felt it flex and expand under her touch and all she wanted was to rip off the towel, hustle him back to the bedroom and start all over again.

"Laters, baby," Aaron muttered thickly as she buried her nose in the soft hairs between his pecs, drank in the sweet, musky, pre-shower scent of him.

Amused, she glanced up. "I don't believe it—you've *actually* read *Fifty Shades of Grey*?"

"Of course not. I watched the movie."

She laid her cheek back on his chest, loving the steady thud of his heartbeat. "Of course, silly me."

He dropped one last kiss on the top of her hair. Alice watched wistfully as his naked back and slim hips disappeared out the door.

*Laters, baby* it would have to be.

~

It was lovely standing waiting for the train to the city. Together.

Lovely the way Aaron didn't exactly hold her hand but looped a finger around hers as they stood together; once, twice. Otherwise they both scrolled through their phones, her on Goodreads, Aaron on Instagram.

It was intimate. Easy. Already she could imagine so much more. Already her mind had galloped ahead: the ring, probably a sapphire, set in a small circle of diamonds; the dress fitting, she'd keep it simple, elegant, not too low-cut. Who would she choose as her chief bridesmaid? Well, that was a no-brainer. Polly, of course.

A woman's voice requesting the time startled Alice out of her reverie. When the woman commented on how pretty her watch was, Alice happily started to chat about how much nicer an old-fashioned watch was than all those beeping things people wore these days.

Afterwards Aaron smiled a little quizzically and said, "That wasn't like you."

"In what way?"

"You don't normally like talking to people in public." He cocked his head and his eyes narrowed. "You seem more—I don't know. Confident, I guess. In public. You've always been fine in the shop because that's safe territory. But, last night outside the bar..." He stepped closer, lowered his voice. "Oof! You were wild. And look at you now, chatting away to that woman like she was your new best friend."

Alice's skin tingled with the obvious admiration in his

voice. How to tell him that amazeballs sex could work wonders on anxiety disorders. That and inventing a fake dad. She decided the concept would probably amuse him. Besides, it was safer territory than admitting that the amazeballs sex had irrevocably changed her forever.

"I invented myself a dad. Polly's idea. I think in some weird way it's helped."

He looked perplexed. "How come?"

"Well…" She hoisted her bag over her shoulder. "You know how it is with me and Poll, how we yarn on about stuff?" Aaron nodded. "Then the other day we were discussing how parents shape you, and I told her I don't have a clue who my dad is, and I reckoned that had something to do with my abject lack of self-confidence and, you know, the anxiety stuff and she said, 'well, invent one'."

"Invent a dad?"

"Yep."

He looked amused. "What did you come up with?"

Eagerly she filled Aaron in on the details and he laughed at her description of how her father's hideously disfiguring injuries came about.

"Your mind is seriously weird, Al. You know that, don't you? You really should write romances or a script for Netflix or something. It would be a hit."

Why indeed not? Her sky was wide and limitless right now.

So limitless in fact that she opened her mouth and out popped, "It must have affected you too, you know, not having your mum around?"

And just like that, clouds rolled over the sun. Aaron's face hardened, his mouth thinned. "Andrea made up for it." He shrugged. "And you get on with life. It's not a missing body part."

"I don't know… Maybe it's not so different, you know—me not having a dad, you losing your mum—it leaves scars, doesn't it? Like, at an emotional level."

Why, oh why was she pushing him? She felt her eyes

smarting as she stared at his face. A muscle in his jaw ticked and he looked over her head, his face expressionless. "It's a long time ago. I choose not to keep dredging it up."

She couldn't stop herself from bursting out, "But don't you think these things make us who we are? Affect the choices we make? Polly says—" She stopped abruptly. This was going hideously in the wrong direction.

The silence between them was filled by a strident passenger announcement. Aaron spoke finally, his voice hard as tintacks. "You shouldn't listen to so much of Polly's psychobabble."

Inside, she wilted. Outside, she pinned on her new, confident, *friends with benefits* mask. "Maybe not." The rumble of the approaching train seemed to shake her bones, but she firmed her legs and stood tall. On the train they did the same things they'd been doing before she opened her stupid mouth— looked at their phones, shared the odd comment—but the wind had shifted direction and the air held a blasting chill.

Why did it have to be this hard all of a sudden? Before all *the sex stuff*, Aaron would tell her things, like the way he didn't get on with his dad after his mum died, how Andrea had made life better when she came on the scene. Admittedly he'd always been sketchy on detail, but it had never felt so hideously awkward before. Now they'd added sex into the mix, it seemed there were "no entry" signs popping up everywhere.

And the problem was, suddenly it seemed so much more important to break them down. Alice sat blindly staring at her phone, aware that Aaron's arm wasn't bumping hers anymore.

Why, oh why did sex have to go and complicate everything?

# CHAPTER 15

Aaron was seeing double. The words on his monitor blurred and bled together.

He was so freakin' tired of this damn case. He couldn't seem to get his usual adrenaline rush. The management of this national beverage company were all dickheads. Prize morons who all needed to do the legal and decent thing by paying their employees their entitlements.

Thank Christ he didn't have to work in a big corporation, like Carts or Dan.

Speaking of Carts… He flicked his wrist and looked at his watch.

Would he go? Heck, it had been running around his head like a rat on a wheel these past few days. The quiz night. Since Alice had doused him in cold water at the train station, he'd been determined to keep some distance. Typical woman. As soon as you brought in sex they wanted to get emotionally close, analyse you, stretch you out, pin you down and pick pieces out of you. It had happened so many times before. That dewy-eyed look full of misplaced compassion. He could almost hear the cogs in their brains turning: "Poor darling, he's so damaged from childhood." Followed by: "I can save you. Pick me, pick me."

He gritted his teeth.

The problem was, his cooling-off efforts had been abysmal. Friday night Carts had flicked him for a family function and Dan had some rugby team do, so he'd gone to the pub with Hamish. But then Jacinta turned up and some others, and they all kept asking after Alice until he wanted to rip out his own fingernails.

So he'd left. Taken an Uber straight to Alice's. Spent five minutes like a burglar checking that Alice was home alone, his suit jacket nearly torn apart by Rowena's frigging rose bushes. Thankfully Polly was out; Friday night was her prowl night. He knew that of course, because he'd seen her often enough when he was on the prowl himself.

But now the only woman he wanted to pounce on was Alice.

She'd let him in with her hair wrapped in a towel, her glasses slightly wonky on her nose. When his eyes slid to her feet, there were those fucking slippers and he'd turned into a wildebeest.

They'd had crazy sex up against her bedroom door; he'd lifted her up and she'd wrapped her legs around him and afterwards he knew she hadn't come. He felt guilty about that—he was a jerk. A great big needy jerk, he'd realised as he went limp against her and his legs would hardly hold him up from the force of his orgasm.

And then they'd made awkward conversation that completely weirded him out, so he'd said he had more work to do and left. Pretended he didn't see the hurt in her eyes. He'd ached—yes *ached*, an almost physical pain he couldn't place at any exact spot in his body—to make it up to her. Kept imagining her face as she broke apart in his arms. The little guttural sounds she would make as she orgasmed, how she'd spasm so tight around his fingers, his cock.

But he couldn't do it. Because then she'd think she owned him, wouldn't she?

Aaron rubbed his aching eyes. Focused again. They'd be well and truly halfway through the stupid event by now. So what? He hated quiz nights; he'd lied to Carts because he couldn't stomach the thought of Carts moving in on Alice. Except now he'd left the door wide open for it to happen.

Well. Marvellous. Carts could offer Alice everything he couldn't. Slavish devotion, hours of endless listening. Real lovemaking. Not just sex.

He checked his phone. She hadn't messaged him. He'd sent her a vague noncommittal message yesterday when he couldn't stand not having contact any longer, when his arm ached from relieving himself in the shower. She'd sent a cool, deeply unsatisfying response.

Now he tapped her a quick "Going to be late. Smash 'em for me."

Alice didn't answer. Probably her phone was on silent.

If he hurried, he could get this report wrapped up in fifteen minutes. He could get there for the last part. Tonight he could sleep with his nose pressed against that little dip in her shoulder blade, inhale the smell of apple blossom. Or at least what he imagined apple blossom smelled like. Just like Alice. In fact, he could almost smell it now…

The outer electric doors swooshing brought his head up in surprise. He'd thought he would be the last one here. Low laughter, a man's and a woman's. Aaron got up, navigated around his desk and peered out of his office to see two heads bobbing along the partitions at the other end of the open-plan offices. One was the unmistakably Nordic dirty blond mane of Archie Bendt. The other was several shades lighter, framing Lauren's perfect features.

Shit on a great big stick. It was 8.30 p.m. Why wasn't Archie at home with his beautiful wife and his two angelic children?

The door to Archie's office closed with a meaningful click. The laughter became muffled.

Aaron went back to his desk and slumped down in a cold sweat. He really didn't need to know about this. He tried to focus on the screen but his mind wouldn't stop going over and over the many little clues: the looks, the way Lauren and Archie's hands would linger over a file passing between them. The way Lauren would lean her breast against Archie's shoulder as she placed a coffee in front of him, the way he'd look indulgently back at her.

Fuck. Fuck. Fuck.

He scrubbed his hands through his hair, down his face.

Suddenly a spine-chilling howl split the air.

A woman.

Christ almighty, was Bendt attacking Lauren? Were Trojan, Bendt and Fink about to have their very own #MeToo scandal?

There was no getting past it; as the screams hit a higher note he knew he had to intervene. He sprinted towards Archie's office and heard Archie bellowing with a level of desperation Aaron had never before heard. And now there were *two* female voices.

"—You scheming, marriage-wrecking little bitch… and you… YOU! I'm going to cut your balls off and ram them down your fucking throat."

"Don't you touch him; don't you dare lay a finger on him."

"Stop it." This from Archie. "Miranda, you've got it all wrong. Stop. For god's sake. Lauren, LET GO OF ME."

By now Aaron had halted outside Archie's office, his mouth ajar. It wasn't pretty in there.

Miranda Bendt was wielding a huge leather handbag like a beauty pageant version of Miss Trunchbull. Lauren had plastered herself to Archie's chest. As for Archie, well, he was trying to prise Lauren off, defend himself and somehow grovel to his wife all in one contorted movement.

Guess his fitness levels helped.

Mid-loop-the-loop with her Gucci missile, Miranda suddenly caught sight of Aaron. The bag clipped Archie's lip and then fell away as Miranda's arm went slack. Archie and Lauren followed her gaze.

Now all of them were staring at him.

Blood oozed from a gash on Archie's lip.

Miranda brushed a wisp of hair off her forehead with shaking, red-tipped fingers.

Lauren crumpled onto the floor, hugged her knees and burst into paroxysms of hysterical weeping.

*Fuck. And triple Fuck.*

You know that numb feeling, when you are in a surreal situation and you keep telling yourself it's a dream and any minute now you'll wake up and go *thank you, god, this didn't actually happen?* Well, thought Aaron, any minute now, his phone would rap out its familiar morning riff and he'd yawn and stretch...

Except it didn't. And now here he was, grimly waiting for Lauren after escorting her out following a hoarse plea from his boss—he could hardly refuse, could he? He'd helped her find her coat and bag, and she'd promptly grabbed the latter and disappeared sobbing into the ladies' loos.

So here he stood, helplessly, while the time ticked away. In the background the rise and fall of voices carried on, accusing, placating, accusing, defending...

Pushing open the door of the cloakroom a smidge, Aaron hiss-whispered, "Lauren. You okay?"

*Sniff.* Of course, she wasn't... "Can I get you an Uber?"

*Sniff,* loud hiccup. "I need a drink."

His heart sank. He could go to the water fountain in the foyer, but somehow he knew she meant something stronger.

Finally, Lauren yanked the door open. Her face was blotchy, eyes red and smudged. She'd reapplied her lipstick but she'd gone up one side of her lip more than the other, making her look like a kid who'd been playing with her older sister's make-up. Which maybe wasn't so far from the truth.

Sympathy tugged at his gut. The kind you had for any other human who had got themselves into an irrevocable mess. And… frustration. He could be with Alice, answering questions on the last king of England to be beheaded, or on what, in economic speak, constitutes the triple bottom line. Letting his leg touch hers under the table.

The tug turned into a painful twist. Relationships. This is where they got you: piled in shit up to your freakin' eyeballs.

"I can't go home yet," Lauren whined.

"Why not?"

Her mouth twisted. "My boyfriend—"

"You have a boyfriend!" His face must have spelled his horror, because her features screwed up, a tear jerked out of one eye and slid down her cheek. A trickle of snot ran out of her nose. Aaron dived into his pocket and found a hanky.

"Clean," he said as he handed it to her. She nodded and scrubbed it around her nostrils.

"Okay. Where do you suggest?" he said lamely.

"Anywhere. Somewhere anonymous."

The sounds were getting louder again from Archie's office, more vitriolic. "… the last time you ever get to humiliate me… I'm going to *bleed you dry…*"

Lauren's face contorted, her body bending towards the sound. They had to get out now or she'd likely pitch into the fray once more.

"Let's go to the Shamrock," he said. It would be reasonably quiet tonight; Paddy would understand and just hand over their drinks without need for an explanation. Gently, Aaron guided her by the elbow and felt her body slumping into him. He snatched his hand away. Life was complicated enough without this, thank you.

He breathed again when, finally, Lauren was seated on the stool next to him at the bar, texting frantically; sending some desperate excuse to her boyfriend, probably. He ordered her a

Cloudy Bay semillon sauvignon blanc as she requested—obviously Lauren could still be picky about her wine even when deeply traumatised.

He ordered himself a small lager and they sat in awkward silence. By her fourth mouthful of wine, Lauren's tongue had loosened.

"He's going to leave her, you know. He's deeply, deeply unhappy."

Aaron stroked his stubble and wondered how to respond.

"He's only there for the kids. We've got a long-term plan."

He stared at her, unable to come up with any words that wouldn't invite a whole heap more information he had no wish to hear. No right to hear.

She gave him a wall-eyed look. "You're judging me, aren't you?"

"No." He hadn't got that far. Who was he to judge anyway? He'd had a brief fling with a woman who had a partner a while back. She'd told him they had an "open relationship" until her boyfriend turned up at his apartment looking anything but open to the fact his girlfriend was in bed with Aaron. Somehow they'd worked it out non-violently. And Aaron had never ever done that again. Strictly no third parties, amicable or otherwise.

Maybe he could have given Archie some tips.

Finally he managed, "What about your boyfriend?"

"We've been off and on since school. It's habit, really."

"For him as well?"

"God no, he adores me." She looked at him pleadingly. "You know how it is, Aaron. It's awful to be on your own."

He didn't. *Hadn't*, that was. Until a couple of weeks ago, when waking up to find a warm soft body curled into him had suddenly felt like the best thing in the world. Ever since, his bed had been somehow too big, too empty, without Alice there.

He slammed down his lager.

"You are definitely angry at me," she said.

"No, what you do is none of my business."

"You *are*, I can tell." Her lip wobbled dangerously. Her eyes filled up, spilling mascara tracks down her cheeks. "W-what am I g-g-oing to do? I'll lose my job... I can't l-lose Archie..."

Suddenly her body pitched forward, her head landing with a *thunk* on his chest. Aaron looked at Lauren's mussed-up silver-blonde hair and wondered how her head could weigh so much.

His hands wavered around the back of her neck. He did not want to put his arms round her. For all sorts of reasons. After a moment's deliberation, he gripped her shoulders and prised her gently off him. He looked into her panda eyes and gave her his best reassuring smile. "It'll work out—"

"YOU ARE—" A vice-like grip on his bicep. Fingers digging in until pain registered. "A PRIZE SHIT!" The voice was familiar, even if the blatant fury in it was not.

Aaron looked up. And up. And there was Carts. Like the wild man of Borneo. And behind him—Christ!—Dan. And for a second, his eyes held two big brown ones full of pain and accusation. Horror swept through him. Then a curtain of chestnut hair shone in the pub lights as Alice spun on her heels and ran out the door.

Aaron's awful evening had just turned into a nightmare.

*Smack, smack, smack,* the hard pavement sent shock waves through the soles of Alice's boots. She couldn't breathe, it was like someone had smashed her lungs with a rock. She had to run faster... faster... Because then maybe she could outrun the image of Lauren Donovan's head snuggled into Aaron's chest. But Alice's body had never been made for running. Her limbs weren't built that way. School sport had been a nightmare of taped knees and hobbling to the sidelines. Letting the team down.

She could cope with letting people down. It was so much easier than the other way around.

At the corner of the street she halted, gasping, bent double, her hands clutching her knees. Aaron and Lauren Donovan. She'd known, hadn't she? From that moment at Aaron's work when she'd seen the look Lauren gave him; of course, deep down she'd known it was only a matter of time...

Hot tears came. Flooding her eyes, threatening to cascade down her cheeks. She wouldn't cry. He wasn't worth it. Truth be told, her heart had been shrivelling all evening. She couldn't even give the answer for the name of the Brontës' brother even though she knew it... she knew *everything* about the Brontës. Next to her at the table, Carts had nudged her and she'd looked at him blankly, her head full of dreadful certainty. Not quiz answers.

After Aaron had turned up the other night and she'd oh-so-eagerly pulled him against her, wrapped her legs around his thighs as he thrust deep into her against the bedroom door... afterwards, that hollow, distant look in his eyes... She realised now that it had signified the beginning of the end.

With a moan, Alice straightened, swiping at her eyes with the back of her fist, her lungs straining for air, everything hurting... every muscle, every joint. It felt like she had the flu—only worse, because people got over the flu, but she would never, ever get over this. She would live the rest of her life with a deep dark crater where her heart should be.

But she would survive. She would. Because people did. All the time.

She started to walk, stiff and slow, then heard fast footsteps gaining on her. Her feet ground to a halt, frozen to the paving stones as a hand closed around her arm. She squealed, yanked her arm up and found herself wrapped in strong arms, against a chest that felt—smelled—so familiar. So *longed* for. So *needed*. More than air. She could do without air, but not without Aaron. Her knees buckled.

"Alice. It's me."

*No. No. No!*

Arms windmilling, she wrenched out of his embrace.

"Alice, you have to hear me out. I can explain."

"I know what I saw, Aaron." They were a few feet apart now, both panting. His hair was an utter mess. Probably because Lauren had been running her fingers through it—which made her want to fly at him and claw his beautiful eyes right out of his beautiful stupid *sodding* face. "Don't come near me. Don't touch me. Do you hear?"

Aaron raised his hands in a placatory gesture. "There's nothing going on between us. You have to believe me, Al."

"Nothing sure has a way of looking like something."

"Al, please, can we go somewhere and talk about this?"

"Oh, yes, good idea." Her laugh echoed around the empty street. "Let's go back to the pub. I'll drag up a stool next to Lauren and we'll have a lively little discussion. Maybe about threesomes?"

"Don't be stupid," Aaron muttered. He started pacing, dragging fingers through his hair. "Lauren's got herself in serious trouble at work. I was asked by Archie to remove her from it. You walked in at the wrong moment, that's all."

"Ha, that's what they all say."

"It's not like that. She's a complete mess."

"Aw, how sweet! Aaron Blake—dragon-slayer, maiden-rescuer."

He stopped pacing. "For fuck's sake, Al, I swear there is nothing going on between me and her." She registered the sudden tug in the centre of her heart, the desire to believe him, and then he blew it spectacularly. "You know I don't date women I work with."

With superhuman effort Alice swallowed her rage. Better to be as dignified as Elizabeth Bennet, as defiant as Scarlett O'Hara. To go out with an Oscar-winning performance.

She lifted her gaze to his, hardened her heart. "Regardless, I don't want to do this anymore, Aaron."

His jaw sagged. "Do what?

"This... us... pretending to be your girlfriend, flirting, fucking each other..." He winced. "Yes. *Fucking*, Aaron. I can choose to have a potty mouth when I want to. And the whole friends-with-benefits thing… well, it hasn't really worked out, has it?"

"I thought—"

"You thought what?"

"That you were enjoying it."

"Were you?"

"Jesus, Al, couldn't you tell?" His arm reached out, and she arced back. If he touched her it would be over. She'd melt all over him.

She clutched her bag in front of her until her knuckles felt bruised. "Yeah, well. Maybe. But the benefits aren't worth the costs."

He frowned. "What's that supposed to mean?"

"I don't feel like we're friends anymore." Those words didn't have enough impact; the urge to twist the knife was unstoppable. "In fact, I don't even know if I like you." For a second then, she saw it and there was nothing she wanted more in the whole wide world than to reel those words right back in: searing pain shot across his face before it went blank. Hard. Cold.

"Thanks a lot," he said, so quietly she nearly missed it. He looked past her with the same stony, dismissive expression. "Anyway, you're safe. Carts is coming to rescue you."

"I'm so tempted to punch your lights out."

Carts and Aaron had been silently watching the tail-lights of the Uber disappear. The Uber that Alice had insisted on ordering. Pleasant and impeccably polite to Carts, ignoring Aaron completely until it arrived, she'd hopped in the back and with one last glimpse of a tantalising slice of leg she was gone.

And now Carts' eyes were gleaming with unmistakable fury. Well, bring it on. His night couldn't get any worse, could it?

"Dare you to, mate." Aaron backed away, holding the edges of his jacket open, exposing his shirt front. He thumped his belly. "How about here?" Jabbed a forefinger at his jutted jaw. "Or here?"

Carts had balled his hands into fists and was doing a weird backwards–forwards dance on his toes. "I'd go for your pretty-boy face. Mess it up. That'd stop you."

"Stop me from what?"

"Hurting any more women."

Aaron dropped his arms. "For Christ's sake, Carts, would you at least hear my side of things?"

"Your bullshit, you mean?" Carts' eyes bulged over the top of his knuckles. "What were you up to with that chick? Why didn't you come to the quiz night?"

"It's complicated," Aaron said.

"Yeah, you're right about that."

"If you stop dancing around like you're practising for a freakin' Celtic dance competition, I'll tell you."

Carts' feet slowed, he dropped his arms, hands fisted at his sides. "Okay, I'm giving you a chance," he conceded. "But this better be fucking good."

Aaron sighed, thrust his hands in his pockets. "I was fully intending to come—you know, to the quiz thing—but I had this report to finish for tomorrow, which I was trying to get tied up, and then I heard Archie come into the office with Lauren."

"Who's Lauren?"

"His P.A. The woman you saw me sitting with at the bar. So, I just put my head down and tried not to notice until suddenly there's all this screaming. And obviously I had to go and check it out, because you can't not, right? And when I do, there's Miranda hitting Archie over the head with her handbag, screaming obscenities."

"Who's Miranda?"

"His wife."

"Christ."

"Exactly."

"When they saw me, they all stopped screaming at each other and Archie thrusts Lauren at me and she's trying to cling to him and he shouts, 'get her out of here, *now*', and you know what? You don't prevaricate in situations like that. You just get the hell out. So I brought her to the Shamrock... and... that's where you found us."

"Man. That's heavy." Carts' fingers unfurled.

A wave of exhaustion hit Aaron. The sudden memory of Alice's shocked face winded him as if Carts had actually punched him. Wearily, he sat down on the edge of the pavement, bent his knees and rested his arms on them. A moment later, Carts folded down beside him, found a stick in the gutter, and began scraping it through a pile of dry leaves.

They used to sit like this waiting for the school bus.

A sliver of gratitude found its way through the haze of exhaustion. Carts had always been fair.

"She was having a meltdown on me. Nothing else, I swear." Aaron glanced down ruefully at the mascara streaks on his shirt. "They've been having an affair for a while, I'd guess."

"Yeah, well, it was obvious she was pretty cut-up about something. I thought it was you. I got Dan to take over before I came to find Alice. He looked like all his Christmases had come at once."

Aaron snorted. Then silence, except for the scrape, scrape of the stick.

"I think she likes you, you know."

"Who, Lauren?"

"No, fuck-head, Alice."

Aaron opened his mouth, but the words were in a pile-up at the back of his throat.

Carts' chin rested on his kneecap. "I was hoping I was wrong. But all evening she kept checking the door. She wasn't focusing on any of the questions, and then when she saw you in the pub... I went, oh fuccccckkk, I get it. And, mate, that made me see red." A pause.

Aaron found his voice. "Well, of course she likes me. We're friends." How unconvincing could you get?

Carts obviously agreed. He made a scoffing sound. "Either you're playing dumb or you've got rocks in your head. She's besotted with you."

Aaron's heart jumped like it had been defibrillated. "That's utter crap."

"Wish it was," Carts said morosely. "I'm getting used to seeing the signs now. Maybe eventually I'll learn to go for a woman who gets that look on her face when she looks at me. Not some other unworthy fucker." He sighed heavily. "I don't know what you've done to deserve her, but if you don't put it right with Alice, I swear..."

"Don't start," Aaron warned. He was trying to digest this new information and he didn't need Carts deliberating on whether to punch him or not.

He groaned.

Carts turned his head and eyeballed him. "I assume you've slept with her?"

"That's between me and Alice."

"Typical. You couldn't keep your dirty mitts off the one truly good person who you *know* won't bounce back from this, won't shrug and move on to the next guy. You break her heart and I swear... I swear, I won't be your friend anymore."

"Don't worry," Aaron gritted out. "Alice informed me just before you arrived that she doesn't even like me. So join the line-up."

Carts grunted and threw the stick on the ground. Stood up and ground it into a pulp with his heel. "I'm going back to stop Dan making a fool of himself with Miss Universe. I'd like to say you have my sympathy over the shite at work, but no doubt you'll come out smelling of roses. You always do. Even though underneath, quite frankly, I'm smelling a whole load of horse shit."

And with that, Carts strode off, his pant hems slapping angrily around his ankles.

# CHAPTER 16

Arms and legs overtaken with weariness, Alice climbed the steps up to the porch.

*Click.* Damn, they still hadn't replaced that stupid light bulb. She fumbled; badly trembling fingers unable to locate her keys in her bag.

After several minutes of frantic scrabbling, she gave up, turned her bag upside-down and dumped the contents on the ground. On all fours she felt around in the pile of pen tops, lolly wrappers and a couple of floral-wrapped tampons until her hand closed around the Rubik's Cube. Her lip wobbled. It was less than four weeks ago that Aaron had helped her locate her keys in the dark, both of them laughing as they made their way to the kitchen, laughing as he filled up Mum's best shot glasses. Laughter replaced with groans of approval when he'd kissed her and stolen the last little sliver of her heart she'd kept safe from him.

The tears she'd forced back this past hour now rolled in a steady stream down her cheeks. They plopped onto the porch, drenching the fingers she used to try to stem them. Finally she located a scrunched-up tissue amid the debris on the ground and blew her nose noisily. Wiped her eyes.

She started to slowly place the items back in her bag and was standing up, door key poised, when she recognised Cathy Brightwater's strident voice.

"Yoo-hoo, Alice?"

Alice jammed her back against the front door. Cathy, their next-door neighbour, was lovely, but made everyone's business her business. Mostly, Alice and Polly were unerringly patient. Cathy had lost her husband in a freak motorbike accident and her son had a drug problem. Cathy needed kindness. But it was 10 p.m. on the night her friend with benefits/fake boyfriend/flirting coach had just broken her heart, and Alice was not in the mood.

Cathy, to Alice's utmost horror, was running up the path in her dressing gown. As she got closer, Alice could detect something large waving in the air above her head.

"I saw your cab draw up and thought I should bring this over. It wouldn't fit in your letterbox so I said I'd take it in for you."

Alice blinked. Crying and contact lenses were an awful combination. Cathy was a blur as she came up the steps and handed the package to Alice. What she could tell as she took it was that it was fortified with reams of tape and heavier than it looked.

Cathy hovered and Alice got the impression she wanted her to open it. Which was ridiculous. It was late at night. It was pitch-black. And her world was falling apart.

She had to assert some clear boundaries. "Thank you, Cathy. I'm really tired—long day. Oh, be careful how you navigate down the steps. The outside light's blown."

Reluctantly, Cathy turned. Alice watched her retreat, one arm out for balance as she teetered down the path. As she closed the gate, she called out, "It says it's from Rowena Montgomery. From some place in England. Lovely mum of yours, sending you a present."

Alice managed a watery smile that she knew Cathy wouldn't see so she called back, "Thanks again, Cathy. Good night."

Inside she threw her bag and keys and the package onto the kitchen table. Then she went to the bathroom, jabbed around until she'd got the little bits of film out of her eyes and groped her way to the bedroom to find her glasses.

She avoided looking at the back of her bedroom door.

She'd probably never be able to look at her bedroom door again; she'd have to feel her way to it with her eyes scrunched shut. It was probably for the best that they'd only made love—correction, had sex—a handful of times. Otherwise the memories would be unbearable.

Back in the kitchen, she stared at her mum's bold, rounded script for long moments.

She was too tired to deal with it now… *except*… maybe if her mum was buying a bookshop in England, well, maybe that was her escape route. She'd go to "overcoming your flying phobia" classes, buy a round-the-world ticket and finally end up in some delightful little Harry-Potter-esque town with spires and magical happenings, and a beautiful young English man—probably an earl or a lord—would burst through the door one day, wanting to buy a first edition of Byron's collected works and—

What was wrong with her? This was like imagining herself a dad. Only worse.

Grabbing a sharp knife, Alice sat down and ripped it through the top of the thick brown paper. Felt around inside. A raft of papers. She pulled them out and scattered them in a pile on the tabletop.

No for-sale leaflets from real estate agents. No photos of a bow-windowed shop with books on display.

Photos, yes, of the same person, and articles… Confused, she frowned as she sifted through them.

*Professor Henry Beacham-Brown talks about his recent research on the life of Oscar Wilde.*

*Henry Beacham-Brown comes out.*
*Cambridge Professor comes clean about his homosexuality.*
*Henry in love.*
*Henry Beacham-Brown marries long-term partner, actor Gabriel West.*

What on earth had this got to do with anything?

Her fingers spread the papers and there, peeping out from beneath them, was an envelope with her name on, again in her mother's distinctive handwriting. Alice ripped and read.

*Darling Alice,*

*This is probably the hardest thing I am ever going to write. A confession. An admission that I chose to lie to you all these years, my dear sweet girl, about who your father really is. As you read the information contained here, I hope you will begin to understand the reasons why I hid it, not just from you, but also from Henry.*

*Of course, it is unforgivable to keep a child from her father, a father from his child. Maybe if you had been less accepting of my half-baked answers to your questions; if you had been a more demanding child, I would have been unable to guard the truth, but you were such a good little thing. You made it easy for me to lie.*

*As the years rolled past, your parentage has weighed heavy on me. This visit to England has been much more than a trip down memory lane. It has been a cathartic journey. Meeting Henry again, telling him the truth—that he has a daughter. (At which, I must stress, he is overwhelmed with joy.)*

*I have his full knowledge and permission to share all of this with you. His life speaks for itself. Hopefully it will help you to fill in some of the blanks.*

*Henry, through no fault of his own, broke my heart. It is not fair of me to break yours by not telling you the truth.*

*Forgive me.*

*Your Mother.*

*P.S. I will be home soon and we can have a chat about all this.*

Alice stared at the letter, the hand holding it completely numb, like it didn't belong to her. She had a father. Rowena had lied all these years. He wasn't Andrew from Basingstoke.

Nor, for that matter, was he a Scottish laird film director with a chronic pain problem. He was Henry with a double-barrelled name. English professor at Cambridge University. He was gay. He was married.

After a moment she spread out the article from *The Times* weekend magazine. Gazed at the photo of the man seated, legs crossed, in a big leather armchair, until her eyeballs felt like they would fall out.

Henry wore glasses. He had a slight build—*dapper,* no doubt the English would describe him. His mouth was small, with a well-shaped upper lip, his smile a little uncertain. Straight chestnut-brown hair fell heavy across his forehead. So much was achingly familiar in his face, and yet she didn't know him at all. Twenty-six years of a father missing in action.

Alice read and re-read Rowena's letter. After a while she folded it into four neat squares. Sentences stood out in her mind, as if written in bright red ink: "Maybe if you'd been a *more demanding* child... you were *such a good little thing...*"

A strangled sound escaped her lips. Clearly, it was her fault she'd never found her father. Because she didn't ask enough questions, didn't make enough fuss... was too *undemanding...* too...

*Scared.* Always, always scared.

Her hands curled until she registered her nails digging into her palms. By default, did that mean it was her fault she'd spent years pining for someone who would never love her back? Someone whose beauty only skimmed the surface, whose way of making her laugh and feel somehow special hid the fact that there was no heart to give?

And why? Because she was simply too terrified... to... what? To ask, to *demand,* to settle for nothing less than what she was worthy of—like knowing who her father was. And being loved... truly loved.

Carefully, Alice organised all the articles and photos of Henry into a pile with neat edges. Tomorrow she would read every word again, find his profile on LinkedIn, search the internet for every possible detail about her father; a man who was clearly not afraid to be truly himself.

But now, there was something else she needed to do. With a purposeful stride she went over to the pine dresser. Took out one of Rowena's shot glasses and searched until she found the stash of alcohol. No tequila, which was a shame, but there was half a bottle of vodka. That would have to do.

Alice filled the glass, screwed the lid tightly back on the vodka and then popped the bottle back where it belonged. Delicately, she took the shot glass between fingers and thumb, tipped her head and knocked it back. Refused to shudder as the alcohol burned her throat. Then she held the glass up to the light in a silent salute, lifted her arm, and hurled it at the wall with all her might.

The sound of breaking glass echoed through the room.

Tomorrow, she would do something about the mess.

~

"Your loyalty… discretion…" Only parts of Fink's words were sinking through the dense fog in Aaron's brain. He shook himself and tried to concentrate. "… will be rewarded."

"Sorry, could you repeat that?"

"Your loyalty to the company, Aaron." Trojan gave him a tight smile. "What Charles is saying is this is the kind of attitude we like to see in future partners."

Aaron willed his features to comply. His lips weren't playing. Since yesterday it had felt like he'd completely lost control of his faculties. The worst of which was clearly his ability to flash his usual charming smile.

But at least, he decided, looking jadedly across at Archie Bendt, the smile seemed to have been wiped off his face too. Not that he could smile easily with that fat lip.

He guessed he should count himself lucky Alice hadn't swiped him one.

*Must not think about Alice, must not think about Alice.*

Truthfully, he'd done barely anything else this past... how long? Not even a day. Twelve hours at most since she'd dumped him. Not that he was counting or anything. On the contrary; he was focusing on what the partners had to say, getting his orders like a good recruit—even though, right now, this minute, he couldn't give a rat's arse if keeping schtum about Archie's sordid affair would advance his career.

"The official line on Lauren—" Archie said, then winced and moved his shoulder around in its socket. Clearly the Gucci missile had met more than one mark. It occurred to Aaron that maybe this wasn't the first time. Maybe Miranda had had previous target practice.

"The official line on Lauren," Archie repeated with a cough, "is that she's had some personal issue come up. And that she'll be working from home for a while."

"She won't be disadvantaged in all of this." Fink was quick off the mark, with a glance at Archie that, for a split second, spelled pure loathing. It was swiftly replaced by the small furrow in his brow that tended to hide whatever was on Fink's mind.

There was a brief period of silence. Fink stood up and went and opened the door. "Clear?" He lifted a brow in Aaron's direction.

"Absolutely." Aaron followed suit. You knew when you were being given your marching orders.

"Good man." Trojan smiled from behind his desk. "One of our star performers."

Archie Bendt said nothing at all.

Back at his desk, Aaron surveyed the files, the mess, the billings sheets winking at him from his computer screen. Today's billings could go to hell. He'd be quite happy to give a few clients a freebie to make up for the exorbitant fees Trojan's charged.

Aaron picked up his phone and his fingers hovered over contacts. Alice's number was on speed dial. Had been since a week after he met her all those years ago.

His scalp went tight. What did that tell him? What did that really, truly say about him and Alice?

He screwed up his eyes and clicked the end of his pen until the sound nearly sent him nuts. What did it matter? He'd blown it anyway. And even if he hadn't, Christ, he didn't know how to do relationships. Had no idea how to... care about anyone long term.

As if from miles away, he heard Hamish's concerned voice. "Aaron, you okay there?"

"Sure." He located a smile from his collection, plastered it on like a clown face. "Just thinking about the new case that came in this morning."

Hamish's eyes lit up. "Really, has Bendt won us another scorcher?"

"Yeah." Aaron looked at Alice's contact details and flicked back to his screen saver. "You could say that."

The day dragged interminably. It was only lunch time. Alice hadn't made contact. By now there should have been a text, the gist of which would be, "I made a mistake. Let's start where we left off." It wasn't like he expected anything too emotional. Alice was eminently sensible; last night had been a weird blip. And, of course, he'd shrug it off. He'd be cool about it all.

Except by 1.30 it hadn't happened, and he was feeling increasingly flat as he went to relieve himself after god knows how many coffees. He'd also been dodging "where's Lauren? Has anyone heard from her?" questions all morning and he was sick to his stomach of passing it all off with a shrug. At the urinal, his shoulders tightened as he realised Archie Bendt was using the one next to him. He stared ahead. Archie stared ahead; did a little shake and zipped himself up.

At the sinks, both washing their hands, Archie looked him hard in the eye in the mirror. It wasn't a friendly look. As he ripped out some paper towels, he leaned forward and examined his swollen lip. "Fucking women, eh?"

Aaron was too gobsmacked to reply.

Archie glared at Aaron's reflection again, harder this time.

"You look like shit, boy. Go take a long lunch break. Charge it to the company card." With that, Archie strode out.

Aaron looked like shit? You had to ask yourself what Archie Bendt saw when he looked in the mirror.

Half an hour later, Aaron found himself wandering aimlessly around Elizabeth Quay. It was a picture-perfect spring day, the brilliant blue sky reflected in the glassy expanse of the river. Easily warm enough for kids to play in the water fountains, squealing with excitement, while their mums sat nearby and chatted.

Usually, he'd be raring to go, pumping to get on with summer, looking forward to lazy days on the beach, wind-surfing when the wind came in and eased the heat in the late afternoon; playing beach volleyball with Carts and Dan and a few other mates…

Beach. Volley. Ball. Aaron ground to a halt, remembering the beach volleyball pitch where he'd first felt the over-whelming urge to kiss Alice. A mere few weeks ago. It felt like a lifetime.

Aaron's hand trembled around his phone. He needed to go for a run to stop these crazy feelings inside him. Why hadn't he brought his running gear to work? Because he was too damn tired from not sleeping and playing and replaying his conversation with Alice over and over like a worn-out ribbon of celluloid.

He needed to talk to someone. Dan was no good. He'd just laugh in his goofy embarrassed way and change the subject to rugby. Carts was usually a sympathetic listener, but after the other night he didn't expect much sympathy there. Carts had made it clear whose side he'd be taking.

Aaron rolled his phone over and over in his hand. His palms were sweating.

Normally—ha!—normally… *before all this…* he'd talk to Alice.

But how could he talk to Alice about his problem with… Alice?

He chewed on the inside of his lip. There was only one person he could confide in. A deep visceral tension churned in his stomach. Around and around, mixing past and present. This person, more than anyone, would likely understand. Surprising, but in his gut he knew it to be true.

Aaron brought up Oliver's number and put the phone to his ear.

# CHAPTER 17

"What in crapola's name happened here?"

Polly stood in the kitchen doorway, wearing a very short tight red dress and looking decidedly seedy. Alice had been up for hours. At the kitchen table on her laptop, she'd searched every skerrick of information she could find on Henry Beacham-Brown. Her search engine had overflowed and she'd clicked and read until she was practically seeing double.

"Nothing, why?"

"Did you two have a fight last night?" Polly surveyed her suspiciously as she beelined for the pantry.

Alice snapped her laptop shut and shuffled together her papers, Henry's lovely smile turned face down on the pile. *Sorry, Dad.* "Why do you ask?" she said cagily.

Polly, two slices of bread in one hand, peanut butter jar in the other, waved the jar at the floor near the dresser. "All that glass."

Relief flooded her. Of course, Polly thought Aaron had come home with her after the quiz night. After all, they'd been discussing for several days how Alice should manage it. What she'd wear, how she'd play it super cool, particularly after

Aaron's rather caddish behaviour when he'd turned up uninvited the other night.

"Panda man," Polly had sniffed disdainfully when Alice told her (sketchily) about the bedroom door incident. When Alice frowned with complete lack of comprehension, Polly elaborated: "Eats, roots, and leaves. Except he didn't have the decency to stay for a meal. Very off. He needs to be taught a serious lesson."

Well, he had, hadn't he? Last night in the street. Alice swallowed a wave of nausea remembering the look on his face as she spat words at him in a tone that would pass for hatred. Shocked. Stunned. Hurt.

She hardened her heart as it threatened to go doughy. He'd brought it on himself with his man-whore behaviour. Everything she said, she'd meant. With a cherry on top.

"It was a little accident." Alice hated lying to Polly. She tried to sound casual as she changed the subject. "Where've you been all night?"

"Oh, just somewhere," Polly said airily as she loaded a knife with peanut butter and slathered it onto the bread, then squished the slices together.

"A Tinder date?"

"Maybe."

Tinder. The nausea was back, bile rising in Alice's throat. It was utterly stupid of her, but she'd kept the piece of paper by the side of her bed with the Tinder profile Aaron had written up for her. Only because it was in Aaron's handwriting. Which was pathetic. She'd bin it. Along with Polly's scribbled equation about amazeballs sex equalling true love that she'd shoved into the back of her dressing table drawer. Amazeballs sex, however cataclysmically orgasmic it might have been, clearly did not lead to true love between Alice and Aaron. Or any love at all for that matter.

Alice scraped her chair back and stood up.

"Aren't you going to fill me in on what happened?" Polly said through a mouthful of bread and peanut butter.

"I promise you don't want to know."

"I promise I do."

"Maybe later. You'll be late for work."

"I don't have any patient appointments booked until ten. Why do you think I still look like this?" Polly held her arms out wide.

Hungover, shagged stupid and in last night's crumpled little red dress, Polly was still utterly glorious. And still her best friend. Alice fought the tidal wave of words rising up her throat. Polly had been her go-to for every problem since they were sixteen. Somehow, though, she sensed Polly couldn't solve this one. This was monumental; the stuff of Greek tragedies. She'd found a father and lost her one true love. Hurled one of her mum's precious pieces of antique crystal against the wall. It was about time she started to work things out for herself.

"I can't be late opening the shop," Alice muttered, clutching the papers and her laptop to her chest.

"Munchkin. Something big has happened, I can tell. Except you're acting seriously weird, so I can't work out if it's good or bad."

Alice got to the door and stopped. "Both. I'll tell you this evening. Don't step in the glass, I'll clear it up when I get home." Stiff-backed, she started down the corridor, but something was niggling at her. Something the old Alice wouldn't have thought twice about. She walked back into the room and focused on Polly's black curls.

"Polly. Please don't call me Munchkin." In her peripheral vision she saw Polly's jaw drop. Her inner resolve wobbled, then hardened. "It makes me feel like a kid." She made to walk off and threw over her shoulder: "And in case you haven't noticed, I'm not one anymore."

Oliver's stride was so familiar, even at a distance. As far back as Aaron could remember Oliver had moved this way: perfectly synchronised, like he was swimming through air. Aaron had always secretly envied Oliver's walk; tried his best to copy it, but he'd never quite got the same grace and economy of movement.

But now, as Oliver approached, something was missing. From him, not Oliver. There were no teeth of envy chewing away at his insides. Instead, a sense of warmth flooded through him. God, if he'd ever needed his brother's help, it was now.

As if Oliver guessed, he slapped an arm around Aaron's shoulders and held on for a few seconds longer than usual. "You want to eat, or you want to walk?"

"I've kind of lost my appetite right now," Aaron replied. "Can we walk and talk?"

"Sure."

Oliver's shoes sparkled in the midday sun. He would have buffed them this morning, his daily habits like clockwork. The shoe buffing would happen after his kilometre swim at the beach and jogging home for a black coffee. For once Aaron didn't care, because Oliver's clockwork precision had got his brother here exactly when he needed him.

Where to start? He cleared his throat and managed a stilted, "Thanks for coming at short notice."

"No problem, I was only editing a chapter of the book. It can wait. You sounded—" Oliver was choosing his words carefully.

"Completely fucking confused?"

"That'll do for starters." There was a smile in Oliver's voice. A kind one.

Aaron took a deep breath. Watched his feet move. One step in front of the other.

"The thing is, Alice and I have been, kind of... dating."

"Ah-ha."

"You guessed, right?"

"Mmm-hmm."

212

"Well, it's got complicated. There's this really bad thing going down at work, seriously messy stuff, which I guess I should tell you about as background..." Aaron paused. "So, anyway there's this woman—my boss's P.A." He felt Oliver stiffen and rushed on. "It doesn't involve me. Archie Bendt, my boss, seems to be having an affair with her and his wife turned up and..."

Oliver made an exclamation. Now the words came tumbling out. All the sordid details of the Archie-Lauren debacle, and then he struggled to find any words at all to explain his fight with Alice. It stung to all hell, reliving what she'd accused him of.

When he'd finished, Oliver stopped and swung round to face him. "So, I'm assuming you've enlightened Alice as to what really happened?"

Aaron ground to a halt, even though his feet wanted to keep on walking. He watched his shoe scuffing at the gravel. "I tried, but she wouldn't listen to me and then Carts—who, it would seem, also has a thing for her—came to find her and that kind of put a stop to it."

Should he explain the whole fake dating deal? The flirting? The friends with benefits? Not now, it would take too long.

He ran his fingers through his hair. Christ. Why did he feel so out of his depth? So *self-conscious*? Like a kid owning up to his first major crush.

"Well, that's fixable."

"Oh yeah?" Aaron's lip curled at Oliver's seeming lack of concern. "How?"

"Explain what actually happened, then tell her how you feel about her."

Aaron dug his hands into his pockets. "That's the problem, I don't know how I feel about her."

Oliver's dark eyes were boring into him. "The way you're acting, I'd say you've got a fair idea."

Aaron fisted his hands and said nothing.

"Okay, use me as a sounding board. What's going on inside you?"

Where to start? "I guess I think about her a lot. To be honest, I think about her all the freakin' time. I can't work properly, my billable hours are dropping, I keep getting distracted. Even going to the gym and running my arse off doesn't help. And I just want to spend time with her. *Shit*—I can't believe I'm owning up to this... and kiss her and... you know... the other stuff..."

"Yep. Sounds like you've got it bad."

"It's just a phase, right? It'll pass. And then what?" He stared past Oliver's shoulder to the city buildings silhouetted against a clear blue sky.

"And what if it doesn't?" Oliver said. "What if that feeling gets deeper and stronger, so all you want is to spend your life with her... what would you do then?"

Silence settled, as all-enveloping as the heat.

"I don't know." Aaron bowed his head and stared at his feet. After a long moment he asked, "Is that how you feel about Leonie?"

Oliver's voice lit up. "Hell, yeah."

"How do you do it? Like *maintain?*"

"Viagra, lots of Viagra." Oliver laughed. "Joking apart, you *have* maintained with Alice. You've maintained an incredible friendship with her for years... To be honest, I'm amazed how long it's taken you to realise you're in love with her."

Aaron's chin retracted. He blinked. "I'm not."

Oliver scoffed. "Okay, let's recap. Here's this couple, a guy and a girl who've enjoyed hanging out together *for more than five years*. Who share the same quirky oddball humour and ridiculous obsession with Monopoly, who have now realised they're unable to keep their hands off each other and when they have their first fight, one of them is so upset that he calls his much-despised older brother for advice?" Oliver mock-stroked his chin. "Let me see... Yep. Sounds like love to me."

A strange prickly sensation seemed to take over Aaron's body, and he nearly missed Oliver's next words.

"What's getting in the way, bro?"

"What do you mean?"

"Something's stopping you. From embracing this." By now the sun was beating down on their heads. Aaron was sweating. Even Oliver had a bead of perspiration on his lip.

"Why don't we go sit in the shade?" Oliver suggested.

They moved over and sat on a bench under a large ficus tree surrounded by a small patch of grass, an oasis amidst the city glass and concrete.

Oliver leaned forward, arms resting on his knees. "Sometimes I worry you haven't got over Mum's death."

Aaron stiffened. "What's that got to do with anything?"

"Maybe nothing." Another silence, both of them squinting against the sun. "Do you remember much about it?" Oliver asked finally.

Aaron shrugged. "Not really. Bits and pieces."

Bits and pieces he chose never to remember. Waiting on the edge of the playing fields as it got dark. Being hustled into a car by a grim-faced teacher. Uniformed police in the house, talking in hushed voices. Oliver huddled against the wall in the study, their dad, their big, strong dad, sobbing.

"Just fragments, you know, about the day… the funeral…" And how much he'd hated the world afterwards, how he'd wanted to destroy everything in it. Break Dad, break Oliver… how he couldn't focus on anything, and how it was so much better when he smoked dope because then he was mellow and fine… and—

"You numbed everything out," Oliver said gently.

Some bearded guy he'd been dragged to by Dad when his truancy got out of control; who'd tried to get him to open up, but he wouldn't, *couldn't*. So they'd given him pills instead.

Why was there a seismic lump in his throat? Aaron swallowed past it. "Changing schools helped," he muttered. A new school, a fresh start, slowly, slowly, feeling like he had a place in the world again.

"Things calmed down for you after that," Oliver said. "And then Dad met Andrea."

Aaron gave a weak laugh. "Yeah, everything kind of got sorted once Andrea came along."

"But did you?"

"Did I what?"

"Get sorted?"

"Of course I did."

"On the surface."

Anger flared. "Christ, Oliver, you're doing it again. The superior older brother crap." Aaron jumped up and started pacing the strip of lawn. He could sense Oliver's gaze following him.

"Yes, it's called *caring* about you, Aaron. And every time I show the slightest bit of interest, you jump down my bloody throat. Don't you get it? I actually want you to be happy. And frankly, Alice is the one woman I've always thought you could be happy with. Everyone sees it. Andrea, Dad, me. Even Gran before her memory went. You asked. I'm telling."

"Well maybe I'm not ready for this commitment shit. Maybe I'm not willing to give away my freedom."

"Or willing to risk it."

Aaron ground to a halt, heels digging into the turf as he yanked two buttons of his shirt undone. Sure, it was a hot day, but this heat was burning him up from the inside. "Risk what?"

Oliver said quietly, "If you don't love someone, there's no chance you'll lose them, is there?"

Aaron crumpled. Collapsed back on the bench and buried his head in his hands.

Oliver's arm came around his shoulders and hugged him hard, rough. Determined. "Mum would be so sad to think that you couldn't grab your chance at happiness because of some misplaced guilt."

Aaron dragged in a ragged breath. Blinked away the blurriness in his eyes. They sat like this, bound together by memories, shared grief, brotherhood. Something stirred in Aaron's chest. Ballooned out through his veins. A throb of hope... and fear... but this time the fear was different. It wasn't threatening to cut off his airways anymore.

"I don't have a clue how to do this stuff," he said finally.

"What stuff?"

"The girlfriend, boyfriend, commitment stuff."

"But you want to? With Alice, don't you?"

*Yes, yes, yes.* He wanted to dive into everything that was Alice, the apple blossom scent of her, her big doe eyes... that smile she had with her head tilted to one side. Her passion for musty old romance books. The way she fingered her hair behind her left ear. Always the left, because that's the way it fell... That weird little hum she made when she didn't know what to say, those damn sexy stupid slippers.

All of it.

All of *her.*

But all Aaron got out was a strangled, "Maybe."

Oliver scoffed loudly.

Aaron gave a lopsided grin in response. "How do I even start?"

"Tell her the truth. That you can't stop thinking about her; that you want to be with her all the time, that this is all new to you and you don't know what to do. And go from there. Just be you. Totally fucking terrified but wanting to make a go of it..."

Automatically Aaron's mouth opened to rebut all this, because... because... why? Because not feeling anything was an equation that added up to no risk. No pain. And no love either.

Hell, he'd played a part for so long, but now, could the real Aaron please stand up? The Aaron who wasn't afraid to feel. The Aaron who wasn't afraid to...

Fall.

In.

Love.

There, he'd let himself acknowledge those three little words. He was still here, still breathing, still alive.

Rising, his legs as wobbly as a newborn colt, Aaron adjusted his collar, picked up his jacket and swung it over his shoulder.

"You're right," he said, the sun warm on his back. "I need to tell her how I feel."

~

Rowena was either dead or had gone to ground. All day, her phone had zapped straight to message bank, and even taking into consideration the time difference, she should have replied by now.

Alice was mad at her, sure, but she didn't want Mum to be dead. That would be kind of horribly ironic. Find one parent and lose the other in the space of twenty-four hours.

Now it was nearly closing time and it felt like she had a pack of squawking parrots inside her head.

There were so many thoughts whirring around that a couple of times she'd been worried that she'd end up having another panic attack. The flippy tap-tap in quick succession of her heart had her hand flying to her chest. It should hardly surprise her. Her life had been turfed upside down and inside out.

Meanwhile, her own phone had pinged with messages all day.

Polly: *Why didn't you tell me you hate being called Munchkin?*

Carts: *r u ok?*

Andrea: *Hi Alice, either this Saturday or next Saturday suits me fine for making the flowers for Gran's cake. Let me know.*

Carts: *One word will do. Yes for ok. No for not ok.*

Polly: *I will never call you Munchkin again. Even if you beg me.*

Unable to bring herself to reply to any of them, Alice finally took the giant piece of wood that was attached to the staff loo key that was shared between their block of three shops and went and sat down on the toilet and made a list.

*7 REASONS TO PANIC*
    *1.I have a dad. Now what?*
    *2.Mum has lied to me my whole life.*
    *3.I have hurt Polly's feelings.*
    *4.Carts may have a crush on me.*
    *5.Mum could be dead.*
    *6.Aaron hasn't contacted me. I hate him.*
    *7.I think I have unresolved anger issues.*

After this she was calmer, if only because she had identified several plausible reasons for feeling she'd been transported into a weird parallel universe.

The rest of the afternoon, in between customers, Alice tried to piece together a picture of one half of her genes and what that meant for… Well, everything.

She'd found out the Beacham-Browns were landowners in Herefordshire going back to King James I. Henry had gone to a top-notch boarding school, where he was bullied; was bad at sports due to knee injuries (oh, how she empathised); and excelled at the Arts (her heart sang). At Cambridge he had started a number of literary societies. At the age of twenty-three he had his first gay liaison while doing his post-grad. He came out to his parents a year later. His father never accepted the fact and was estranged from him. Henry went on to lecture at Bath university before being offered a position at Cambridge. Currently he was writing a biography on Oscar Wilde, relating it to Victorian prejudices towards homosexuality. He'd recently married his partner of fifteen years, actor Gabriel West, who had just landed the part of Phileas Fogg in an upcoming remake of *Around the World in Eighty Days*.

Yes, she'd got some answers, lots of them, but they raised

more questions. Including the most important one: how had she been conceived?

Finally Alice closed up shop and left for the day. She'd just pocketed the key when a shadow stepped out of the doorway of *Quirks and Perks*, the uber-trendy gift shop next door.

Two flashes of intense blue, a broad chest almost skimming her breasts. A mouth she ached to kiss.

"God, Aaron, you scared me!" To hide her crazy heartbeat, she demanded, "Why didn't you just come into the shop like a normal person?"

He smirked. "Maybe because I'm not normal." When he saw she wasn't smiling, his jaw tightened and a pulse ticked on his temple. "Sorry, I didn't mean to scare you. I need to talk to you without having to dodge customers."

She couldn't answer. Aaron hijacked her senses—just one step and she would be in his arms... and despite everything, her knees went weak with lust.

She jerked as reality kicked her in the ribs. Was her memory that bad she'd just wiped out yesterday like it never happened? Miss Scandinavia's beautiful silky head had been resting on his chest. The same chest she'd lain on, blissed out after he'd made her come three times in a row and she'd returned the favour. Alice squared her shoulders and stomped away.

"Will you please listen, just for a minute?"

"One minute. Okay. Talk fast."

"Al, please don't do this! Are you trying to piss me off?"

*Nothing compared to how you've pissed me off. Bastardo.*

"Okay. Five minutes. Literally. That's how long before my bus arrives."

"Can't you catch the next one?"

She sighed heavily. "No, I'm very tired. I didn't sleep well."

"Because of us?"

"No. Something else. Much, much more important."

He looked felled.

They were at the bus stop now, and thankfully no-one else was waiting. Alice turned towards him, huddling her face into her scarf. Her mouth would not be available for any possible kiss-attack.

Aaron braced against the wind. It blew the blond hair off his forehead, making him look achingly young and suddenly lost. How she yearned to reach for him. She didn't, of course.

"Lauren. The woman at the pub with me. She's Archie's P.A."

"I know."

"Right. Well, I was packing up to come and join you guys when she and Archie came into the office. The vibe was sort of weird and *too* friendly, but I tried to ignore it and finish off because, despite what you might think, I did want to join you at the quiz night."

Alice jiggled on the spot. "Four minutes left."

"*Jesus*, okay." He sucked in some air. "Then I hear all this screaming. So I rush to where the commotion's coming from to find Miranda Bendt hitting Archie over the head and Lauren splayed across him like a human shield—well, the long and short of it is he's been having an affair with Lauren, probably since before I joined the company, his wife found out, the shit hit the fan, and Archie told me to get Lauren out of there before somebody got killed."

Alice tried to hide her shock. Archie cheating on the impeccable Miranda? Impossible to fathom. "That still does not explain why you were cuddling her," she grunted out from behind her scarf.

"I was *not* cuddling her. I took her to the pub because she needed to calm down; she told me all this shit about her life I really didn't want to hear, and then she fell on me."

Her chin jerked up. "Fell on you?"

"Well, her head did."

"And you were conveniently close enough for her head to fall on you."

"Not intentionally."

Alice sniffed; it was getting colder and her nose was going to run any moment. She yanked at her scarf, ready to go back into hiding. "I guess that shoots the family values out of the water, doesn't it?"

Aaron frowned. "Sorry?"

"With Trojan's. The 'Our reputation is built on family values' rhetoric. All that's been made a nonsense of now. Which means you really don't need a fake girlfriend anymore."

"W-what?"

"Well, they can't exactly hold it against you for being a player when Archie is fraternising with his P.A., can they?"

Aaron chewed at his lower lip.

"Therefore," Alice added with a brightness so sharp it made her teeth hurt, "we can call off the girlfriend thing. Guess we're quits on the flirting too."

"And the rest?" he asked softly, his eyes glinting in the evening light.

*Tap-tappity tap.* Her heart gave its irregular beat. She had to get out of here; she must not have a panic attack in front of Aaron. The new Alice didn't succumb to anxiety.

She glanced up and saw the bus and suddenly it all felt too hard. The enormity of everything piling in on her like the sky caving in. "Look," she gasped out, "something has happened in my life and—"

"Is it Carts?"

Her eyes rounded. "What? No. No. Not at all."

His features relaxed. "Tell me. Maybe I can help?"

The bus drew up. One of his fingers touched hers, trailing a line of fire up her arm. "Talk to me, Al."

He stepped closer and she almost swayed into him. How easy to just give in. The old Alice would. Except giving in to temptation would only be putting off the inevitable. Because if it wasn't now, with Lauren, it would be later, with someone else.

She lifted her chin. "I don't want to talk. I haven't even begun to process it myself."

He looked bewildered. "I have to see you. Soon." He sounded urgent, desperate almost.

"Come on, you love birds. Make your mind up. Are you on or off?"

Their heads jerked up in unison. The bus driver guffawed. "The bus. On or off?"

Alice ripped her hand away. "I'll call you. Tomorrow." His face turned up to her as she took the steps and waved her card at the machine. "We can go for a drink, a meal, there's something I need to—"

*Swooooshhh.* The bus doors slammed shut.

Alice stumbled along the aisle, her eyes swimming in tears, groping for a seat.

Thank goodness, there was one left. On the street side. She slumped into it as her glasses fogged up.

Either way, she wouldn't have to see Aaron standing there as the bus drove away.

# CHAPTER 18

*Tell her how you really feel—good one. Thanks, Oliver.*
Aaron found himself staring glumly after the departing bus. Alice had effectively dragged the rug out from under him. He reminded himself of one of those cartoon characters, feet pedalling so fast they turned into spinning wheels. Going nowhere fast. The past twenty-four hours churned inside his head as he strode off down the street.

Alice behaving like a ball of prickles towards him, surely that was significant? Hadn't he learned enough to know when a woman got angry it usually meant they were hiding a truckload of hurt feelings? The truth was, he'd never cared enough in the past to try and put things right. Now, wanting to put it right was tearing him apart.

Except, he reminded himself, she'd told him it had nothing to do with him. He racked his brains some more.

Whatever had stopped her sleeping, it was a big deal, something she couldn't—or wouldn't—discuss with him. Despite what she'd said, he couldn't dislodge the thought that maybe the big deal *was* Carts. Aaron's forehead squeezed. No, that was completely illogical. When he'd suggested something was going on between them, she'd looked genuinely surprised. And there was no point phoning Carts to find out. It had already caused a rift in their usually solid mateship bond. If this went on, he'd lose all his friends.

Hurting Alice, arguing with Carts, Miranda Bendt causing grievous bodily harm to Archie. Lauren falling for Archie's false promises. His bosses twisting his balls to get him to comply with their story.

What a fucked-up mess.

*You aspired to be Archie Bendt.*

Yowch!

The beautiful day had turned icy cold by now. The sky was clear, pricked with evening stars. Hands dug into his pockets, Aaron wrapped his jacket around himself and walked faster. He didn't want to be the next Archie Bendt.

He wanted to—what did he actually want to be? What kind of man? He was going to have to re-invent himself piece by piece like those Lego sets he'd been addicted to as a kid. He wished he could buy one ready to assemble. A kit for a man who treated people decently. A man capable of real feelings, or even—icy fingers curled around his spine—love. It still made him want to shut down, saying that word to himself. But he wasn't going to. He was going to breathe deeply and try to work out how to sort out this mess. Tomorrow he'd text Alice.

No, damn it. He'd text her right now. So what if it left his underbelly exposed?

Aaron wrenched his phone out of his pocket and typed in: *Can I see you after work tomorrow?* Paused, then with slow deliberate fingers added, *I miss you.*

No emoji. Just the words.

He pressed send.

～

*Ping.*

She would *not* look.

*Ping.*

Not under any circumstances.

Her phone could burn a hole in her bag, through her coat, sear the skin of her leg. She would give herself up to a closet full of boggarts before she'd check it.

Besides, it was probably only Carts responding to the "YES, ok" she'd texted him before she left the shop, to stop him from worrying.

Alice laid her head against the window of the bus and closed her eyes.

One day, this would stop hurting; it would be nothing more than a distant memory. She imagined herself walking through the cobbled streets of Cambridge—they had to be cobbled, didn't they?—her arm looped in her dad's, barely remembering that man she'd foolishly thought she was in love with back in Australia.

She needed to focus on the issue at hand: tracking down Mum and making her tell her how Henry Beacham-Brown had become her father.

Deep in thought, Alice nearly missed her stop. She got off the bus with an apology to the driver and trudged up her street. She found her key remarkably easily for once, and was just about to open the front door when a laugh bounced down the hallway and stopped her. It was a laugh that used to make her cringe as it bellowed out at school sports days and assemblies.

Rowena was home.

Her fingers flimsy as rubber bands, Alice fumbled to get the key in the lock, and didn't bother to close the door behind her when she belted up the wooden passage. Polly and Rowena sat at the kitchen table, a teapot between them. Rowena's signature fuzz of strawberry blonde peppered with grey was crammed haphazardly on top of her head. Her large pale grey eyes rose to meet Alice's, and it seemed for a moment that time stood still. Then Rowena's face crumpled like she might just burst into tears. She jumped up and held her arms open. "Darling girl, I'm back."

Alice felt herself crumpling too. Without conscious thought she moved into Rowena's embrace.

Her mum's arms, always so strong, trembled as they tightened around her.

Polly got up. "I'll go and close the front door. Leave you two to talk."

Once they were alone, Alice sank down on a chair and flung her bag onto the table.

"I've been phoning all day," she said, trying to keep her voice calm. "Why didn't you answer?"

"I was on the plane, sweetie."

"What about in Singapore? You could at least have messaged to tell me you were on your way home."

"My battery ran out."

"You were avoiding me, Mum."

Rowena had the grace to cringe a little. "I'm sorry, darling. Cup of tea?"

"No, Mum. I want you to tell me about my father. Everything. No excuses. No more lies."

"Goodness, sweetie, I've never heard you be so... assertive."

Alice's eyebrows shot up. "*Demanding,* you mean?"

Rowena looked perplexed.

"You wrote that you'd probably have told me a long time ago if I'd only been 'more demanding'. Remember?" Alice said flatly. Rowena didn't get how her breezy approach to life could hurt people. Honestly, it was a wonder their relationship hadn't come to grief years ago except, of course, Alice had never chosen to rock the boat. Right now she was prepared to sink it to get to the truth.

Rowena was flapping around, refilling the kettle, pulling out teabags and another cup from the cupboard.

"Mum, stop. Sit down. Talk to me. How did you and Henry meet?"

Rowena let out a gusty sigh. Slumping down at the table, she pulled a tortoiseshell comb out of her hair and dug it in higher up her head. "You've read everything I sent you?"

"About a dozen times. And searched him on the internet. But that tells me nothing about *you* and Henry. There are gaping holes you need to fill in here."

Rowena picked up her teacup and rolled it around in her hands. They shared the same hands. Pointy fingertips, small neat nails all with half-moons. Otherwise, like always, it was hard to see the resemblances between them. Now at least, Alice knew where her looks came from.

"We met soon after I got to Cambridge for my post-grad year. It wasn't exactly love at first sight. To be honest, I thought Henry was a bit scrawny." Rowena laughed. Alice didn't join in; as far as she was concerned, Henry looked perfect. "Anyway, it took us a little while, but we became friends. I thought him a snob initially with his super posh voice, but the poor darling was just shy. I think he found this loud Australian woman rather overwhelming, then intriguing. But, oh… when I got to know Henry he was so eloquent, so quirky and funny. God, we laughed!" Rowena's eyes shone at the memories. "And no-one knew more about nineteenth century English novelists than Henry. We'd run poetry readings. Keats, and Byron, and twentieth century greats like Sylvia Plath. I guess you'd say I became his muse. Before long I was head over heels in love with him. Not just his mind but all of him. Loving Henry consumed my life."

Alice's heart lurched. She knew exactly how that felt.

Rowena grimaced. "You know me, darling. Never one to hold back. I informed him I'd fallen for him—I had to; it was eating me up. When Henry told me he thought he was probably gay, I was utterly devastated. But I accepted it. What else could I do?"

For the first time since the Henry-package had landed in her hands, Alice felt a surge of sympathy for Rowena. "I don't get it. Henry being gay… how on earth did I happen?"

"Things aren't always black and white, sweetie… particularly where sex is concerned…" Rowena nipped at her lower lip, her cheeks even rosier than usual. "It was at a May ball that you happened. Do you know what a May ball is?"

Alice shook her head

"Every year after exams, Cambridge and Oxford hold balls, sort of like formals, only better. Each college has one. Everyone dresses up to the nines. It's all there. Live bands. Champagne, feasting all night. The fact they happen in June is neither here nor there…"

Rowena was stalling, Alice could tell. "Go on," she prompted, impatience building.

Rowena huffed out another sigh. "Henry invited me as his partner. We got pretty sozzled. And I dared him to test his hypothesis. So we kind of, well, *did it*, in a meadow on the banks of the River Cam as the sun rose. I remember the grass was very itchy. And…" Rowena stopped, took a noisy slurp of tea. "I was so impetuous and silly. Contraception didn't occur to me for a second. I guess I hoped, you know, that I'd be the one to change his mind. But for Henry it confirmed that women were not where his passions lay. I never let on how hurt I was. Soon after, he came out to his parents. It was a huge shock to them—such conservative people, very prominent in society. The Beacham-Browns were *Honourables*, which is just off from being a viscount or some such." Rowena clunked her cup down in her saucer, filled it from the teapot again. "To say Henry's father didn't take kindly to the news was an understatement. He disowned him. It was horrible for Henry. *Horrible.* So when I found out I was pregnant, I decided not to tell Henry. He was going through too much already."

"Why didn't you get rid of me then?"

Rowena looked aghast. "My precious baby girl. It never even crossed my mind. My post-grad year had finished about the time I found out, so I fled back to Perth. Henry wrote to me, but after a few months I told him I had to sever all contact because I was still in love with him. It was the truth, but equally I couldn't tell him about you. It would have complicated everything. Then your nanna was diagnosed with cancer. I had to focus on helping her and Pops; keeping all our heads above water."

"I guess it must have been hard," Alice conceded. Both her nan and pop passing before Alice even remembered them would have been a huge sadness, though Rowena rarely mentioned it. Then starting up the Book Genie when Alice was barely out of nappies, well, despite the major fibbing, she had to admire her mum.

Rowena shrugged. "I was young. I got on with it. I tried to forget all about Henry. I pretended to everyone, Nan and Pops included, that you were the result of a one-night stand."

Alice felt her lips twitch. "Andrew from Basingstoke."

"Mmm. So, of course, when you started to ask questions, it was easy to keep up the lie." Rowena gave a little shrug. "By then I think I'd almost convinced myself of it too. It's amazing —if you do it enough, you start to believe your own lies. Now, darling, I'm not saying I'm proud of it. None of it. As time went on and I saw Henry in you more and more; the way you smiled, your poor little knees that kept getting injured. Your eyes—" Rowena sighed heavily. "The passion you have for the Brontës and Jane Austen, oh gosh, it tore me into shreds."

"You never showed it, Mum. Ever."

Rowena waved her hands in the air. "Ta-da, Rowena Montgomery, Mistress of emotional disguise."

Huh, like someone else Alice knew. She hustled thoughts of Aaron into a dark corner of her mind and slammed the door. There were parallels opening up between her and Mum that she didn't need to investigate right now.

"What made you decide to go find Henry? Without telling me?"

"I just thought if Henry was unhappy about being a father and I'd already told you, the pain of him rejecting you would be too much for you to bear."

"You don't know that, Mum."

"I know, darling. I *assumed*. I always assume, don't I?"

The truth hung between them, acknowledged but unspoken. The assumption Alice would work in the Book Genie after she graduated. The assumption she would be happy for swathes of her salary to be funnelled back into the shop, the assumption she would keep on living at home with Rowena.

"It wasn't hard to find Henry," Rowena continued after a moment's silence. "To be honest, I'd been internet stalking him for years. When I turned up, he was so happy to see me. And then, oh goodness—" She sandwiched her cheeks between her palms. "When I told him about you, he cried. Openly wept, poppet. He is so happy to be a father, and so is Gabe—by default."

"Gabe?"

"His husband."

"Oh, yes, the actor."

"I have a letter from Henry for you in my luggage," Rowena added, almost as an afterthought.

Alice was about to demand it—yes, *demand*—when Rowena's next comment floored her. "He's here. In Australia."

Her eyes flew wide. "Henry's in Perth? *Now?*" she almost squealed, jumping up from her chair.

"Not quite. He's the keynote speaker at a conference in Sydney. But he's planning to visit Perth on the way back to meet you."

Black dots swam in front of Alice's eyes. Totally overwhelmed, all she could do was sink back into her chair. "Oh, god, when?"

"On Sunday."

Only five days from now. Trip-trippity trip went her heart. Alice's head nose-dived between her legs. *Breathe deep and slow, in for two, out for three...*

"Oh, sweetie, has all this started an attack?"

Alice got it under control. Brought her head out from between her knees and pressed a hand to her breastbone.

She knew what she had to do. "I'm fine. But I don't want Henry coming to Perth."

Rowena looked shocked. "Darling—why ever not?"

"No offence, Mum, but I need to see my father on my own terms first. Without you there." Resolve fortified Alice's spine, one vertebra at a time, until she was sure she was sitting taller. "I'll fly to Sydney to meet him."

Rowena's jaw dropped. "But you're terrified of flying."

"There's a lot of things I've been terrified of, Mum." Alice got up and placed her hands flat on the tabletop. "But as from now that's changing." She met Rowena's saucer-stare. "I'm going to Sydney to meet Henry. End of story."

"Oh, oh, oh. Goodness." Rowena was pushing threads of wiry hair off her face. "This is all so *new*."

Alice quirked a smile. "Funny that. It's all new for me, too." She got up to search for her laptop. If she waited a second more her resolve might slip. "Can you bring me Henry's letter as soon as you unpack?" As she walked away, she heard Rowena calling out in a perplexed tone, "Darling, what's all this glass doing on the floor?"

Alice's smile spread, bunching her cheeks. "I really have no idea."

Later, she'd tell Rowena the truth. And she wouldn't wait twenty-six years to do so.

～

"Have you noticed the really tense vibe here the last couple of days?" Hamish said as he got into the elevator next to Aaron.

Aaron eyed his reflection in the strip of mirrored glass next to the elevator control panel. Features drawn and tired. He scraped a hand through his hair but it refused to fall in its usual languid fashion over his forehead.

Crap. He didn't want to meet Alice looking less than his best.

He shrugged. "Too busy to notice, frankly." He hoped he

sounded casual and disinterested enough to put Hamish off the scent.

Clearly he hadn't, because Hamish said next, "Heard any more on Lauren's disappearance?"

"Nope."

"The word is family stuff. Maybe she's got boyfriend issues. Must be bad to keep her away from work, though."

Aaron pulled at his cufflinks, the Batman ones Alice had bought him for his birthday. He hoped she'd be impressed he was wearing them. "Could be a sick parent."

"Maybe." Hamish's pleasant face broke into a smile. "Anyway, how's Alice?"

Aaron felt a daft smile hijacking his features. "She's good. Catching up with her now, actually."

She'd sent a curt "ok" to his text about grabbing a bite to eat tonight, with no acknowledgment to his "Miss you" comment of yesterday, then proceeded to floor him by suggesting the food markets on Nevis Street. The markets, with their plethora of stalls and cramped together tables, tended to be a place Alice avoided. Not the best arena to talk, either, but for once he wasn't going to argue the toss. He just needed to see her.

The lift pinged at the ground floor.

Hamish flicked up the collar of his jacket. "Say hi from me. We'll catch up soon, eh?"

"Sure." Aaron resisted the urge to cross his fingers for luck. Next he'd be trying to locate a black cat and bribing it to run across his path. Oliver hadn't mentioned the strange personality changes that overtook you when you found yourself in this L-word situation.

Saying his farewells to Hamish, he resisted the urge to bound down the road, tempered his pace to a brisk walk and headed for the markets.

Alice was waiting outside the entrance, neatly buttoned into her coat. Glasses on. Hair tied back, her mouth as buttoned up as her coat.

His heart sank.

Where was he supposed to start? Especially when it appeared he'd had a charm bypass in the last few days; all his usual lines had completely dried up on him.

"Hi, sorry I'm late."

"You're not. I was early." She stared at his left ear.

*Awkward.* Now what? He ducked his head and gave her a peck on the cheek. Alice retracted her head and he drew back, frowning. Small talk was probably the safest bet to start off with.

"What do you fancy, Indian, Chinese, Thai?"

They deliberated for what seemed an agonisingly long time, but finally he chose Vietnamese and Alice decided on The Raw Rage. Maybe the title was fitting for how she felt about him at present.

Seated at a small table away from the other few Tuesday-night diners, he asked, "So what's the big thing you wouldn't tell me about yesterday?"

She stared down at her plateful of green leaves with the odd piece of capsicum and sunflower seeds thrown in. "I've found my dad."

"Is he a Scottish film director?" he joked. By the look she flashed him, jokes were not in order. But at least she didn't have a thing going with Carts. He wanted to punch the air— probably not the moment for a testosterone-fuelled gesture, either. He forced himself to sit dead still and listen.

"No. He's a university professor. At Cambridge."

Now his mouth went slack. "Seriously?"

She nodded, nibbling on a piece of greenery.

"What happened? I mean, how did he find you?"

"He didn't."

"You found him?"

"Nope."

Aaron frowned, perplexed. "What then?"

"Mum," said Alice, and he saw the tiniest quirk at the corners of her lips. "Seems her trip to England was about a lot more than foraging for old books."

Half an hour later, Aaron was realising he enjoyed listening to Alice. Not in the way they'd talked before, the easy camaraderie of long-term friends. This was different, more *intimate* somehow, like he was listening with his whole body. He had a sudden fantasy of snuggling on the sofa with her, a fire burning, her head resting on his shoulder as she told him about her day. Found he'd got a little lost in the scenario, and had to backtrack. "Sorry, did you just say you're going to fly somewhere? As in a plane?"

She nodded. "Yep. I'm flying to Sydney to meet Henry. This weekend."

"On your own?"

"All on my own."

"Wow!"

A huge smile cracked across her face and a bolt of something delicious shot down his spine. Glasses, no make-up, hair tied back: she was beyond beautiful when she smiled this way.

He wanted a zillion more smiles like this one directed his way.

By the time Alice had finished explaining, Aaron was fidgeting. It was amazing, mind-blowing in fact, that she'd found her father after all this time, but right now he needed to set things straight between them. Needed to start the herculean task of telling her how he felt.

They'd finished eating and Alice was making noises about leaving.

Desperation clawed at his chest, rose up his throat. "Al, are we okay? As in, you and me?"

She stilled, then shrugged.

"Have we—I mean, did what I tell you yesterday clear up the misunderstanding?"

Alice was staring at his left ear again. "I suppose so."

"You don't sound convinced."

"What are you trying to say, Aaron?"

"I guess—er." He gulped in a mouthful of air. "I think I'm

trying to say I—um—like you." He laughed too loudly. "But you know that, right?"

"Yes, I know that," she said slowly. "You've always *liked* me."

"Well, since we started, you know, the *benefits* thing, maybe you could say it's a bit more than like."

"What does that mean?" Her face was flushed. He was sure his was too, by the heat that was radiating out of him. This was torture. How did you tell someone after years of being friends that you were a mess of badly fitting parts because of them? That those parts had been put in some kind of blender, whizzed around and put back inside you completely differently—so differently that you were finding it hard to recognise who you even were anymore.

How in fuck's name were you supposed to explain any of it?

"I mean... I—*like you* in the sense of... if... you wanted to continue the benefits thing for —um—longer, then I would be up for that."

She jerked back like he'd made to hit her.

The nuances of the term "foot in mouth" were beginning to sink in when she replied coolly, "Thank you, Aaron. I'm flattered."

He shoved a hand through his hair. "That came out wrong."

"On the contrary, it probably came out exactly right," she said. God, you could tell she had aristocratic British genes in her.

"Al—" He tried to reach for her but she snatched her hand back.

"Actually, I have a confession to make too. I've decided to turn over a new leaf," she continued icily. "I've promised myself not to behave like Rowena, not to lie and disseminate. To be scrupulously up front and honest henceforward." Where in hell's name was she going with this? With a toss of the head, Alice looked him squarely in the eye. "So, Aaron, since we're baring our souls to each other, here's my take on things. I've enjoyed it too. The whole fake dating thing, flirting practice—the benefits arrangement. It's been very nice, all of it. I've learned a lot; some wonderful new positions, found out what butt plugs are, even. But I don't want to continue with it." She paused and his eyes fell on her breasts rising and falling sharply.

"Why not?" he croaked out.

"Because I've a lot more than 'liked' you for a very long time."

Aaron's brows creased. "I'm not sure I understand."

Her head bowed and he found himself staring at her neat parting. Slightly to one side of her head. An achingly sweet little wisp of chestnut had escaped, and she tucked it around the back of her ear.

"Do you remember meeting me?"

"Yes. Of course." He laughed nervously. "A girl going blue in the face behind the lecture theatre is not easily forgotten." Wrong again, if that flash of a sad smile was anything to go by.

"When I looked up and saw you, and you talked me down from my panic and counted with me and gave me your phone number and said any time I needed to talk… I knew… I kind of…" She stopped abruptly, her throat moving like it was hard to swallow. "Not *kind* of—I absolutely did fall in love with you."

"You fell in love with me?"

"Yes. And I've been in love with you ever since."

He stared at her, his mouth dropping open.

Alice had been in love with him for *five years!*

And great big doofus that he was, he'd never realised. Never even thought… all the times… Christ… all those times he'd taken advantage of her generosity, dossed on her sofa, eaten her food, got her to hide his keys so he wouldn't drive drunk and borrowed towels to cover his naked morning glory… All the times he'd hurled expletives at her when she'd whipped Mayfair and Park Lane from under his nose; the tips he'd asked for on how to nicely extricate himself from this woman, that woman.

He groaned. "Oh god, Alice. No." Her eyes widened behind her glasses. "Not, like no bad, no, I mean—"

He was flailing wildly for words as she sprang up, hands clenched tightly at her sides. "I get it, Aaron. I get it. You're about fun and frivolity and three months maximum. But the problem is I'm not that kind of person. I'm much more like Rowena than I thought—a one guy for life kind of person. And the trouble is, you're not the guy to be having 'for life' feelings for. "

He winced. He'd never realised how being called out on that could cut so deep—when you actually cared about the person saying it. "I think I could be—"

She sucked in an audible breath, her eyes suddenly blazing dark behind her glasses. "*Think* isn't good enough for me anymore, Aaron." She bit her lip and looked down as if trying to compose herself.

A hundred and one words formed inside him, but none of them seemed capable of making it to his lips before Alice continued, "So, I'll say what *I* think, shall I? I think it would be best if we don't see each other for a while."

He wanted to shout, "*No, no, no. I don't* think, *I* know. *It's you I want. It's only ever been you.*" But the problem was he had no track record. No evidence. The enormity of the task floored him. How did you compare five weeks to five years? As a lawyer, he knew the truth was unequivocal. Guilty as charged. He had been a superficial, commitment-phobic jerk.

And he didn't deserve her love. Not even her little finger's worth.

"H-how long are you talking about?" he managed finally, lamely out of dry lips.

Alice shrugged. "However long it takes for me to see you and not love you. To only 'like you'. Better still, to be completely indifferent to you. I'm going home now." She raised her hand as he made to get up. "And no, I don't need you to come with me. I'm absolutely fine without you."

Helplessly, he watched as she weaved her way through the tables, ponytail bobbing down her back until she disappeared onto the busy street.

Absolutely fine without him.

# CHAPTER 19

"*Please return to your seats and fasten your seatbelts as we begin our descent into Sydney Airport.*"

Alice guessed a quick victory dance along the aisle wouldn't be allowed. Besides, they weren't safely on the ground yet; she'd heard take-off and landing were the riskiest times.

Still, her heart swelled with triumph, because she'd almost done it.

She beamed up at the air hostess collecting the rubbish. "This is my first ever flight."

The woman smiled back. "I hope you enjoyed it."

"Loved it."

It was true. At take-off the last vestiges of anxiety had vanished as adrenaline whooshed through her body. Her back flattened against the seat, the engine roared in her ears like a dragon and instead of fear all she'd felt was exhilaration. Sure, the online course she'd found, "Flying Without Fear", had done a lot to help these past few days, as had Polly's pep talks. (Even if Polly was handling her like a new and strange species, possibly at risk of biting.)

In contrast, Mum had definitely *not* helped. She'd fussed around at the airport, hovering while Alice checked in until Alice was completely discombobulated. She'd sighed with relief as she'd watched Rowena's tie-dyed skirt disappear, half convinced Mum would re-enter through another door and stow away in some unsuspecting passenger's luggage. Rowena was deeply disappointed not to be there when Alice met Henry for the first time. And while Alice got that, she and Henry had a lifetime to catch up on.

Rowena owed her that much.

*"Cabin crew, please be seated for landing."*

Alice closed her eyes, let the downward pull flow through her stomach into her legs. When the wheels touched down, she couldn't help digging her heels in like she was hitting the brakes. She guessed it didn't hurt to give the pilot a bit of help.

And then they were taxiing in.

*Hooray!*

But when she arrived in the terminal, the vastness of it, and the people milling in all directions, was more overwhelming than she'd expected. Her breath quickened. A man stepped forward from the crowd; the words "Alice Montgomery" bobbing on a board in front of her eyes.

Alice stepped back in surprise. "I—I wasn't expecting to be met."

The man smiled. "Professor Beacham-Brown arranged our chauffer service to pick you up."

"Oh," she said, her chest ballooning with pride. "How nice."

She was due to meet Henry at 7 p.m. As she finished checking in at the five-star hotel, Alice realised that was only one hour from now. Henry was staying in the same venue for the conference. They'd had a short phone conversation last night, their first ever, somewhat surreal and stilted as they discussed the arrangements. Mum had been right; Henry *did* have a very posh voice—one notch down from royalty posh. Alice found herself musing over the term "plum in the mouth" after they'd hung up, wondering whether elocution lessons really did involve putting pieces of fruit into children's mouths. Was there something significant about a plum or would an apricot or even a cherry do just as well? Maybe she'd experiment some time. And then she'd smiled to herself; this was clearly a displacement activity to stop herself thinking about the enormity of meeting Henry.

In her room now, she unpacked her carry-on bag—she was only here for three days, she didn't need much. Put her toothbrush in the bathroom. Rubbed the luxury bath towel against her cheek, then padded back into her suite and hurled herself backwards onto the bed.

And that did it.

A lightning flash of throwing herself onto another bed, her skirt riding up her legs, arms reaching towards the most beautifully ripped male torso she'd ever set eyes on, and—

NOT NOW!

Not ever again.

A wounded little sound pierced the quiet. Startled, she realised it was her. She bounced off the bed and started pacing, nibbling at her thumb. She'd done so well until now. Was it really only three days ago she'd told Aaron that she'd loved him all these years? Every time she'd recalled the shock on his face, the sound of his horrified rebuttal, she'd flushed it out like a ferret chasing out a rabbit from its burrow.

She pressed her trembling fingers into her eyes. Admittedly she'd allowed herself the bitter satisfaction of her grief that night, sobbed into her pillow for literally hours before falling into an exhausted sleep. Which meant she'd had to wear sunglasses to breakfast.

"Are you all right, sweetie?" Rowena had asked as she stirred a pot of porridge at the stove.

"Migraine headache," she'd mumbled into her cup of tea.

Later that day, Polly had appeared in her bedroom doorway and said, "It wasn't a migraine. Rowena gets migraines. You don't. Do you want to debrief yet?"

"No. Thanks very much." Alice tried not to be snappy; things still weren't back to normal since the Munchkin episode. The Henry thing had been hard on Polly, too. Of course Polly was happy for her but when she'd given her a congratulatory hug, Alice thought she heard a little sniffle; fathers were a fraught subject for Polly.

And as for the other problem... No, she emphatically did not need to talk about it. All she had to do was banish any thoughts of bright blue eyes, a flash of blond hair, that panty-melting smile, those wickedly clever fingers—

Alice dashed into the bathroom, turned the shower full blast onto cold, ripped her clothes off and ducked under the jets.

Sometimes extreme problems required extreme solutions.

An hour later she sat sipping a glass of sparkling mineral water at the hotel bar. In her pocket was Henry's letter, which she'd more or less pleated into a fan the amount of times she'd folded it. It was short, succinct, beautiful prose that highlighted his surprise and delight at finding out he was a father. He'd said that despite teaching the written word for more than a quarter of a century, all words had utterly deserted him at the gravity and honour of the role he now found himself in. Her eyes filled up every time she read it.

What if she disappointed him? If they had nothing to say to each other?

And then she lifted her head and there he was.

Small, neat, with a purposeful stride, making his way across the marbled floor. His posture was upright, and yet... that slight downward tilt of his chin belied his step, as if Henry Beacham-Brown was both sure of his place in the world and wanted to escape from it.

Her heart felt almost painful with the emotions swirling around.

This perfect stranger who, in some place deep inside her, she'd known her whole life.

Alice stood up and reached out her hand as he reached out

his. A warm firm grasp slid over hers and there was a moment of self-deprecating laughter from both of them, then Henry's head bobbed forward and he kissed her cheek.

She'd wondered earlier if he would hug her, should she hug him, but as he stood back and smiled, this felt enough. Enough for now, anyhow.

"Alice." The way he said her name made it sound almost like "Ell-iss". "Shall we sit?" Henry waved a hand at the chairs in a sweeping motion. She noticed the wedding band on his left hand and thought of Gabe—her stepfather, she guessed. There was so much new information to take in her brain resembled a super-charged bouncy ball. Her search on Gabe had been much less extensive, but quite exciting. She hadn't realised he'd had a part in *Downton Abbey* and she was planning on a rerun binge just to watch him.

Henry flicked back his jacket as he sat, his movements neat and measured. She wondered if his knees were okay. They seemed to be as he crossed them with ease and then said, "Where to begin?"

Alice picked up her glass and mumbled something about a whole lifetime being a long time to catch up on.

The waiter came and Henry ordered a gin and tonic and asked her what she would like, but she stuck with her mineral water, for now. She couldn't afford to go fuzzy and miss a beat of what they shared.

"I think you do resemble me," Henry said after a long moment, his eyes behind his glasses searching her face. "As much as one can tell how one looks, of course, which is always difficult. The mirror only reflects so much." He made a face, his mouth turned down self-deprecatingly. "Ah, my dear, I'm at risk of talking gibberish. It's not every day a man gets to meet the daughter he never knew he had." He leaned back in his chair. "How have you been all this time? Seems woefully inadequate, doesn't it?"

Alice smiled so hard her jaw hurt. "Maybe we should start

with something current, like your keynote address, and work our way backwards. Oscar Wilde, I love Oscar Wilde." She was gushing, but that was to be expected. Henry was so amazingly clever. "Tell me about that?"

Henry looked relieved. "Yes. A man ahead of his time."

"Aren't you writing his biography at present?" If she pretended she was discussing books with a customer, she could do this just fine.

"Indeed. It has been a labour of love." He looked like he'd be quite happy to dive into this subject, then pulled himself up short. "No, Alice. Don't start me on Oscar Wilde. He can wait. This is about you and I, and we must not waste a precious moment of it." Alice's heart melted at the warmth in his voice. "Your mother says you have a passion for English literature. You studied it at university? First-class honours I believe?"

She nodded, feeling herself growing rosy-cheeked with pride.

"A woman after my own heart, what a delightful coincidence!" When he laughed, his laugh had a lovely warm timbre and an infectious undertone, like he could be quite mischievous once you got to know him.

Henry's drink arrived. He stirred it gently with the swizzle stick and picked it up. His hands, fine-boned and long-fingered, shook noticeably as he put the glass to his lips.

Did Henry have an anxiety problem? Surely not. He gave lectures to hundreds of students, spoke at conferences around the world. Stood up at gay rights rallies, had been interviewed on television and radio, even made regular appearances on a British book review program. No, he couldn't have.

"Have you ever had a panic attack?" The words blurted out of her mouth before she could stop them.

Henry drew the glass from his lips, his expression surprised… and then, relieved.

"Oh, yes, they've plagued me for years."

"Do you still?"

Henry put his glass down. "Not exactly. I can get palpitations when I'm nervous."

"Feeling like your heart is tripping over itself?"

Henry nodded, grimaced. "Ghastly things."

"Oh, I know," she answered with feeling.

He gave her a look of sympathetic understanding. "You too, then?"

"Yes. Mum has never had one. So the first time I experienced one she didn't know what to do. She thought I had some strange neurological problem. She took me to all sorts of people to try and cure me. The problem was so many things terrified me, even the idea of things. Witches that might peer in through the bedroom curtains if I left a crack open. Goblins under the bed."

Henry laughed. "Dust mote demons."

Alice blinked across at him. "Sorry?"

"Invisible creatures that lived in dust motes. Some were good, some evil but I never knew which were which because when the sun shone there were so many of them waiting to pounce if you put a foot wrong. I think it was my own variation of A.A. Milne's poem: *And the little bears growl to each other, 'He's mine, as soon as he's silly and steps on a line.'*"

Without even thinking, Alice finished, "*—and some of the bigger bears try to pretend that they came round the corner to look for a friend.*"

Henry grinned with pleasure. "I was five at the time, so I could be forgiven for thinking there were evil creatures hiding in the barn of an old house we lived in. My mother, a frightfully unimaginative woman, was unable to reassure me. Luckily, I had a very good nanny with a great many variations on killing dust mote demons by stealth."

Now they were both laughing. Shared neuroses, it seemed, were a wonderful ice-breaker.

After that their conversation flowed easily about all manner of things, from *Winnie the Pooh*, and how Alice was Eeyore according to Polly, and Polly was Tigger. And her favourite subject, the Brontës, of course. Henry insisted Alice come to his keynote address to find out his take on Oscar's life. Finally, the waiter told them their table was ready in the restaurant.

As they sat down their phones dinged simultaneously with a message. Their eyes met.

"Rowena."

"Mum."

"She's awfully cut-up not to be here," Henry said with real affection in his voice.

Alice's lips quirked. "I know. It must be unbearable for her. She has the worst FOMO in the world at the best of times, let alone…"

Henry inclined his head, shook out his napkin and laid it neatly on his lap. "And you and I—what's the term I heard the other day—?" His face lit up. "That's right, JOMO. Joy of missing out."

"Oh yes." Alice rolled her eyes. Great big missing pieces were being slotted into place. "Was Mum like that when you met her?"

"Exuberant, you mean?"

"I guess," Alice answered. Overbearing would probably sound too mean-spirited.

"She was the absolute life and soul of every party." Henry's features softened as if recalling happy times. "She'd breeze into a crowd of us earnest young students discussing Sartre in hushed voices and shout, 'Forget Sartre, what about Simone de Beauvoir?' and suddenly everything would get lively and interesting. She was the one who suggested the three Ps Club."

"What was that?"

"Poetry, Philosophy and Pimm's. Best summer of my life. Reading and talking along the banks of the River Cam, Pimm's in hand. The world was our oyster back then."

Henry looked at her, suddenly serious. "You need to know I loved your mother. Very dearly. I still do. But I wasn't made to love her the way she wanted me to."

Alice fussed with her own napkin. "Obviously she's told me a bit."

"Of course," Henry said without any sign of embarrassment. "I hope you will forgive her for not telling you the truth."

Alice was silent. She would. In time. But there was a hefty accumulated debt here. "I will, Henry, it's just all very new. How about you, have you forgiven her?"

"I could never be angry with your mother. She helped me through the worst period of my life. She told you about that, I presume?"

"The way your parents…" Alice trailed off, not wanting to get her facts wrong.

"Disowned me?" It was a question that held its own answer.

She nodded, placed her napkin neatly on her lap just as Henry had done. "She said when you came back from meeting with them, she couldn't bring herself to tell you she was pregnant."

Henry looked surprised. "Oh, but she was there. With me. When I told my parents."

Alice's eyes rounded.

"She didn't tell you that?"

"No." More omissions. Would she ever be able to trust Rowena again?

As if Henry read her tightening features, he said gently, "Your mother is a good woman, Alice. She may have been misguided in not telling us, but her heart is as big as an ocean. Even when I'd dashed her hopes, she insisted on coming with me to tell my parents. They had always assumed that Rowena was my girlfriend. They didn't approve, naturally." Henry rolled his eyes. "I mean, a girl from the Antipodes, god forbid. You'd think she'd just got off a convict ship. However, that was better than having to swallow the unpalatable truth that their only son was homosexual."

They stopped talking as their food arrived. As the waiter

left, Henry resumed. "I think my father would have set the hounds on me but for the fact your mother stood up to him. She was amazing. A lioness. She let him know what a bigot he was, how he didn't deserve me as his son." His expression went distant for a second. "I will never forget it—how she stayed with me afterwards, helped me through the toughest few weeks of my life... and then..." Henry snapped his fingers in the air. "Gone. She went home to Australia. I wrote copious letters. Finally, she broke off all contact. I had to respect her choice, even though I sent her Christmas cards for years. I assumed she'd moved on. I was sad, but the strength her actions had instilled in me never left me. It gave me the courage to let the world know I was gay, which, when you're in an establishment like Cambridge, is not the easiest of things, believe me. Eventually I learned to shout it from the rooftops. Well,"—he laughed—"maybe shouting isn't quite my style. I just knew I never wanted another young person to go through what I did. But still, it happens..." Henry shook his head, his brows drawn tight. "Even now, it happens... the prejudice, the lack of acceptance."

"Did you speak to your father again, before he died?" Alice asked quietly.

"When he was very sick we made peace of a sort. It wasn't exactly what one would call cathartic—there was no deathbed reunion, no 'I love you, my boy'. No apology. He was a product of his generation, I get that. But we said our farewells." His face brightened. "And Mother and I are good friends now. She adores Gabe. I think once she was out from under my father's shadow she could be more the person she really is. A bit of a strange bird, but basically a jolly good soul."

"Do I have aunts and uncles?"

"You have an aunt. My sister, Hilary. Five years my senior. She's married to a pig farmer in Wiltshire and throws pots." He laughed. "Not literally. She's a potter. Her daughter, your first cousin, Felicity, is as close as I thought I'd ever get to having my own child. She's a teacher. But now there's you..." Henry's face creased into delightful upward lines as he smiled across at her. "And here we are!"

"Here we are." Alice felt a lump in her throat. As they both raised their glasses in a toast, she added, "Perhaps we should text Mum back. She'll be wondering what on earth is happening."

Henry got up, placed his napkin on the table. "We'll send her a photo of us at dinner, shall we?" He winked. "Make her a teeny bit jealous." As the waiter came back with their drinks, he asked, "Would you mind taking a shot of my daughter and I? Her mother is expecting it."

He came and leaned over her chair, his hand gently resting on her shoulder, their heads close together.

On a whim, Alice let her hand creep up and felt the warm, reassuring squeeze of Henry's fingers around hers.

The camera flashed. The waiter showed them the results. Two slightly startled smiles. Light reflecting off two pairs of glasses.

Her and Henry. Two peas in a pod.

Later, as they said goodnight at the elevator, Henry said, "Having you at my keynote tomorrow will give me courage."

"Do you still worry about talking in public?"

"Often. But one learns to manage these things. The things that do not kill us make us stronger."

Alice nibbled her lip and nodded. There was so much truth in that. It had taken two very huge events in quick succession— one heart-lifting, the other heart-breaking—to catapult her into the world. There was no going back now.

And if one part of her felt like there was still a bottomless hole waiting to swallow her up if she tripped; well, she was going to step right over it and keep on walking, wasn't she?

"I think we should have a hug, don't you?" Henry said.

Alice moved into his embrace. He smelled lovely, of sandal-wood, and wool and the tiniest hint of mothballs. Suddenly she wanted to open her heart to him about Aaron. Let out all the pain. She was sure Henry would understand in a way Rowena never could.

After the conference, she resolved, she would tell him.

She gave him a little wave as the lift doors closed, and Henry waved back, his hand held close to his body in the same way she'd done since she was a child.

Yes, Henry would definitely understand.

# CHAPTER 20

"Which do you prefer, the marzipan or the icing sugar version?"

Aaron sauntered over to Andrea's kitchen work surface and tried to put on the deeply serious expression of a *MasterChef* judge. "The marzipan one looks a bit 1970s-ish."

"That's the whole point," Andrea explained eagerly. "Marzipan decorations were all the rage when Gran was in her prime. You could buy all these wonderful little marzipan apples and oranges in patisseries. They made little marzipan eggs on Simnel cakes."

Aaron had no idea what a Simnel cake was.

"Okay, you're going for the retro look. I see." He rubbed his jaw. He wasn't in the mood for edible flower judging. Nor was he in the mood for a family lunch. Truthfully, since his dismal attempt at imparting his feelings to Alice on Tuesday, he wasn't in the mood for anything except hibernation.

He'd gone to work on automatic pilot, weathered an atmosphere you could cut with a knife, carried the can for Archie's frequent absences; shielded call after call from angry clients. The pinnacle had been an awkward meeting with Fink yesterday to work out how to manage Archie's cases while Archie managed his failing marriage.

It was so bad he'd started to toy with the idea of searching for another job.

Andrea darted a look at him out of candid hazel eyes. "Are you okay?"

"Sure."

"You seem a bit flat."

Aaron spluttered out a hollow-sounding laugh. "Tired, that's all."

"Pity Alice couldn't make it," Andrea added like it was an afterthought as she fussed over her edible flowers.

She didn't fool him for a second. Aaron blanked his features. "She's gone away for a few days."

"Yes, I know, she messaged to say she was going over east at short notice. Do you know why?"

He shrugged. "Maybe a book fair." He had to field the overwhelming urge to blab the real reason, but it wasn't his news to tell and it seemed suddenly the most important thing in the world to do nothing that would make Alice despise him more than she did already.

His stomach bottomed out. Yes, the unequivocal evidence was that she now despised him. She *had* loved him, a fact he'd been dumb enough to miss for five years. After his stupendously awful attempt to express his feelings, he knew he deserved her contempt. And he couldn't work out, however much he tried—biting pen tops and crushing numerous takeaway coffee cups at his overflowing desk—how to make it up to her. The more he thought about it, the messier it got, in direct correlation to the pile of crap on his desk.

"Whatever one you think will make Gran happiest," he said finally. "That's the most important thing."

Andrea looked relieved. "The marzipan version then."

Aaron forced a smile. "Yep. Definitely the marzipan."

He couldn't meet Andrea's gaze any longer, so he stared out the window at the garden. Dad was coming up the path from the shed, the wisp of hair that usually covered his bald patch whisking around in the wind. He was carrying a box.

As the door opened, he literally blew into the kitchen. "My god, it's howling out there."

He looked up, saw Aaron, and his smile spread into a genuine grin. "Hi, son. I've been going through some old photos for Gran's party and thought you might like to see some. You and Oliver both. Come and join me; there's a fire in the lounge."

Aaron hesitated. Old photos. *Gah.* Delving into the past. The last thing he needed.

Andrea motioned with her head as David strode off towards his study. "Your dad would love you to help him go through them," she said pointedly.

Reluctantly, Aaron followed.

In the lounge, Oliver was clearly on a phone call to Leonie, going by the syrupy tone of his voice and the "love you", followed by "love you more", which made Aaron want to hurl.

But when Oliver put the phone down and jumped up to give him a friendly thump on the back, his gut curled. It wasn't Oliver's fault that Leonie was the love of his life. Or that his advice to Aaron had gone pear-shaped. That was *his* problem. He was the love rat. The abject failure in the commitment stakes. The one who'd blown his chance of happiness with the only woman he'd ever—

Oh, for fuck's sake. He had to stop being such a sook.

Eight weeks ago—less—seven, he'd been blissfully ignorant of this other loved-up world that so many people seemed overjoyed to inhabit. Now that he'd fallen into it, however briefly, he didn't seem able to forget how wonderful it felt.

Aware of Oliver's eyes on him, he made sure he sprawled casually in a wing chair on the other side of the fire and stretched his legs out. Maybe there was some way he could get back to being the old him? The him that skimmed the surface of relationships, that never got close… and never got hurt. Surely he could do it? He almost patted his body to reassure himself it was possible.

Then David Blake put the box on the coffee table, opened the lid and dragged out a wad of old photos.

Of him. And Oliver. And *Mum*...

And that other world, that world where he actually *felt* stuff? That world full of painful, beautiful stuff? The world he'd just tried to convince himself he wanted no part of?

With a loud whooshing in his ears, Aaron fell right back down the rabbit hole.

~

The Opera House in the flesh (except you couldn't call it flesh when it was actually lots of shiny tiles, could you?) was more beautiful than Alice had ever envisaged. And the way the Harbour Bridge formed an arching backdrop... the photos just didn't prepare you for how breathtaking it all was.

She and Henry had attended a showing of *Carmen*, getting last-minute tickets, and she'd sat enraptured, wiping away tears surreptitiously after every spine-tingling aria. And now they were walking along the promenade, and Henry had bought them both an ice-cream and it was the sort of thing Alice guessed he would have done with her a zillion times when she was little if they'd only had the chance.

By now, they'd got so comfortable with each other that she didn't think twice about linking her arm in Henry's as they walked. The past three days had been pure magic, but tomorrow she would fly home and Henry would fly back to England. He had lectures and events to attend but they were already talking about next time. In England.

*England!*

She was going to visit Henry in England.

And really, once you were on that plane, what was the difference between five hours and twenty? Either way, you were up in the air with your feet resting on a bit of metal with nothing else between you and 42,000 feet of nothingness.

They'd talked about so many things these past days. Henry had asked if she had a partner and she'd been noncommittal. She'd been waiting for the right moment, but now the desire to tell him about Aaron was bubbling up inside her with more urgency the closer she got to leaving. Henry was so wise. So compassionate.

"So, did you enjoy it?" Henry asked about the opera.

"It was divine. But Don José murdering Carmen made me mad. I mean, why are women always so hard done by in operas?"

Henry pulled back and took a hard look at her. "Said with true passion."

"I've learned the hard way, that's all," Alice mumbled.

She must have curled her fingers tighter round his arm. "I sensed some reserve when I asked if you had a partner the other night. Has someone hurt you, Alice?" Henry asked this with such kindness that her eyes smarted with tears.

"Yes," she said, a lump lodged in the back of her throat. "Quite recently, actually. That's why it's all a bit…" She swallowed hard. "Why I guess I'm a bit reluctant to talk—it's still painful."

"Do you want to tell me about it? Or perhaps you'd rather not." His reticence was so quintessentially English, Alice had to smile despite herself.

She drew in a deep breath. "I've been in love with a guy for five years. And I found out he will never be able to love me back."

"Oh dear. That sounds frightfully like history repeating itself."

It took her a moment to digest and then she replied, "Oh, no, not like you and Mum! Aaron loves women. Rather too much, that's the problem."

"Has he been unfaithful? Believe me, that problem doesn't differentiate whatever your sexual orientation."

She shook her head. "No, he hasn't been unfaithful, that's the weird thing. It's complicated..."

And suddenly she was sketching out a brief history of her friendship with Aaron. "Then a few weeks back things kind of got weird between us," she sighed.

"What kind of weird?" Henry enquired.

So then, of course, Alice had to explain the fake dating and Polly's amazeballs sex and love equation, to which Henry couldn't help but chortle. And the change of clothes and wearing contact lenses—and Henry said he sympathised, as he hated contact lenses too, they made his eyes sting to buggery. And when they'd finished commiserating on that, then she filled him in on the flirting deal and the kiss (she naturally skimmed over things you didn't tell your father about, however open-minded he was).

By the time she'd got to the Lauren Donovan incident, they'd reached one of the oldest, most picturesque parts of Sydney, The Rocks, and decided to go into a pub for a drink.

"So," said Henry after they'd ordered a couple of glasses of white wine. "You say he came chasing after you?"

"Yes. And naturally, I assumed the worst, and the very same night Mum's package arrived with you in it. Well, not literally *you*, but all the articles and features about you, and obviously my life changed. And I had this light-bulb moment, this amazing clarity that I couldn't put up with waiting in the wings—hoping, and praying, though they're actually Polly's words not mine, but that's apparently what I do. I realised I had to be true to myself and not settle for anything less than the real deal." Her shoulders slumped with the effort of getting all that off her chest.

"Have you spoken to him since?" Henry asked.

"Oh yes, just before I came here he said he *kind of* liked me, well, more than liked me, and would I consider continuing with the arrangement."

"I see." Henry's lips twitched. "The—how did you describe it earlier?—friends-with-benefits arrangement?"

Alice nodded. "And I stupidly told him how I'd loved him for five years, ever since we met, basically. So I couldn't ever be accused of behaving like Mum and hiding the truth." She bit her lip and gulped. "And all Aaron said was 'oh no'. That was it. Just 'oh no'."

"Then what?"

"Well—nothing except a bit of bluster on his part. So I got up and left."

Henry played with the stem of his wine glass. "Do you think it's possible you might have misunderstood?"

"*Oh no* seems quite conclusive, don't you think?"

"To be honest, it doesn't sound like you gave the poor fellow a chance."

Alice stared at him, suddenly lost for words.

"When I was first with Gabe, we had a big fight. I'd been with someone who was unfaithful before, and Gabe being a flirt and so theatrical made me very insecure. He was showing off by being over-friendly to some other fellow at a party. I'm not proud of it, but I stormed off and wouldn't let him explain. Wouldn't take his calls, then when I did, we kept saying the wrong things, putting our foot in it. But we were just talking at cross purposes, because underneath we were totally smitten with each other. It took us a while to sort out, backwards and forwards..."

Alice couldn't help smiling. "Like the Push-Me-Pull-You?"

Henry looked perplexed.

"Out of *Doctor Dolittle*. The Push-Me-Pull-You."

Henry's eyes crinkled with sudden recognition. "Oh yes, I remember, I took Felicity to that film when she was a little girl. The weird creature that resembled a two-headed llama?"

"Yes. Polly said that's what love is like, especially at the beginning. You both push and pull and get kind of stuck."

"I agree," Henry said. "I think I'd like Polly."

"Everyone likes Polly. She's loud and beautiful and unfailingly optimistic."

"Remarkably like Rowena, then?"

Alice's lips quirked. "Yes, they could probably be clones."

Henry laughed, and when Henry laughed the whole world seemed more manageable somehow.

For a moment he looked thoughtful, as though considering her statement. "In the early stages when you're dancing around each other, yes, I'd grant there's a fair bit of push and pull."

"So how did you and Gabe resolve it?"

"Eventually, we sat down and talked and talked, and argued and made up. And we did that quite a few times, if I remember rightly. But finally, we worked out it was our insecurities getting in the way. Our fear of rejection. Past traumas. My father's rejection. Gabe losing his mother as a teenager to cancer. Gabe was extremely close to her and it hit him very hard."

Alice's heart did a strange flip-flop in her chest. "Aaron lost his mother too, when he was twelve. In a car accident. He's never talked about it to me, not in any detail, but then Oliver told me just recently that—"

"And Oliver is?"

"Aaron's older brother. Oliver said it affected Aaron a lot. He even said I was the only girl Aaron had ever formed any real connection with."

"Interesting."

Alice chewed on her lower lip, a glimmer of hope in her heart. "I guess." She thought about that morning, after the amazing night where they'd made love for hours, that wonderful feeling of closeness, of intimacy, of belonging. Before she'd blown it all by asking Aaron how he felt after his mum died. Maybe she'd dug too deep too soon? Maybe he'd needed more time to process it all?

And ha, she could hardly take the moral high ground, could she? Look at her, ears primed for rejection, stalking off like a bristling cat. What if she'd kept her cool, stayed put, listened properly instead of cutting him off? Could they have sorted it out?

Mind you, Aaron hadn't texted her since, not even to ask

259

about how meeting Henry had gone. Which, you could argue, was the biggest event in her life if you didn't count being born; no, he'd shown not a skerrick of interest. Surely that was proof he didn't care?

Except, of course, she'd told him not to contact her, that she only wanted to see him when she could feel—what had she said? Completely *indifferent to him.*

Alice groaned and dropped her head in her hands. "I didn't give him a chance. I was too hurt and angry."

"And that, my dear, is entirely understandable. But you and Aaron have been good friends for a long time. Before all the other stuff happened. That bond will still be there."

They sat and stared at their drinks for a long moment. Picked them up and took a sip in unison. Then they looked at each other with exactly the same quirked eyebrow and burst out laughing.

Henry reached over and patted her hand across the table. "It sounds to me like the poor chap has fallen for you jolly hard. Frankly, I think he's drowning."

Alice stared at her father helplessly. "What should I do now?"

"Throw him a line, Ell- iss," Henry said gently. "Give him a chance to save himself."

# CHAPTER 21

W hen the doorbell rang, Aaron was ready. Decked out in his running gear, he pressed the intercom button in the hallway.

"Hi, it's me." The voice, tinny through the speaker, was still unmistakably Carts.

"Come on up," Aaron said.

His apartment was spotless. He'd spent the last few days cleaning. Everything was in its rightful place. Clothes folded, dishes washed and put away. Apart from the table that was scattered with photos. Family shots, going back to when he was a kid. Of him and Dad and Oliver—and Mum, her blue eyes shining, blonde hair tied into a ponytail, all of them at a ski resort somewhere in Japan. Of him, minus his front tooth, standing proudly grinning next to Mum on his first day of school. Of all of them with Gran and Gramps at the beach.

With Oliver's help, Aaron was in the middle of putting together a photo board for Gran's birthday. And the weird thing was that the more they sat and arranged photos, the more they snipped and smeared glue on the back and pasted, the more it seemed the muscles down Aaron's spine uncoiled. And even weirder, as he and Oliver reminisced about Mum—the games she'd make up with them, the way she had of telling stories in so many different voices (*Where the Wild Things Are* had been her speciality), the happier he felt.

When his vision had gone blurry, Aaron had felt his eyelashes. They were wet. He'd looked over at Oliver to see him wiping away a tear of his own and they'd both laughed, a gruff, look-at-us-grown-men kind of laugh.

And you know what? It had felt so fucking good to feel it all. Even the painful, difficult stuff. And after that, over a beer, they'd talked about Alice. Oliver heard him out about his seismic gaff, patiently helped him make sense of it all, and had given him some sound advice. Which was kind of why he'd invited Carts over this morning. To clear the air.

He couldn't afford to lose his best mate because they'd both fallen for the same woman.

*Rat-a-tat tat.*

Aaron took a big breath and opened the door. He had to fight not to burst out laughing. Carts was decked out in a strange combo. Purple and black quick-dry shorts halfway up his long thigh bones, fluoro green runners. A one size too small T-shirt showed a strip of midriff, the classic image of Che Guevara emblazoned on the front. Purple sweat cuffs circled his wrists, another one round his head. He struck Aaron as a 1970s-tennis-pro-cum-Argentinian-revolutionary-inspired-cheerleader.

Carts grinned. "How do I look?"

"Interesting."

"So where are we going?"

"Up to the lookout and back."

Carts' face turned dubious. "How far is that?"

"Well, if we go the short route, about 3 kms."

"I'm not so sure about this fitness gig, after all." Carts strolled into the living room. His eyes zoomed in on the dining table. "What's this you're working on?" His eyes narrowed as he got closer. "Can I?"

"Sure."

Carts shuffled photos around. "Is that your mum?"

"Yep."

"You're the spitting image."

Aaron felt the familiar tightening around his chest. Breathed through it. "So I've been told."

"You've never really mentioned her," Carts mused. "I guess it happened before we met you, so I never, we never…"

"Guess teenage boys don't tend to talk about the difficult stuff."

"Dan and me sort of knew it was a no-go zone." Carts shrugged. "Something you didn't mention."

Aaron smiled. "Well, now I do."

Carts nodded thoughtfully. "Good to know," he said.

He took one more look at the photos. "She was beautiful."

"Yes. Very." Aaron's throat knotted, and he said, "Maybe we'll break in Mum conversations gradually."

"No worries," Carts said.

"Okay, then, shall we go? We can grab a coffee after."

"Don't you have to be at Trojan's?'

"No rush." Nope, Aaron certainly wasn't falling over himself to get to Trojan's. Not these days. A radical shift in his priorities had taken place.

Carts looked pleased. "I've got until 8.30. My suit's in my car. If I can change into my work gear here, we'll have time."

As they ran, Carts spluttered and complained. Stopped every five minutes and dropped his hands to his knees, puffing loudly. Drank from his water bottle ten, maybe fifteen times? Aaron waited patiently each time. He could forfeit his fitness regime for once. It gave him time to think about his text exchange last night with Alice.

Aaron: *How did it go seeing your dad?*

(Yep, he'd had his heart in his mouth sending that.)

He waited, no answer, so he got out the vacuum cleaner, then *ping*.

Alice: *Amazing. Thanks. (smiley face)*

Promising. Hope flared in his chest.

Aaron: *How's the indifference going?*

Alice: *????*

Aaron: *As in, r u indifferent enough to me to meet up yet?*

Alice: *Maybe.*

Aaron: *It's Gran's birthday party next Saturday.*

Alice: *I know.*

Aaron: *Are you coming?*

A long, long silence, during which Aaron had vacuumed under the coffee table, around the couch, under the couch. With frequent stops to check his phone. Finally, he couldn't stop himself.

Aaron: *Gran would love it. I would love it.*

Come on, come on…

Alice: *Okay.*

Aaron: *Meaning?*

Alice: *Okay, I'll come.*

His heart had done a tap dance. Oh, what the hell; he'd sent a kiss-blowing emoji. After a couple of minutes, Alice sent a smiley face back. Okay, no kisses, he'd worked out he'd have to earn those from here on. He was prepared to work his butt off just for one sugar-coated marshmallow kiss. More than that, Aaron refused to think about. Not if he wanted his fly to do up.

By now, Carts had stopped panting, hands still on his knees as he looked up from behind a slick of sweat-drenched hair. "Christ, you never said there would be hills."

Aaron grinned. "That's not a hill." He pointed to where the path wound steeply through thick bushland. "*That's* a hill."

Carts groaned. "Pleeease, someone kill me now."

Forty-five minutes later they were both showered, suited up and perched opposite each other on high stools at the coffee shop next to the train station.

Aaron steeled himself. "I think we need to clear the air."

Carts looked dubious. "What about?"

"You know *who* about."

Carts stared at his coffee cup. "Right-oh."

Aaron's throat didn't seem to want to get the words out. "Alice and I—" That sounded weirdly formal. "I mean, me and Al—"

"You can cut the crap," Carts butted in. "I already know."

Aaron frowned, his heart pounding against his ribs. "Know what?"

Carts let out a big huff. "Sunday I popped round to see Al. I hadn't realised she was away. Or that Rowena was home. Or any of the stuff about her dad."

"It wasn't common knowledge," Aaron said stiffly.

Carts shrugged. "Yeah, well, anyway, Rowena had a migraine. She told me the whole history of Alice's conception with an ice pack over her eyes and a towel wound round her head, which was a tad strange but I got the gist of it. Polly wasn't home, Rowena couldn't move off the sofa, so I went to pick up Alice at the airport."

A spasm of jealousy hit Aaron in the solar plexus.

It must have flitted across his face because Carts said, "Don't get stroppy, mate, you don't own her. Anyway, I met her at the airport and she's so excited and tells me about meeting her dad—sounds like a nice bloke, by the way—and we get home and Rowena's kind of wailing and crying and laughing all at once. She is seriously melodramatic, that woman. So anyway, as Alice walks me out, I kind of hint."

"Hint?"

"Yeah, you know, *hint*. Like the, 'how's things with you and Aaron' hint? The hint that someone else might be interested if…"

Aaron scowled. Carts ignored it. "Anyway, as soon as I mention your name she goes all kind of soft and mushy and says she's got to give you a chance to explain yourself and… then she gives me this frowny stare, not like Alice at all, and asks was I trying to ask her out? So I said, 'yes maybe', and she said—these were her words, I remember because they were kind of harsh—'I really like you, Carts, but it will never be in that special way'. So I asked, 'Have you got that special feeling for Aaron?' and she goes bright red. And so then I say, 'Don't answer that.' And that was my cue to make myself scarce."

A huge grin swept away Aaron's scowl. Carts looked disgusted. "So it's serious then? This thing between you and Alice?"

"Yes."

Carts sniffed like there was a garbage bin close by. "Thought as much. Never seen you like this around a woman before."

"Like what?"

"A total mess. Even your hair's gone to shit."

Aaron took a sip of his coffee to hide the way his blush seemed to be spreading. How his neck, his cheeks, even the tips of his ears were burning.

Carts looked away, as though Aaron the colour of a ripe tomato was equivalent to him stripping his clothes off in front of a café full of customers. Then he sighed heavily. "Well, anyway, I was feeling a bit depressed after Al told me I was permanently friend-zoned, so I went and saw Polly."

Aaron nearly dropped his coffee cup. "What for?"

"A bit of advice. I caught up with her at the hospital. She took me into one of those counselling rooms. It was pretty calming. Pictures of mountains with sayings like 'Be your best self'. Tissues. Flowers, though they might have been plastic. Not what I imagined a psych ward would be like at all. And I tell you what, she's good. If you need counselling, Poll's the real deal."

"Think I'll pass on that," Aaron muttered. Christ, he couldn't think of anything worse than opening up to Polly. She'd break a guy, have him on his knees, weeping like a baby.

Carts continued, "She gave me a bit of a serve, in a nice way. Told me I was in love with the idea of being in love. That I had to start taking care of myself, respecting myself, stop letting women walk all over me."

"She broke your balls, right?"

"It was a wake-up call, to be honest." Carts grinned. "So

that's when I thought, right, that's it. I'm going to stop drinking eight coffees a day, wiping myself out every Friday at the Shamrock. I'll drop the carbs, go for high nutrition foods. Exercise. Build some real muscle. It's time. I'll never find the right woman if I don't respect myself first."

Aaron's lips twitched. Carts looked happy. Like he'd been scrubbed clean.

"So I'm taking a six-month hiatus from women."

"I think that's a sound decision."

"I'm going to find the real me," Carts said. "Might even take up yoga."

"Go for it." Aaron kept a straight face. "Though maybe drop the Che Guevara T-shirt."

Carts frowned. "What do you wear to yoga?"

"I don't know. Leggings? T-shirts with Buddha heads, maybe? Om signs?"

"Man, I'll end up a freakin' hippy at this rate."

They got up, both laughing. Aaron decided not to suggest that anything was preferable to Carts' current exercise gear. Instead he threw an arm round Carts' shoulders as they walked towards the train. "Thanks, mate," he said, feeling a thickness in his throat. "You're a real friend, you know that?"

"Yeah, well…" Carts cast him a sideways look. "I have your promise you're not going to break Alice's heart?"

"You have my solemn promise."

"Bloody oath." Carts grinned. "One more thing—and dude, this really is the litmus test."

"Go on."

"I want to be your best man."

Aaron didn't even flinch.

Alice stacked the last of the job lot of Penguin classics on the shelf and turned back to the shop. She'd felt calm since she got back from Sydney last week. She was at a crossroads and whichever path she took, her life had purpose. Meaning. Direction.

She knew the direction she *wanted* it to take. The path she wanted to tread was with Aaron. But if he didn't feel the same, she knew beyond doubt her life would be fine. She was exploring doing a masters, then opening up her very own Book Genie. Maybe in a cute little English town somewhere with a hyphenated name. There were so many options; something she'd never really believed before.

Even so, she'd been trembling at the idea of contacting Aaron, so when his text pinged onto her phone, her heart had leapt.

Aaron had made the first move.

Her spirits had soared at the possibility that they might be able to sort this out.

She spent the rest of the week trying not to be irritable at her mum's constant questions: "Did you discuss Henry's work on Oscar Wilde? When are we going over there together, darling?" At work she finally taught herself how to use the computerised accounts system properly. To top it all off she'd bought Rowena an antique crystal shot glass on eBay, identical to the one she'd smashed. Anger was not worth holding on to, she decided; love was so much better.

But maybe ask her again after Gran's party.

"Hello, Alice." She swung round at the sound of a well-modulated woman's voice to find Delia Trojan smiling at her. Delia, Alice remembered, had been the nicest and most relatable of the Trojan wives. Even if the other two had talked over her unmercifully, she felt she and Delia had formed a rapport. She was as immaculately groomed as only a Trojan's wife could be, in navy blue slacks and jacket, but her eyes were brighter, her face more relaxed somehow.

Alice beamed. "Oh, Delia. How are you?"

Delia huffed out a sigh. "Things have been better. I guess Aaron would have told you the whole story?"

What to say exactly? Situations like this were always

awkward, like the person was fishing to see how much you would divulge.

"Mmmm?" Alice left a question mark hovering; it was up to Delia to interpret.

It was clearly enough. "You've heard, then? About the Archie debacle." She made it sound like the *Bourne Conspiracy*; then proceeded to look over her shoulder as if to check there were no Trojan spies around before hissing, *"The affair."*

"Oh, yes." Alice rolled her eyes, then tried to tone it down. "Aaron gave me a brief account." Understatement of the century. Like the whole thing hadn't blown her and Aaron's fledgling relationship into tiny pieces and scattered them into the stratosphere.

"It's got really nasty." Delia's tongue clucked on the roof of her mouth. "Geoff is trying to sort it out, but it won't be good for Trojan's image once this gets out." She sighed heavily, her eyes travelling over to the crammed bookshelves.

"Will it get out?" Alice asked.

"You met Miranda. She will not go quietly, I can assure you." Delia's smile was the kind you wore to funerals. "Anyway, enough of that. I've been meaning to pop in and have a look around your lovely shop." She moistened her lips. "Actually, I'm after some law books."

"We have a section of business and legal to the right at the back," Alice said briskly, more than happy to change the subject.

"Ah, good," said Delia. "There's some family law texts I'm having trouble locating; I thought you might have second-hand copies."

"Quite possibly. The students bring in their textbooks when they've finished their degrees."

"Wonderful!"

Alice watched Delia's high heels tip-tap determinedly to where she'd pointed. She was gone so long—a good half hour —that Alice actually thought she might have left the shop, until she landed a big pile of textbooks with a triumphant smile on Alice's desk.

As Alice added up the prices, Delia leaned over the desk conspiratorially. "I've been offered a position with Hatchers, the biggest family law firm in Perth."

Alice made sure her fingers didn't falter. "Really."

"I'm so excited, I think I could burst. I haven't quite plucked up the courage to tell Geoff yet. It's all such a mess with Miranda filing for divorce and that girl being pregnant—"

Alice's eyes widened. "Pregnant!"

Delia shook her head. "I know, I know. And now, Archie looks like he'll be going out on his own. Not sure how big the offer was to get him to agree... the three of them were squir-relled away in a meeting for hours, but... it's going to rip a hole in the firm." Delia laughed hollowly. "Anyway, I started to think about *my* needs in all of this. And realised I have to work or I'll go insane. There's only so much organising hockey tournaments and baking cupcakes for school fetes a woman can cope with. By your fourth it's a bit like *Groundhog Day*."

Alice nodded, even though she could never imagine feeling like that about her children. But really, who was she to walk in another woman's shoes?

Delia pulled out her credit card. "Geoff and I will need to have a serious talk. I am going to stand my ground no matter what he says."

"You must. Absolutely," Alice agreed. Delia may be whip-pet-thin, but she had metal in her bones after all. "Good luck with telling him."

"Oh, don't worry." Delia smiled sweetly. "I'll win."

As she turned on her heels to leave, she looked younger, more vibrant somehow; there was none of the wistfulness in her eyes Alice had noticed when she met her. As if Delia's life had suddenly become an adventure. It struck Alice as the look of a woman who had finally had the courage to follow her heart.

As Delia reached the door Alice called out, "Oh, Delia, I forgot to mention, I've found you a copy of *North and South*."

Delia turned with a perplexed frown.

"The book by Elizabeth Gaskell," Alice explained. "We discussed it at the cocktail party. Would you like it?"

Delia hesitated. Glanced down at her bag bulging with family law books. "You know what, Alice, I'll give it a miss. I'm not going to have time to read novels for a while."

And with a wave she was gone.

~

The house looked stunning. Even Aaron could appreciate the lengths Andrea had gone to.

The flower arrangements were gargantuan; streamers cluttered the usually simple walls, his and Oliver's picture board stood on an easel in the drawing room. Yes, he was proud of his efforts. The only worry was his hope that Gran wasn't having a forgetful day and would remember who everyone was. But apparently, Andrea had told him, reminiscence therapy really helped to ground people with dementia.

He hoped he'd done Gran's life credit.

Dad was in a great mood, helping cut egg and cucumber sandwiches, his big hands working with unusual finesse under Andrea's careful instructions.

Mini quiches. Cheese and pineapple on sticks. Tiny prawn cocktails with fanned out avocado drenched in bright pink sauce. It was retro heaven. Good on Andrea. She had a knack of making things special.

Then the guests started to arrive. All ages, but mostly over eighty. He hadn't realised how many friends Gran had. How many people adored her. He guessed she'd done bring and buy stalls at Christmas and Easter, and she'd campaigned tirelessly for better road safety after Mum's death. She'd given her unconditional love to all who crossed her path and now they were all here to give back to her.

Aaron's chest filled with a warm, fuzzy feeling. He took a breath. He was beginning to get used to this emotion stuff.

Finally Gran arrived, leaning on her stick, dressed in lilac and looking remarkably like the Queen.

Aaron strode over and kissed her.

"Aaron." She smiled sweetly, her face a map of crinkles. She'd recognised him, had got his name right. So far so good.

When Oliver went over, though, she called him David. Did that mean his fiancée Leonie would be mistaken for Mum? That could be awkward.

But you had to trust a woman to remember her own daughter. Even though Leonie was willowy and blonde, she clearly wasn't Mum.

Gran frowned. "Where's Andrea, David?" She directed this in a rather outraged tone to Oliver. "Flaunting your new floozy like this. It's just not on." She was just about to give Oliver a rap with her stick when Dad raced over. Finally the situation was explained to Gran's satisfaction. Ten minutes later, after a cucumber sandwich and a nice cup of tea, Gran was beaming at everyone and tapping her foot to Frank Sinatra.

The doorbell rang.

"I'll get it." Aaron ripped fingers through his hair and dived into the hallway. It had to be Alice.

It was Alice.

Standing smiling up at him, she stole his breath. Eyes wide and dark, lips shimmery pink, her hair glossy and—shorter, much shorter. A neat bob with a straight fringe that made her look like she'd stepped off the set of *What's New Pussycat?* All she needed was a leopard-skin outfit and knee-high boots. As it was, she was wearing a chocolate brown velvet dress with a hint of cleavage, and pearls… *those* pearls. Red-hot lust flew to his groin as he remembered the last time she'd worn them at the art gallery. Well, this was potentially embarrassing—particularly among a group of octogenarians.

Aaron stepped forward and kissed her cheek, caught her apple-blossom scent. "Love your hair," he managed.

"Oh, you do?" Alice cocked her head and her hair hung heavy to one side, just below her left ear. "I had it done in Sydney. Dad persuaded me it would look nice shorter."

"It does. You look amazing."

She blushed and it made her even more beautiful. Aaron's blood fizzed around his veins, hammered a crazy beat in his ears.

He grinned at her like a loon then stepped back, subtly rearranged himself by tugging at his belt. As he took her bag their fingers grazed and everything revved up again. It wouldn't do to drag her into a cupboard at Gran's ninetieth, would it?

Luckily, before lust got the better of him, Andrea swooped. "Alice, you must see the cake before I bring it out."

Alice cast him a little smile that spoke volumes as Andrea hurried her away, both of them whispering.

He stuck his hands in his pockets to hide any residual evidence of arousal and stilled the urge to bounce up and down on his heels. He'd planned his and Alice's own special afterparty, now he just had to cool his jets for an hour or so longer.

Taking a deep breath, he strolled over to the laden dining table and picked up a plate of sandwiches.

"Mrs Braithwaite, isn't it?" he queried the lady on the sofa with the pink rinse and the toy poodle on her lap one shade lighter.

"You're Betty's grandson, aren't you?" When he nodded, she beamed delightedly. "Do call me Edith."

Holding out the platter, Aaron gifted her his most charming smile. "Edith, can I tempt you to a cucumber sandwich?"

Edith winked as she reached out a blue-veined hand. "Thank you, dear boy. Consider me tempted."

Clearly there was no such thing as being too old for the game.

# CHAPTER 22

The party was all but over. A few stragglers were picking at the remains of the cake. It made Alice think of a citadel that had been stormed and well and truly conquered. David Blake had taken Gran back to the residential home with a Tupperware container full of marzipan violets.

The last two guests finally said their farewells, Andrea fussing and getting their coats, and then it was just the five of them: Oliver, Leonie, Andrea, her—and Aaron, standing so close that all Alice would have to do was sway a little and they'd be touching.

Halfway through the party Aaron had asked her to stay on afterwards so they could "talk"; he'd kind of hovered behind the rim of one of Andrea's best teacups, blue eyes unblinking and earnest and quite un-Aaron like. Other than that, they'd had little contact besides some seriously hot glances while Alice zoomed around with a plate of cheese and pineapple sticks and Aaron offered Gran's hard-of-hearing friends mushroom vol-au-vents in a very loud voice.

The superhighway was now a speedway it would seem, if

the clenching of her internal muscles, the buzz and hum *down there* were anything to go by.

And Henry's words kept ringing in her ears. "Throw him a line, Ell-iss, give him a chance to save himself."

She'd throw out a whole net if she had to. Send out a lifeboat. Because she still loved Aaron desperately. She would never let him drown. It was that simple.

"Just look at the sparkle on that diamond!" Andrea was saying now as Leonie displayed her engagement ring, moving her wrist this way and that to catch the light.

"One and a half carats." Leonie smiled beatifically.

Oliver was gazing at Leonie's face with exactly the same look that Aaron had worn when he'd looked at *her* these past few weeks.

The Blake look of devotion.

*Oh don't be silly.* She was definitely getting ahead of herself here.

Finally, Aaron said, "Alice and I are going for a drink."

Alice was certain a knowing smirk passed between him and Oliver.

"Oh yes," Andrea enthused. "You've earnt it. Thank you both so much. I'm sure Gran went home happy. Aaron, you were clearly a hit." Andrea's breathy laughed tinkled with delight. "I swear Edith was on the verge of proposing."

"Maybe I'm already taken," Aaron said. And he looked at Alice. Straight at her. Oh god, she was at risk of melting into a great big puddle.

Farewells said, a hug from Oliver, an air kiss from Leonie— there was just something a bit Trojan-wife about Leonie, lovely though she was—another big hug from Andrea. "You two go and have some fun," she said as she waved them away.

And then they were alone, taking the steps from the front door in the cool early evening air. On the pavement next to his car, Aaron said, "I don't really need a drink. I'm pretty much marinated in Earl Grey tea. Can we walk along the river for a bit?"

"Okay."

They walked, and he asked lots of questions about Henry, and she found herself happily telling him the details (leaving out her heart-to-heart about Aaron, of course).

She sensed Aaron stiffen when she said she was going to England sometime in the future.

"For how long?"

She waved a hand in the air. "I don't know; that depends."

She felt his eyes boring into her. "On what?"

"Oh, you know, how long I can leave the shop for…"

He nodded thoughtfully. "Do you mind if we sit?" he asked, suddenly.

Alice followed his gaze and noticed a seat nestled in a small hollow with a sweeping view across the river. They perched side by side. For a second she thought Aaron was going to take her hand, but then it was like he thought better of it, and sat forward, elbows on his knees, staring out at the boats returning to their moorings like nesting birds in the early evening glow.

Was this the lifeline Henry had talked about throwing him? Just being here, waiting, willing to hear him out?

"I—um." Aaron frowned. Blinked, shucked back his hair with twitchy fingers.

"Go on," Alice prompted gently.

He let out a low whistle through tight lips. "Okay… what I wanted to say is—"

*Sit still, wait, listen.*

"Remember that day when I first met you?" She made a little noise she hoped was encouragement. "That look on your face… when you were trying to get your breath… bottomless fear… I knew that feeling… I'd been there. I had this immediate sense that I *got* you." He paused and stared at his clasped hands for long moments.

"I've never talked about this, but after my mum died, my life fell in a huge hole. I went kind of crazy there for a while. Couldn't focus on anything, couldn't study, kept getting into trouble. I literally hated everyone, everything. Dad used to drop me off at school; I'd wait for roll call, then escape through a hole in the fence. They'd find me, phone Dad, give me detention, and then I'd do it again. After a while, I got involved with a bunch of older kids who were doing the same thing and one of them gave me some dope. So I smoked it. It made me feel so good, so mellow—like nothing *hurt* anymore." He paused. "But then things kind of went from bad to worse; one day I was found with a stash of dope on me and got suspended."

"How old were you then?"

"Fourteen."

Alice groped for his hand; she couldn't help herself. Grabbed and squeezed it. He squeezed back, gave her a fleeting, thin smile. "I had the pleasure of being dragged to counsellors, then finally a psychiatrist. In the end he diagnosed ADHD and depression. I don't think it was ADHD. Not really, though it probably looked like it. You see, I couldn't tell them. I couldn't tell anyone Mum dying was my fault."

"It wasn't your fault," she exclaimed. "How could it be your fault?"

"I was supposed to catch a lift home after footy with another kid. I was mucking around, no doubt trying to impress, knowing me, and the kid's parent thought I'd gone with someone else. I phoned Mum, and she was on her way to pick me up when... when the guy ran the red light. If I'd just done what I was supposed to... she... she wouldn't have died."

"You could never have known that, Aaron. That's like saying every second of every day each one of us is responsible for every single event in the whole world. Like we're God or something. It doesn't work that way."

"I know that. Logically. Why do you think I studied law?" His smile was shaded with so much sorrow it tore her apart. "But deep inside—" He fisted a hand to the centre of his chest. "In here, when you're twelve years old, you don't understand things that way."

He sat, rocking backward and forward gently. "Finally, Dad

put me in a different school that was more supportive of my needs, I guess. He met Andrea; I made some friends—"

Alice's lips quirked. "Carts and Dan, right?"

"Yeah." He laughed, his face relaxing a smidge. "Jerks, both of them, but loyal mates."

They sat quietly for a long beat. "Life gradually got better after that. I think the medication did help me focus; my grades improved. I joined a gym, started running, then entering marathons, until I gradually got off the medications when I was at uni. I felt okay. Life was good. I dated lots of… well, you know that. As long as I avoided getting close to anyone, I felt I was safe. And then you came along. And suddenly I had something more. A girl who it felt good to just hang out with, who made me laugh. Who made the best hot chocolates and beat me at Monopoly and laughed at my bad jokes and saved my bacon so many times I've lost count. And I cared…"

Alice sniffed. "Just not *that* way."

Aaron flashed a grin. "You were always kind of nerdy cute."

"Thanks," she said with heavy sarcasm.

If Aaron got it, he didn't let on. "The problem was I had two identities; the player who had flings, one-night stands. Whatever. And then I was this other person… the one I was—am—with you."

"And never the two shall meet, right?" She tried not to let the bitter note creep in, but her heart was dropping like a stone. He was telling her he cared about her… just not that way. Not in that special way.

Well, she could take it, she was strong enough now. "I get what you're saying, Aaron." She tried to pull her hand away.

He looked up at her, brows furrowed, eyes clouded, and held on tighter. "Let's go somewhere else."

This was getting confusing. "Where now?"

"You'll see." He jumped up, and with his hand still clasping hers, Alice had no choice but to follow. "Trust me."

"Really?"

"It's only a short drive. Come on."

As Aaron strode purposefully along, his hand around hers, Alice's pulse spiked, her heart thundered against her ribs. It felt like a tornado was brewing.

Was Aaron feeling it too?

She prattled on madly to hide it. "Delia came to the shop the other day. She told me all about the Lauren thing—oh, and she's going back to work, but I don't think she's told her husband yet, so maybe don't say anything."

Aaron nodded. "Yes, it's mayhem at work. The whole affair with Lauren is out. Apparently Miranda's spilled everything to the press. There's a double-page spread coming out sometime next week."

"What are you going to do?" she asked as they got into his car. "Will you stay after your probation period finishes?"

"I'm looking at my options." Aaron started the engine. "I'm thinking about maybe stepping sideways. Going into legal aid."

Her eyes popped wide as she turned and stared at his profile. "Wow, that *is* a step sideways."

His tone was level as he said, "Yeah. I guess you could say I've had a few major eye-openers lately."

Quickly, Alice looked out the passenger window. She shouldn't read too much into those words; the things he'd told her had helped her make sense of the past, but hadn't made her think they had a future. If anything, it was the reverse. And yet the softness in his eyes... the way he'd looked at her all afternoon, the steady grip of his fingers around hers...

"Oh, gosh," she realised after a few minutes. "We're at the beach."

"We are indeed."

"Isn't the Bendt's house just up the road from here?" She almost expected to see sparks flying off the roof.

"Don't worry," Aaron said, "we're going the other way."

As they exited the car, once again Aaron took her hand firmly in his. Alice let him lead her down to the beach. Ahead of them the volleyball pitch was all lit up and party to a few gathering seagulls.

She looked around, puzzled. "This was where you brought me when—"

Aaron grinned. "—You were getting over that panic attack after our first date."

"*Fake* date," she corrected, then giggled nervously. "And you gave me a flirting lesson and I was hopeless, if I remember rightly.'

Their feet sinking into the sand, Aaron turned to face her.

"I thought maybe we should have another go at it."

Speechless, she gazed at him as her heart bumped into her mouth.

Aaron settled his shoulders, composed his face, put his hands in his pockets, took them out again. "Okay, a bit of back story here. So there's this guy who's spent some time with this girl, lots of time, actually, over quite a few years." He stepped closer, took one of her hands and threaded her fingers through his. A flurry of firecrackers exploded inside her and she frowned to try and hide it. "And here's the thing... this guy, he kind of screwed up. Badly. Took the girl for granted, always expected that you'd be there for him, basically behaved like a selfish, conceited prick... and..." He stopped, stared up at the darkening sky. "And then one day..."

His fingers squeezed hers tight, and she saw his throat work. Maybe she needed to give him a little help. "Go on," she nudged.

"Okay, in role now." Aaron cleared his throat. "I had a great time with you today."

Alice swallowed hard. "Me too."

"I'd really like to see you again."

"That would be nice..."

Aaron lifted his free hand in the air, as if raising the bar. "How about 'that would be wonderful'? Or 'I'd love to'."

Alice nibbled on her lip, trying to focus on his words. "I guess that depends..."

"On what?"

"On his intentions."

Aaron shook his head. "No, no, not third person, not 'his'. Talk to me." He tapped his chest with his free hand. "Ask *me*, Aaron, about *my* intentions." His eyes traced her face until she knew she was blushing madly.

Alice swallowed hard. Here they were. Finally. "Are they honourable?" God, here was the moment she'd been waiting for and she sounded like she'd just walked off the page of a regency romance!

Aaron threw back his head and laughed. Then his hand came up and stroked her cheek. Fingers grazed her lips. His eyes dived into hers, bright and brimful of something unbearably wonderful as he murmured, "Deeply, deeply honourable."

Emboldened, she let her lips nip at his finger and heard him inhale sharply.

"So honourable, in fact," he whispered, "that this guy... finds he's... he's..."

Alice's heart beat its wings and threatened to burst through her chest. But all she could say in a kind of weird gruff squeak was, "You've gone out of role again."

"Arghh, god, this is hard!" He threw his head back and dragged in a deep breath. "Okay, here goes. I, Aaron Blake, am totally, utterly, irrevocably in love with you, Alice Montgomery. Will that do for starters?"

Alice wasn't sure if her smile was going to split the top of her head from the rest of her body. "For starters," she mumbled, because it truly was hard to speak through a grin as huge as the entire universe.

Later she knew there would be more talking to be done, but right now she couldn't stand being apart from him a moment longer. Going up on tippy-toes, she wound her arms around his neck and kissed him with everything she had.

A long time later they managed to pull apart, both of them breathless and panting. "I think that broke the ice," Aaron gasped.

Alice smiled as she nestled her cheek against his chest, relishing the tightness of his arms around her, the *ka-boom ka-boom* of his heart.

"Is making love on a beach illegal?" she asked, peering up at his delectable chin.

"Most likely."

"Probably deemed lewd behaviour."

Aaron laughed and tightened his grip. "You and your weird phrases."

She raised her face to his and he kissed her mouth hungrily, which stopped all conversation for another couple of minutes.

"My place?" he asked when finally they drew apart again.

"Yes, please."

"You haven't said it back."

"What?"

"That you love me."

Alice pulled back, wide-eyed. "I thought that was patently obvious."

"But I'm an insecure guy. I can own that now. I need to hear it. Probably every day for the rest of my life."

She reached up and stroked the hair away from his eyes; eyes that were as wide as the ocean—open and vulnerable and beautiful. "I love you," she said tenderly. "Totally, utterly and irrevocably."

Aaron's arms squeezed her so tight, Alice almost lost her ability to breathe. "Promise me?" he whispered.

"What?"

"You'll never stop telling me that."

"I promise."

As he released her, a sudden wicked grin shaped his lips. "Let's get out of here. We've got five years of lost time to make up for."

Alice said, all mock-innocent, "What did you have in mind?"

"Let's just say it involves an awful lot of time in bed,

completely naked. And maybe the odd post-coital game of Monopoly."

Alice grabbed Aaron's hand and breathlessly, laughingly, tugged him up the steps towards his car. "Come on... I'll race you!"

# EPILOGUE

9 MONTHS LATER

"No!" Aaron rushed forward ready to tackle Dan, who was about to land all 110 kilos of his bulk onto Aaron's suitcase. Dan grinned, and desisted.

"How long are you going for? A year? Two?" Carts grumbled, lifting the lid and peering inside. "Do you really need that many shirts? And sweaters? And what in fuck's name is this?"

He pulled out the striped pale blue and navy jacket on top with a disgusted look on his face.

Aaron flicked an impatient hand through his hair. "It's a blazer. Cambridge colours."

Dan's jaw dropped. "What for?"

"For when I take Alice punting."

"What in frig's name is punting?" Dan asked.

Aaron resisted the urge to feel insanely stupid. "Punting," he said airily, "is what you do in Cambridge. On the river. A flat wooden boat which you stand on the back of with a long pole."

Carts smirked. "Appropriate for you, then."

"Like rowing?" Dan screwed up his face.

"More like being on a gondola, I guess," Aaron supplied.

"Jeee-sus. You've gone soft!"

"Yeah. Pussy!"

Carts and Dan puffed out their chests and did a joint impression of the two tenors. It was so bad, Aaron's eyes almost watered. Finally he shut them up by shouting, "*Stop, you're destroying my fucking eardrums!*"

"You're probably over your luggage allowance." Dan eyed off the suitcase again.

"Throw out the blazer," Carts suggested.

"No way." Aaron shook his head. The blazer had a special purpose. Realistically, he could have bought one over there, but he'd sent for it online, along with a pair of white linen pants, a la *Brideshead Revisited* (which, incidentally, he'd just finished reading).

He had a plan.

Instinctively he felt in his pocket for the small velvet box. He could have waited to buy the ring over there too. But he needed everything to be worked out beforehand: the champagne, the picnic basket, the punt... legal brain stuff.

Proposing to the woman you loved couldn't be left to chance.

"Come on," he said impatiently. "If we go easy the three of us should be able to get this baby closed."

Three pairs of hands landed palms-down on the lid; three sets of strong arms pushed down; three faces grinned at each other and *click click*, the locks were snapped.

"You going to wrap it in plastic?" asked Carts, ever the cautious one.

"Nah," said Aaron. "The valuable stuff is staying with me."

He turned the box around in his pocket. A sapphire surrounded by diamonds. Just like Alice had dreamily said one night after some seriously acrobatic lovemaking and he'd just happened to ask her favourite gemstone… as she drifted into sleep.

He wasn't even sure if she remembered telling him.

"Okay, guys," he said, as he hoisted the suitcase off the bed with a grunt. "Let's go."

∽

Polly hugs were really hard to breathe through. Probably because of all those tightly packed curls. Suffocation by hair.

"Oooh, I'm going to miss you so, so much." Polly squeezed Alice tighter.

"It's only three months," Alice mumbled through a mouthful of curls and Diorissimo.

"Another six weeks and I'll be over there too," Rowena bellowed, elbowing Polly aside.

Alice felt like a pass the parcel as she finally extricated herself and righted the glasses that had been pushed sideways off her nose.

"Wish I could come," Polly said, a little glumly. "But I can't really miss Dad's seventieth." She grimaced. "Or Jake's wedding. Neither event is filling me with anticipatory joy."

Alice gave her another hug. Polly was not her usual ebullient self of late. Jake had got engaged after a whirlwind romance with a girl Polly had introduced him to. "There goes my fuck buddy," Polly had complained when it was patently clear Jake was smitten.

"You'll meet someone soon," Alice said. The weather was going to change in respect to Polly, she felt it in her bones.

"Munchkin!" (They'd got back on to Munchkin footing. After a while, Alice had to admit she missed her nickname.) "I don't want to meet someone," Polly refuted hotly, then grinned. "Not that way. Just a muscle-bound six-foot-three ex-marine with amazing prowess in the bedroom who I can dial up whenever I need him. Send him away when duly pleasured."

"Hear, hear!" Rowena beamed.

Alice gave Polly a sly glance. "Fibber. In your heart of hearts you want to fall in love."

Polly's green eyes flashed. "Never going to happen."

Alice turned away to hide a little smile. Maybe her and Aaron's happiness these past nine months had given Polly pause?

Maybe.

And then she looked up and there he was. Or rather, there *they* were. Striding forth across the departures area like the Three Musketeers. Her very own tamed rake taking centre stage and smiling at her like she lit up his world.

Just as he did hers.

Carts hugged her. Dan nearly crushed her bones. It would be good to get on the plane just to recover from a bad case of over-hugging.

Now Aaron's arm was around her shoulder, his presence as dear to her as the air she breathed.

A few more woeful wails from Rowena and they swept through the departure gate, tears pricking Alice's eyes as she finally lost sight of her little band. She looked at Aaron and saw his features working. Since they'd been together her man had proven himself capable of the full range of emotions. In fact, he seemed to delight in them.

She kissed him and he laughed and said gruffly, "I'll miss those bastards."

"Me too."

Waiting for their flight to be called, they sat reading their books, Aaron on his Kindle—finally she'd got him interested in something other than Instagram posts. In point of fact, he was proving to be quite a voracious reader, as though discovering his feelings and reading novels went hand in hand.

Well, she'd known that for years, hadn't she?

"So," Aaron said when they were clipped into their seats on the plane. "What are you looking forward to most?"

"Being with Henry, of course; meeting Gabe. Going to Paris

and Italy. Seeing all the things I've dreamed about... how about you?"

"Punting."

Alice screwed up her nose. "Punting?"

"Yeah, I've been looking into it. There's quite a knack, apparently. I can't afford to fall off." He grinned at her. "I'd look like a prize twat, isn't that what the English say?"

Alice shook her head. "You are honestly turning weirder than me. What about the Eiffel Tower? The Trevi Fountain? Seeing the Mona Lisa face-to-face?"

"You and me and art galleries get into all kinds of trouble, if I remember rightly." Aaron lifted her hand to his lips and kissed each finger. "Though we probably should do it again, for old time's sake."

Alice bobbed up and down in her seat. "Well, funny you should mention it; I've got an itinerary planned."

Aaron groaned. "Oh god, I'll be cultured out."

*"Cabin crew, cross check and prepare for take-off."*

As the plane taxied out, Aaron whispered, "Nervous?"

"Only a teeny bit. I loved flying when I went to Sydney."

"You adrenaline junkie!" Aaron laughed and kissed the top of her head.

"Hardly." She lifted her face and he kissed her again, softly on the lips, with the barest stroke of his tongue. Aaron kisses made her insides melt without fail. She would never tire of them. They were a superhighway to her erogenous zones, for sure, but more than that, they went straight to her soul.

No need to pass go.

Or claim two hundred dollars.

She would always be his. Always.

As the plane whooshed into the air, and their hands held on tight, Alice couldn't help a big smile curving her lips. The words "amazeballs" slipped into her head.

She whispered it out loud.

Aaron didn't hear, not over the roar of the engines. But he kept squeezing her hand and that was all that mattered.

She was going to see her dad. She was flying. With the man of her dreams by her side.

It was truly amazeballs.

All of it.

# ALSO BY DAVINA STONE

## THE POLLY PRINCIPLE

*Sometimes love is unpredictable*

She's running from love… He's just running away.

Social worker by day, sex siren by night Polly Fletcher has a clear set of principles that guide her life; her Tinder app, her Jimmy Choo shoes and a strict no commitment rule.

So when she meets a sexy, silver-eyed stranger at a friend's wedding, all she's after is a wild night between the sheets.

Solo Jakoby has his Ducati motorbike, a backpack of his belongings, and a disaster he's escaping in Sydney. And sure, he's wildly attracted to the curvaceous beauty, but he has a job to do, and some unpleasant memories to forget.

So what if their time together blew his mind? It was just one night, right?

But when Solo and Polly are flung together in quite different circumstances, it seems the chemistry between them won't let up. And as they start to uncover each other's secrets, maybe this crazy attraction is set to turn into something deeper? Something that might just challenge Polly's firmly upheld principle—to never, ever give away her heart?

Find out in this steamy, heart warming second novel in the Laws of Love series.

## A KISS FOR CARTER

### *Sometimes love is a tall Story*

One kiss… one crazy week… is Carter Wells' luck about to change?

He's six-foot-six of soft heart, bad hair days and dating disasters. But now Carter (Carts to all his friends) has met his dream woman and he's determined to make it work.

Judith has always settled for sub-par love, played peace-maker between her mum and sister and baked brownies to keep everyone happy. But now she's falling for Carts and she's determined to put her own needs first.

But when their first date turns into a disaster of gargantuan proportions and major family dramas erupt around them, it will take more than one magical kiss to save their budding relationship.

Are Carts and Judith destined to be apart forever? Or will the universe take pity on them and intervene?

Find out in this heart-warming third novel in The Laws of Love series.

## THE FELICITY THEORY

*Sometimes love is a journey*

He's grumpy… She's sunshine… And they're about to take a road trip across Australia.

Successful, handsome and a little bit OCD, finance guru Oliver Blake believes he has the perfect life. Until his fiancée leaves him on their wedding day, and his carefully constructed world crumbles around him.

Still trying to piece his life together six months later, the last thing Oliver needs at his brother's wedding is a bubbly British bridesmaid plunging his life into more chaos.

Felicity Green doesn't believe in perfect. She's had enough disappointments to prove dreams don't come true. She has a theory — life is what you make it, and she's determined to make her trip to Australia one big adventure.

Somehow, Oliver and Felicity find themselves in a Kombi van traveling across Australia. As they share confined sleeping arrangements and nights under the stars, it's not long before the chemistry between them is sizzling off the charts.

En route to Sydney it seems that Oliver and Felicity may have stumbled on something almost perfect after all. until they meet a hurdle that just might be too big for either of them to overcome.

Will they find a way through this, or has their love met the end of a long dusty road?

For fans of Christina Lauren and Tessa Bailey comes this steamy heart-warming fourth book in The Laws of Love series.

**Paperbacks available through Amazon.**

**E-books available through all major on-line booksellers.**

# THE POLLY PRINCIPLE SAMPLE

CHAPTER ONE

With her champagne flute poised, it flashed through Polly's mind that she should be on a retainer for the number of couples she'd delivered to the alter. Would a wedding planner hire her? Or a swanky venue? Her track record for pairing off bridesmaids with stray guests was impressive. She could single-handedly keep the bookings up for cakes, dresses, hire services . . . honestly, the list was endless.

"Please raise your glasses to the beautiful bride and the ugly groom." The best man's words cut through her brilliant career plans. Laughter, murmurs of *Jake and Lou,* and the clink of glasses filled the room. Jake kissed his bride, the couple wearing matching, only-have-eyes-for-you expressions.

Usually Polly's heart did a happy dance right about now, so why was there a stabbing sensation just above the waist of her vintage Suzy Perette dress? It couldn't be the food. She'd been super careful not to overdose on smoked salmon blinis and chocolate-drizzled profiteroles. She might as well be wearing a hair shirt instead of her Spanx, as far as self-denial was concerned.

She took a gulp of champagne and bubbles fizzed up her nose.

Then it struck her.

*Polly Fletcher you are jealous.*

Which was patently ridiculous. Sure, she could probably get a Ph.D. in matchmaking, but all this commitment stuff was never going to be her gig.

*Piss off, I am not.*

"Excuse me?" The woman next to her stiffened in outrage. Polly grimaced. Clearly another of her brain-to-mouth malfunctions. More than three glasses of champagne and they became a rather regular occurrence.

"Sorry," she hiss-whispered. "Emergency call from my brother. Amazing things, smart watches, aren't they? I'll take it outside."

Wrist pressed to her ear, (it was actually a fake Patek Phillipe she'd bought in Bali for two dollars, but who'd know at a distance?), Polly squeezed through the crowded room. Stumbling onto the hotel patio, she heaved a sigh of relief, downed the rest of her champagne, and muttered, *"Idiot."*

"Who's an idiot?"

The voice was husky, male and very, very close.

Polly swung round. Luminous silver eyes fringed by black lashes met her gaze, crinkles of amusement fanning the tan skin at each corner. Quick as a flash she took in the rest of his face. Not exactly handsome. Short, dark hair, nose a little crooked; a lean jaw shadowed with stubble, but add in a mouth that looked like it was made for pleasuring a girl and Polly's powers of speech promptly sank into her vagina.

Hot. As. Hell.

The guy cocked an eyebrow, brought a cigarette to his lips, and took a slow drag.

Hot he may be, but a vice like that was too good to miss.

"Well, you are, clearly," she smirked.

Both eyebrows shot up this time. "Why?"

"For smoking, Mr *Dinosaur*."

Hot-as-hell turned his cheek, and exhaled. Which allowed Polly a once-over of his bod. She almost groaned out loud at the intoxicating sight of broad shoulders gift-wrapped in leather, long, denim-clad legs, and dusty bike boots.

He pointed at her champagne, "Why's that's any better?"

"*Hel-lo*. You don't see smoke coming out of my glass, do you?" Polly wiggled her glass in his face.

A sudden grin carved a groove in his right cheek. " Just a different choice of poison."

Polly narrowed her eyes. "Implying what, exactly? That we're all stuffed up one way or another?"

"That's an assumption that says more about you than me."

"Oh, very clever."

"What?"

"The way you turned the tables so I'm the one with the problem."

Hot-as-hell laughed and tapped ash off his cigarette. "You're a guest at the wedding?"

"And clearly you're not."

His pupils dilated, black blotting out silver. "How do you know?"

She allowed herself another lightning scan of his body— purely for research purposes, of course. "You've got oil stains on your jeans, and red dirt caked on your boots," she said airily. "Not exactly hard to work out. Besides, my job pays me to observe people."

He dropped the cigarette butt and ground it under his heel. "Really? What do you do?"

"Why would I tell you?" That came out snarkier than she'd meant, blame it on rampant lust.

"No reason. Except I asked."

"if you want me to enter into a conversation, a name would help."

"Solo."

"Ha-ha, where's R2D2?"

He dead-panned her. "Yeah, I get that a lot. More often Luke Skywalker, but that's the name I go by."

Cheeks on fire now, Polly propped her butt on the wall and crossed her arms. It was just too . . . *arousing,* standing facing him. He must have noticed her nipples like little bullets pointing at him from under the flimsy fabric of her dress. "Do you live up to it?"

He sat down next to her. "What do you mean?"

"Do you fly solo?" It was out of her mouth before her brain cells could engage.

He chuckled. "Are you hitting on me?"

*Fuckity fuck.* "God. No! I just meant, are you a loner?"

"That depends," he said. "And you?"

"After that apology for an answer, I'm not telling."

"Ah, right. So, if a girl wants to ask personal questions, that's fine, but if the guy makes a move, he gets a bad rap."

*Holy shit, is he? Making a move?*

A quick sideways glance snagged on a firm muscular thigh almost nudging hers and it took all her energy not to whimper.

Solo gave an exaggerated sigh. "Anyway, when I said *and you,* I meant what's your name? Only fair—I told you mine."

She hesitated. "Polly."

"Nice."

She let out a snort.

"I mean it. I like your name. Come on, you've just ridiculed mine and I'm being genuinely complimentary about yours. Why are you so tetchy?"

He had a point. She was being a prize cow. Too much alcohol because her fuck buddy had got married when she'd come to the erroneous conclusion he'd always be single, and now her complete mess-up of an introduction to the sexiest guy she'd encountered in months, possibly years, wasn't something to be particularly proud of.

Pushing off the wall, she shoved a curl off her forehead and faced him with an apologetic smile. "Okay, I admit it. Champagne makes my tongue muscle misbehave. Let's start again. My name's Polly and I'm here at my friend Jake's wedding, and when I'm not being a complete bitch to men I've just met, I work as a social worker."

She thought a brief shadow passed over his face, then his lips once again tipped into a grin. "Nice to meet you, Polly. Passing through on my way to take up a three-month contract in Perth. No offence taken. I quite enjoyed sparring with your bitchy alter-ego."

"Thanks, I aim to please. What are you doing in Perth?"

Again that miniscule misting of his features. "Working on a building project."

"Designing?"

"No, labouring."

Polly frowned. Somehow it didn't add up. Sure, he looked fit enough to do all kinds of manual work but . . . the way he spoke . . . he sounded as if he was more, what . . .? *Educated . . .?* Hell, she was grossly stereotyping, wasn't she? A sudden vision of Solo naked to the waist and glistening in sweat as he heaved girders over his shoulder sent her into another near meltdown.

On second thoughts, manual work it most definitely was.

Flustered, she turned and leaned her elbows on the wall. Beyond the hotel's reticulated gardens, great swathes of wheat spread out towards the red ball of the setting sun.

"It's still freakin' hot, isn't it?" she said. *Pathetic.* Surely she could do better than the weather. "So, if I'm allowed to ask, where are you from, Solo?"

"Sydney."

"Sydney." Polly couldn't help a surprised glance. "How did you end up in Western Australia?"

"I rode over."

"Oh, yeah? Where's your faithful stead?"

"Parked out the front. The red Ducati."

An image of those strong thighs draped around a big shiny bike made her mouth go dry. She feigned interest in the sunset. "Yeah? How long did that take?"

"Two weeks. I camped on the road."

"One more day and you'll be there, then."

"Yep, decided to go luxury for my last night. Only to realise I was gate-crashing a wedding. I was surprised the hotel had a room spare."

"Most people are staying at the bride's place," she said lightly. "Her dad owns a zillion hectares of wheat out here."

He leaned his hip against the wall, studying her. "And you?"

"What about me?"

His proximity brought with it the smell of warm musky male and miles of Australian bush. It made her want to pounce and rip him out of those dusty clothes.

"Are you staying at their property?"

Polly kept her eyes on the sun as it slid lower "Um, no."

"Why not?"

"I—um,. . ."

"Too awkward, maybe?"

*God the guy was astute.*

"No, not at all." There was no need to explain how her long-term *friends with benefits* arrangement had ended abruptly six months ago when she'd introduced Jake to Lou. And that while she was ecstatically happy for them, she wasn't staying in the same building while they got on with their conjugal duties.

"Here you are, I've been looking everywhere—they're about to cut the cake."

Polly supressed a huff, not sure whether to be annoyed or relieved at her friend Judith's appearance.

Judith beckoned. "Come on, quick."

Polly started to back away; realised she had a ninny grin on her face and gave herself a mental slap. "Mustn't miss the cake being cut. Nice to meet you, Solo."

His lips twitched like he could see right through her. "Likewise." Had his gaze darkened, or was that just the fading light? "Catch you later, maybe."

Polly's heart did a little rap, the kind with really inappropriate lyrics. "Maybe." And with that she almost scampered after Judith.

"He is *gorgeous*. Who is he?" Judith said as they headed into the reception.

"Some random."

"Oh, really? You seemed to be having a very cosy chat. I wondered if he might be your new love interest."

"You know I don't do love, Jude."

Spotting a waiter nearby, Polly made a dive for his tray of drinks.

"You may not." Judith grinned, following her. "But there's a battlefield of Polly Fletcher slain hearts out there."

"*And h*ere's to the one that got away," Polly said, raising her glass as Lou and Jake's hands combined over the knife to slice the cake.

"You didn't want Jake that way," Judith hissed in her ear over the cheers. "And you know it."

Polly sculled her champagne. True enough, she supposed. All she'd ever asked of Jake was a warm, cuddly friendship with some pretty good benefits tagged on the end. But . . . it was just, *well* . . . where was she going to get regular sex with no strings attached, now that Jake was off in married-la-la land?

A pair of beautiful silver eyes danced into her head, along with a sensual mouth that she'd bet would be capable of getting up to all sorts of mischief.

Polly placed her glass back on a passing tray and smiled sweetly at the waiter as she grabbed another.

*Poison of choice, my arse.*

How, she wondered, did you find out the room number of another guest without looking like some sex-starved stalker?

Information on where to buy
The Polly Principle
and Davina's other books can be found
https://davinastone.com/

# ABOUT THE AUTHOR

Davina Stone writes romances about flawed but lovable characters who get it horribly wrong before they finally get it right. They also kiss a fair bit on the way to happily ever after.

Davina grew up in England, before meeting her very own hero who whisked her across wild oceans to Australia. She has now lived exactly half her life in both countries which makes her a hybrid Anglo-Aussie.

When not writing she can be found chasing kangaroos off her veggie patch, dodging snakes and even staring down the odd crocodile. But despite her many adventures, in her heart, she still believes that a nice cup of tea fixes most problems- and of course, that true love conquers all.

**Please Review This book.**

Reviews help authors to keep writing and help readers to find our books. If you enjoyed *The Alice Equation*, please consider leaving a review on Amazon or Goodreads.

**Why not drop by and say hi?**

Want to read the story of when Alice and Aaron first met? Sign up for my newsletter and get the prequel to the first in the Laws of Love series, *The Alice Equation* FREE. You will also get updates on new releases and a little bit of once-a-month silliness (cute pics of kangaroos may be included on occasions.)

Check out my website at https://www.davinastone.com/

Connect with me on …

- facebook.com/DavinaStoneAuthor
- instagram.com/davinastone_
- tiktok.com/@davinastoneauthor
- bookbub.com/authors/davina-stone